T0322282

A Little Trickerie

A Little Trickerie

Inspired by true events

ROSANNA PIKE

FIG TREE
an imprint of
PENGUIN BOOKS

FIG TREE

UK | USA | Canada | Ireland | Australia
India | New Zealand | South Africa

Fig Tree is part of the Penguin Random House group of companies
whose addresses can be found at global.penguinrandomhouse.com.

First published 2024
001

Set in 12/14.75pt Dante MT Std
Typeset by Jouve (UK), Milton Keynes
Printed and bound in Great Britain by Clays Ltd, Elcograf S.p.A.

The authorized representative in the EEA is Penguin Random House Ireland,
Morrison Chambers, 32 Nassau Street, Dublin D02 YH68

A CIP catalogue record for this book is available from the British Library

ISBN: 978-0-241-64606-9

www.greenpenguin.co.uk

For Oli and Rex

A roof in return

Somewhere near Newmarket

May, 1500

Ma had said she would give the cordwainer man a baby – the thing he could not get from his dull-as-ditchwater wife – and we would get a roof in return. That baby-child would be born, and when it was out then the cordwainer would discard the woman called his wife by-hook-or-by-crook, and we would live there in that neat stone house and eat from clay plates like the kings we were. Or so said my ma who was oftentime mistook.

'Finally, Tibb!' she did holler with a big hoot-hoot and 'Fuck knows we have waited for it!' And we did dance like two lunatics from the madhouse since we had dreamt of a roof for all-of-time. I can't say how long the cordwainer man would have lived there with us, since my ma was partial to that naughty game of throat-slitting by then, but in any case, that question did not matter one piece.

The problem went like this: there we were these months later outside our soon-to-be house, and the baby still had a purple rope hanging from its belly and my ma was still walking with her legs apart like a duck, and the cordwainer man did look like there were two perfect strangers standing on his own doorstep. He was like a bun on two legs. Perhaps there was a pudding stuffed up that fine wool doublet.

'It is me!' said my ma, and she was all pale in her lovely face and sweaty since it was only recently she was saying, 'O-O-O, Tibb!' and cursing around like a sick pig while that person called my sister climbed her way out.

'O, yes . . .' he said very slow. And he did examine her with his bead-eyes and say, 'A girl? I did not order a girl, dear.'

Well that was some sinking feeling and I did wonder if my stomach was tumbling out of my arsehole. And such a waft of leather at the door from his shoe-making business, my nose was wrinkled up like a currant.

'I shall tell your wife,' she did hiss, for my ma had some sharp tongue on her, though never for her own Tibb.

He fingered his chin which was covered in fluff. 'Well I cannot see my face in this child at all. I will deny that thing, and furthermore, I will have you both corrected since don't you know vagrancy is outlawed?'

I scowled, because he did not mind it so much when he was wriggling around on top of my ma. Did you think of that then, sir?

Bang went the wood door and we did disappear towards that barn where he kept us those last months in secret from his boring wife.

'I should have known it, Tibb,' she breathed. 'And have I not always said to beware the fuckers?'

Ma was leaning on me like she was an old crone and she was getting closer and closer to that trailed-with-blood ground so by the time we were back she was mostly crawling. Perhaps she truly loved the man. I couldn't be sure, since Ma was always bending to the left and the right with her thoughts and she did fall into love and out of it too quick to keep up.

Now this hay is all red in here and sticky from that birth but she is sitting on it and I am crouching in front of her, and that baby is going suck and suck for its little life.

'This is some horse-shit, Tibb,' she croaks. 'And would you pass me that beer?'

Well she is reaching out for that wood tankard which we pilfered from an inn some time back for the purpose of collecting water, but more commonly beer for my ma. In fact there is only goat milk in it now and not much of it left besides.

That tiny baby called my sister rolls off her chest and cries on the ground so I pick her up, and this bleating life is all hot and squashed in my hands and I should hope I'm not breaking it.

'There is no beer, Ma.'

'Aaw!' she says in a long string like she is a cockerel because beer is medicine for my ma. Then, 'I have never given you a roof, Tibb!' And she says sorry and sorry, and I am starting to leak from the eyes.

'Would you find a nice roof, Tibb?' she whispers. 'And would you take your sister there too?'

'Ma?' I say, because I don't much like how she is talking – like she is going somewhere – and nor do I like that shiny blood which is leaking out of her underneath-part and making the hay turn redder. And then she is all still like she is formed of stone and the baby is squawking like there is a bull in here.

I say, 'Ma! Ma!' like this might wake her. She has been threatening that thing called death for so long and wishing away this shit world, and now it is here, but I am not ready for that. And my knees are stuck upon with the blood-hay while I poke her about her lovely face but she does not open one eye and wink at me because this is no joke, Tibb.

Waste-of-money shoes

Here I am on this hay still and I cannot think I will ever move. I have stopped saying, 'Ma,' and I have stopped shaking her because it is clear the fuckers won and she is not speaking back ever again.

That sun is beating down outside this barn like it cannot see what has happened in here. And some birds are doing their morning song like they can't see it either, but this sound is muffled in my ears like it is very far away. And this baby-cry is muffled too. Really I can hear only my own breath which is too shallow owing to the black snake which has wrapped itself around my body and most particularly my heart and my throat. That squeezing pain is something hollow and my mind is hollow besides. I do not see that fat man the cordwainer till he is swaying above me.

'Ah,' he says, 'but childbirth is something truly perilous.'

These words are travelling across the seas to reach me and that grin crawling up his doughy cheeks looks like it would jump upon the clouds. Here is some victorious fucker.

'Well then, would you get gone already, child? And would you take that screeching baby before my wife comes to this tannery and hears it all?'

I don't answer that. Maybe I will not ever speak again.

He returns with a spade and then he is digging a hole out there in the soil and muttering to himself, and I am thinking this is no kind generosity, sir.

'You are a crook and a liar,' I wish to say, and I wish to find a blade and ram it into his throat as I did see my ma do oftentime. But I am just sitting here and watching with my eyes wide like two moons and I have wrapped my new sister in my own apron. Perhaps the snake will kill me. Clouds traipse across the sky out there like they are watching too.

Now he is dragging out that lovely woman called my ma by the bare feet so she is bumped into that hole and my heart is aching like it will turn black and stop beating. And I want to tell him to be gentle but those words are stuck inside my throat. He throws soil on top.

'Well I am going this day to sell my fine shoes and when I come back here you will be gone.'

His mouth is moving at a different time to these bad words he is saying, and his finger is wiggling to some other tune besides.

Gone. Gone without her?

The baby is doing some thrashing with her head like she wants to say, 'Would you feed me, Tibb?'

'You will be gone, child,' he says again, and these words squat in this death-air, and I do not much like the way he is holding that spade out like it is a sword. Then he squints his eyes and he says, 'And if you are not, then I will turn you in myself and you will be strung up like the vagabond you are.'

Well there is some thumping inside of me as he stomps away and that nowhere-voice is saying, 'Would you move, Tibb? And here is the first rule of vagrancy: do not stay long in one place else the fuckers will catch on.' And that should be my ma's own voice except for the fact she is dead.

Suddenly this baby-wail sounds louder in my ears, and there is some urgency to it that I didn't hear before. I do drip the last of that goat milk into those baby-lips from my finger, which is hard because my eyes are leaking. Drip and drip into her little mouth and I am blinking like the world is new. Would you get your sister a roof, Tibb?

My legs feel like someone else's legs and I am not standing on them like I did before she died, but more like a fawn or a drunk man. And I gather up our things which are the blanket and the tankard and the canvas bag and I stagger out of here with the snake upon my shoulders and my legs apart like it is me who did just birth this person in my arms. Do not look back at that new-on-top soil, Tibb, else you will never leave.

In the distance I can see the cordwainer man, off in his horse-cart all stuffed with his waste-of-money shoes. The crickets are shrieking in these grasses, but there is something else ringing inside of my head. A subject my own ma did think to verse me on called revenge, Tibb. Even at the worst-of-times.

Better milk

Clouds scud across the sky but the sun is too hot for May. Those flames and that stench of smoke are all behind, since I did set alight to that man's dry thatched roof while he was at the market. He did not keep his promise of the roof, so why should he have one himself?

These fields look like they have never once been trod in and these long-like-weeds grasses are scratching at my knees. I can feel it like they are knives sprouting from the ground. Villages stomp past, else the odd mostly-mud hut which is better than no roof at all, Tibb. And some scatterings of peasants in fields, but no cows. I am walking on with my wide-apart eyes and I am thinking of this word *cows* like it is stuck upon my head because if I do not think of cows then I would crouch down and let the snake finish me off. This black feeling is swelling and swelling and making my legs feel heavy and my head is so full that it's just empty.

'Henrietta,' I say, and that voice sounds strange. 'I will find you cows.'

Ma and I were loitering around this place called Newmarket these past months to wait for that baby and the cordwainer's big promise to come true, but I can't remember these near-enough fields because the world has gone a terrible shade and everything has been turned over and stuck back on upside-down. Either that, or the cows did fuck off and die like Ma.

This name Henrietta is after our own King Henry VII, though Ma said he is the person who has declared vagabonds like us to be called *criminals*. But I cannot think of any better name since I do not know many people to fill me with ideas and thinking is something hard right now.

She is too small inside the apron-swaddle and I am not sure of the best way to hold her since there is no sturdiness to her body. Now she is looking over my shoulder and I am stroking that soft furry bit at the base of her neck because this is making her be quiet and it is smoothing over that barbed ache inside of me which is gathering up armies. Sometimes she is rooting around for a great pair of tits to suckle on but my chest is flat like a board though it is high-time for tits or so said my dead ma.

'Henrietta,' I say. 'You are growing backwards.'

I think she is even smaller than when she climbed out.

Fingers of light are sticking down and I want my ma back out of that hole. The hem of my dress has unstitched itself and is hanging below my knees. I have worn this thing every day since we pilfered it from that second-hand clothing market at Melksham which is far away from here. I could be the daughter of a nobleman in this costume because it is white with a laced apron, but it is filthy and it stinks like a cheesecloth.

Move, Tibb, before this evening sun is chased away by the black clouds. This canvas bag of mine slaps against my back and I want to wrench it off. I am dipping that tankard in a stream but this water is not making me smile because my ma is not here. Henrietta does not enjoy water either.

'Henrietta, I will not let you die.'

By the time I spot that shock of black and ivory lounging in a field I am somewhere deep into the land of Norfolk and that is all I know. I squat in a dense hedgerow while the rain hammers on to the mud, making streams like the ones outside the butchers' tents but those are formed of blood.

I wring my hair out like a rag. White, thin hair which hangs straight like a poker to my waist. 'Your ma was knocked up by the big-man-God himself, Tibb!' she said, because I was surely an angel with my doe eyes and this ghostly complexion. Then she laughed because there is no God. 'The world has been hoodwinked, Tibb!'

Thoughts of my ma are feeding the snake.

The string-bean farmer gathers those cows into their barn and Henrietta looks like a doll there on the peaty soil. I think she is too small for this big world.

'Look,' I tell her, and 'I am going to fetch you better milk.'

Night is the time for all shady business, Tibb, or so said my ma and she was well practised to know it.

I am skittering with the wood tankard like there are flames beneath this mud and this shit-smell is so rank that I could spew. There is something like terror in these fingers of mine while I do pull and pull because this milk is more than one nice supper, Tibb. The other cow-friends watch me like I am here to do murder. Perhaps it is them who placed that iron trough in the shadow so I crash into it.

Well that farmhouse door is thrown open and that bean-man is out here again, and with two dogs this time. He looks like he would thrash me on the whipping post himself.

'I see you, urchin! Thieves must face the pillory!'

Now those dogs are chasing me and snapping their great teeth and my breath is too quick, like it is going to scamper away completely and leave me empty. Fuck this hair and this ghostly skin – I must be like a speck of light darting over these dim fields. The sight of the milk on that black dirt is something truly bad and Henrietta is under the hedgerow and perhaps the dogs will get to her first.

Eventually the farmer whistles and those dogs retreat but the milk is lost already. Henrietta is wailing and that is something urgent and terrifying so I tip her head back and pour in the not-much-left of it but I can tell she wants more.

'Henrietta,' I say, and I wrap that apron-blanket around her tighter and I am pushing her down the front of my dress so she is warm. Those mewlings are not so urgent as they were before and maybe that is something good or maybe it isn't. I should find her more milk but my eyes are closing because of the walk and the snake and the cloud which would smother me.

In the morning the cold wakes me; this bulging soil and some bad teeth-chattering of mine. The bundle on my chest called Henrietta is all wrapped up and next to my skin and I clutch her in my cold hands like the cherries did ripen and we pinched the lot and there is some deep swooping inside of my guts.

I stare down at her velvet head. Up there, those birds stop jabbering and the branches stand still and mad thoughts are rattling through my mind and snapping at each other and pulling there. Feelings which are stretching and stretching and these don't have names until they all mount up to one thing called relief because you still have this person to care for, Tibb Ingleby, and if you didn't then there would be no point to you.

'Henrietta,' I say, and that name is clumsy on my tongue like I did learn to speak just now. 'You know we still have each other?'

She looks up at me like she knows it too.

Don't beg

I did see that thing called ecstasy pass over my ma oftentime – mostly after she did threaten to leave this shit place by the slitting of her own throat – but I did not feel it myself till now. And such a shame to boot because here is some sweet highness inside of me. I should say it is like one great sunrise in there because of all the things Henrietta and I will do together in this life and I am not thinking of my dead ma in the hole because she wouldn't want that either. Henrietta does gurgle like she thinks the same and like there are things she would say to me besides.

'We should go!' I tell her.

So we do.

I know where we're off to and I could skip with all my big hopes but these wild-flower meadows reach up to my skin-and-bone thighs and 'Ha! Would you slow a good girl down, dears?'

Well I am not looking for mushrooms today, Ma, and I can spot the best too, but I am pulling up some of those fine buttercups because when Henrietta wakes then she will like the colours.

In fact she is sleeping in the soft sling I have made with that apron of mine and she is all nestled on my front like I have got my own baby and not just a sister. I stroke that silk-hair and I hold those dangling-down legs in my palms. This walk could last years and I shouldn't give a fuck since I am full up with all the ecstasy thoughts.

'Would you close your ears, though?' I laugh, and I cup my

palms over her tiny petal-ears because the big-man's bells are louder than ever since the day is Sunday. That noise is making the grasses go limp and the leaves shake.

Of course I am avoiding the churches in these speckled-around villages since those people flooding in and gossiping might see a vagrant called Tibb Ingleby and her small sister and don't you know vagrancy is outlawed? Well I am picturing them all up on their hind legs and saying, 'Sturdy beggars right there!' and pointing and puffing around to send their watching-men after us though my ma did say, 'We don't beg, Tibb. However much we want that nice roof.'

'That's some horse-shit too,' I whisper to Henrietta behind this faraway peeping-tree but she is a baby so she can't understand and she is sleeping besides. 'Why should the big-man-God have so many houses, when we do not have even *one*?'

This is something my ma did ask oftentime though we made our home in a barn for a whole month once, before the farmer there realized he had two naughty lodgers in that warm hay.

In fact my own ma did favour churches when they were left unlocked, and even if they weren't then she had a way with the rectors. I am smiling at that naughty thought and I am remembering how she would say, 'It is the least they can do for us, Tibb, because the big-man-God didn't help me when I asked him because he only cares for money.' And she did say, 'Why pray to something in the sky when the things we need are here, if only you are crafty enough to get them?'

On we go and the sun is chasing us. I wish her dangling-down feet were not so cold in my hands, but why do you think those bad thoughts, Tibb, and ruin such a day?

'Henrietta?' I say, and I hold her up to my ear. 'More milk you say? Well you are one sneak-rat like your sister Tibb!'

This dairy-farm is riper for pinching since the farmer is at the church-place too and I am opening her lips and trickling in the milk and I think she likes it a lot. Then I am stroking those rosebud lips and this soft little face which must be called perfect.

'Henrietta, I could look at you longer but we are off and I know where.'

Those fields turn wilder and there is some deep silence. 'Would you bark a ditty for a baby?' I do shout to those flapping birds but they don't answer that. 'Ah, you're all good-for-nothing!'

Up these hillocks and finally that sea is winking down there like it would have us dive in. Wink and wink and 'Would you look, Henrietta? You know this is what we came for?'

Sit up and howl

The dead woman called my ma did love the ocean once. 'Those naughty waves are so cold,' she did laugh, 'they would have the corpses sit up and howl!' And she would rush in and out and throw her head back, and I would trot in behind to feel that freezing water around my twig-legs and we did laugh some more. But after we left the land of Weymouth she couldn't look at the ocean again because the sea did remind her of that man called Farmer O.

'Would you smell the salt, Henrietta?' I say, because I am not thinking of Farmer O now – in the same way I am not thinking of my dead ma – and she is wriggling like she can't wait either.

Now these tracks are all sandy under my feet and here are some marshes and little riverways with ducks hiding there. Has the ocean been tucked away to play a trick on wanderers? All these narrow walkways and sand-hills and this sea-bracken is sharp under my heels but who gives two shits?

When I finally reach that bay it is like this place is cut off from all the rest of the world behind the dunes and it is flat like it is going on forever. The colour of this sand is white and it is warm from the sun. Perhaps this is what the Spice Islands look like or else that nice place named Constantinople that I am hearing of.

'Henrietta,' I say and I am peeling her from the sling, 'would you look at that?'

I am wading into this shallow sea with my dress on and I dip her tiny feet in this great ocean and, 'Henrietta?' I say. 'Don't you like that?'

Well those waves roll around my ankles and turn white but I am finding the ecstasy feeling is slipping away and now I am turning black and the snake is winding itself around my body again.

'O, but I did think you would enjoy it better,' I whisper.

My sister is not giggling like I hoped she would and she is just still.

There is a thudding inside of me and this water is making my toes go numb and I think all the joy will never return and why would you take a baby into cold water, Tibb?

'Ah, what was I thinking?' I laugh. 'You must be too cold now!' and I kiss her head. 'I think you shall like it better when you're older and you might run away to boot!' Then I am pulling up that sling higher because of this wind and tucking her in once more and I do laugh like ho-ho-ho despite my small battle with a snake.

By the evening I have walked up a short length of the wet beach which is being slowly covered in a low-lying mist and my feet are carrying on like they will never stop. I am talking and talking because Henrietta likes that and these words are tumbling out like: 'I shall teach you to skip when you are old enough for it, and that is some little joy in the world' and 'We won't loiter near towns since that would spell some trouble.' And: 'You shall need more milk soon, my dear.'

When I don't talk there is just the wind and the waves breaking out there and that is when the black fog creeps in and the snake does play its squeezing game some more. That grey cloud up there is wispy like a beard. It is shaped like a beard too. Like the beard of that man called Farmer O but you are still not thinking of him, Tibb Ingleby.

In crawls this tide and my feet are making imprints on this sludge-sand and the beach is getting smaller because of the coming-in sea and I don't like these dark thoughts or this pain inside my chest.

'At least I have you, Henrietta,' I say, or perhaps I just think that, and I wrap my arms around this sling because here is something good to live for so why doesn't the snake fuck off now?

Soon the bay cleaves inwards and turns rocky where before it was all soft, and the sea-water is trickling into this inlet so here is a kind of sludge-lake.

I stop. Bang and bang says my heart like it has been saying since we arrived at this place but here is some new reason for it. A man. Sitting up on those rocks above this almost-lake.

Men will eat you up and spit you out, Tibb, but I don't know if this is really a man. He looks like he has started the process of growing up and is somewhere around half-way through or a little further. There is some nearly-invisible wire which he is sliding between his fingers and he pulls up a crab with all its red legs wiggling. I have not seen many alive-crabs in all the skulking-round-towns-in-search-of-the-fuckers which Ma and I did often do. Mostly they were dead on the benches or other times they were not there at all.

Would you put your arms around this sleeping sister and fuck off, Tibb? But I don't do that thing because this man-boy doesn't have the stern look of churchly men or the hungry look that my ma warned against but also liked a lot. And that gaping blackness which is threatening to bury me whole is not so large when I am gazing at him because he seems peaceful sitting there, a slight curve to his posture, and he is looking at me and there is something gentle in those blue eyes of his, and this open face. He shuffles along on his rock, as though to let me sit beside him. So I do that.

'Ivo,' he says in a deep-but-soft voice which is not a boy's voice, and he holds out a hand to me. I notice he has muscly forearms and they are covered in pale wiry hairs like a man's arms already.

'What's your name?' he asks me when I don't take that hand.

I say, 'Tibb,' and he looks at me like I said a lot more than just my name.

There is something different about this person. His edges are hazy like mine, and 'What's in the sling?' he asks.

I shake my head and I hold it closer because she is sleeping in there.

For a long time he looks at me, then he says gently, 'Do you eat crab, Tibb?'

Some good nourishment

The sun is all packed up and Ivo has made a fire within those big dunes. We are nestled in, amongst sea-grasses and sheltered from the winds off the ocean. I have not done one thing to help but just stood here with my arms around the sling and there is something good about being near this person which makes no sense. But my nice thoughts about Henrietta and the fact she needs me are blurring and there is a spiked feeling which is digging in.

Ivo's face is angular and soft in all the right places and there is a kindness to it which is making me sure that he is not one of the fuckers. He has pulled his braces down and they hang there by his sides, flapping against his trousered legs, and I wonder why he wears them since he clearly doesn't need them.

'Would you sit, Tibb?' he asks and he pats that sand beside him. Then he says, 'How long have you been on your own?'

'Since my ma is dead some days back.'

This hoarse voice doesn't sound much like mine.

He looks sad, like it is *his* ma who is in the hole somewhere outside Newmarket. He pushes back his blonde hair. At the front his shirt gapes open and I can see there are some blonde hairs poking out of his chest muscles too. I am thinking of the person in the sling and there's a dragging feeling inside of me.

He pulls the legs from the dead crab, though keeping all the shell on it, and he throws the body and the legs on to the fire which makes a crackling sound and the flames climb up higher. After a while he pulls all those things back off again on to the sand with two sticks.

I have a feeling Ivo has been living here some time. A few weeks at least judging by that sun-licked skin and burnt-a-bit nose. And he knows what he is doing with the crab and already there was a fire laid at this exact point on the beach. Some of his belongings are stacked up by the fire too, like a blanket and some leather shoes which do not look like they were knocked up by the same cordwainer who dragged my ma into a hole.

'Crab is some good nourishment, Tibb,' he says, and he smiles.

I am not moving my head much. I am not really moving any part of me.

Now he pokes at it with his own hands, breathing on it like he wants to make it cool down. There is some white ooze seeping out the edges of that shell-body and some smell I do not find pleasant but there is an emptiness inside of my belly that is growling because when did you last eat, Tibb?

He pulls bits of shell off and scrapes them away, and then cups some white flakes in his palm which he holds out to me.

I take a few and poke them in my mouth and that soft pulpiness on my tongue is disgusting. I eat some more and watch this smiling person named Ivo until his nice face turns all wobbly in those flames and there is some urge to speak a little more.

'But I had someone else for company, Ivo.'

He looks interested and my heart is banging around in there.

'A sister,' I say. 'Henrietta. I will need to find her milk soon but she is just sleeping now.'

Ivo shuffles nearer to me and then he wipes my cheek with a finger because maybe I am crying.

My fingers open the sling just enough for a peep, though I don't look inside myself. His body freezes a bit but he doesn't jump back and declare me a lunatic-person or someone who has never attended that place-called-church.

'She is very pretty,' he whispers.

'Yes. But I should have got more milk.'

Now my throat is stinging and I am gulping the air.

His hand is wriggling into mine and he says, 'I think you were a good sister.'

Why does he say that?

He puts his arm around my shoulders and it feels heavy and strange but I like it there, then slowly he edges this sling and the person inside of it from my grasp and he takes it into his hands and I let him do that.

'I'm tired.'

'Then you should sleep, Tibb.'

And my head is being guided down on to something soft and I can feel there is something soft on top of me too, like a blanket, and Ivo is there because I can hear him breathing.

Leominster, Herefordshire

Five years later

The man has been dumped into this cellar with all the ceremony of a shit in the woods, and he is sitting on the wet hay like a new donkey would, with his legs bent beneath him. It is a manor house in the town where they have brought him. The cellar is rented out to hold prisoners awaiting their sentencing, and that is what he is now. A prisoner.

His head feels heavy in his hands, fingers rifling through his fair hair, and those grooved lines across his forehead seem to burrow deep into his flesh so he looks older than he is. The smell of damp and piss is so strong, he wonders if he might pass out from it.

The Justice of the Peace squints in the dim light of the lantern, banging his cane on the stone floor, making the rats scatter. Disturbing the puddles of stagnant water. 'You won't be long in this place,' he sneers. 'Once the King has been fetched then you'll be on a pyre out in that town square. You'll find kindling a good deal more comfortable than hay, I hope.'

The prisoner doesn't answer that because if he opens his mouth he will hurl. It seems a cruel joke that this man has the word 'peace' nestled in his name.

'Do not give the man bread for a day,' he says to the young warden beside him. 'And when you do give it, be sparing with the portion.'

The warden nods, wide-eyed.

'You see, we shouldn't want to kill him before the horses have returned from London with the King on the saddle. Burning is worse than starvation.'

Burning. His skin puckers; like the flames are licking him already.

The Justice seethes. 'You know you are not the first. Others have angered God with their fraudulence and their dishonesty, but they only faced the block. Nothing but the flame can meet the evil you have done, and time is slipping away . . . sir.'

He smirks at that word: sir. The cruelty buried within its letters. The prisoner glances round at his final home. At the water dripping down these mouldy walls. The grime beneath him.

Images – snippets of memories – race through his mind. Sandy feet. A bowl of money, placed by a door. He sees the back of a boy's head, wispy hairs at the base of a neck. Two little girls, their heels pummelling his chest as he carries them on his shoulders through the woods. And his mother's soft body, sleeping behind a broken curtain. The shiny surface of her eyes – open just for a second. Or did he imagine it?

The Justice turns to his colleague. 'In fact, make it two days, Marcus, before you bring refreshment.'

When they have left so has the light, but the prisoner can hear the rats scratching too close. He draws his arms around his body. Muscular shoulders which have held up the weight of the world. He grimaces, terror etched across his chiselled face. He is formed in strong, sharp lines.

He takes gulps of rancid air and stares into blackness. Evil. Perhaps his father was right all along. Perhaps evil is truly what he is.

Some slice of evil

When I wake my thoughts are sluggish like they were dipped in honey. I have slept extraordinarily deeply on this soft sand and the sea is so far out that I can barely snatch a peek of it. But those bad memories are catching up and sinking their claws in and there is some taste of bile in my mouth which wants to come out and splatter the sand.

'Henrietta?' I choke, and Ivo is beside me so quick, it is like he was waiting. He holds my hands and looks into my morning-eyes.

'She is peaceful now, Tibb.'

Those tears are falling and this bad feeling is so strong I wonder if it will eclipse my whole body. There is a sense that I am floating and this is vivid like a memory though I have never floated once before so that is confusing. 'I had a thought that the waves would make her sit up and howl but my ma did tell some bad lies there to boot.'

He nods like this makes a lot of sense.

'It was a deep hole, Ivo?'

He nods a lot and says, 'It was very deep and calm and she was sleeping.'

The cold wind is whistling across my face and I look into it for a time. Then, 'Ivo,' I whisper. 'Do not tell me where that hole is.'

'As you like it, Tibb.'

And still he is there beside me when I am closing my eyes again. And there begins some half-life of mine, because if sleep is all you do, are you even living?

If I wake in the day then I am finding that Ivo has draped his shirt over my face to stop that bad sun turning me to ashes, and if it is night when I stir, then I am finding I have a blanket all tucked around me. And always Ivo is nearby with something like a crab for me to eat and some fresh water there for me to drink because Ivo is not one of the fuckers.

My dreams are broken up into shards except the face of Farmer O which is round and hairy and clear and that is unsurprising since he has not fucked off yet after all these years. I am hearing those words he said when he did climb into the mattress, like: 'You are a bad girl, Tibb Ingleby. And you are some slice of evil.' Well you had it right, Farmer O, because I did let my sister die just like I drove my own ma to ruin and I must be the worst person who did ever walk in this kingdom called England because who buries two corpses in quick succession and calls the thing chance?

I don't know how much time has slid past but those bells are ringing through this land from the place-called-church as though the big-man-God is saying, 'Would you wake up, Tibb Ingleby, you lazy fuck?'

The sun is low, like it did stay put just for me, and Ivo is there because he is always there.

'Ivo, how many days have I been sleeping?' I ask, and he passes me some water.

'Five, Tibb. I think you were very tired.'

'I think I was.'

It seems that the snake around me has loosened from all the sleep but mostly I am pleased Ivo is still here. I sit up.

'I have found us eggs, Tibb,' he says with a smile. 'When you cannot catch a crab then there will always be eggs if you know where to look.'

In fact he has cooked those eggs on the almost-gone fire, so now they are hot and I watch as he peels them and he gives me one. This springiness is something pleasant to eat. We did snatch things often, my ma and I, but not really eggs. I am eating it slowly, like my teeth and my tongue forgot how to do it.

'Do you feel better?' he asks me.

I nod, but I want my ma. And I want to tell her sorry for what happened to Henrietta. Ivo puts his big warm arm around my shoulders and there is nothing strange about this even though he is almost a stranger. Really he is something quite beautiful with his blonde hair and those blue eyes and I wonder if this person is formed of golden stuff.

Soon that sky is turning black and he is lying next to me, very close.

I say, 'Thank you,' and he says, 'No thanking, Tibb.'

I am listening to his breath.

'You won't go anywhere, Ivo?' I whisper.

'No, Tibb. I won't go anywhere.'

There are some birds singing their long-enough notes behind this beach.

'I miss my ma,' I whisper, and there is a hard ball in my throat which is swelling up.

'I know, Tibb. Would you tell me about her?'

I shrug. 'It is strange to talk like she is not here.'

He nods like he understands. That sharp-edged jawline is some perfect thing.

'My ma was either up or she was down and there was not much in between. And sometimes she made us dance in the rain and other times she cried and said she wished to die in a ditch like a dog.'

He says, 'That must have been hard.'

'Not really. And she did go to such lengths to find us our roof, since we have not ever had one. She would go from man-to-man for this end and sometimes it worked for a while.

Farmers mostly who would hide us in their barns or their chicken yards and come and do that naughty thing with my ma which was never very quiet. Or else she would find some merchant who would give a little money for a lodging room till his wife did find out, and when that did not work she would just do some fucking for money.'

His kind blue eyes are all glassy in this moonlight and they are looking straight at me.

'And afterwards she would hold it in her fist and say, "Well I am saving it all up for our nice big roof, Tibb," and she meant every word. But then she did require a great deal of mead with that money or else some nutmeg to soothe all those worries, and I would stand and wait till she was better again. This was not her own fault though, Ivo, but that of the fuckers.'

He nods like he knows those fuckers too.

'And what about your father, Tibb?'

I smile a bit which feels odd because this is something I have not done much of recently. 'My ma did joke that she was knocked up by the big-man-God himself.'

He nods and smiles and watches me. And then he says, 'You know, Tibb, your ma is not really gone.'

'She isn't?' I say, and I am looking around like she did jump back to life. Like that man called Jesus who I am hearing of.

Ivo smiles and points up to the big sky. 'I like to think that those stars are in fact angels, just hovering.'

Well I had not noticed them up there till now because of the snake and the sleeping-all-the-time problem, but this dark sky is spotted all over with stars and they are shining up there like they have gathered to dance a jig.

'Angels? I have not ever seen one of *them*.'

'No?'

'No. That stuff is just lies, I think. My ma did tell me, "Tibb – you cannot see the big-man floating around in the sky as much as you cannot see the grand place called Heaven with all the dead people sitting there." '

He nods a bit, like he is thinking things and I should ask him, 'Do you see the marsh-birds assembling in the grasses there to discuss the price of butter too?'

Eventually he says, 'Perhaps. But I think of it a little differently. I can't imagine angels are fully formed in their white robes, but rather, they are like a soul.'

Now here is a word my ma did not think to verse me on.

He is reading my no-ideas face and he explains: 'Like the thinking parts of a person, not the bodily parts. And that's the bit that lives on once someone has died.'

It seems unlikely that thoughts can exist when they don't have a person's head to hold them in, but I am listening to Ivo because he is kind and he has listened to me a lot.

'I can imagine the souls all bright and calm up there, flickering as though to tell us they are not really dead at all.'

'Can you?' I say. Now I am squinting up into that dark sky besides.

'I can, Tibb. I can see my grandfather . . . just there.'

His finger is dancing in this clear air as he points upwards.

I say, 'Ivo, they just look like stars.'

That nice face of his has disappointment scratched all across it. The waves are slurring in the distance and the birds are calling in those behind-the-beach grasses like they would sing a lullaby.

'I really believe it, you know,' he says. 'That your ma and that sweet sister of yours are up there, and they are watching you from their great height and they are thinking of you all the time. And one day, a long time from now, you'll join them too.'

Will I? I am considering it when a thought smacks me round the face. 'But . . . is it not only *good* people who become angels, Ivo?'

Of course I am thinking of that man called Farmer O and the fact I am a whore-bitch. I am thinking of those rough fingers and all that blood and my black magic.

'You are a good person, Tibb.'

'I could have saved my sister, and I am bad besides. I have given it a lot of my thoughts.'

Now he is quiet.

I say, 'Anyway, how can you know for sure that the angels are up there? And how did they get so high?'

He smiles again. 'It is just a nice thought, Tibb.'

Is it?

Flood the world

Ivo is sleeping and I am listening to those far-off waves which did not wake up the corpses. Then I am climbing up that sand-hill behind us to be closer to the skies myself, because if my ma is really up there like an angel-person – her thinking parts at least – then I need to see her and I need to tell her, 'Would you come back now?'

There is some lonely feeling with this night-cold sand beneath my feet and those sharp grasses poking up. They did not seem so sharp when I was trekking to this beach with a dead baby on my front and the ecstasy feeling inside of my head.

I stand at the top of this mound like I am the only one left and my white hair is blowing in the breeze and this dress is looser than it used to be. I cannot think the snake will ever leave, or this heavy emptiness inside my chest.

'Ma?' I say in a nearly-whisper, because it seems wrong to ruin this not-a-sound night. Up there the stars are still bright like a thousand yellow buttons but I cannot think which one is my ma. How did Ivo notice his grandfather in that great swarm?

No answer.

'Ma,' I say again, but a little bit louder, and 'I want you to come back.'

Still nothing. I had hoped she would flicker brighter or dash across the sky to show me she was listening. A big stone is rolling into my throat again and making my eyes drown. 'Ma? Would you answer me?'

Here is a black space. It is inside my skull and this is loud and quiet and it is making me feel like I will never be happy again. And here is a great banging in my chest and I am rubbing at my face because of all these hot tears, and this breeze is too cold. Henrietta and Ma and the cordwainer man and the dairy-farmer and those wolf-dogs; they are all piling up and up inside of my body and I don't want them there at all.

'I'm sorry!' I say, but that ragged voice is not travelling into the skies. 'It is all my bad fault, Ma. Just like he said!'

I cannot know if these mad tears will ever stop.

'And I am sorry I did not keep Henrietta alive! I did try but I was chased with those big dogs and the milk spilt and then I was asleep and maybe she cried but I didn't wake up!'

Ma isn't answering because she isn't there.

Well I am crumpled on this dune because there is no angel after all. And then I can hear Ivo is coming at a run and his sandy hair is poking in all directions and there is such a lot of worry sprawled across his kind face.

'She isn't up there, Ivo!' I tell him. 'You said some bad lie!'

I think I could punch a fist at him, but he is putting those almost-man arms around me and he is picking me up like I am a small baby myself and he is carrying me back to our sand-house.

'You lied!' I say again, and I am pounding at those hard chest muscles of his like that would stop the pain and these tears are dripping out and perhaps they will roll across the sand and flood the world.

Oysters have a roof

In the morning, Ivo is watching me when I wake up and he smiles gently with those eyebrows all furrowed. That no-reply discussion with my ma last night is bleeding back into my memory like some ink was spilt.

'I thought today we might go on a ramble, Tibb.'

'A ramble? What is the meaning of that word?'

He smiles. 'A walk. A walk to find oysters, because this low tide is perfect for it and I need your help.'

'Oysters?' I say.

'Never eaten oysters?'

I shake my head.

We walk together a mile or so and I am noticing more things like the little worm-piles on this wet sand and that stalk-leg bird who is strutting like someone just stuffed a crown upon his head and I am trying to forget about the stars which did not answer a girl named Tibb.

We turn into a place that Ivo calls the saltmarsh. This is some flat puddle of water, with islands of grass floating here and there and black mud at the edges. He speaks a lot about the sea and the tide and it is nice to listen to his chatter. It doesn't climb up or down like the voice of my ma which was oftentime roaring and other times mute. The steadiness of this noise is making me feel less sad since nothing about it reminds me of her.

'How old are you, Tibb?'

'Who knows, Ivo, but I should say somewhere around fourteen.'

'O,' he says, 'you are little for fourteen.'

I shrug. 'I am built this way. I believe I will always be little.'

'I like that about you,' he says. 'You know I am sixteen according to my mother, though she has some poor skills at counting.'

This makes me stop.

'Why are you wandering, Ivo, if you have a mother still?'

And there is some big worry inside of me saying: Tibb, he will leave and go back to her!

He looks out towards that hiding-sea for a long time. 'Because my family had plans for me that I didn't like.'

'Plans?' I say. 'But it is your own life. And you must never sell yourself to a rich man, Ivo. Rich men will eat you up and spit you out and you will die seeing only the inside of a scullery or the bottom of a wheat-field and you will never see your own children when they do come along.'

He smiles a lot, like he wants to laugh, and I cannot think why. There were many things my ma did say of little sense, but this was not one of them.

'What?' I ask, my head cocked.

'These are *some* words,' he says. 'I will have to heed them. Who told you?'

'My ma. And she did have many thoughts on life besides, though hers was not ever as she wished it.'

He nods but there is something sad about his face and I am thinking Ivo is not telling me everything. He puts a hand through that golden hair like his head is full up of worries and he would catch them with his fingers.

'Do you have other family left over?' I ask.

He shrugs. 'Just an uncle who might like to know me still, but he is moved to a place called Leominster I hear and he is a man of the cloth these days.'

I do not know what that means as much as I do not know the whereabouts of Constantinople.

'Look, Tibb,' he says though. 'Oysters.' And he is pointing to some rocks which are overhanging a sludgy sort-of-marsh, forming a low, long cave.

'See, in that small space the oysters sit and wait.'

I peer in. Well that is no grand home for princely people, but those oysters have a roof and that was not ever really true for my ma and I.

'There are worse places to live,' I say and Ivo laughs again.

'What are they waiting for?' I ask.

'For the tide. You see, they breathe in and out with the tide.'

Ivo rolls his trousers up and jumps down and his ankles are muddied at once but this does not seem to bother him. He crouches and reaches in and selects a few flat shells which he passes up to me. They feel rough in my hands and I make a little pile on the ground. I have seen oysters sold on market benches but these ones are far larger.

I can see his manly-arm does not stretch far in though, so I jump down too and climb right into the cave by way of squatting and dipping my head between my bent legs like a frog. I pick a selection of those big ones right at the back, all clumped together on their rocky mound, and I put them into the laced apron of my dress which is now almost black from this splattered mud. Ivo watches like I am casting spells in here.

'Tibb, you are small enough to fit in! But how can you make your body so creased up that way? It is a fine talent!'

His voice echoes a little in this low cave and I am all pink in the face from my folded position.

I say, 'That is nothing, Ivo!' But I am liking his smile and his warmth and it is making me forget all the bad things which have happened these last few days.

After, we walk back to our little camp-home and drop the oysters there. The mud has dried and is itchy on our legs so we wade out into the shallows. The sun is hot though, and I feel that the skin on my face is getting tight.

Ivo says, 'Your fair skin will turn like a strawberry in this sun, Tibb.'

I like how he speaks – like we are old friends. And he removes his shirt so he is just in his trousers and wraps it round my head to create a kind of turban-hat. It is warm from his skin and smells of him, and I like this scent and the fact I have a living and sweating companion like Ivo beside me. Those not-so-boyish hairs are covering lots of his tanned chest.

I say, 'I think I should look like a queen this way.'

'No,' he says. 'Rather an angel, and this is your halo!'

Later, we sit to eat the oysters and Ivo prises the two shells apart with a blunt knife. He has the knack for this, driving it into the little gap, then offering it to me. I did not know that someone could be strong and gentle in equal measures as Ivo is. He shows me how to send this slimy oyster-creature down my throat all in one, but this salty taste left in my mouth makes me wince. I think it is mostly sea-water within this barnacled shell, but I am so hungry that I am having another.

'Why do you study the inside?' I ask him.

He smiles. 'I am looking for a pearl.'

'A pearl?'

'Like a small gemstone. I should like to give it to you.'

'And how do I use such a thing?'

'It is just something to make you happy.'

'It looks pretty?'

He nods.

'And it is worth some money?'

Here is your own ma talking, Tibb Ingleby.

He nods again.

'Then I would like one very much.'

When it is the night he spreads out the blanket on top of me and asks, 'Are you warm?'

'I am, Ivo.'

He lies next to me. It is silent except for the waves licking the sand some way off, and those marsh-birds saying cheep-cheep just a little.

'Ivo,' I say quietly into this night air. 'I don't know what you are running from, but can I run with you?'

His almost-manly hand is finding mine in the darkness and those stars are bright and he says, 'I would like that, Tibb.'

Church-going man

Days slip by on this beach. Calm, warm days while the months become June and then July, or so says Ivo who knows those things. I think my heart is healing because of him, and that black snake is unwinding itself and I am finding I can breathe again, but in a different way than before. Not bad so much, just different.

We move slowly around the headland – towards Suffolk, Ivo says – stopping at each cove for a few weeks so as not to draw attention from any of the small villages which are speckled behind this vast coastline. Some of the names I learn, like Blakeney and Salthouse. Mostly I just like to be with Ivo.

Occasionally we spy some vagabonds like us though my ma did say, 'There are many thousands of vagrants in this country of England, Tibb, but you will never see them.'

Some feign madness, holding out their palms for money on empty-lanes and stuffing chicken heads in their ears, while others travel in groups and we must be wary of them since they can be what Ivo calls *hostile* and they carry wood sticks.

On Sundays we are hearing those bells ringing out from the church-places because that sound has a way of travelling in the wind so even the sultans of Constantinople can hear it, or so said my ma. It is on these days, when the people are all tucked away and doing their prayers, that Ivo and I go to pick early-enough berries from near the villages.

'I thought you would be a church-going man, Ivo,' I say, stuffing these sweet berries in my mouth, 'since you know a lot about things such as angels.'

He shrugs. 'I used to attend with my mother and father and my sisters. But not any more.'

'Why not?'

He stops and thinks about this, like the answer is very difficult to form. He looks so beautiful to me, with that stubbly beard growing and his blue eyes, but those lines creasing his forehead are something sad on such a perfect face. I wish to smooth them all out with my fingers. Finally he says, 'Well I realized God was very unforgiving.'

'Unforgiving of what?'

He thinks on this. 'Of difference.'

We pick some more and the birds are chattering above us.

'I do not have any regard for the big-man myself.'

He looks like he would laugh and that is some improvement.

'No?'

'No, sir. My ma was having some bad turn, you see, because she did fall in love with a painter from the land of York and she loved him a lot. He was not married and I think she believed he would make her his wife because she was quite beautiful, my ma. But men don't want a bastard daughter when they pick a wife because that thing called pride is something terrible. And then she did see him flouncing around town with that gob-like-an-onion woman who he decided to make his wife.'

He is all wide-eyed like I am sharing some big bad secret or some story that should make the clouds weep.

'Ivo, she couldn't move for three days straight, though the local people did squawk that they would have the watching-men take us away. Well I was quite desperate and I marched to that very same church and I said, "You God-man! Would you make my ma better?" And I really meant it, which I hear is important. But nothing happened, because my ma was right. The big-man isn't up there at all.'

Ivo nods and nods like he understands, then he says, 'Well? Did you get out of that town?'

I swallow my berries and wave a hand. 'In the end. I did have some good knowledge of those dark moods and I learnt how to shift them though sometimes it took me a while.'

'Tibb,' he says, 'you have seen a lot of this life already.'

I think that is a strange thing to say.

'No, but I *have* discovered what will make my heart sing, Ivo. My ma did speak often on this subject, though hers did not often sing. The roof would have done it, I think.'

Ivo smiles. 'And what will make your heart sing, Tibb?'

'To stay here, Ivo. Near you and Henrietta. And to live on these beaches and eat those crabs and these nice berries.'

He reaches for my hand. 'Then we will stay here if you like it.'

These words make me feel warm inside, like there is nothing to worry about.

'And what will make *your* heart sing, Ivo?' I ask.

I can tell he is pondering this question, then: 'I am not sure, Tibb. I think it's a little confused in my mind.'

In the evening those stars are brighter than I have seen them on account of the no-clouds sky. They are blinking up there like a million cat-eyes and those thoughts of rooves are crawling back like when Ma was here.

'It is strange, Ivo. My ma was looking for a roof for us ever since I can remember, and I did want that thing too, and yet I should say this covered-in-stars roof is the best one I have ever had, and that is not really a roof at all.'

Ivo reaches for my hand.

'I think your ma was not looking so much for a roof, but a home.'

That is not making any sense since surely the two are exactly the same.

Ivo rolls on to his side to face me. 'I should say your ma wanted to find somewhere she belonged. Or someone she belonged to.'

Now I am doing the thinking.

'So are you saying that perhaps a home does not need a roof?'

'Perhaps not, Tibb. And besides, home can be a person as much as a place.'

'I think you are my home then, Ivo.'

He looks all watery in those lovely eyes and he says, 'And you are mine, Tibb.'

Very perfect way

Months sail past and it should be winter soon but this sun is still too hot for all that. I am walking around in the almost-sea with my shirt-turban around my head and the cool water lapping around my ankles. My toes like the feeling of these ridges under the water: this sand has been raked with a giant comb, I think.

Again we have upped-sticks to another small cove because Ivo says it is important we do not get that thing called a reputation. He is thinking like a vagrant these days.

'The people of England were fighting wars against each other before you did come along, Tibb,' that woman called Ma did say once. 'And those two princes were murdered in a tower because of it all, and when that fighting was done, King Henry wanted more so he did make vagabonds the enemy instead though we have done nothing so bad.' Well that stuff is true enough, but I don't care about being an enemy so long as I'm with Ivo, and wandering with him is different than it was with her.

My back aches oddly this morning, and now I feel something dribbling out of me, between my legs, so I lift up this dress of mine and cast my eyes down to the place where I am now sporting that nice patch of downy hairs, and I am seeing there is a shock of red upon my thighs.

I stand very still a moment, the sun beating down. I could faint with that shock, but my ma did tell me that here is something which makes you into a fully-grown person, Tibb Ingleby, though blood in my mind is not ever good.

I walk back on to the beach with some dull thumping inside my skull.

'Ivo,' I say. 'I believe I am a woman.'

He is sitting by the graveyard of last night's small fire and he is plucking the feathers from a marsh-bird which he jumped upon this morning.

'Then I should congratulate you, Tibb!' he says, which is not what I expected him to say.

'But I do not find it such a wondrous thing, Ivo,' I say, sitting next to him. For some reason there is a sadness settling on my shoulders, not unlike the heaviness of the snake, and these small buds on my chest are painful to touch. 'This nuisance thing will stop me hunting for oysters anyway.'

He looks at me a while then he jumps to his feet and wipes his hands on those wool breeches. 'I have a plan, Tibb!' he says, and I watch as he is scampering around on the sand like a dog and collecting all the straggly pieces of seaweed which stink, and then as he sits again and plaits them into a sort-of-belt. The end of his tongue is sticking out between his lips because he is concentrating hard. I think he could shift the sun with all that effort.

'Here!' he says, and he ties it around his own waist like he is thinking hard still, and then he takes the shirt from my head and rips a long piece from the arm and ties it to that belt so it hangs underneath him between his legs.

'This will be a blotter, Tibb!'

He turns and turns, looking down at that thing, and he says, 'Try it!'

This seaweed-and-shirt invention is thrust at me but I am too stunned for a moment to move any part of me. Some slick of red does creep across Ivo's cheeks and then I throw my arms around his neck because I think he must be the kindest person who has ever lived in this kingdom called England

and I cannot think why his family made plans that would drive him away.

In the evening we sit as usual and have our marsh-bird dinner and a little egg each and Ivo leans forward and says, 'Here.'

There is something round and whitish between those tanned fingers of his.

'What is it?' I say.

'A pearl. I have been waiting to give it to you, Tibb, and today seems the perfect time.'

I take this thing with watery eyes, studying that ghostly sheen. How smooth and hard it feels to me. Uneven, but in a very perfect way.

Carefully, I put it into the pocket of my lace apron which is now much too small. And when Ivo is sleeping that night, I am looking up to those always-above-us stars and I am holding that thing up to the moon in case my ma is really up there after all.

'Would you look at this pearl, Ma?' I whisper, and she is answering me with a hoot-hoot in that sea-air, like: 'Fuck, Tibb! And this is some momentous day!'

This church-place is all corrupted

It has been one cold winter but I should say it's over now. Some nights we did find a barn and lie in the hay together, which I did oftentime with my own ma too, but it was different with Ivo. I didn't have much of that scared feeling because we weren't hiding there like the bad secret of some slimy man who would pop in and out for the fucking dance and who Ma might possibly kill with that bad knife.

When we couldn't reach a good barn then Ivo and I did sleep in cattle-wagons or wedge ourselves into the row-boats which were left out in the water-ways, covered with a canvas. Or we found caves and made fires in them even though that made us cough sometimes.

Right now the sun is sitting on top of our heads and Ivo says the month is March and we are hiding behind some trees near the coast at Slaughden which is in the land of Suffolk. This place has early shoots and flower buds sticking up in its roll-on-forever meadows and I am thinking soon it will be coloured in like a painting, and I wish to ask Ivo about those tiny birds which are gathering in the trees here since I haven't seen birds so little and blue like that before, but this is not why we are here. We are here for the purpose of watching a church. It is Sunday and the man called the priest is standing outside in his dress and he is telling all those people who go in that the big-man-God is arrived and ready for them which is a lie because how would the big-man fit in that small building?

'Come on, Ivo,' I say when those people are all inside, 'trust me.' And I drag him forward till we are huddled outside this door at the side of the church-place.

'Tibb,' he says with some wobbly note in his voice. 'Are you sure this is a good idea?'

He is not looking quite well just now, not like his usual self. I have brought him here by-hook-or-by-crook and it is quite clear he would rather be anywhere else. I press my ear to this tiny door and I can hear the strange language called Latin which the priests like so much, and I am watching Ivo's face turn to ash.

'What is it about churches, Ivo?' I ask. My friend has not ever wished to try a church on those coldest nights as Ma and I did oftentime. 'What are you scared of?'

He says, 'Nothing!' But I am not believing that too-quick answer one bit.

'Don't you want to have a nice sip of wine and a piece of bread?'

'It's just . . . this is stealing, Tibb.'

I grimace because stealing is not stealing if you really need that thing. And I have done this with my ma many times over. 'That one is a door for rabbits, Tibb!' she would say. 'You know they do never lock it.'

I tell him, 'We'll wait until the end and when the priest is gone home for his pork-dinner, then in we go by way of this little door and we will be feasting upon that bread and wine which is always left over on Sundays.'

'They could catch us,' he whispers with a tremble in that voice. 'Besides, the Church is in charge of every law in this country and we are quite clearly vagrants which is not lawful. We are climbing into the lion's den!'

'Trust me, Ivo.'

I think he does not trust me one piece.

That priest is speaking English again, and: 'Behold this toe-nail, o good people of Slaughden!'

A toe-nail?

'This, I have received from a man returned from the holiest land, and do you know it is the toe-nail of Joseph?'

Who is Joseph? I am wondering. And I am pressing my ear against that wood because I am hearing some great ruckus besides.

'Ivo,' I say. 'I believe there is an auction going on.'

He shakes his head. 'That is some poor deception, Tibb. He will have plucked that nail from his own toe this morning.'

'You think so?'

He shrugs. 'Those priest-men make relics from clay, and they are lifting water from wells and selling it off as holy. And they are charging such a lot of money for seats in Heaven.'

So my ma was right. This church-place is all corrupted.

Ivo whispers, 'And they are doing worse things than this.'

'What?'

He shudders. 'Bad, bad things, Tibb.'

I don't know what he means but my friend Ivo is scared just like I thought. Can't he see this place is like a treasure chest for empty stomachs?

Eventually those people clear out and the priest too and this door is not locked as I thought. They don't expect thievery in churches since the big-man is also the big judge-of-right-and-wrong and you would be some mighty fool to steal in front of his own eyes. Ha! It is warped with the cold though and I have to push hard to get it open.

'This is a good church, Ivo!' I say, and I have seen a few. My eyes are poking out on stalks like two crab-eyes at that painted ceiling, and this dusty smell is making me remember my ma. 'This is some cavernous bedchamber, Tibb,' she would say. 'Would you make yourself at home and ho-ho-ho?'

Ivo is not moving.

'Tibb!' he says. 'Get your bread and let's go!'

I trail a finger over the dark-wood seats and some merry tune is whistling from my lips and rising up to the rafters. At the front, there is a table all dressed in a white sheet like a big woman in a skirt and this is fucked-up since these church-places are no friends to women, Tibb. My ma was speaking of the adultresses who are hauled out each week to do their shame-walk in their nothing-at-all clothes, even though there are two persons in that naughty dance and Ma did vouch for that herself.

'This is the place for bread, Ivo,' I say, and I am eating those crusts and swigging the dregs of that sweet wine, but he is still rigid at the rabbit-door.

'Ivo?' I say, holding out the bottle. 'You will really not have any?'

He is all tetchy, glancing behind him. 'They will put two-and-two together when they see us, Tibb, and they will make four!'

'Fine,' I say, and I cram the rest of those crusts into my apron and then we are gone from here, but Ivo does not say one word all the way back and I am trying to work him out and this strange mood of his. What bad thing has the church-place done to Ivo?

Leominster, Herefordshire

His mouth is parched. He is imagining wine slipping down his throat. He imagines gulping it down till his teeth are stained. Rolling it around on his tongue till the whole bottle is drained.

He cannot know how much time has passed. Since he arrived here he has been plunged into darkness, and days and nights don't exist. There is no hole in the stonework to let in skinny beams of light and remind him that the sun still shines, because he is underground with the rats.

Perhaps he should pray but praying has never changed a thing for him. He lays his head back down on the wet hay, memories floating in and out of his mind like stormclouds. Himself. But a boy still. Stuffed into the pew beside his father, praying to be different. Praying that by the end of the service, he would walk out of that place somehow changed. But that never happened.

Footsteps jolt him. A key in the lock. Why? It can't be time for his sustenance yet. He sits up, his heart pounding. Is the King come already from court? There is a heaving in his chest; his hands shake.

The dim light of a lantern casts an oval on to the squalid floor and the pale, doughy face of the young warden is like a moon in here. White and round. He has a heel of bread and a cup in his hand and he holds out those things and glances around like someone might catch him at it.

The prisoner blinks. 'It's been two days already?'

The warden shakes his head. 'Barely one,' he whispers.

'Then why?'

He shrugs. 'I have my own opinions, whatever the rest of them should say about you.'

The prisoner takes the bread and the beer. 'Thank you,' he says, and he drinks deeply, the whole watered-down cup, savouring the warm sourness as though it were nectar.

'You're a good man,' the warden says, an earnest look across his face. 'And even good men fall foul of cunning women and witches.'

That word is squatting in this rank air. How easy it would be to play along; to take this story as his own. To feign ignorance. Innocence. He was duped by a witch! He shakes his head. 'The King?' he asks and the warden looks guilty, like all this might just be his fault.

'The message will be half-way to London by now, I should think.'

He nods, and he feels a fool that for a moment there was a glimmer of hope in that image when really he is simply counting down to his own death.

Once the man has gone, he is thinking of those stark words. Witches. Well she's no witch, but he can't get away from the fact it is her fault. That if it wasn't for Tibb he wouldn't be here at all. She cannot see that the world is formed in black and white; in straight lines carved into stone. But why would you fear rules when you have never been governed by them?

Why did he let everything unravel as it did? Why did he dare to believe that there was something grey in all that black and white? Something softer? This anger sits hard and strange inside him, like a stone in a nest, because how should he feel towards her now?

No tincture like it

We don't go back to the place-called-church, and these pesky seasons skip on and sneak up. Ivo and I trail around the coast all the way down to the land of Felixstowe and back up again and we watch as the leaves fall in the thickets behind the beaches, and then as all the birds do up-and-leave, and we are still wandering when they make their return to these marshlands.

Crabs and oysters make some fine-enough dinners and sometimes little fish which we do spear with a sharpened stick. Ivo knows how to spot the seaweed which is good to eat besides, and I have learnt to like that thick texture and the salty taste.

We hunt for eggs on the marshland and when the wading birds come to stop, Ivo is wringing a skinny neck and we cook that thing and feast away like two rich men with a hoo-and-haa. And even when the blood does think to arrive, I have been climbing into the oyster caves and running up dunes as usual with my fine seaweed belt. And every night, wherever we sleep, it is always close together, with Ivo's big arm around me.

Now we are returned to King's Lynn which is the place we met and Ivo says we have been together for two years now but that time has gone quicker and quicker which is not making much sense.

I should say I look quite different. Not much taller, but I have grown to have two fine bulbs which sit upon my chest like gargoyles and make my laced dress pull and stretch. Ma would say,

'Tibb, you are like a Queen of Constantinople!' Though she did not know much about that place any more than I do.

Ivo has changed too in that he is more muscly than before and bronzed to boot in this summer weather. 'You have been sculpted like a statue, Ivo!' I tell him as I chop his too-long hair and beard with the oyster knife. 'If only my own hair was thick like this. Why does it hang so thin and straight around my face like a white veil for a bride-woman?'

'A bride-woman?' he repeats, and he is thinking about this.

Later, when we are on a little walk, he says, 'Tibb, do you think you might take a husband one day?'

'A husband?'

'Yes, and have your own children to wade in the sea with?'

I have not thought of this idea even once.

'O, I have spent most of my life thinking of my ma, Ivo, and her own great hankering for a husband-man who might give us a roof.' My thoughts turn to Henrietta, cold dead under the hedge that morning. 'And I don't think I would be such a good ma anyway.'

'I don't think that is true, Tibb. But would you want that . . . a family, I mean?' He laughs a bit but it sounds hollow. 'Surely everyone wants that? To find someone to love as wives and husbands do . . . ?'

His eyes are searching me. Why does he ask me all these questions? Does he wish to get rid of me already?

We walk a while in silence and a tightness settles inside my chest because of Henrietta who is buried near here but I'm not sure where. I couldn't leave her. And I couldn't leave Ivo. Why would he even suggest it?

'Ivo, I like our life.'

He squeezes my hand but I am staring at the sand because of another thought which is slithering up. Perhaps Ivo asked me those questions because he does wish to marry me himself! This hot feeling is spreading up my neck and I think all the flowers in the world did just pop open at once.

He smiles. 'Tibb, can't you recognize where we are? We are back at the very rock where we met!'

Well that is something true enough. I remember him sitting there with his crab-wire and his almost-manly arms.

'But you are a great deal happier,' he says. 'And that is truly wonderful.'

I shrug. 'But Henrietta is still dead.'

I should say to Ivo that I think often of that dairy-farmer who had me spill the milk and those are no happy thoughts, but he is nodding at me like he often does and looking into my eyes like he can see beneath, at all the skull-bones and the feelings inside of them.

Then, 'Ivo?' I say slowly because I am thinking that farm is a half-day's walk from here in some direction. 'Would you come with your friend Tibb on one small errand?'

He is looking very shifty like I just brought out a knife.

'Tibb?' he says.

Here I am, back in the hedge near that bad dairy-farm. The morning is Sunday and I am feeling like I felt those two years ago with a dead baby in the soil and that snake choking me just the same. Here is a trip to the Hell-place, Ma.

Ivo squeezes my hand. 'What will you do, Tibb?'

'I will teach him a lesson.'

'Revenge?'

I nod because that thing did always make my ma feel better. 'There's no tincture like it,' she did say.

'Well you should do what you have to, Tibb, but I don't know if revenge will ease your grief.'

I want to ask, 'What do you know of grief, Ivo?' But there is something sad in his lovely blue eyes and I think – as I often do – that Ivo has not told me everything.

I say, 'I don't know either, my friend, but I wish to try it all the same.'

Won't you stake your claim on this land besides, Tibb? Don't you have a right to be here?

'Look,' I whisper, and we are ducking our heads because that bean-man is leaving his stone farmhouse with his fat wife who is shaped like a bucket herself from too much milk probably, and off they go in the horse-cart to the place-called-church to see the big-man. But those two snap-dogs have spilt out besides and they are prowling around the barn.

O, I am remembering these creatures like they chased me yesterday but you have shit for brains, Tibb, because did you not think they would do it again?

Ivo is rummaging in his trouser pocket, and he takes out one big dead crab.

'Ivo? I did think you smelt too much of sea! But how did you know where we were going?'

He shrugs. 'I had a feeling.'

Now we are creeping up and Ivo does toss those dogs that smelly crab. Such a whining and a scratching at the shell for the meat inside – I should think they will be there till the sun goes down.

Well we open the gates and let out those big creatures so they wander off and follow the best of the grass. Traipsing through that shallow river and far over the fields till some other farmers will catch them and claim them as their own even though nothing in this life comes for free, Tibb.

'Share your milk with my sister, you fucker,' I say quietly. 'Or you will not have any yourself.'

On the walk back Ivo puts that arm around my shoulders and I'm glad I didn't do this thing on my own.

'Do you feel better, Tibb?'

I think a while and I can't look at him. The sky is spitting on us.

'Not yet,' I say. 'Maybe tomorrow I will.'

A V upon your foreheads

We are lounging in the shallows. Not swimming, though Ivo has taught me some good-enough strokes, but we are lying like two mermaids and the month is June so we are hot and I have unbuttoned my dress and pulled the sleeves down so I am all bare-chested to this sun and Ivo has taken off his shirt too. But here is a great shouting from the beach and that man is panting down like a bull.

'Vagabonds will be outlawed! We have seen fire from this part!'

Ivo freezes – I have not seen him go so pale since we went to the church-place. My fingers are fumbling as I pull up the sleeves of my dress.

'I will have you branded with a V upon your foreheads!' the angry man is shouting towards us. 'I will tell the Church about you both, and you will be forced into labour of the very worst kind! And this is to be shamed besides . . . this fornicating!'

He storms off with many cruel tidings about returning with a torch-fire party and villagers to boot, and Ivo says we must run. There is a look of terror in those blue eyes and it doesn't suit my Ivo who is shaped like a man and who has protected me from everything. He is stuffing on those shoes that he never does wear on these beaches then he takes my hand and pulls.

'Ivo?' I say, but he is pulling me all down this beach, so fast that my eyes are watering in the wind, and my thoughts are turning red and black and the sand is turning red too, like all the crabs are scuttling along behind.

'Ivo!' I pant, turning round to stare at that one-time home. 'We left the tankard and the blanket!'

He doesn't answer me because he is grit-your-teeth-running.

'Ivo!' I shout again and that wind makes my nose stream. There is panic clawing at my throat when I think of that fire of ours with the tankard and the blanket beside it because those things were Ma's and without them I don't have anything left of her. And then another thought slaps me across the face and I am tripping over my own feet since now I am formed of wood too.

Henrietta. Don't you know Henrietta is back there?

Above, the sky is darkening and I am following Ivo along dirt tracks while the sun goes to its west-bed. Henrietta. She is all I can think of.

Eventually we are stopping at a thicket in a small woodland and Ivo is making us a little home within the bushes, but this place is not our home because the sea is all gone and that stars-roof too. I can hardly look at him and we don't speak for a while but the sky is moaning for the both of us. There is a sagging in the clouds, like they need to piss out all that hanging-water.

'Ivo,' I say eventually. 'Why did we have to leave like that?'

He says, 'Would you trust me, Tibb?' But he doesn't look at me.

I cannot make sense of any of it. This forest smells musky and damp and nothing like that salty sea-air. I think it is going to collapse on top of us.

'What is *fornicating* anyway?'

This is the word which the man said. And he did say it with that hiss-of-venom and a face-like-thunder.

Ivo shrugs. 'Like to kiss and lie with someone as wives and husbands do.'

My eyebrows furrow. 'But we were not doing those things. So why did he say that?'

Ivo doesn't answer but I notice he is all red in his face. He scratches wood for a fire but not very well and those pieces keep slipping from his hands.

'Ivo?' I say. 'We were doing nothing—'

'I know!' he snaps, and this tone sounds all wrong from Ivo's mouth. It is making some tears rise up into my eyes and those bright and calm days we shared are sliding away like they have somewhere else to be.

He says quieter, 'Of course we were not,' and he sharpens that stick some more.

We stay like this in the silence and the moonlight is worming its way through these thick trees. The forest sounds are so different from the usual bird-callings of the beaches. These scurrying noises and the hootings are pressing in on us and my ma is not hanging up there any more.

I watch him from the corner of my eye. Squatting all hunched against a tree-trunk; the steeliness in his eyes. Like this fire-stick is some foe to him. What is going on inside that lovely head? He never tells me a thing. Not why he was running in the first place. Nothing about his family. And he knows everything about me. He catches my eye then he looks away because we are in separate countries now.

Hoot-hoot says the owl and that sounded close. Wise owls, said my ma, and you are no wise owl, Tibb, but perhaps you were right the other day. When Ivo asked about husbands. Perhaps he is angry now because in fact he *wanted* to be fornicating with me and this is the reason for that crinkled brow of his.

This thought is squatting inside my head like it would grow roots there. Perhaps Ivo has loved me all along and I have missed those signs. Why have I shared with him all my secrets about the new bulbs, and allowed him to make me a belt for when the blood was coming? I watch as he blows on a small flame and I should say I am seeing him in some different way. Like the colours changed.

Standing up, he stretches his broad back like the world is something heavy to carry and all men want a wife to give them babies, Tibb. A son in any case, judging by the cord-wainer man. Well I am copying that lip-biting which my ma would do when she was busy making someone love her and I do stand on my tip-toes and press my lips on his.

For a moment he just stays very still with big open eyes. He doesn't put his arms around me like when we sleep or when we are laughing, but how can I blame him when he has been angling all along to be more-than-just-friends and I didn't see that thing staring me in the face? I am attached like a big white spider and he holds me up so I don't fall, but then he places me gently back down on to the damp floor of this woodland and the barely-there sun falls out of the sky.

'Ivo?'

'It isn't you,' he says.

There are tears gathering up in my eyes as I turn away and he holds on to my shoulders like he wants to yank me round and eye-ball me. 'Tibb! You have to believe me! If I wanted a wife, it would be you!'

I say, 'All men want a wife, Ivo,' and I am remembering Farmer O and those things he said when he climbed into that mattress. Like: 'No one loves you, Tibb.' And I am thinking that man was right all along.

Perhaps a tanner

In the morning I can't really look at Ivo for all those shame-thoughts. That was some long night and the rain was dropping on me like it would say, 'Serves you right, Tibb. You thought Ivo would take *you* as a wife?'

Now he reaches for my hand and he says, 'Tibb, do you forgive me?'

His eyes are searching me all worried like he really means it so I nod and he breathes in deeply like he is truly very relieved. Then he gives me a soft leaf which he must have buried in a cup-shape into the ground because it is full up with cold rainwater. I gulp it down.

'We cannot carry on living how we have been,' he says. 'I'm worried what they might do to us, Tibb. What that man said . . .'

'Ivo, I have been a vagrant all my life and no one has put a V upon my head yet. We just need to move on, that's all. Perhaps we will go down south?'

I think these words are made of feathers, the way he shakes his head and stares right through me.

'Tibb, we cannot be running and hiding forever. It was always going to end sometime.'

'Why? You said yourself a home is not always a roof.'

He looks at me a long time. 'I promise you we will have an even better roof than the starry one. And a table, and a mattress.'

'Ivo, I have never had those things before. Mattresses and tables. I liked the way we lived.'

There is something happening beyond those blue and now tinged-with-red eyes and I can't work it out. I want to tell him: 'Ivo, that angry man and his words about the church-place have scared you, and now you are all changed!'

He leans his back against this tree like standing is some great effort to him.

'I think I must learn a new trade,' he says. 'Not to farm that is, but something in town.'

'A *trade*?' I repeat, like this is some bad language. 'In *town*?'

Towns are bad places with their watching-men and their pillories and we only went there when my own ma needed to make monies by the deed of whoring.

'A trade like what?'

He shrugs with those droop-eyes. 'Perhaps a tanner or something. A blacksmith . . .'

'And what would you have *me* do, Ivo? Girls cannot learn any trade like you can, but only to be a man's serving maid.'

'Tibb!' he says, like this is some terrible thing. 'I would not ever see *you* bound up by work. That would kill me, I think. You are a free spirit.' He shakes his head. 'You can pose as my maid. You see I have it all planned out.'

'Your maid?' I repeat. And here is the fucked-up truth of it: my own Ivo would prefer to have me pose as his maid than call me his wife. That is some big puff of shame just there. I can hardly see through it, and I am cursing these skinny arms and legs of mine, and this strange colouring. These eyes which are too big for my face.

'Tibb, once I have a trade – something useful – and the respect of people, and a reference for my character, the world will open up for us.'

That weak smile doesn't look right on Ivo's face, because it is false and he is not telling me a thing. I cannot understand what terrible thought is whistling through my dear friend's head, but there is some yawning-empty hole inside of his heart because of it.

He holds on to my shoulders and bends so his lovely eyes are glaring into mine. Searching me with that worried look again. 'Can't you imagine it, Tibb? Can't you see that future? A house all of our own with a roof like your ma wanted for you?'

Why don't we have that nice wood roof like the rest of them, Ma? I asked that question once and I think that pierced her deep but she just laughed and said, 'Tibb, don't you know what's good in this life such as the sun rising and setting and the rain on your skin?' And sometimes she would have us stand on almost-mountains and hold our hands out to catch the droplets, but mostly she just cried about the no-roof problem. The up and the down and the nothing-in-between was something hard to predict with my ma but I got skilled at that. She said, 'Tibb, don't you see me trying?'

I sigh. 'Then I guess I must be your maid, Ivo.'

He hugs me, but his warm, muscular arms are not very sure like they used to be. These are some terrified arms and there is a gap widening between us that my ma would call a crevice and I think somehow it is all my fault.

Not so angelic

The town Ivo speaks of is going by the name of Peterborough and I do not think this is somewhere I have been before.

It takes us the day and the next morning to walk there and we are not so easy with each other because I am busy pinching my lips and my cheeks and I cannot imagine Ivo going to work every day. What will I do apart from miss him? Then I am thinking of Henrietta and the fact we are walking away from her. What if she would wake up and call for me? O, you have shit for brains, Tibb Ingleby.

When we arrive at Peterborough the time is afternoon and it is market day and the noises of this place are too big and too close and there is sweat forming under my own arms. Such a heaving throng of people over this wood bridge – I am seeing a dozen water sellers already. This one is all pinch-faced and dancing in front of me, and would you offer it to those poor pack-horses instead, sir?

'We mustn't look like vagrants, Tibb. Keep your head up, like we know this place and like we have a right to be in it.'

O, we don't have two rights to rub together, my friend.

We traipse through skinny alleys which are cold and sunless like the God-man got upset. This dirt stinks like shit and I am stepping in it without shoes.

'Mud is not so pleasant to the feet as sand, Ivo,' I say hopefully, like this might make him change his mind and announce that we can leave again.

In these wider cobbled streets I am too hot and sticky and there are a great many tents of cutlers and mason-people and a big pavilion of leatherworks which is reminding me of the smell of the cordwainer's own house. Here are live pigs and dead pigs and pedlars of every kind with mirrors and pins and ribbons. The smells from these tables of fish are making my stomach turn, and I have some feeling of being watched besides.

'I think people can see we are not from around here, Ivo.'

He smiles softly, shaking his head, and there is a glimpse of my old friend again. 'I think it is the case that people think you beautiful, Tibb.'

But *you* don't think me beautiful, Ivo.

This square is heaving and I am studying the people as they line up for their honey and their fine spices like they think this is London. There is even a goldsmith's bench at this place!

'Which is your best offering, sir?'

'The price is too dear!'

Why do rich folk always haggle over prices? The ones dressed in fine broadcloth doublets with capes, and with those rolls of spare fat on their necks? This is making little sense, but then nothing is making sense to me since we left that beach.

'Ivo,' I say. 'Would you wait for me here?'

Bread, Tibb. Bread and beer. So said my ma on the subject of survival, though she did live mostly on the second one alone.

'Fuck!' they call, and 'Get the hens!' because those chickens are pecking around outside their pen and while every merchant is diving to help, I am feeling the floury surface of two buns in my hands.

'Where to, Ivo?' I say when I am back.

He looks at my bulging apron like I did just slice a man up.

'You took them, Tibb?'

I shrug. 'I let the chickens out to distract them. That wood bridge. We can sit under there.'

And we do, and at least the sun cannot catch us here, and Ivo is eating his bun despite saying, 'Tibb, would you be careful, since I would not ever wish to see you on the whipping post.'

'Ivo, my ma did teach me well.'

He smiles weakly and says, 'You are not so angelic as you look, Tibb.'

A farmer called O

When that hot sun turns red for the evening then Ivo and I are staring up at our under-the-bridge roof which is in fact rotting, and there is a heaviness crouching on my chest and some bad words inside my head that are hard to ignore since those words are in the gruff voice of Farmer O. He does always speak to me when things go wrong. And he says, 'You are some slice of evil, Tibb Ingleby, and have you heard of just rewards?'

'Perhaps it is my fault, Ivo,' I say quietly. 'Perhaps the big-man-God is real after all, and perhaps he sent that shouting man on the beach to scare us away.'

Ivo turns towards me, and his lovely face is all drawn. 'Tibb?' he says. 'What are you talking about?'

There is a dull beating inside me because it is not often that I speak of Farmer O. Not ever in fact.

'Maybe I did not deserve that nice roof-of-stars and that wondrous beach-life, because I am a bad girl and I do bad things.'

'Who said that to you, Tibb?'

Well that old friend called the black snake is slinking back on to my shoulders and making my breath grow shallow.

'Ah, when I was young, my ma did have us stay some weeks with a farmer called O.'

'Farmer O?'

'I do not like to say his whole name, Ivo, since something happened at his farmhouse in the bad land of Weymouth that I shall never forget though I try to. Something I did there . . .'

I am not looking into those glassy eyes of his, but I am

twisting my thin white hair around my fingers like each one has a noose.

'And would you tell me?' he whispers. I should say every breath in this world is held just now.

I swallow hard. All those bad thoughts. 'Well most nights he did spend with my ma doing their under-the-blanket dance, but one time that all changed. My ma was snoring away, and Farmer O did slip into my on-the-floor-bed instead, and he ran his big farmer hands all down my body and I lay there stiff as a board, Ivo, because I did not like that thing a bit and there was some white fear in me.'

Ivo's face is so pale and still, I should say his jaw is carved of chalk. I don't like to think what he will make of his old friend Tibb once he does know the real truth.

'And then he did whisper to me, "I have a thought you are some slice of evil, Tibb Ingleby. You have been tempting me all day to do this thing and have me betray your own loving ma." So I told him, "I did not tempt you, sir," and he did say, "You don't even know you did it since you are bad to your bones and this cruel streak is in your blood." And he had some probing hands and his fingers were like iron-fingers, Ivo, and they pushed and pushed up inside of me till my eyes were streaming with that pain and the sheet was splattered with my own blood. And that made him all breathless and crazed in his eyes.'

These words are tumbling out of my mouth quicker and quicker, like they have been waiting a long time to escape.

Ivo is staring at the ground and he says slowly, 'And did the farmer put his own part inside of you?'

I shake my head. 'No, because that dance is loud and my ma would have heard it. But he put that thing in my hands and then in his until he was quite done. And after he did whisper that I should not ever tell my ma if I loved her, because it would ruin her life to think her own daughter had betrayed her like that.'

Ivo nods lots of times, like he is choosing his words.

'Tell me you told her, Tibb.'

'I didn't for a while, and this thing did happen some more because I was encouraging it, so said Farmer O. And then he threw my ma away as all the men did, and only some years later did I speak of it.'

'And?'

'O, she took us marching back down this country to Weymouth because she had a thought to slice his neck, but he had fucked off and who knew where?'

Ivo looks like the world has ended under this rotting bridge, and now I have said it, I have some strange wish to know what he thinks of all of this business.

'But, Ivo, Farmer O was right, because I told my ma and in fact it *did* ruin her life, because after that, she was never the same again. She drank and drank and she did start to kill other men who were not really deserving of that thing. Like the men who paid some money to have a quick fuck. I remember the first time it happened. "Money for our roof," she said as she did slip behind the King's Arms at Doncaster. She did not return with mead though, but a dead man who she was dragging by the feet. "Fuck!" and "What did you do?" I said. And she told me: "Well he did have the same eyebrows as that farmer person, Tibb." Then she was sobbing away because she didn't take it lightly. And that same thing would happen many times after but I could not think her bad for those throat-slittings, because that was all *my* fault.'

Above this bridge I think even the sky has its listening ears out.

I shake my head. 'I should never have told her. And I should not ever have tempted him in the first place.' I stop here and

I put my head into my hands. 'O, this thing always hurts my head. There is too much thinking to be done on it.'

'There is no thinking, Tibb. None.'

Ivo guides my head up and has me look at him by cupping my face in his warm palms. There is something calming in this. 'This farmer was a terrible man and you were right to tell your ma. He told you a lie, Tibb. He made you think *you* were evil when in fact *he* was the truly evil one.'

I am thinking about this. I am thinking of the fact I killed my baby sister, or at least that I did not keep her alive. Then I am thinking of nothing at all.

'But sometimes, Ivo, when life is bad, I think of those words. And that is why I said I will never be an angel and see that woman my ma again.'

'I think you are an angel, Tibb,' he says, and he is so very sure that it is making me a bit more sure too.

'And not all men are bad, you know.'

'I know. Because you are a man and you are very good.'

He is looking at me a long time and then he says, 'Come on, Tibb. We are not going to starve here.'

Now he is taking off one of those leather shoes which do not suit him and he is pulling out one coin. 'An end-of-the-world coin,' he says. 'For times like these.'

The Lamb and Boy

Ivo takes me to that tavern which is a noisy building and those black timber frames look like spider-legs wrapped around it. He says this place is going by the name of the Lamb and Boy, because Ivo has a little bit of the great skill-of-reading.

I have stood outside enough taverns from my ma's days of charging-for-it and that bad habit of murder which sometimes followed. And other times I dipped inside those places to drag her from the table when she did drink enough liquor to make her words come out like sludge and I never did like to see the men laughing and poking at her while her eyes closed. But now it is different because Ivo says we are here for the good times.

It is teeming with men in velvet breeches and craftsmen with dirt streaked down their shirts, and all of them bumping up together like this is one cooking pot. But we enter like the two vagabonds we are and we are not fitting into either of those camps. My no-shoes feet are something like a sore thumb in this place with its stone benches and its nice wood tables and I am wondering if Ivo and I will really be finding the good times here amongst these shout-a-lot town-people.

'Hold your head up, Tibb,' he whispers. 'Like we belong here.'

But we do not belong here since Ivo is all beach-tanned and the two of us do not belong anywhere except under the covered-in-stars roof with my dead sister nearby and my ma in the sky.

'We will have some beer, if you please,' Ivo says to the nice-bulbs maid. 'And some meat stew too.'

Meat stew? Well maybe the good times are edging closer after all. In fact my body is feeling a great deal lighter since I told Ivo about Farmer O.

We sit at a table next to two men and this feels mighty strange. I could be the Queen of Constantinople sitting to dine like this, though my feet don't reach the stone floor. Ma did make us an eating-table once too, right on the edge of a moor when the fog was low. She turned over a cattle trough and she put two leaves out like we had plates and she said, 'Those rich folk do thank the big-man-God whenever they sit at a table, Tibb, and that's some horse-shit right there!' And we did eat our cold mushrooms and they tasted different than usual, coming from the table.

My eyes wander over the stone walls and the oak barrels stacked up against them and the men who have gathered around one of the tables and who are banging their fists down all at once. Then over the skinny fiddler-man who has started playing by the fire, a small dog by his ankles.

These table-fellows are both very jolly and jovial and I like their smiles. One is pale and gangly and he says his name is Samuel; the other is big and round with a bald head that looks like the shiny duck eggs we were pinching oftentime in the sweet lands of Norfolk and Suffolk. This person is called Ewan, and my ma did once have a man called Ewan who we were stalking and she was sometimes fucking but this one is nicer already.

They ask, 'Are you new in the area?' and Ivo says, 'Yes, friends,' because he is very kindly like this.

They are doing lots more smiling and Samuel says to me, 'You are very beautiful, madam.'

'She is,' says Ivo, like he is very proud of me. 'This is Tibb.'

'Tibb,' they say and they are shaking my hand which has dirt trapped under every single nail. 'Well what a lucky man your husband here is!'

'O, I am not her husband,' Ivo says quickly, like this would be a very shameful thing to him, and those words are all jagged around my heart. He is studying me like he feels guilty already.

'We're staying here,' Ewan says. 'Just a few nights and then on to another tavern.'

'You are travelling the country?' I ask.

'Something like that. We do not like to stay put long.'

This seems strange, since they are clearly not vagabonds like us. They can afford to stay at inns for a start, so why do they not buy their very own roof? And do they not wish to take wives? They are older than Ivo and me after all.

'Are you brothers?' I ask, but it seems unlikely, since they do not look like brothers.

'Just friends,' they say, and I do spy for a moment Ewan's hand holding Samuel's beneath this table so they must be very good friends indeed. I should say my Ivo has seen that thing too and his body is softening next to mine like perhaps he was a plank of wood before and that is something strange.

'Fuck, Ivo!' I say when my meat stew arrives and a big loaf of cheat-bread beside it, and those sad feelings are slipping away. I should say I am not good for any more talking. It has been mostly fish these last two years so meat is something like nectar and this bread is no cheating thing from where I am sitting. I am licking that plate clean and then I am belching by accident and those two nice men smile because you are no lady, Tibb Ingleby.

'Would you have another?' Samuel asks and I shake my head because Ivo and I spent the money now. But Ewan does stop that maid and say, 'Another plate of it! And four tankards of beer, please, madam!'

'We cannot pay you for that,' Ivo says quickly, but the egg-man waves a hand like he is saying, 'No bother, my friend!'

Now these three men are chattering away together and Ivo is smiling and he hasn't done much of that since we left the beach. I am going outside to piss with this beer swishing around inside me and all that fine food. Would you piss on your own feet, Tibb?

By the time I return, my Ivo seems even lighter. Like all that worry he had today about becoming a blacksmith or not becoming a blacksmith has just drifted up towards the clouds. I think he did borrow that grin from our table-friends.

When we do walk back to our under-the-bridge house, I ask, 'What are you thinking, Ivo? There seemed to be such a good feeling between the three of you and perhaps I missed something important.'

'O, nothing much, Tibb. It is nice to speak to other people. I think I do not feel so much alone now.'

'Alone?' I say, and I am standing on those cobbles by the river like he just slapped me around the chops. 'But you are never alone with me!'

'I know that!' he laughs, and this makes very little sense but I approve of anything which makes Ivo laugh.

We lie under our rotting-bridge-home and Ivo puts his arm around me and he says, 'Soon we will have a proper roof, Tibb. I promise.'

I wish to say that I liked the stars-roof more than any other roof, but perhaps he is right. I can't imagine it would be some sweet thing to have a great V across my head, all burnt into my skin. Perhaps that stars-roof was too good to be true.

'Goodnight, Ivo,' I say, and he is giving me a soft kiss on my forehead.

Then: 'Ivo, do you promise me one day we might go back to that beach just once, because I did not say goodbye to that sister of mine.'

He says, 'Tibb, I promise.'

Most deplorable way

In the morning, I follow Ivo around as we make enquiries for his big new job at those cutlers and tanneries and those tents of metal workers and he is asking after those things called *apprenticehoods*. There seems to be a shortage of openings. Inside my head some bats are circling because of last night's beer-drinking. I think my own ma must have been warding off the bats every day of her life.

In a blacksmith's workshop they have Ivo flex the muscles of his lovely arms and then swing a great hammer upon a beam of metal but we are stopped short, for there is a pealing of bells outside and that is no normal sound but something urgent and bad. A stomping of feet and a hollering from the square.

Like everyone else in their aprons and their wool caps, we surge forward with the crowd, all crushed in like this is a pen for sheep. Wide-eyed about something. But what?

In the centre of those dirty cobbles there are two men, thrashing, held with their arms behind their backs.

'Ivo,' I say, and I can feel some coldness crawling across my skin. 'It is our friends from last night!'

He is not answering, and now the crowd is closing in and that prattling is all muffled like someone did cover up my ears.

'Ivo, what's happening to those nice people?'

Samuel and Ewan are twisting and squirming like there is fire beneath their toes.

'Shh, Father Brian will speak!' some town-people say.

It is a slight man who steps forward but he seems to shut

these crowds up by just being there. He doesn't wear a hat like the other churchly men but if the rain fell I think it would roll off that slick hair in droplets because he did pat it down with duck fat and part it with a knife. There is a great hush like the world did pull its curtains.

'The transgressions of God's people is shameful. It has become clear to me that sins such as lust and adultery which are punished often are not the very worst sins against nature, but that there is a vice more evil which has wound its way into this kingdom. A different, more unspeakable sodomy. And now the demon of the spirit has entered two men who would travel through this parish and has bound them together like spouses.'

It is strange – his voice is something quiet and high-pitched but these words seem to poke holes in this town square like they are formed of barb. I do not like the creeping of this silky voice around my neck or this feeling that terrible things will occur because of it.

'What's happening?' I ask Ivo again, because all those long words did pass over my own head, but my dear friend is white beside me like he is a corpse-person. Like Henrietta looked when she was stiff on the soil that morning.

Father Brian continues. 'It is my understanding that they were found this day at the tavern of the Lamb and Boy not twenty yards from this square, caught in the most deplorable way in an upstairs chamber by the fire-lad, a Master Vaux himself.'

That smirking boy is standing like he has discovered gold in this very ground and I want to box him round the ears because I am piecing this story together and this stranger-word called sodomy. But I am worried for Ivo beside me who is breathing from the corner of his mouth like there is something obstructing his throat.

Samuel, who was so calm and smiling just last night, is

moaning on the cobbles like he is bound for the slaughter house. Will they make an animal of him here?

'If the Lord did make these urges inside of me, then you are saying our creator is not himself perfect, though the Lord of your reckoning is most perfect!'

Here is a fine-enough point, but his words are quickly stolen; at Father Brian's nod, he has been cast down by a mighty bludgeon and I am covering up my face because this is something truly evil. The cold feeling is winding around me and sucking at me, and I am seeing those cruel faces of Father Brian and his henchman who did that thing and that boy Master Vaux like they are puffed up with air. This is some terrible barbarity. The scorn in the faces of these fuckers, and the anguish of the poor men who bought us ale and meat stew from their own pockets. 'Tibb,' Ma said when she met the cordwainer, 'time to bury that knife since my bad days are over.' In fact, I would like the knife right now, Ma, to do some good damage of my own.

'These words are Godless themselves,' Father Brian says with that silky voice, and his head moves too fast, like he is a sniffing-dog. 'For you have both perverted the course of nature. God did not create you this way, but rather you have succumbed to the ways of the devil, Lucifer.'

I am thinking that the long dress Father Brian wears is making him the ruler-of-everything.

He turns to the crowd. 'They will be marched into the farrier's just there, to be castrated so they might never do another act of this nature as long as the sun shines upon this Earth.'

Those two kind men start to writhe like snakes but this cruel crowd of people are enjoying it, or at least they seem to be. I cannot bear to be amongst them and watch this awful thing happen. What is wrong with the world, Tibb? And did the blackbirds swoop down and pull the sky to the ground?

'Ivo,' I whisper. 'What can we do?'

Perhaps I am made of iron with this new sadness and this thrumming inside my belly and my head.

He doesn't answer me, and it is some bad shock when I glance there to find him on the floor like a puddle of jelly, his hands all stiff and his fingers sticking in every direction like two splayed forks.

'Ivo!' I say. And 'My dear friend, Ivo!'

So simple in your eyes

I have dragged my friend Ivo to our rotting-bridge-home which is a hundred yards or so from that square. Even from here the crowd is testy with the spiky shards of what has just happened, and those screams from the farrier's tent are squatting in the air like they will never blow away. The sun is setting on this river like the water is bloodied too.

I look down at Ivo who is lying grey and slick with cold sweat. His eyelids are fluttering, as though something bad is happening underneath them. Is he dreaming of those men?

I climb down the wide bank of this river and lean into the shallow stream, wetting my hands, and I rest them against Ivo's face until he opens his eyes.

'Ivo,' I whisper. 'I feared you would die.'

He sits up very heavily, blinking like this is some new world. Like when my ma would say, 'Did the watchmen cart me off, Tibb?'

'Those men,' he says. 'Is it . . . done?' He whispers like the wind shouldn't hear it.

'It is done, Ivo. I believe that the golden-dressed man named Father Brian made up that punishment from some very dark place inside his head.'

He sits very still and very white. 'There is no limit to their power, Tibb,' he says and then he touches his forehead and his cheeks over and over again like he is checking all the parts of him are still there, and he lies back down.

'I wish you had told me, Ivo.'

His eyes are closed like he doesn't want to see anything of

this world. I think he is deciding whether to admit this thing or not. I take his hand. My dear, kind Ivo who has cared for me and who has never left me. That he should have to hide anything of himself is something truly fucked-up.

'But, Ivo, all those people boo-ing . . . there are more fuckers in this kingdom than I knew.'

'People are just frightened, Tibb. They will do and think anything the priests tell them, because the power of the Church is something truly fearsome.'

Well my ma did warble just those same notes and I can see now why Ivo did not like my tricks of snatching the bread and the sweet wine from the church-place. Then I smile. 'I should say I am relieved, Ivo, that the reason you do not want me as a wife is not because I am very ugly and strange-looking indeed.'

'This is what you thought?'

I nod.

He smiles lightly, though it doesn't travel into his eyes as it usually does.

'Life is so simple in your eyes, isn't it, Tibb?'

'It is, Ivo.'

I put my arm around his broad shoulders, which feels odd because usually it is the other way round.

That afternoon passes in some quiet way, and I am snatching us more buns which Ivo won't eat. He lies looking up at the bottom of the wood bridge, all crumpled like a rag, and that cold sweat glistening on his perfectly-sculpted face. There is a silent lull in this town of Peterborough, like the birds are in protest. When the moon comes up he is hugging me extra tight, like I would crumble into the air. And then he is watching me while my eyes are closing and closing.

'This is some dangerous world,' he whispers. 'Tell me you would never wander it alone . . .'

'Ivo?' I mumble, and 'What are you talking about?'

He says again, 'If anything ever happens, will you promise me that?'

I open one eyelid. 'Those priestly men will never get you, because they will have to come through Tibb Ingleby first.'

He smiles.

'Why are you watching me, Ivo?'

'No reason, Tibb.'

Leominster, Herefordshire

Time has passed. Hours. But how many? The beer and bread seem like months ago. He kicks his foot out at the damp, pissed-on hay like this should make him feel better. Memories and thoughts are plaguing him, multiplying to fill this tiny space. Soon there will be no room to breathe and he knows that feeling well. It's why he went to the beach in the first place.

'We'll take your son for a bag of grain each quarter.' That's what the petty school demanded of his father and so he went. And he sat behind a boy called Robert whose mother was a widow. While the teacher spoke of great philosophers and transcribed Latin prayers, he studied the back of this boy's head. The waxy whiteness of the scalp beneath his short brown crop; the curly hairs around his ears.

They became friends, running to the woods after school, playing in streams. They started pressing their lips on one another's – just to practise for the wives they would marry when they were old enough. Then they agreed they didn't want a wife. They wanted each other.

But that woodland was no island as they thought and his father's prying eyes were everywhere, observing those two boyish hands entwined. He remembers the feel of the stick against his back. And, a while after, that name: Catherine. A girl produced to make things right again. But unlike Robert, who was married off and sent to live out his days in Harrogate, he found he couldn't do it.

He remembers the night he ran away. Gathering up his things, waiting for the moon to climb higher. Slipping out quietly while his sisters slept. At the front door he walked carefully around the bowl of coins his mother kept there. She had counted them that evening, as she did every night. Even now he can recall the sound of her muttering as she added them up; the metal clinking. Money to give the priest for their seats in Heaven.

He coughs. This damp is making his chest heave. Maybe death is preferable over a life spent hiding. Maybe he should be grateful for what Tibb did.

A familiar kind of shame settles over his body, sinking into his skin. Into the clothes he wears. Into the hay and the crevices in the walls. For a long while, he believed he was entirely alone in the world. And then a glimmer of hope; the presence of others like him. The relief had been overwhelming – he was solaced – but that feeling was lacerated so quick and left to bleed out.

Footsteps again, and more than one set but no cane. He sits up, a drumming gathering inside his chest. Thundering there. And a swooping in his guts that perhaps he will be hauled out and burnt in a matter of moments. But the iron door creaks opens just a little and the cellar is bathed in golden light. His breath has stalled.

'You came?' he breathes.

'I paid off the warden,' the other man says. 'Ivo, we don't have long.'

Inside my innards

When I wake, there is a feeling like I am falling through clouds and that the ground will rise up to meet me. Ivo. He is gone.

The morning sun has turned black and the world is shivering. Some taste of metal is flooding my mouth and my ears are beating and beating like the crows did descend. 'Ivo?' I say but I can't hear it much.

I stagger up and 'Ivo! Ivo!' says a bad voice, louder and louder, and it doesn't sound like it is coming out of my own mouth but someone else's. This panic has the market-people gawping like fish.

'Ivo! Ivo! Ivo!' I shout and it is getting less sleep-crackled and more urgent. I think this word will drop off a cliff if I don't say it enough. 'Ivo!'

That merchant of belts and leather stuff stares like I am naked just here. In the blacksmith's I scream, 'Ivo! Ivo!' because maybe he is just doing his new job. 'Fuck off!' they say, and 'Would you shut your trap?'

I am squawking this sweet name beside the milk urns till that word is making gashes in my throat and the man with all his linens does shove me out the way in case I should put off the customers. But customers and milk and linens don't matter if Ivo is gone. Why does nobody see it?

'Ivo!'

They are whispering about me in groups on these cobbles but I am existing somewhere outside of my body and watching on and I should say it too: 'Would you shut that trap, girl?' Because deep down inside my innards, I know he is gone for good.

Ivo. My own saver-of-life man. The man who is called my very own home. My heart is torn in two so I am split down the middle and I am all prickly with confusion and terror because this is alone, Tibb.

I return to the bridge-house like my feet are seizing up and I am forming a ball under here with my pale twig-arms around my knees and I am shutting my eyes on this world which is in fact some dreadful Hell-place with this Ivo-shaped hole in it.

The snake is back. It is winding around my body like it never left and squeezing in all those same places like my ribs and also my throat and don't you know evil will be punished, child? Right again, Farmer O.

I drag myself into that river – the shaded patch beneath this bridge – because I need to check I can feel the wetness of it, and by that I mean to check I am still alive. I squat here. Like the wading birds that lived in the marshes but with none of their own gracefulness and just with full-up eyes which perhaps will never stop leaking.

Where are you, Ivo? Why did you leave? The market behind is too noisy for my ears so I hold my hands over them. Perhaps I will stay in this water till I die. I am still here and shivering when those young children come and begin their river-play. They try to rile me like a monster under their bridge.

'You don't *look* like a vagrant,' one says to me. Her little face is cocked to the side like her neck has been severed.

She comes closer and touches a hand to my long white hair. 'Are you an angel?'

Disturb the ants

This is some dark-enough forest and I am up inside this tree-hollow, folded in like I should be a white owl. Three days like this. Like a wild creature. Ever since I did leave that shit town called Peterborough and its rotting-bridge-house.

Something like terror is rippling through me but it is silent now and dull, like it will stretch on forever. Between my fingers that pearl feels smooth and bumpy and I will never sell this thing because otherwise that life with a man named Ivo never happened at all.

My stomach is hungry in a low, scratching kind of way, but until the sun sets then I am not stepping down on to that forest floor. These woods are empty enough but who knows what could happen now Ivo is gone? My mind is playing some evil tricks and I think if my toe meets that cold soil then this whole forest will burst into flames and the fuckers will descend. Fuckers like Father Brian who is formed of pure evil, and like those hungry-for-a-fuck men who my ma did warn me to stay away from, Tibb. Perhaps this tree will swallow me whole.

That sleep-a-lot problem has called again and I am drifting in and out of it like I am very ill, and the moon is there and then it is gone. And Farmer O is here to boot and he is saying, 'Tibb! You are some bad bad girl.' And now I am something like six years old but who can know for sure? Well I can feel those hands of his on the blanket like he is truly here, and then over my skin where I never did want them. Those rough farmer-fingers poking at my chest which was a little-girl's chest, so there was nothing to find. And I can smell his sour beer-breath and I can feel as well that sinking guilt because I did tempt this man without even trying since I am made of evil stuff. 'Did the devil send you?' Well perhaps he did, because everyone I love is leaving, as you said they would, and this can't just be chance.

The sky turns red and orange and black and a hole is burrowing into my skull and making it all turn blacker still. And that star of my ma is up there and then it isn't.

'Ivo,' I say to the owl-hooters and the moon-face. 'How could you leave me?' And that snake is winding around my heart because tomorrow no one will say, 'Oysters today, Tibb!' or 'A nice crab for lunch!'

What happened to spending our lives together? To getting that forever-roof he spoke of? He did not trust me with his secret, and though he was *my* own home, I was not his.

I slide from this tree with my eyes wide like the fuckers will jump out. Moving is no small pain and this soil floor feels damp under my feet. I tip-toe on it like I must not disturb the ants.

Eggs, Tibb. When there is nothing else, you can rely on eggs. But there are no eggs here and there is no Ivo either. I scour the woodland and eat three blackberries but they are mostly sour.

The moonlight is pushing its way between the trees and reflecting off the water and I stand with my feet in that weak stream because it is some safe feeling to have water around my ankles again. 'Ma,' I whisper, and I am searching that sky for her star like she would up-and-leave me too. 'Would you stay with me here?' O, are you a simpleton, child? That woman did leave this shit world at Newmarket.

After, I am heaving myself up the tree again like I am a too-old person.

Henrietta. Why did I not ask Ivo where he buried her? Why

did I not go and sit on top of the grave-place even once? I think that makes me evil, and now she is in Norfolk, alone beneath the sand, and I am somewhere outside of Peterborough and towards the middle of this big country of England.

I wish for the end to swallow me whole, Tibb.

I wish it too, Ma.

Oblivion, Tibb

The sun has dropped out the sky and I have walked to this village from my hollow like a wading bird. Like these legs of mine are made of twigs. Oblivion, Tibb. Well oblivion is something I am after too, Ma, and the bottle worked for you in times like these. I am on my way to oblivion already and these hiccoughs are turning to belches. I tried four churches on my way and I did drink the dregs of a bottle, half of another and a whole jug of sweet wine in the last one. I have been pissing like a horse and I am enjoying this feeling inside of my head, like all the thoughts are gone to bed, and I have a great thirst for more of this stuff to knock me out cold so I might never wake up and face this no-Ivo life. Can you see the pretty colours, Tibb? O I see them now, Ma.

I do not like this village and all its wood houses and their thatched rooves shaped like hoods, and the smell of pottage which is puffing out of their chimneys. My ma would say, 'Tibb, don't you know these people are all thieves and murderers?' even though she was both of those things herself. But there is a tavern here and she did like taverns well enough.

I watch from the lane. The way those fat men do spill out the front of their drinking-place, holding their full tankards, and my head is swimming and this need for beer is bobbing around in there and saying, 'Get on with it, Tibb Ingleby!' when all the other voices like Ivo's are just mumbling and I can't hear them much any more. There is a flatness inside of me, like I am not really here.

A man goes round the back to piss and I hover like a fly

beside him as he straightens up those wool breeches. Don't you know there is something men do enjoy even more than beer, Tibb?

'Fuck!' he says, because I startled him. 'Where did you come from?'

'You would pay a groat for a quick fuck, sir?'

I think I do not want to push out my bulbs for this man and his round face and his drunk-too-much nose.

He looks at me carefully. 'For *that* price you should be a virgin. Are you?'

I nod. And I am feeling like those nice colours which the wine did paint upon the sky are fading and those white hairs on my arms are standing up and Ivo's voice is getting louder where before it was muffled by that nice drink called wine. 'Stop, Tibb!' he is saying, but what do you care, Ivo? You left me already. O, I am thinking of the bottle.

'Well, sir, that is settled,' I say, and I turn so I am facing the back wall of this tavern where he just pissed and I rest my head on the timber frame and I am waiting for that man to pull up my costume.

'Ha! A virgin who knows the ropes too well. I'll give tuppence and that's all.'

I say, 'Fine, sir,' and I think of the beer, but my cheeks are wet and this is not so easy as my ma did make it look those times.

He lifts my dress and smacks my white buttocks and that hurts. 'There's nothing of you, girl! Don't you eat?'

Not recently, sir.

O, those stars up there are getting brighter and I am thinking of my ma just now. I am thinking of how she did keep that little knife inside her pocket to slash the fucker once it was over because she did never get her revenge on Farmer O and she couldn't help herself. And I am thinking I should never have told her the truth of it and ruined her own life. And then I am thinking of the fact that Farmer O did ogle at my buttocks just like this man and whisper, 'Do not say a word of it, Tibb Ingleby.'

He is saying, 'Well and well,' and fumbling at his crotch but I think I can hear my own ma out there on the lane crying, 'Tibb, I did it again! When will the end come and chew me up?' Those words are so clear that I wonder she did plunge from her starry-perch. And the memories are swatting me round the face like a swarm of bees. Ma. The knife. The dead ankles which we did drag too often to a ditch. 'I won't do it again, Tibb. Never again. And would you take the bottle away?'

My thoughts are all soupy inside my head, and I am turning to look at this face-like-a-pig man, his breeches around his ankles already, pumping away at his little prick. But his face is all different and he looks like Farmer O now. And my ma is calling from the lane: 'Run, Tibb! Did I not warn you about the fuckers?'

This kick is coming from somewhere deep inside of me – from the bad places where I keep those memories of that farmer – and he cups his groin in his hands and 'Ah-ah-ah!' he grunts. Those cheeks are glistening like two plums popping out of his face. There is no oblivion now – I think I must have pissed out all the wine because everything is clear as day.

'You little—' he shouts after me but I am running because my ma did teach me something good.

Fools to leave a rabbit

These woods all look the same, Ma, and I have found myself a bigger hollow so truly I am an owl now, except owls don't cry and they don't drink wine or charge for a fucking either. I have been here since last night and now the sun has left again. My head is thumping still from that wine. I think the big-man has whacked a slice of wood against it for all that stealing I did think to do.

They arrive when my eyes are too heavy. These noisy forest-hackers with their bags and poles. I am rigid in this high-up hole like there are some murderers down there. Like here are the owners of the hot rod which will brand you a vagrant, Tibb. The low dullness is suddenly sharper. My red eyes are staring through the branches.

'Ambrose!' they say. 'Luke!'

These leaves are shrouding my vision but I should say they are all different shapes and sizes and one is even a woman who is smiling and very big around the chest and this is giving me some calm feeling. And there is a very tall and long-limbed man who is carrying a lute of all things.

Canvas tents are popping up and my eyes narrow. Are they vagrants too? I have not yet seen vagrants with tents to live inside.

'Now,' says that woman with a big booming voice, and 'Would you catch us a rabbit, Penn? Lay a trap, would you?'

This man called Penn does go off through the trees, all smiling, and I like his sloping shoulders. He looks young in the face, turning back to holler things at his friends and to make them laugh. I think this is the kind of man my own ma would say is good for more than a fuck, Tibb.

'We should expect some great audience in Oundle,' another says.

An audience? Then these people are actors! And actors of the travelling kind. I did see actors with my own ma in the town called Cambridge and she did have a wish to join them since acting is some easy-money, Tibb.

Well Penn returns and they cook the rabbit soon enough and the smoke is rising. I should say the spit gathering in my mouth will spill out on to the dirt floor and make a flood like the one I am hearing of which that man Noah did navigate with his hundreds of animals and his fat ark. I have eaten only berries.

They are laughing and joking still and I like that sound. And here are some words exchanged about those two princes in the Tower who are all gone and probably murdered, and this is a topic my ma would speak on oftentime.

'What do you think of it, Maria?'

'Ah!' she says. 'I have long believed the rumours that it was King Richard who committed such a heinous crime since his was a piss-poor claim to the throne and he had money on his mind.'

I should say Maria's throaty voice is certainly not from this shit land of England but somewhere else and I like that meaty roundness to her words, as though they were roasted up in a pan with onions.

'Impossible!' says another.

Maria throws her hands up. 'But of course it was him! If anyone was ripe to do murder it was Richard. The man was born with a full set of teeth – does that not make you shiver, my friends?'

Now my ma did have her own thoughts on this bad crime.

Mostly she did talk round in circles of the fuckers and murderers and the innocence of babies, and don't you know you can't trust anyone, Tibb?

Penn, the rabbit-catcher, says, 'I should say the Duke Henry Stafford is the one.'

Then another man who is shrouded by trees says, 'No, no! It was our own King Henry! Did he not kill John of Gloucester besides?'

On go those accusations of murder and I am thinking of those small boys. I am thinking of their bodies because some fucker must have dragged them off. Then I am thinking of Henrietta's tiny body and those floppy baby-legs in the big sea at Norfolk. And this is not some idle gossip but something different and dangerous.

Once those down-below people are all done with their hot rabbit then there is some lute-playing by the tall man who I cannot see so well between the leaves. But I haven't heard music like it. This is no droning organ-song from the church-place. Here is music so natural and flowing that I should say it is moving like air. It is making me think of Ivo and Henrietta and Ma, and it is making me think sad thoughts of poor Ewan and Samuel who did not deserve to be butchered in a farrier's tent, but I do not want that person to stop playing either since these nice notes are something special in my ear. A brief glimpse and that man seems to be covered in rouge or some other face-paint and it all makes sense I suppose.

When they are sleeping I slip down because my stomach is growling. I am tip-toeing like they would wake and cook me too, but I don't get too far because here at my feet is their own rabbit carcass. And tossed so close beneath my tree-home!

I take that thing like this is some strange treasure and up in my hollow I suck on those nice bones which are not well-stripped at all. Such fools to leave a rabbit this way.

In the morning they are packing up those tents and speaking of the good town of Oundle where they are heading, and all those fine coins they should make there, and my heart is thudding when I think of the silence which they will leave behind.

'Would you get a move on?' I am hearing from that wide-brimmed-hat man, and that is some West Country accent if I have ever heard one. Why is it they are calling him Signor and Signor Perero, when he is clearly from this very kingdom of England?

Go quietly would you, Tibb? Well I am walking behind like a shadow-dancer.

One says, 'Do you hear that crunching?' And these trunks between us are doing me some favours.

'It is nothing!' says the lute man who does not trust his own ears. 'Would you keep walking, friends, else the sun will go down.'

Snort and splutter

These are not actors at all but strolling-players and perhaps that is some easy-money too, Ma. At least this discovery is burying my thoughts of Ivo and the fact he did leave me alone. In fact I am stuffed between the town-folk for the purpose of this fine display.

'My juggler!' says the man named Signor.

That juggler is as thin as a string-bean but he doesn't stoop like the dairy-farmer who was also a bean. He looks young and bendy and he is all dressed up in emerald tights and red breeches and holding three leather balls which he is tossing into the air and catching again with his two hands. And the smiling man called Penn is coming out next and flipping his body around in somersaults. And then the two are joined top-to-tail and rolling so one is up while the other is down.

'Lambert!' Signor shouts and a third man comes out on to the cobbles and this one has not got much hair but he has a very fine beard. He crouches and Penn sits up on his shoulders and another acrobat comes out who Signor is introducing as Luke and who has sandy hair like Ivo, though I am not thinking of Ivo, and he is somersaulting across the ground and then he is pulled up so he is also in the man-tower. And I would not think that thing could grow any taller when John does get hauled up and he stands at the top to do some more of that sweet juggling. If my ma were here she would be running into that circle because there is no party without me, Tibb! Well that was true for half the time.

Too many people are standing in front of me but Maria

walks out at eight foot tall so this doesn't matter. She is all legs under that long skirt and I am thinking there must be two blocks of wood underneath but she slinks around so gracefully, it is like she is a real giantess-person, all brown-haired and large-chested and smiling to the children, and I am thinking Henrietta would have liked to see this trick besides.

The little man called Signor Perero is announcing these people like he did cast them all from clay himself, but now the music comes. That lute again, and this town with its high smells and sharp corners is not deserving of the beautiful melody. 'There!' and 'Look!' those people cry and finally that man called Ambrose walks out to this crowd, and here is some breath caught up inside me. How naturally those fingers move upon the strings.

In fact he is reminding me of Ivo in that he is a muscular person, though much taller, and he is a different colour to Ivo. A different colour than any I have seen, because that was not rouge I did spy from my hiding-hole but a stain like blackberry juice all down one side of his face and neck and one of his lute-playing hands besides. Here is something quite special, because if I could pick an opposite person to myself it is this man who is tall and broad and patchwork against my bland white-ness. Stare like a simpleton and they'll cart you off to Bedlam, Tibb, and perhaps that is true but I am thinking of how much I would like to be painted in this way and not ghostly pale all over.

Does that lovely colour go all down his body? I would like to know the answer. And I would like to know how he did land himself that brass-buttoned jacket since that is a garment of some great expense by the look of things. Like the livery of a rich person's staff.

'Fuck – there is something the devil spewed out!'

I do spin around to see that crowd-watcher shout it, and

then another: 'Sir, are you mottled with ink?' And there are more of them laughing besides.

Ambrose keeps playing, and after he does bow at those rude men and his face is polite and he doesn't look angry. It's like all their bad words did not even scratch his surface. Don't you wish to land a punch on them, sir? He pushes his curly red hair from his face and I think I could look at him forever.

The man named Signor Perero has removed his big hat to reveal a thinning-on-top head, and he is weaving around with this thing like it is a begging-bowl. The people in this crowd are sliding away and soon enough those players are walking off too. I am thinking of the hollow and the silence and the fuckers on the fire-floor. The fact Ivo did up-and-leave me.

'Wait!' I say quick and that word tickles my throat. 'I wish to join you.'

The man called Signor turns and his eyes are darting all over me. The last of the crowd-stragglers turn as well and they look too interested, like perhaps there could be more entertainment on offer just now.

'What's your talent?' he asks.

Nothing is swimming into my head except the thought that his skin is dry like a scaly serpent. Those patches on his neck require a good measure of beeswax upon them, or so my ma would say if she wasn't dead in a hole.

'Well?' he says, and he tuts like I am something irritating. 'Would you spit it out yet?'

My heart thuds for the lack of ideas and these nosy townfolk have some flapping ears, I think. I bury my hands into my apron pocket to feel for that pearl because this is some small comfort.

He turns and his scalp is all flaky at the back under those wispy hairs. 'Back to camp, would you?' he says to those acrobats who are studying me with some pity there. Not the berry-coloured one though; that man doesn't bother to look at a girl called Tibb.

That small sliver of hope is dwindling inside of me, but my fingers fumble around this not-quite-round shape which they know so well and I think there is a beam of light shining into my skull.

'Oysters, sir!' I say, and my arms are hanging by my sides like two skinny weeds.

His forehead creases. *'Oysters?'*

The last of the crowd-people are sniggering.

I say, 'I can fit in oyster caves.'

He is scowling even more and he does look to these nosy watchers so they snort and splutter. 'We are town-players, dear! Have you hay between those ears?'

'Any small space, I can fit into!' I call after him with that thing called desperation swilling around in my belly.

'That is no talent!' he shouts back and he hollers to his acrobats, 'Are you hearing it? This creature wishes to sit in oyster caves and she believes it my business to care!'

Some studious deliberation

Canvas rooves are not for you, Tibb Ingleby, because you are a dirty vagrant. Yes, sir. And I am watching that through-the-trees camp with my back against this church because who gives a fuck what these town-people say and maybe a V upon my head will suit me. Don't you know you caused this, Ivo? This hot summer rain is making puddles form upon the ground like miniature oceans. I think there will be whales and mermaids soon enough.

For a while the woman called Maria who wore those wood stilts was walking around in the clearing, flat-footed again, and I liked the look of her big bosoms and that smile, but she has gone into her own canvas roof now on account of the rain.

'Would you give it up?' I shout upwards so my face is drenched, but that hammering continues and my white dress is like a roll of parchment around me. The rabbit-door to this church-place is locked too because the priest must be a fucker besides.

This town is smaller than Peterborough and the houses are bulging out and leaning on one another like they drank too much wine. There is both a stocks and a whipping post and I wonder what Ivo would say about that. I wonder where he is right now and if the rain has fucked him too.

'This is all your fault, Ivo!' I shout into that grey sky and there is some grumbling in answer. My own ma did like the lightning-and-thunder storms more than anything else since that great banging did smother her own noise for a short while. And she would be skipping and skipping under that rain which made me happy and also sad because the down came after the up as I learnt time-and-again and then she would threaten to leave this dull place by the slitting of her own throat. I do not have the urge to dance.

The rain is dripping off my white-enough eyebrows and on to my eyelashes and soaking into this too-small dress, and I am thinking about that man Ambrose and the fact he did not seem to care that those people were saying some bad and wicked things. And I am remembering how those town-dwellers did tell my ma, 'That child of yours is something strange!' and she would bare those teeth and say, 'Fuck off to Hell!' though she didn't believe in that place, and yet here is a man who is half-spilt upon with wine and he doesn't seem to give one fuck and nor should he since he is quite beautiful where I am painted in white and plain all over.

I am not seeing that figure till he is right in front of me and the rain is jumping off his wide-brimmed hat like he is a fountain.

'Show me, then,' he says, in those West Country tones.

Is this some apparition, Ma?

'Sir?'

'Show me your talent!' he says again, and he is shouting over this rain. 'I think what you described is a kind of contortion and perhaps I packed you away too quickly. You know I have partaken of some studious deliberation.'

Now those words are making fuck-all sense, but I am hunting around for something like an oyster cave though we are not in Norfolk any more. The rain is splashing off the stonework. There is a collecting-box outside this church, because the priests do not pass up the opportunity for monies even when the big-man is not inside. This wood box is the size of a small apple crate – the kind my ma did upset for the purpose of distraction and then snatching – and I turn it over so the rainwater spills out on to the stone path. Then I am folding myself in with my knees up by my ears and my chin pointing down against my chest.

Signor Perero peers down at me like he is peering into my tree-hollow and he says, 'Shi-iiit,' in a very long-drawn-out way like this is something truly surprising.

Dining like a sparrow

The woman called Maria puts her big thumping arm around me. 'Would you come for a wash with me, Tibb?'

We have walked this day from Oundle to an even smaller town and now the sun is disappearing again.

'I'll say it's some mighty fine change to have a woman in the troupe,' she says, setting those brown eyes upon me, but I think she is addressing the trees around her with that booming voice. 'How old are you?'

'Almost sixteen now, madam, I should think.'

'Almost sixteen! And unmarried, such a shame. A pretty girl like you!'

She says it like she is joking, with all this cheery laughter, but I am not understanding that thing.

'Where did you come from, Tibb?'

'O, all over.'

'All over?'

My belly lurches because what are you saying, Tibb? She will stink out a vagrant like they all do.

'Well, I was living in the area called Norfolk a while. Until I wasn't any more.'

She nods and nods and smiles with that nice wobbly chin even though those words of mine are not patched together with many threads.

'I'm from the Low Countries myself, and I came here seeking the work of a cloth weaver in London-town, only to end up a stilts-woman in a big long dress in this troupe of outcasts.'

Outcasts? So we are all the same?

Again that rolling laughter which makes me warm to this person named Maria very much.

She takes off her tunic so she is naked and she marches into the river and lies down flat, looking up at the sky. That stream is so weak that the water hardly flows over her. She is like a dam in there, and the form of her body is all different than mine besides. Two enormous bosoms and wide hips and then a great bush of hair at the top of her legs and under her arm-pits.

She leans her head back and she rubs away at her scalp and says, 'Ah-ah-ah!' like this is truly something wonderful.

I lie down also like a dam in this trickle-of-water river, and those birds are tweeting above like they would have a good look at the both of us.

'You will see that the life of a strolling-player is not so very bad, Tibb.'

'Yes,' I say.

'But you are melancholy it seems.'

'I do not know the meaning of that word, Maria.'

'You are sad about something.'

How can she tell?

'Well,' I say slowly, because the snake makes it painful, 'I had a great friend who I am separated from – who did leave me in fact – and this is weighing on me ever since for it was a betrayal and I cannot figure it out one piece.'

'Tibb?' she says, with some look like a stormcloud. 'Your own husband is it? He has done that dirty thing and gone to another woman's bed and turned you out for good?' Now she brings out a thick finger. 'Well you listen to Maria and you say to yourself: "Fuck the bastards!" '

This sounds like something my ma would say and it is making the snake squeeze harder. 'O, well it is not so much like that, Maria . . .'

'It isn't?'

I shake my head. 'Not the husband-love, but a different kind.'

She cocks her wet head, and I should say those brown strands of hair are stuck to her round face like weeds. 'Like a friend?'

'Closer than that.'

'A brother?'

I squint my eyes for the purpose of not-crying. 'He was another half of me really, since he did save me after my ma and my baby sister died. And we had plans for a fine home together forever and ever, and by that I do not just mean a roof.'

Maria puts those no-clothes arms around me, with all those warm and extra parts of flesh, and she says, 'Nothing lasts forever, Tibb. Think of the future not the past. Do you think I shed tears over my old life? Anyway, perhaps he did that thing because he loved you.'

Here is a riddle to turn the tides.

She says, 'I left my mother in the hills outside Antwerp since she was sick to death with the lot of us and she saw in our faces the look of our father. It was the kindest thing to do.'

I say, 'There was nothing kind about what Ivo did.'

We are quiet for a while then, and I don't like that pity in Maria's eyes.

'Anyway,' I say quick, and 'I was just on my way to that family of mine up in the land of Leicester, and then I found you here.'

My ma would speak often of this same family when the no-roof problem got us some bad attention, and those people did not once exist but would you have the pity of peasants too, Tibb?

Maria is looking at me with her deep brown eyes and I don't know what she is thinking. Then: 'Look,' she says, 'you can share my tent since you won't take up much room. I think you are more like a wafer than a person and we shall make that a very sweet home!'

I nod, though I will never find a home without Ivo inside it.

'Tomorrow you'll watch us perform once more and then Signor will be thinking upon your act and the props for it.'

I don't know what are props.

'Why do we call him Signor?' I ask instead. 'I have not been in Spain oftentime, but I have been in the land called Somerset more than once with my ma, and I am certain I recognize the accent.'

Maria rolls her brown eyes. 'He thinks it makes him sound very worldly-wise. You know his real name is John Payne?'

We both laugh at this. I want to ask about the lute-player with that fine and purple skin and how it is that he did end up here too. And did he have a ma who told him to ignore the fuckers and their shit-for-brains opinions?

When we get back to that camp there is a nice haze-light around the fire and we are in a good clearing which is allowing for the pink sun to peek through, or the last of it which remains.

'Such a smell!' those acrobat men are saying.

They are all very pleasant, Penn and Lambert and Luke, though I believe it will take me a while to know which name belongs to which clever acrobat. The juggler-man who is named John has found berries just like the ones I would eat with Ivo. I am feeling for the smooth and bumpy pearl again between my fingertips.

'Tibb,' Maria says, and 'Would you eat a thing or two? You are dining like a sparrow.'

'Ah, but I have lost that thing called an appetite most late,' I say.

I am watching Ambrose with his beautiful colours but he is

the quiet one in this party and I think he hasn't noticed me here at all. I catch his eye and he looks away so quick I wonder if I imagined that. Now he is peering into those flames with something like calm in his eyes and he is big all over like a real giant who doesn't need stilts.

'What do you usually have, then?' says John. 'For dinner?'

I can feel all these eyes upon me but I do not wish to speak about that time in Norfolk with my dearest Ivo.

I shrug. 'An egg sometimes.'

I can picture him saying it. With that sandy hair and those lovely blue eyes: 'There will always be eggs, Tibb, when the crabs won't bite.'

When we are in our tent later I am looking up at that canvas above us and wondering if my ma would have counted that as a roof or not. Maria is speaking of props and shows and hay-bales, but I am thinking of something different.

'That man Ambrose does not speak much, Maria.'

She turns so she is facing me and she lets out one loud holler. 'Ha! All the girls take some great interest in Ambrose! He is like a guilty secret, I think, since people can't know whether to lust after him or be disgusted. You know, in London-town he had a whore beg a night with him free of the charge, just to see what was lurking beneath those clothes – whether he is painted that purple colour all over. And the size of that thing between the legs of course, since he is large everywhere else!'

Well I am thanking the sun for fucking off because my cheeks are burning. What did that whore look like? Nicer than you, Tibb. Did he take her up on the offer? I have a feeling that Ambrose would be skilled at that fucking dance but in a quiet kind of way. Quieter than my ma did like to do it.

'Night, Tibb,' she says.

'Goodnight, Maria.'

*

In the morning Maria has woken up and gone already and there is an egg outside this tent. A small and pale green one that was not laid by a sea-bird. I pick it up and it lies in my palm like this is some fine treasure from a pirate. Those clouds are in a race up there and I lift my egg to my face, studying it right up close. At those thin veins which are criss-crossed on it like someone used the scribing pen.

This egg is not hot because my Ivo didn't put it on the fire, but I am cracking it into my mouth anyway and there is some nice feeling about the way that liquid slips around my teeth and down my throat because an egg is an egg if it's cooked or not. Tears are filling up inside my eyes and making my throat sting because that person Maria has some kind heart and the heavy snake is shifting a little so it is not quite so tight around my rib-cage.

Leominster, Herefordshire

Ivo takes Flavio in his arms and the two men are knitted together so tight, it is like they were sewn this way. It is dark in here. Pitch-black, and for once they don't need to hide. He can feel Flavio's heart thudding under his clothing.

'Were you followed?' Ivo whispers.

Flavio shakes his head and they stay like this, melting into one another. They don't say anything because nothing would help, but time slackens and wanes.

Eventually Ivo straightens up when the warden's footsteps can be heard out there. 'Run. At least one of us might not die for this piece of trickerie.'

No answer, but a faint smile. Why does he not take it seriously?

'Go! Go anywhere. Distance yourself from all of it.'

Flavio puts his hands on Ivo's shoulders. 'Don't you know of fig trees and bats?' he says with that Spanish lisp. 'On their own, those things cannot exist – they need each other to live. And I don't exist without you.'

To this, Ivo can't muster a response. The warden is out there, fumbling with the keys, the light from his lantern creeping under the iron door.

'I'll come again.'

'No! It's too dangerous.'

Flavio doesn't look like he will heed that advice either. He says, 'Don't be angry at Tibb. You know she never meant for this, and without her, we would never have become the fig tree and the bat.'

He is thinking on this as the warden rams the key into the lock and Flavio looks at Ivo. A long time, because they both know this could be the last time. Is it not worse, he wonders, to have seen how beautiful life could be? To have experienced this kind of love, even for a short while? Surely it would be easier to die not knowing at all.

Without Flavio, he feels even worse; the kiss lingering on his lips. The taste taunting him; that word dancing a jig in his mind. Sodomy. The worst of all sexual misdemeanours – worse than fucking horses or sheep – that is why they don't speak of it. When they do, it is described only as an act – an ill-judged moment. A glimpse of madness. But what if it's not?

When he fled his home that night, he had paused in the thin corridor, listening to his father snoring on the mattress behind the curtain. The fabric was broken on the railing so the end of it hung down, leaving a gap of about an inch or two. He is plagued by the image behind it. His mother, lying there with her eyes open, looking straight at him as he made his escape.

How many times has he played out this moment in his mind? Two shiny eyes in the darkness. Silent, united. Colluding. Telling him – without speaking at all – to pursue happiness, not to be trapped in a life like hers where suffering and righteousness are bundled as one. Where passions must be subdued.

He stretches out, aware of the coarse stone beneath him, the feel of the damp against his back. Sometimes he wonders if she was awake at all. Is he simple? Why would she care about his happiness when she too was splattered with his shame? He feels there is a yawning space in this cellar. He feels empty and hard like a carapace. Like a shell.

No fine carpentry

'What can be hiding in the shell?'

We are here in the town of Corby and the people are whispering out there like this is the greatest mystery of the world.

'Now, ladies and gentlemen!' and that is the voice of Signor, as he did warn me. 'Would you clap along, so that the shell might be persuaded to open?'

This flour-and-water mixture which is pasted on to my face is starting to itch in the heat. And this white costume which is in fact just strips of linen all wrapped around my body is itching too. I am curled up in here like Henrietta did curl up against my chest.

Signor says those words, 'Reveal yourself!' and this is the signal to push open my on-top shell.

Up I rise and I should look some spectacle with this sheet of white hair and this flour mixture and these strips which are pasted over me so I could be cast in chalk. 'Do not speak, dear,' so said Signor, 'since you haven't a knack with words as I do.'

Those people are gasping away and shouting, 'A pearl, a pearl!' and clapping like they would bring the houses down, and they are asking, 'How did she fit in there?' to boot. But I am looking for a head of blonde hair amongst these staring town-people. And two beautiful blue eyes.

'A pearl indeed!' Signor says, and he is hopping around at this grand reception and these delighted faces, and wiping his hands on his breeches in this hot sun.

'But what is wrong, fine pearl?' he asks loudly, because

I have pinned that sad expression on my face like I was told to. 'Was that oyster too large a home?'

I just nod, and these watching-people all gasp some more and they nudge each other and listen like the big-man-God has come to walk upon the Earth.

'Who would watch my pearl squeeze into a smaller house?' Signor says, and there is some hooting like: 'It isn't possible!' and 'It cannot be so!'

Now Ambrose is bringing out one slightly smaller wood oyster and placing it on to these cobbles and the clapping starts again. It was only yesterday that Signor came back from the carpenter's tent saying, 'Tibb, I have commissioned for you three oyster shells which will make the act complete! Did you not speak of oysters before?'

A cave, sir. Not a shell.

In fact, these wood contraptions are no fine carpentry but I fit inside them just fine. They are like two cupped palms, joined at a hinge, making a rounded cavity within. The smallest is the size of a large hare.

'Will she fit her pearly body into this oyster, madam?' Signor asks one spectator.

That woman's cheeks wobble like she can't form the words.

In I climb to the next and I pull a rope-string on the inside to ease the top shell over me. Those people are gasping like I did walk upon the water too. Then we perform that whole sequence again until the town-people are asking, 'Who is it?' and 'Where did she come from?'

'Well here is a pearl of some magical properties!' Signor says, and those small girls wish to come and touch my hair and they are staring like I am something truly strange and wonderful, and I am thinking that my ma would have approved very much of *this* type of attention.

When it is time for Ambrose to do his lute-playing, my

breath has scampered away. That instrument looks too small in those large and two-coloured hands of his. I should say it did give me some strange feeling when he carried me in that shell and put me on the cobbles to open the show. But you are some fool, Tibb, since this big-and-quiet man is dreaming of those whores who have a wish to fuck him in London-town. He is not thinking of you any more than Ivo is.

Ambrose's gingery curls fall over his eyes which are soft in the same way that dew is soft, and that song is something beautiful. But I am hearing all these whispers again like: 'Has he spilt the red wine?' and 'There is a monster among us!' And these words are making me want to turn and blacken some dull eyes with my fist. Again he bows to those nay-sayers when he is quite finished, and that eye-gaze of his is not wavering at all. Signor is gathering coins from the cobbles like he would lap them up with his lizard-tongue.

Very proper talent

It seems we are creeping west across this kingdom of England, far away from Henrietta, but in a wandering, looping kind of route. The sun is staying put for longer and longer since the month is August and then September or so says Maria, and we are going through the same towns so often that I am thinking the man called Signor Perero has in fact exaggerated his important skill-of-navigation. That map he consults oftentime is not doing us all much good, not least my own two feet, since trudging in the summer heat and these too-long days is giving me blisters. You must have silk for skin, Tibb!

Being with these people is better than living in the hollow, but those thoughts of Ivo will never go away. Every place we stop I am looking for him. I am looking for his cut-with-a-knife jawline and his sea-blue eyes. I am looking for him when Maria and I walk through those villages to spend our money on meat pies. The back of a fair head and my heart speeds up like the tigers would chase me. But those men who turn around are never Ivo. They have weak chins and sagging bellies and they are not sculpted by artists like Ivo is.

When I am not thinking of Ivo then I am thinking of Ambrose and I am watching him like a sneak-peeper. At how well he holds himself; like he deserves to be here. I do not think that man was ever a vagrant.

There are two mysteries troubling me besides, and one is how the lovely juggler-man called John can eat so much and still look like a tooth-pick, and the other is the hair belonging to the man named Luke, because I cannot decide whose is more golden – Ivo's or his.

Now we are in some village named Geddington and we have set our tents beside a nearly-gone stream. Drought will be the end of men, Tibb.

'O, I cannot think the King Richard will have done it,' says Maria.

We are talking again of that thing which did shock the world regarding the two vanishing princes. My feet are all blistered and red.

'I should think he had bad-enough blood inside him,' I say, since those were my ma's own words and she knew one thing or two about throat-slitting herself.

Maria says, 'Well they were murdered in cold blood by *somebody*. I think we are joined in this country by pure evil, my friend.'

I wish to ask, 'Maria, am *I* pure evil?' And I want to know whether not-keeping-something-alive is the same as killing it. But Signor stops itching a moment and snaps, 'Ladies! Would you speak of those things which you understand, and leave the rest to us?'

Maria is puffing out her cheeks and I wonder if she might open her mouth and belch real fire.

We sit around a while longer until Signor says, 'To the tavern for ale!' and sleep does knock upon our heads and now it is just Ambrose and I.

The moon is sneaking over like it would say, 'Tibb, I can see you blush!' It is some odd feeling I am getting around this person named Ambrose. Like a good thing and also an uncomfortable thing. There is one jolly dance going on inside my ribs and I am wondering if he can hear that. I did not ever have this feeling with Ivo but I am not thinking about Ivo now. And there are so many questions I have for this same-as-me-but-entirely-different person.

'Your talent, Tibb. It is unusual, I believe.'

'Yes,' I say, and I am feeling my face turning hot at these soft-spoken words. His eyes are partly green and partly brown, like a painter did mix up the colours. 'Though it is perhaps not so much a talent as a fine stroke of luck that I can bend these strange ways.'

He nods, like he is truly thinking of this. I push out my bulbs.

'But yours is a very proper talent, Ambrose, and I should like to know how you learnt it.'

I should like to know a lot more than that, I could add. All the girls he has held in those multicoloured big-and-gentle hands of his.

He smiles. 'I was taught to play the lute when I was still a boy. My parents were rich people and my father insisted I was taught on the virginal too.'

'Well that is some fine gift for any child!'

'Ah, they did not wish to see me much, and that's why they kept me busy in the school room.'

He shakes that head and those gingery-brown curls fall over his face so nicely. We have never spoken on anything other than which bird he has cooked for us all.

'Would you tell me why, Ambrose?'

He cocks his head like I am joking, then his face changes. 'It was a deeply shameful thing for them to have created such an unnatural child. Sometimes my father would try to beat the colour out of me but that didn't work either.'

This is making my heart hurt and, sir, don't you know those bold colours are something glorious to me?

'But your mother? Did she care for you?'

He says, 'At first, but it never sat quite right with her. And there were more and more whisperings that she had birthed a cursed child. Anything that became of the town, such as floods or storms which were not infrequent in that part of the country, were all put down to my doing. By the time I was six or thereabouts, she was so worried she might be thrown into a river and drowned as a witch that she cast me out and I never saw them again. At least I was given my father's old lute to make a life for myself.'

Well here is something, Ma! Ambrose was roof-less like us and look at him now! The player of perfect tunes and lovely notes!

'And has it?' I ask. 'Made a life for you?'

He thinks about that. 'I suppose so. I have played for many rich and noble people as their musician and the wages were good enough, though I was always more of a spectacle than a musician. And of course now they are employing black-skinned trumpeters from across the seas and these people are even stranger than me, so there is not such a great demand.'

'I see. So now you are here.'

'I am, and sometimes I think it would not matter if I couldn't play a note, since most people don't speak of the music but my skin.'

Now that is true since I heard it myself.

'You do well to ignore those cruel jibes, sir.'

He smiles and then he looks abashed and stares some time at the flickering last-flame. I could add that I like the way he bows to those fuckers and he doesn't curse and holler like my own ma would have done, or pump his fists and puff out his great chest though he has the big muscles to scare off a bull, I think.

He shrugs. 'I've learnt to hold my head up.'

I nod and he leans forward like he has something to tell me urgently.

'It's important to stick up for yourself, Tibb, however you might feel inside. Because no one else will do it for you.'

Now these are some sound-enough words to live by, though I am thinking of my ma who would chase off those Tibb-starers and tell them, 'Don't you know she is an angel-child? You ask the big-man since he did knock me up himself!'

'And that smart costume?' I ask him. 'You were gifted it?'

He nods and smiles a little bit. 'Before joining this troupe I was playing at the great house of the Lady Astor who is dear friends with the Lady Margaret Beaufort herself.'

'The King's own mother? Did she hear you play?'

Ambrose shakes his head. 'She was more devout at her prayers, miss. She doesn't allow herself pleasures such as music and dancing. Mostly she has taken herself away from society and locked herself up at Collyweston to live like a nun.'

'Why?' I ask.

He colours and says, 'Who knows.'

I think perhaps that *he* knows, but I couldn't give two shits about the woman called Margaret Beaufort when I wish to know every single thing about this person called Ambrose. The exact thought which is sitting in that gingery-haired head of his at this precise moment. And every thought he has ever had besides. I want to know what it would feel like to have those big lute-playing hands plastered to my bulbs, and those long arms wrapped around me. But would you stop all that dreaming, Tibb?

'I have lived some small life compared to yours,' I say, and I should tell him, 'Don't you know I am a dirty vagrant, sir?'

He dips his eyes. 'Now this I don't believe.'

A parrot's own plume

The lack of Ivo is losing its sharp edges and that is because of Maria and these nice people and also because of the music. Autumn did visit and the trees are all splattered with rouge like fine ladies and I would have been a long time in the hollow by now.

We are performing each day in towns like Desborough and Rothwell and Harborough, and my own ma had some shady-enough view of towns, though we did find ourselves inside them oftentime. I wonder what she would say if she could see her Tibb living in these places and performing for the town-folk to boot?

It seems these people of England are so fed up with their dreary lives and the praying they have to do and the toiling-away-to-get-to-the-Heaven-place, that they are all gasping for a good show. We are pulling in bigger crowds every time and this oyster-act is so piss-easy that I could do it in my sleep. My body is so used to folding itself into each wood shell that I am certain I could make myself become far smaller still. Once Ambrose has carried me out – and I like that part the best – then the thing is so dull to me that it comes as a strange surprise when those town-watchers say 'oo-and-aah' as I reveal myself. And all the little girls who want to touch my mane of white hair and run their hands down it.

'Who in these parts has dreamt of finding a pearl in their oyster supper?' Signor asks. But there is always that tinge of sadness inside me because it was Ivo who took me to the oyster cave and I will never forget him while I do this act.

Mostly I like to watch Ambrose play his lute since this music is making me feel warm inside and forget those memories about Ivo and the feel of that stiff person called Henrietta who did not howl in the ocean. Every melody he plays is different and though he is very big, the noise he makes on that lovely instrument is not so very big at all, but slow and gentle.

When we are not performing then we are trudging to the next village or town and I do like the countryside better because this reminds me of my ma and I like to hear those bird-ditties instead of all the market-shouters. But we are not going near the coast and perhaps that is a good thing because I don't wish to feel the sand between my toes.

If we are not trudging then we are sitting together round the fire and eating and I should say this life of a strolling-player is not so very bad after all. My ma did say work was some terrible vice but at least I am not working for a rich man who will spit me out and have me inside a scullery for the rest of my days.

Maria and I are bathing or wandering to markets often enough too. It is some strange thing to brandish this earned-money of mine and to give it to the pedlars like a high-up lady, taking that nice fruitcake or that slice of ham in my hands and not hiding it inside my pocket and fucking off quick. I am spending these monies like that stuff would grow on trees! My ma was right though – there is nothing like the big thrill of a little sneakery, and I do wonder that a stolen fruitcake does taste all the more sweeter.

In the mornings Maria is off and away and practising her favourite task which is carrying haybales on her shoulders until those farmer-people shout at her to fuck off. 'Must work these muscles, Tibb,' she says, and this is something of a mystery to me.

I am liking the company of Maria very much and these little

gifts of eggs she is leaving outside my tent each morning before she goes off lifting her haybales. I should say it is because of Maria that the snake is loosening, and now we are at that big second-hand clothing market in the land of Lutterworth.

'It is high-enough time that I traded in that old dress, Maria, since I have grown some fine bulbs and these are popping out.'

'Ha!' she says. 'I had two bosoms like yours when I was still in my cradle!' She weighs her great bulbs, one in each hand. 'You know, I used to bind them flat.'

'No?' I gasp. Why would anyone bind a pair of great tits such as Maria's?

'But I am pleased for them now, since those men give more money when they watch my stilts show.'

Well we are feeling some good linens here and some nice wool aprons, and 'How about this, Tibb?' she says. She is holding out a red-and-yellow dress in some thick yarn with long puffed sleeves to boot. 'This will have belonged to some grand little lady, I think! It is like a parrot's own plume!'

'A parrot?' I repeat.

She leans in. 'Tibb, I am speaking of a wonderful and strange bird which I spied in the harbour at Antwerp. All colours of the rainbow.'

This sounds a very fine thing to me, and Maria is bartering that price down till the dress is mine.

'And would you get some boots as well, Tibb?' she says, and she looks down at my feet which are thin and white and covered in dirt. 'I noticed you do not wear much in the way of shoes.'

'O, I lost the last pair, Maria, and they were some lovely red ones. You know my family up in Leicester are fine boot-wearers too.'

She nods and nods but lying feels sharper than usual. She scours these benches for some old pair which she is tying on my feet with those long laces and I am walking back to our camp in these leathery things like a baby deer. Why does the world wear shoes when they hurt like this? I will have a crop of new blisters and that is no sweet thing. Maria is hoot-hooting like she never saw anything funnier.

Later I put the dress on and Signor has some slick of surprise on his face and the acrobats and John say, 'Bravo!' but I am looking at Ambrose because I want to know what he makes of it. But he is just looking at my big boots because you are something quite ridiculous, Tibb Ingleby.

No place for big women

Since I bought my parrot dress I have been receiving those stare-eyed looks from Signor like he has only just met me, and now we are the two of us alone by this fire.

'Tibb,' he says, and he picks those head-flakes with a finger and flicks them on to the flames so they sizzle. 'This is no world for a girl all alone.'

I shrug. 'We travel as a group, sir, so I am hardly alone.'

'Ah, but I have been in the business a while and people can leave this company at the drop of a hat. So many jugglers I have been through, I can hardly count . . .'

'Truly, sir?'

'Of course,' he says, and he extends that skinny neck with its dry patches. 'And I have let go of many mummers since that fashion grew old. Tastes change when the King dictates it. Soon enough no one will wish for a pearl any more, and I should have to lay you off too.'

Fuck. Here is some panic rattling through my skull. Is it back to the hollow with you, Tibb?

'That is why I tell you that you should find a husband, dear. Because otherwise when you are let go, you will be in danger of becoming a vagabond.'

He peers at me under those flaky eyebrows like he would say, 'I know what you were.' Then he says very quiet, 'I was the one to take a punt on you, dear. Without me, where would you be?'

I am not sure what to say to that.

'My dear,' he whispers, and he is taking my skinny arm and

planting this on to his own leg and those birds are tweeting slower and the river is flowing like there is just sludge inside of it. My heart is slowing down besides but in a heavy way and maybe it will stop like Henrietta's did stop.

Signor is pushing my hand towards his crotch and this cold weather has just got colder somehow. I can feel a wiggly worm under this wool which is giving me the feeling like I could spew up over the campfire. His moustache is sprouting hairs and now he looks like Farmer O with that terrible bushy beard.

'I have been thinking that you are not such an ugly bird, Tibb. In fact, I should be glad to make a wife of you.'

There is something very large and black creeping around my neck and that creature is nothing new there, Ma.

'I don't know about that, sir,' I stumble. 'I have not much wish for a husband.'

'Ha! You are speaking rot, dear. You will not survive on your own.'

Perhaps he is right. Mushrooms are no fine snack and do you want to charge-for-it, Tibb?

'Besides, you won't find many men who see an inch of beauty in this strange appearance. You should be lucky with my offer.'

I am finding my voice. 'Then I will think on it, sir.'

Suddenly Ambrose appears out of his tent and he says quite loud, 'Well I am sorry to disturb you both, but I would sleep outside tonight, since the air is too stuffy in there.'

Stuffy, sir? When the summer did stomp away already?

O, it is some relief to see Signor sidling off to who knows where.

In our own tent Maria is grunting away and I poke her awake and whisper, 'Maria, do you think of some life after this troupe?'

She rubs her eyes. 'O yes. And do you know what I dream of, Tibb?'

My heart is sinking now.

'A little picture in my head, of that life I should mostly enjoy. I will have a small plot of land, and I do not mean to rent it from a great lord and thus be his peasant and at his beck-and-call, but to buy a plot outright, far from anything or anyone. And upon this land with my own hands I intend to build a small house in which to live. And then for my sustenance I will have one of each of these animals: a chicken for eggs, a cow for milk, a sheep for some fine cheese. I think I won't be slaughtering a thing, since I can live well enough on these foods. Besides, I will go out and fish for dinner. It is a simple life that I have in mind, Tibb. I have no ambition for more.'

I think my heart is plummeting. Maria would leave me?

'Build a house? You think you could do that?'

She laughs. 'I am a big country girl. And have you not thought why I wish to work my muscles each morning by the lifting of haybales?'

Now this is making a whole lot of sense.

'This world has no place for big women like me who wish to build houses, and I don't intend to be sewing and making stew, my friend. But why do you ask? You will be off with that family of yours in the land of Leicester I think you said?'

Would you have the crickets feel sorry for you, Tibb?

'Ah yes, Maria. That's where I will be.'

All the signs

The leaves are brown and I have been thinking of Signor Perero's offer. We are in some copse just outside the grand town of Northampton where we have been performing and now Maria and I are having a moonlit dip in this nice lake. The water is stinging-cold and I am trying to forget the person who taught me to take these strokes with my arms. Maria's great bulbs are floating at the surface like lily pads. A way off through the trees there is a rustle and I can see the shape of Signor slipping off towards the town from our camp.

'Signor Perero must have quite a nose for business, Maria. Every one of these big cities and he is off to find us work, I think.'

I am searching out the good things about that man which is some tricky-enough job.

Maria says, 'Ha! You cannot believe that, Tibb?'

I cock my head.

'He will be off at the brothel of course and that is what he spends his money on since no good woman would suffer his frowns and his dark temper.'

'Really?' Now my mind is whirring with some bad thoughts, and 'Maria,' I say. 'You know Signor Perero did offer me some marriage contract and I have been thinking of it? After all, I am no good-looking woman and he did take a wager on me—'

'A wager!' she cries. 'On *you*? He did no such thing!'

'He didn't?'

'No! It was Ambrose who persuaded him to find you in all that rain.'

'Ambrose?'

Well she is laughing again with that throaty ho-ho-ho. She is laughing so much that those bosoms are slapping on this cold water.

'You are a blind bat, Tibb, since you are missing all the signs.'

'Signs?'

Now she is knocking on my head like my ma did rat-tat-tat upon that man the cordwainer's door.

'Tibb, my friend, but you have gone all soft in that sweet skull. You are a fine and beautiful person with those big blue eyes and I should say any man would like to have you in their bed, and one most especially!'

Now I am not certain of a thing, Ma, but there is a small bead of hope inside of me which is sprouting wings.

More of that hearty Flemish laughter and my friend called Maria says, 'Tibb! I see you looking when he is playing that lute, but you cannot know that when you do your act, *he* is looking straight at *you*. The problem is, he thinks of you as you think of him. Like you are beyond his reach.'

Some hand has swung down from that dark sky and has smacked me about the chops. 'Maria,' I breathe, and 'Would you stop this nonsense head-filling stuff?'

But she is just laughing and laughing, and then I am thinking of something else.

'Maria,' I say slow, 'I am right in thinking you are the gifter of the fine bird eggs I am waking up to oftentime?'

'Bird eggs, dear? What bird eggs?'

Fuck, Tibb. This smile spreading up my cheeks is going to poke the low sun and I am bobbing around on Maria's lovely head and we are saying hoo-and-haa together like we are two silly children in this lake-bath. And the rain is coming again because all this land called England does is rain and rain some more.

That purple part of you

Here I am in this tent belonging to a man named Ambrose who is fast asleep with his flickering eyes and that wild hair across his face. And I bite on my lip like my ma did do in the hope of securing a barn but this is different, Tibb. Would you wake up, sir?

Now I am an inch from his face and staring like an owl. He is something truly beautiful in here, without his shirt on, and that chest which is in fact half-purple too. He has nice muscles like Ivo but his skin has fewer of those wiry hairs. In fact there are no hairs at all on the purple side.

'Tibb?' he says, sitting up sharp. 'Are you well?'

'Of course I am,' I say and I swallow hard. 'But would you tell me straight, sir? Does my friend Maria speak some truthful things or are you having a cruel joke?'

'A joke?' he repeats, and he pushes back those gingery curls. He grabs his shirt and pulls it on like he would hide that colourful part of him and this is some baffling thing to me.

'You gave me the eggs?' I say. 'Those things were from you?'

He looks abashed, like the floor is of some great interest. 'Well you were not eating much else, Tibb. And did you get that snack of the rabbit carcass underneath your hiding-tree?'

Well I think my face is pulling every which-way and don't you know you'll stay like that when the wind does change, Tibb?

'You saw me up there?'

He nods slowly. 'I didn't want to alarm you, but I am glad you thought to follow on.'

'And you did say to Signor, "Would you take on that girl?" '

He nods again.

'*Why?*' I say. 'What was the meaning of it, sir?'

He pauses a moment. 'Well I feel a great need to protect you, Tibb,' he says quietly. I think everything Ambrose does is quiet except maybe the lute-playing. 'I told you that a person must stick up for themselves, but to tell the truth, I have had a wish to do that job for you, if you do not mind too much.'

I wonder if my heart is going to beat out of this chest of mine and crawl across the forest floor. Ma up there – are you hearing this stuff?

'Maria says you have been looking at me during the show besides. Is that something true also?'

He blushes some more on his white-side. 'Well it is, Tibb. And carrying you out in that oyster to open each show is my greatest privilege.'

I say, 'Sir, I cannot think of why.' But my voice has petered out to a whisper and I don't really know if I said a thing.

'Tibb, you are a beautiful person, inside and out.'

I shake my head because this is not what Farmer O said and it is not what Signor said either. And I can't imagine how Ambrose can tell me this when I do not have this nice purple colour and in fact I am pale like a ghost.

He says, 'Perhaps I must tell you till you believe it.'

Well here is a blush for the boys, Ma! I say, 'But you had that whore in London-town who wished to see you in your no-clothes outfit.'

He smiles. 'There was nothing beautiful about *her*, Tibb.'

There is something like hot air squatting between us in this tent. Those hazel eyes of his are all patterned like snail shells. He takes my hand like he should be the nervous one, and it is soft and big and mine is somewhere inside of it and we just sit like that for a while.

'Ambrose, those people in your village were wrong. You are no more strange with your purple mark than I am with this ghost-white skin of mine.' It is quiet between us, then I say, 'Might I touch that purple part of you?'

He says, 'If you like.'

Gently I put a finger on that lovely face of his and it is all soft like a flower-head on the purple side. For once he is looking straight at me and those nice lips are coming closer and this is not the kind of kiss Ivo did give me each night upon my forehead in the land of Norfolk but a different kind altogether. This isn't friendship, and nor is this what Signor was after. There is a great stretching inside of me, and then he pulls back and he says, 'You know I love you, Tibb.'

Leominster, Herefordshire

Of course he loves Tibb. He can't be angry with her, not after what she did for him. Her belief in love. Flavio's words are ringing in his ears. About fig trees and bats. Perhaps Tibb was right about all of it – that exquisite future she painted. The thought of it was almost too sweet to fully comprehend but now he allows it to swell and become clear in his mind. Flavio's hand in his, warm water lapping around their ankles, the sun on their backs. He imagines the feeling of being free and light; of the shame being lifted from his shoulders.

Soon the warden returns with bread and beer and something metal in his hand. 'I'm afraid I'll need to put you in chains,' he says, looking guiltily at Ivo down there on the floor.

'Chains?'

He holds them up. Thick irons to tie his prisoner's wrists to the hoops on the wall. 'So when the Justice returns, he'll see you're suffering.'

Ivo nods, since this man has been kind to him. He holds his arms up and the warden ties his wrists so they are fastened a foot above his head, muttering all the while. 'You were fooled like the rest of us and it's some bad business. I wonder why that madwoman did it though? Surely there are easier ways to earn money – would she not take a room at the bawdy house like a good wench?'

He laughs and Ivo feels heat rising up his neck – he doesn't like to hear anyone talk about Tibb and bawdy houses in the same sentence.

'She's real,' he says but his voice is flat. His torso feels sapped of all its power like this. Stretched. The hairs on his stomach poking through.

The warden looks at Ivo with pity in his eyes, as though his prisoner is the most gullible of all.

'Thank you,' he says quietly. 'For letting in my . . . cook.'

The warden nods. 'He paid me off.'

'And could I pay you off to let me out?'

The warden's face crumples. 'Sorry,' he whispers, and Ivo just nods. It was worth a try.

'How long left?' he asks.

'I hear the horses have arrived in London.'

Thousand dead guards

This breeze has one chill edge but Ambrose and I are keeping warm, lying in a meadow and watching the clouds sneak across the sky. These skinny plants are tall around us but they are gone limp and golden like straw-people, bending too much in the wind, and each one with its little head, tufted with cat's whiskers which have mostly fallen off, or else flowers which have dried and gone crisp. I wonder we have one thousand dead guards to keep us secret in here.

I am resting my head on his chest and it is pleasant – this sensation of moving up and down as he breathes. It is clear to me now what it means to be in love – not just to love like I did love my ma and Henrietta. Like I still love Ivo. But the different kind of loving.

'I think I was waiting for you,' I tell him because this new love is something like a roof.

It is making me sad to think my ma had wanted this so much and she did chase this feeling with all the bad men but she never had someone like Ambrose. I like the way he moves those big branches out of my path when we trek through woodlands, and how he does check upon Maria and I and say, 'Let me carry those heavy things for you.' And he plays to me from his lute and has me stare into streams while he asks, 'Do you believe it yet, Tibb? How beautiful you are?' This man would have me think the sun is shining from my arsehole.

He wraps that arm around me and squeezes me tight. 'Well I was waiting for you, Tibb. Only you – in all this kingdom. Because you understand how it is to be different and you look at me differently than other people do. I think you can see people under their skin.'

Well that is a foul thought but I smile and I reckon those circling birds up there are wondering who are those two opposite-people amongst the dying meadow down there – one half-purple like a berry and the other white as a ghost.

'Ambrose,' I say. 'Would you play another?'

I wind my white hair around my wrist and I think I could listen to his tunes forever. This melody he is playing now sounds like water and sand. Like the tide and the sea-air. It sounds like time is sliding past, escaping through my fingers, and it is something shameful to me that tears are dripping down my face. Thoughts of Ivo and Ma and Henrietta. The fact I'm so happy with Ambrose and Maria and yet I do miss those gone-already people just as much and how can that make any sense at all? Did you know music can shift the mountains, Tibb?

Ambrose lowers that lute, his face crumpled with worries. 'Tibb!' he says. 'Would you tell me what's wrong?'

More tears do come though my ma did tell me, 'You are one ugly crier, Tibb.'

I say, 'You know there was a baby once who I did not keep alive too well, which in fact means I killed her—' but these words are all choked up and escaping in little bursts.

'Tibb?'

'She was my sister, Ambrose, and I thought I should tell you this so you can know who it is that you are loving so much.'

He smiles a bit and I can't think why. 'Tibb,' he says, laying his purple hand on my cheek. 'Life is hard, and you are a kind person.'

I sniff and sniff. 'How do you know it?'

He tosses those gingery curls from his eyes. 'Because I have seen many unkind people, and I know you are not one of them. I can tell it from a mile off.'

I lie back down and he does too and I am not gulping for air any more.

'How?' I ask him.

'Lots of things. Because you worry when Penn is gone too long with his rabbit-traps . . .'

'Well my ma did warn me of those groups of wandering-men who will jump upon a stray just for their own sport!'

'And because you offer your meat to Maria though you must be hungry, I think.'

'Ah, now she does like it more than me, Ambrose. And she needs muscles for her grand hobby of lifting.'

'And because you had some stern words with that woman in the crowd at Bedford who shouted that I was cursed by Lucifer.'

'You heard that?' I say, and I wipe my face. 'I think you don't miss a single thing, Ambrose.'

He chuckles and squeezes me tight. The mostly-bald flower-heads bob in the breeze and it seems Ambrose is a very wise person. He doesn't have the scared feelings which followed me and Ma around like a shadow, and most of all Ivo. I think Ivo did have those scared feelings more than anyone.

Perhaps even a gale from the big-man himself would not rock Ambrose. It's like he has faced all the bad stuff of this world already and that has built him up rather than cast him down, and I think I could lean on this pillar-person and he would hold me up forever. Ivo's face is in my mind. If only he could have some of Ambrose's sureness – but why am I wishing that when Ivo up-and-left me? Would you mother a snap-dog, Tibb?

'Please don't leave me, Ambrose,' I whisper.

He rolls on his side and looks me in the eyes. 'Tibb,' he says, 'I will always be right beside you,' and I do want to believe this promise, Ma, except a man said that to me once before.

Waiting for nothing

Men are like leeches, Tibb. They don't survive on their own because a man is not a man unless he is fucking one of us. Well that is what my own ma did say and I can see that is the case with the serpent-man called Signor Perero and how did I not see it sooner? Had my ma come across *him* in her days of charging-for-it, then he would have been first in line for a throat-slitting. But I am not finding it to be the case with Ambrose.

In fact, after that sweet kissing we have been doing, then he is just holding me very close and I am feeling safe. Like I haven't felt since Ivo left. But if my ma was right, then Ambrose should be wanting a bit more than this.

'Ambrose,' I say. 'There is something on my mind.'

We are hiding in a barn since this weather got colder. Those chickens in the corner are no bother and that roof is some nice vaulted thing. I am staring up at it now like an angel should pop out because wasn't the big-man born in a barn?

He says, 'Tibb?'

'I think you do not want to do that fucking dance with me.'

He looks like he would laugh. 'O, trust me, I do, Tibb. But this is an important thing for a young woman, and I should not like it to be done in a trice.'

'Ambrose,' I say. 'I have been doing this thing in my head with you since I first saw you.'

He looks happy about that, so I am peeling off all these clothes of mine, and then I am peeling off his, and he holds me by my shoulders and he says, 'Are you sure about this, Tibb?'

That great turnip of his is certainly sure. I am quite shocked by the size of it.

'O, would you get on with it!' I say, and those gentle hands are lifting me up to sit astride him and I can't think of anything better – but then something is swooping over me like a bat. This barn is swimming in a flood and I am thinking of Farmer O. I am thinking that these are *his* hands around my waist right now. And Ambrose's lovely face is all sweaty and dotted with black over his nose like Farmer O. He is sprouting with hairs like Farmer O too and his breath is reeking of beer just the same.

'Tibb?' and 'Tibb?' I hear. Now I can't see one thing but I can hear my chest is heaving up and down and my limbs have gone floppy and I can't really feel them. And my head is not here at all but all the way back in the bad land of Weymouth, under a blanket with a fucker called Farmer O who I did tempt with some black magic even though my own ma did love him and was sleeping just beside us. Then there is some cool air on my face and I am feeling some dense soil under me which is a nice relief. This world is returning like a patchwork – square by square – and I can see Ambrose is crouching next to me with all that concern streaked across his forehead. He has carried me outside and that barn door is hanging open because he cares more about a girl called Tibb than those chickens, and now they are pecking around in this soil-field because here is a feast of worms they didn't bargain for.

'Tibb,' he says, 'you had me terrified.'

He has left all our clothing inside that barn and we are out here in our nothing-at-all suits.

'Don't leave me, Ambrose,' I say. 'I promise you won't be waiting long for the fucking to start.'

'Tibb, I am waiting for nothing.'

Trees will chatter

This January weather means no haybales and so Maria is lifting a fallen tree-trunk and I am watching her. We are somewhere in the forest near Daventry but who knows where that is? She drops it with a grunt and then she flexes those big muscles.

'I will be all ready to build myself a very fine home soon enough,' she says, and she laughs with a great ho-ho-ho and her breath is forming puffy clouds in this cold air.

A sheet of thin ice has gathered at the base of this tree and I push the heel of my leather boot down so it breaks into pieces like I just smashed some glass, and I am thinking that the cordwainer's shoes did not have good soles like mine since he did not have one honest bone inside that bun-on-legs body.

'You won't mind to be alone?'

She shakes her head a great many times and then she has a little half-smile appearing too. 'I would not be alone, Tibb, for while you have been with Ambrose, I have been up to some naughty tricks with John.'

John? I did not hear her speak of John even once.

'The juggler?' I say and she nods.

Well here is something I did not expect and these green-all-the-year trees are gasping besides.

'You are a sly fox, Maria!'

This patch of forest seems to take one great breath and those trees do shrink so the sun can poke through.

She laughs some more. 'I intend to have a brood of

strapping boys and you will visit us, Tibb. If your family in Leicester will spare you?'

I nod but she cocks her head.

'Tibb, you have not been yourself recently.'

'You noticed, Maria?'

She sits down beside me. 'Friends notice the small things.'

I shrug. 'I think I am not deserving of that beautiful man Ambrose because of something bad I did with Farmer O which was my fault after all. And Ivo did make me feel better for a short while but then he left too so the farmer was certainly right.'

Her brown eyes widen a lot. 'Tibb, you are making no sense at all. Who are you talking about? Who is this Farmer O?'

She repeats it far too loud and clear and I flinch because the whole forest will know what I did and all of those trees will chatter together about it.

I make a line on the ground with the toe of my leather boot. If I had the grand skill-of-writing then I would scribble it all down so I didn't have to say it.

'I think if you knew then you would not claim to be a friend of mine any longer.'

She puts those cushiony hands around my face and she says, 'What rot do you speak, girl? Now you will stop all this nonsense talk and you will tell your friend Maria all about this person named Farmer O.'

Well the tent is all sweaty and I am lying on top of Ambrose's big body while we catch our breath because Maria was right. I did tell him all that stuff and it was something like a miracle-cure. Now his arms are wrapped around me like he would never let me go and I am thinking this tent is some small paradise.

I say, 'Well I enjoyed that, Ambrose!' and he smiles a lot.

The owls are hooting out there and those night-stars are winking at me through the little holes in this canvas roof like they would tell me, 'What a show!'

'I would like to do this all day long and never be a pearl again.'

He sighs deeply. 'Me too. I think my best audience would be no one at all.'

I lie on my side so I am facing him and I trail a finger over that kind face. 'It would? I thought a player of your talent would quite welcome all the listening ears. You must be used to fine audiences of important people.'

He shrugs. 'The lute has given me the means to survive and for that I'm grateful, but I don't want to perform all my life.'

'Because there are cruel comments too?'

'O, not that – truly they slip over me, Tibb. I can hardly hear them. But even the good comments don't mean a thing. Perhaps they once did, but not now. It doesn't make a difference any more if a man I have never met and will never meet again tells me he has never heard anything sweeter. I don't need their compliments to make my life richer.'

I think about this. My ma did need the compliments of all the men to bring on her ecstasy, but she hated herself for that too.

'Maria is finding a piece of paradise, you know. And she is leaving the world behind to live with John and have a brood.'

He nods. 'We could do that, Tibb. We could save our monies and get ourselves a house. Would you like it?'

I am not answering for a moment. The thought of it is too big and too beautiful to fit inside my head because I have thought oftentime of rooves but I did not ever think there was one so perfect as Ambrose who would jump across the ocean for me and shift the mountains if I needed him to. I would feel safe in a sinking boat with this person. But there is something sad about it too because my ma did not ever realize how wonderful and peaceful a roof could truly be.

'I would,' I say, but I am thinking of Ivo's words about belonging and rooves-not-always-being-rooves, then I am remembering that nice weight in my arms of the baby who I called Henrietta and I do so wish to feel that sweet heaviness again. But how could you think to be a ma yourself, Tibb, when you did kill a baby?

I whisper, 'Though perhaps not the brood part since I would not be good for the job.'

He props himself up and says, 'Tibb, I think you would be perfect for the job.' And these tears are knocking hard because they want to come out.

We lie a while longer like this and there is something else nagging at me. I say slowly, 'It just seems strange that anywhere could be a home without Ivo.'

'Ivo?'

I can see that look in Ambrose's face like he would say: 'Now this doesn't sound like good news to me.'

I shake my head. 'He was more like a brother. And the people who he loves in a marriage-way are in fact other men. I think without him I would not be here at all because he kept me alive when I just wanted to die.'

Ambrose wipes that tear with a purple finger and he wraps me up inside his manly limbs. 'Well in that case I am full of gratitude for this friend of yours.'

'Ambrose . . . perhaps we might leave a sign outside when we live in our own paradise, just in case Ivo should come looking? I think you have the good writing-skill after all.'

He says, 'Of course we can, Tibb.'

Of the sex kind

This winter passes quick because I am busy at church. And by that I do not mean the place-called-church, but rather the church-of-Ambrose since he is certainly a God of the sex kind and perhaps he will go down in history for all the naughty things he can perform with those white-and-purple fingers of his.

We are doing this thing everywhere including Bedworth and Coventry and Kenilworth and all those small villages in between. Would you stake your claim on every inch of this kingdom, Tibb? Sir, I would.

Signor is doing a very poor job of not-caring. I think he has cast me so many angry looks that he has grown a new wrinkle to join the others between his flaky eyebrows. And now he speaks loudly about those poor women he fucks in the brothels like this should bring tears into my own eyes.

When spring arrives it is too hot and Maria calls it *unseasonable* which is some long word besides. I do not have that turban Ivo would make so now my scalp is scorched in this sun. And always these crickets running-amok and shrieking bloody-murder in the grasses. O, God-in-the-sky, would you blow away this swarm? And would you send the rain again to boot?

Every evening Ambrose and I take a walk so we can be quite alone, and we are climbing hills to see the nice views and watching new lambs take their first steps. Sometimes we follow rivers as they wriggle like snakes across the fields, staying out till the sun goes down, but Ambrose always knows the way back and he is not scared of darkness and the shady deeds which happen under it. He could scare off a whole group of fuckers with his great stature and all his muscles, though I can't imagine it too well because he is what my ma would call mild-mannered. I like the way he holds my hand in his and how big and tall he feels beside me.

'I do think there is a lot more beauty in this kingdom than my ma let on,' I say when we are sitting and watching a pink sunset in the place called Walton. 'Only you have to know where to look and when.'

He smiles and his speckled-like-an-egg eyes smile too. 'Doesn't it make you wonder about all the beautiful sights we will never see across this Earth?'

'Like Constantinople?' I say, because this is somewhere I have heard of from my own ma. 'And the land of Antwerp?'

He smiles even more. 'Yes, exactly. But even further besides. All those rich folk I used to play the lute for would talk endlessly about their travels. And I took a lot of interest in the amazing things they collected.'

'Like what?'

'All sorts, Tibb. Bowls of spices that smelt sweet and hot all at once, and dried pods taken from the cocoa plants that rattle when you shake them. Huge leaves, each one the size of an eagle and spiked with tiny needles. And soft bird feathers as blue as the sky. There are whole worlds out there we'll never see.'

My eyes are like two round buttons just now because my ma did have some thoughts on Constantinople but she did not mention anything about feathers and birds and spices apart from nutmeg which she had her own bad use for in fact.

'Would you tell me more, Ambrose?'

Leominster, Herefordshire

The warden looks down at him with pity. 'Listen, do you have family I might tell?'

Ivo shakes his head. He is remembering his sisters. The games of make-believe they played behind the house when they were young, digging small pools in the mud; lining them with leaves and scooping in water from the brook. They built bridges with sticks so the ants might march over. They demanded shoulder rides and piggy-backs. To be spun around till they went dizzy. He never said goodbye.

He went back there once. After he left Tibb; before he came to Leominster. He returned to that village in Kent and he hid in the copse, watching the small house where he grew up. His sisters were gone already – married, he supposed. Marriages arranged for the sole purpose of breeding.

The scene at Peterborough had rattled him to the core; convinced him that some feelings cannot be given the space to surface and breathe. He would plead youth or insanity or both, and he would marry after all.

First he watched his father go off to work, those fists opening and closing by his sides. Why were they always pumping that way? Then he observed from afar as his mother began her day, in and out, seeing to errands. When she was inside he could picture her so clearly, just fifty feet from him. Was she thinking about him? Was she counting money for his seat in Heaven?

How close he was to walking in there and holding her in his arms. Telling her how much he missed her. That it was all madness back then and he had returned to do the right thing.

Somehow, though, he couldn't. He just stayed there, behind the trees and the hawthorn bushes, until the sun went down again. Wishing he could ask the only question he truly needed the answer to: Did you see me that night? Did you open your eyes?

He looks at the warden who is still waiting for a response.

'No family,' he says.

Fine head-crowns

Another winter did pass and then another one and they were made a lot warmer by my own sweet Ambrose and Maria and the acrobats. I have been part of this almost-a-family troupe a good three years and our own King Henry is still perching there on his big throne though my ma did say that man is as weak as a rat's cock. His wife did think to die of course and they say he might marry again but Maria tells me that no one should want him. And people still do talk and talk about those little princes who were killed and maybe by him. So perhaps the no-wife problem is a fitting punishment from the big-man himself.

We have been down to Oxford and up to Birmingham and to every place in between and now we are in a large town going by the name of Stratford-upon-Avon which does stink in this June heat. The council here has requested to extend our stay since our act is bringing in a great many people to the markets. I should say they are speaking in that crowd of the big stilts-lady and the pearl-person before we even show ourselves.

Right now they are clapping and those acrobats are tumbling some more, then Signor is talking a long time to a man in the crowd. This person is all dressed up like a robin in a fine doublet lined with scarlet silk and a red velvet cap though the weather is far too hot for it. Those pennies are glinting on the cobbles but Signor is still simpering with some serious-and-important look under that wide-brimmed hat. Then they are shaking hands and he is sidling back towards us, puffing out his little pigeon-chest.

'I have secured you all an evening at the home of a real nobleman! A wealthy Lord Fielding, as he is known around these parts, and of close connection to courtly men.'

He waves a small piece of parchment in our faces like this does contain the directions to the King's own jewels.

'He has given me here the details of his great house in the area of Wilmcote where he should have us perform in two evenings' time. Entertainment, you see, for a great many of his wealthy friends, who may then wish to copy the same. And he is hiring us at a good price too.'

'How good?' I ask, and Signor scowls back.

'You can leave the business to me, dear, and do your work, and if you do not wish to, then feel free to enter a life of service or find some employment as a wheat-picker.'

I glower because I am the naughty owner of that thing named gall these days. I do think all those scared feelings I once had for this face-like-a-rat man did drip into the dirt since my own Ambrose became my protector-person. And what do you think of that, Ma?

'The Lord Fielding has requested a play of virtues as they have at the King's court. A morality play that is.'

Well this is some slick of irony right there, and I can see my friends in this troupe of ours are thinking just the same. What does Signor Perero know of those things called virtues since he is the proud owner of not one of them himself?

'But we are no grand actresses of the stage here, sir,' I tell him.

'You can play any part if you have the right costume.'

Maria whispers, 'But your hat is not enough to convince us you are Spanish,' and I stifle a big snort.

'Shall we begin our practice?' he says like he is the King-of-the-world with this new business deal of his. 'I am thinking that Maria will play the part of Diligence, owing to those great muscles. And you, Tibb, are to be Chastity for those obvious reasons of your appearance.'

I could point out that there is nothing so chaste about me, sir. I was writhing around on top of my big Ambrose just last night!

'And Penn and Lambert and Luke will be something in the way of Justice and Prudence and Faith. And John will be Charity. And then Ambrose of course might be named the devil himself who will be chased away by all of you. This should do nicely!' and he claps those scaly hands like all the problems of this kingdom are solved this day.

'Wait,' I say, since there is some anger bubbling up inside my body. 'Why should Ambrose be cast as the devil?'

Signor looks like he wishes to take a pick-axe and swipe my head off. 'Because, dear, that strange colour lends itself to the part so nicely.'

'I do not agree, sir!' I say, and the other players are all shaking their heads besides but Ambrose is glaring like he would tell me: 'Tibb, would you give it a rest?'

Now that scaly face of Signor is right up close. 'Dear, you do not need to agree, since this is all my own reckoning and not yours. Now, I will be going to the blacksmith to commission some fine head-crowns so you are all trussed up like real actors.'

If my ma was here she would raise those arms and give this man Signor some great smack about his dry head. And would you watch the fuckers win, Tibb?

Her polished cane

This enormous house in the place called Wilmcote is a beautiful sight indeed, all straight-edged and formed in reddish stones. I should say those latticed-like-a-pie windows are fitted with real glass. Then there are paths around it and all manner of trees which have been cut into shapes like slabs of butter which tells me the Lord Fielding is a very rich man indeed. As do all those poor peasants who are hacking away in the fields beyond in their sad tunics.

Drudgery. Now here is a topic I am well versed on from my own clever ma who was not all sponge inside that sometimes-scrambled head. The rich and the poor and the nothing-in-between, Tibb.

'O, I am all worn out, Signor. I should like to sit down.'

I am certain now that this man cannot read a thing since we have been walking in circles all day with Lord Fielding's map. And this thin skin of mine is no good at walking in the summer and never will it be. I am cropping up with big blisters between my toes like here are some sweet cushions.

He ignores me.

'Lord Fielding did say there are some twenty-four hearths inside of this great stone building!' He rubs those sandpaper palms together. Perhaps he thinks the man will gift him this very house after our performance, and, Ma, I am beginning to see the appeal of that throat-slitting hobby you did favour.

We set our tents up in the gardens with that pink sun for light and this heavy crown is no fine costume. Poor Ambrose is wearing wood horns upon that lovely head and this is some bad, bad day.

'I don't like to see you dressed up in this stuff, Ambrose.'

It does not suit him a bit. He is too tall and upstanding to be made into a mockery.

'It's you I am worried about,' he says. 'I didn't like the look of Lord Fielding and I have seen enough of rich people to spot the truly rotten ones.'

We enter the house through those kitchens which are bustling and hot and I should wish to stick my head into that fine-looking jelly and to guzzle those bowls of meat and buttery stuff. How many friends does the Lord Fielding have here tonight? And how much are they planning on eating? I am tripping over my feet for staring at these too-many cooks and all the nice-smelling steam.

Up some wide-enough stairs and I have not walked up stairs too often in this life. 'Stairs are paths for queens, Tibb,' my ma did say and she told me, 'One day we shall have our own set to boot.' But these ones are so flat and long that I am putting two feet on to each step before I can climb to the next. Ambrose slips his hand into mine just for a secret moment.

The dark corridors are all perfectly laid with plaited rushes and high-backed chairs and wood chests but this place has some creepy-enough feeling. All the beeswax candles which aren't lit and the good-for-nothing little models of strange beasts cast in brass. My ma would be slipping things inside of her pockets because these people have no need for it, Tibb, and I am thinking I wouldn't want a roof at all if it was dingy like this one. In fact, I am imagining all these dark-wood chests to have skeletons lurking inside them and I have an urge to wrench one open and check for myself. There are some minstrels playing somewhere and I don't like the sound of it one piece and neither do I like that smell of hot meat which is marching down the corridor towards us like we are in a pie-shop just now.

'The hall, sir,' or so says the kitchen boy who opens a heavy wood door, and here is some noisy feast already. Three long tables all stuffed with people, and the wine is all flowed out or otherwise spilt upon the floor, and those heavy scarlet curtains and Turkey carpets are not soaking up one part of the din.

My eyes do drift along the big tapestries which are hanging all around the oak walls and this is some fucked-up story they are telling. The stitched-in-gold peasant people who are hacking away at the wheat in the first tapestry are being whipped in the next, and in the one after they are all of them lying dead-as-doornails, their spilt blood sewed in gold besides. I think every white hair on my body is standing up just now since the Lord Fielding is formed of rotten stuff as Ambrose did suspect, and this stupid crown is making sores behind my ears.

'So for my troupe!' Signor announces, and this room is lively with applause for our own grand entrance. The minstrels have stopped their playing and that is one good thing at least.

In we go, but I am wandering my eyes over these ladies very carefully. At those stomachers and kirtles hiding all manner of bloated bellies. And all of them necking back the wine like tomorrow shouldn't come, and the fat men amongst them belching away in their jewelled ear-rings and ruffs as they do watch us enter. This dining room stinks of meat and fat and it is mingling with the sweaty scent of these people and I don't like it one bit.

Signor stands between these tables and puffs himself up like he has sprouted feathers. 'Lord Fielding and esteemed guests . . . I, Signor Perero, do beg you to make yourselves ready for surprises a-plenty!'

If he thinks to call himself Signor to these people, then at least he might attempt a Spanish accent for the occasion.

'You are joined here at your fine home by the virtues of the good book, and some cruel devil. And would you watch, dear guests, to see which will triumph?'

Now on we go with that strange play which Signor did have us practise. Mostly this is just twirling and charging at one another, but these people are clapping nonetheless and such is the cheering that if Signor were not a sneak-rat we should all be made as rich as kings from this performance tonight. Down goes poor Ambrose who is no bad actor and then the Lord Fielding is standing up and swaying on his fat-enough legs.

'Bravo, sir! Bravo! That ugly brute the devil was all chased away!'

Ugly brute?

'We will retreat now, us gentlemen,' the Lord Fielding slurs and he is wearing his scarlet robin-hat again. 'To some other chamber for the purpose of brandies and wagering with my dice and cards.'

All the men are staggering to their feet and I am thinking that we will now be released which is some slice of good fortune since I've had enough of this dark place and these fat people for a lifetime.

'We will split your players, Signor,' he says. 'These two women will come with us and the men and that devil will remain in here to entertain my wife and her lady-friends while they take their hippocras and their sweetmeats. You said he has some talent at the lute?'

Signor says, 'Yes, he will do his penance and give you all some lovely music and ha-ha-ha!'

I am not liking this plan. Why should we be split up? And my Ambrose is not looking so delighted with that lute thrust into his hands while the acrobats and John are being jostled around and stuffed on to the benches between these women and poked at like they are something to eat besides. One old noblewoman reaches out and prods Ambrose with her polished cane. 'Well? Play then, boy!'

Now I am come over quite icy cold, but 'Move!' is the word hissed into my ear by that awful man called Signor Perero. I see he is all wonky at the moustache and stern-eyed in his efforts to shepherd Maria and I out of this eating-hall so we might do as the Lord Fielding has asked.

I move slowly, like a snail moves, meeting eyes with my Ambrose and I can see he does not much like what is happening either and that snake is lounging across my shoulders like it never really left.

Our hairy parts

That serving boy is taking us down corridors to the gambling room and at the same time trying to peer down Maria's dress with his roving-everywhere eyes. What is waiting for us? I did have this same bad feeling when my ma would say: 'Tibb, this one will be different! Do you know he will leave that wife for us?'

Outside the door Signor says, 'The Duke would see you dance for his pleasure.'

'*Dance?* But I cannot dance a step!'

He shoves us both inside and this place is dark like a cave. But not like those nice caves where Ivo and I would sleep in winter because they were something cosy and they had the sound of the sea for music. In here there is just the noise of men belching and slurping and beneath my bare feet there is the striped skin of a wild cat with jewel-stones for eyes. The fire is too hot and smoky and there is hardly enough air to breathe as these men prepare their drinks or else help themselves from that table, forming little heaps of spiced sugar on miniature plates though they are spilling most of it on to the striped cat. Do these people ever stop eating? I do smell nutmeg in those spices besides and that is no good memory, though my ma did have a little habit to smoke hers from a pipe.

'Gentlemen, we have two visions of Aphrodite just here,' the Lord Fielding says, eyeing us, and those men all laugh and laugh.

'Exactly!' Signor cries. 'Exactly that, good sirs!'

The man is a weasel.

All the jewelled collars in this small room are making my eyes squint in the candle-light and those cat-eyes on the floor are glinting like they would tell me: 'Run already!' Maria is frozen beside me and Signor Perero is watching us like he has some hawk-eyes on his face.

'Settle, settle,' the Lord Fielding slurs. His scarlet cap has come clean off and now he is revealing his greasy mop of black hair. 'The big one will dance first, since I could not see her full-figure well enough in there.'

There is a great cheer to this though not from Maria. In fact, her honey skin is like a pallor. We could be sisters just now.

'There is no music, sir,' she says, all wobbly-voiced. 'You have separated us from our fine lute-player. Perhaps we should fetch him back?'

Lord Fielding looks around and bangs a friend on the back who starts some low singing and a great bashing of his fat hand against a table.

'Now there is music, dear, so dance!'

Still Maria doesn't move an inch and Signor steps forward and yanks the sleeves of her dress down further. 'Dance!' he growls, all low in her ear, and those men push her up on to the table.

In fact, my friend Maria, who is made of strong Flemish stuff, starts spinning like a graceful swan despite those big bosoms and that large bottom of hers and the fact she is terrified of these peeking-men. But when those hands reach out to slide beneath her dress and up her legs then she kicks them away and stops her dance.

'No!'

That was Signor and he is all testy and jerking like there is a wasp beneath that hat of his. He pulls her down and slaps her round the face and she is sent back up on to that table all hot and blushing and I am blushing for her. This lion's-den will eat us up, Ma.

'Now now, man!' the Lord Fielding laughs, patting Signor on the back like they are brothers. 'I will see to law and punishment here.'

I do not like how this man's teeth are sticking out and overlapping. They are like apple-seed teeth, or else wolf-teeth. I can picture them sinking into my own flesh and I am thinking of the tapestry with the whipped peasants and the gold blood.

Still the fat friend is chanting his dire song and perhaps he should be gagged instead of making this cat-wail sound. My heart is jumping and jumping.

'My gentlemen friends have requested to see the other girl have a try,' says the Lord Fielding. 'To have them dance together in fact.'

'Of course, good men!' says Signor, and he does order me: 'Now get up there, Tibb.' And I do since there is no other choice, but I am doing such a terrible job that Signor Perero withers, his face in his hands. 'I apologize, for this one has the grace of an elephant and she does not dance so well as my other girl, I am afraid. Is there nothing else she might do for you?'

Such a raucous braying from these tubby-tummed friends in reply. It seems they have many ideas of what I might do for them and I was not born just yesterday either.

'Dance!' the Lord Fielding says again, though he is not so jovial any more. 'Are you deaf, you women?'

This jig is some pitiful scene, though it is nice to hold Maria's hands and squeeze them tight in mine. But those men are bored and there is a gathering instruction for my dear friend Maria to be taking off her clothing and to be dancing for them in her nothing-at-all outfit. And there is Ma sitting on my shoulder saying, 'Tibb! Would you stand for that?'

'My friend Maria and I are experiencing that monthly blood which is called the menses, sirs,' I do announce. 'Perhaps you have heard of it, and that is no pretty sight when you see it all trickling down our legs and stuck there upon our hairy parts.'

Well these disgusted faces are something sweet to behold and Signor Perero could well have fire billowing from that crooked nose of his. He drags us out of the room and says, 'Fuck off, and consider your wages to be docked for a month!'

I can still hear Ambrose playing in that feasting hall as Maria and I run through this house and down to the back door like two criminals escaping the gallows with a great ho-ho-ho at my fine excuse.

Out in that camping-field she says, 'But you are so quick-thinking, Tibb! I did not know this about you!'

'Ah, but I had to think quick many times, Maria. Like when my own dear ma snatched a farthing-cake from a stand in her too-much-ale stupor. Or when she thought to plunge a knife into a bad-man's neck outside a thriving tavern.'

Maria nods and nods and she does not say, 'Tibb!' and 'What an unholy cow was your ma!' because friends do not do that judging stuff.

Outside the tents we eat a little of the salty porridge gifted from that fine kitchen, but this evening is too hot. Honey mead would be a finer thing.

'I am sorry about the wages, Maria.'

'Tosh!' she says. 'You stopped a terrible evil happening in there, my friend.'

She puts those big arms around my shoulders and she smiles her lovely smile which does hail from those Low Countries.

'Not too much more of this travelling life, Tibb. Soon enough we will be free from John Payne and we might look forward to a much finer life in our own homes.'

'Maria,' I say quietly. 'You know I do not have family in Leicester? I was a vagrant in fact.'

'I thought so,' she says.

My own pet

My ma is up there but she is not winking much tonight through the hole in the tent.

'Ma,' I whisper. 'You would not have liked that roof either.'

When will Ambrose be back? This is what I am wondering as my eyes are closing and I am wondering the same thing when that strange light outside does wake me up. Did the moon topple out of the big sky besides?

'Ambrose?' I whisper. 'Is it you?'

How long have I been asleep?

'It is me! Signor!'

'Signor?' I repeat, and that lantern light is getting brighter and his scaly head is poking in here like he would clamber through the gap.

'But where is Ambrose? Still he isn't back?'

O, there is a sinking feeling inside of me, like my guts would be dragged down to my feet.

'But that is why I am come for you!' so says Signor. 'He is asking for you, dear.'

'Asking for me? Where?'

Signor nods and nods. 'He is waiting in front of the great house for you.'

Now this is a strange-enough thing to say and I am feeling that seed of something-like-doubt. His pig-eyes are darting around and he has lit up this small tent like a lantern itself. The moths will be flying here from Constantinople.

'Ah, you cannot know a good thing when it slaps you about the face, dear.'

‘Fine,’ I say, because I need to find my Ambrose, and I am pulling on those leather boots.

This night air is cold and I am crossing my arms over my body. Little stones say crunch and crunch beneath me and I wonder I shall wake the whole house up with this crunching. I don’t much like the swirling in my belly either. Like wolves might jump out of those trees and snap their big teeth.

I squint. Now this figure who is waiting down the path is not a wolf and neither is he the shape of my lovely Ambrose, but shorter and far more blubbery at the middle. He is almost at the entrance gate, standing there beside a carriage.

‘Madam,’ he says, bowing, and here is some repulsive sight. He is all limp and drippy except for that round, stretched belly. I wonder that a pig’s bladder has not been blown up and shoved inside of that waistcoat and he drums his fingers on it excitedly. I recognize him from the gambling room.

I say, ‘Signor Perero has sent me here to find the lute-playing man called Ambrose. So where is he, sir?’

‘Ambrose?’ he says, like he is all confused. That thin hair is stuck to his forehead with sweat and his lips and teeth are all stained with red wine. ‘Ah yes, yes! Ambrose, that strange-coloured person! I shall take you to him if you would just shut those eyes, no peeking now.’

‘This is a stupid game.’

‘Do you wish to see him, madam, or no?’

I have barely shut my eyes before I am feeling something very wrong indeed. A big thwack around my head and a knee in my stomach and I keel right over on this path. I want to thrash like a wild pig and to squeal for Maria to come running, but I cannot do either on account of this pain in my belly and this sensation of being only half-awake. Such a pain that

I cannot move an inch. That fat man is squatting somewhere close because I can smell his breath and that out-of-puff groaning.

'I think Signor Perero set a low price on you. In fact, I would have paid him double to have you as my own pet.'

A songbird of no sweet music

A little drip of water on to my head. Drip. And another. Drip. And then drip-drip-drip till it trickles down my nose and into my stinking-like-a-dead-rat mouth. This is no water, Tibb, but wine. And why should I be tasting wine?

Now I am prising my eyelids apart but this is a struggle owing to the great clunking and aching inside of my head. I wonder I have been struck by a wagon, else that someone is driving a poker into my skull. Then some rush of panic, since I do not know this place at all. This sad nothing-in-it room. Ambrose? Where is Ambrose?

I try to sit up but I cannot do this either since my hands are tethered to the posts of this bed like I am a prisoner here.

The dripper of wine lounges next to me, his sweaty face all smiles, and those half-memories are crashing back into my head like the bull was let out. And the fact I am now laid out in this bleak chamber in my nothing-at-all costume, lit only by a candle. And Ambrose is not here beside me.

He grins, a crumbling row of yellowed teeth, and 'Lie back,' he says, starting the dripping game again but this time over my chest. He wants to dye me red, this man. 'Now you have had a long night's sleep, you lazy slug. It is noon already!'

'Why am I dressed in nothing?' I ask, though my voice is all crackly like a crone, and I can see enough of myself to notice the great bruise across my stomach. 'I will scream and your servants will come running.'

'O, there are no servants to hear you, my dear, for I dismissed my household months ago owing to my fondness for the dice. It is some stroke of luck besides since the noises I will be making shortly would scare off the hounds.'

Fuck.

I scour this room. A woman is never without a weapon, Tibb. Well you are wrong there, Ma, for I see nothing here to make my weapon. Not one wood pole nor anything formed of metal to bang against the back of his sweaty skull. In fact it is completely bare and clay-floored and really there is only this bed and the bucket he has left for the purpose of pissing into, I imagine. Judging by the brighter paint left in big squares, I should say there were once tapestries tacked upon these peeling walls and this four-poster bed would have been something truly grand till it had all the curtains wrenched off.

He chuckles. 'There is nothing here to aid you, dear.' He cracks his knuckles. 'And luckily we are quite hidden in this part of the countryside. It is like a retreat from all life! Consider it your new home.'

'It is a prison to me, sir.'

'Yes, yes, I suppose it is since your owner did sell you to me!'

'I had no owner.'

'Ah, now every poor-man has an owner. I have one myself, and that is the gambling dice.'

He shakes his head, then he is trailing a finger down my arm which is making me want to hurl up the nothing-in-my-belly. 'Now I have had a good look at all these parts of you while you have slept here and I am glad of everything I see. I am sure you will prove to me I have not wasted my money, won't you, dear?'

I say, 'I will prove no such a thing, and who are you besides? You were there, I think, in Lord Fielding's gambling room.'

'Mr Gerald Manners, dear.'

'Manners! Since when is it good manners to steal a person?'

He waves a hand. Those fingernails are bitten down so low, his finger-flesh does hang over them like little hoods.

'I did not steal you, as I said already. I have bought you as a pet. A bird in fact, judging by that nice costume you wore in the carriage. But can you sing, dear?'

'Ambrose!' I say. 'Where is he? The lute-player?'

He baulks. 'That stained man? Who knows.' Then he squints those grey eyes. 'And why should you ask me again of this man? I think you spoke his name last night too.'

'Because he is the man I do love, sir.'

Mr Manners recoils like he is truly hurt. 'No! Now that good man Signor Perero told me you were a virgin. You were the chaste one in that play! I think he fed me some great lie!'

'That he did, sir, so why not cast me aside right now to avoid the disappointment?'

'Ha!' he says, rising and shaking his not-much-left hair. 'You are some quick-thinking bird, and a songbird of no sweet music, I see. At least you will have a thing or two to show me since you are well practised at the sport of love.'

Love? He thinks there is some stench of love inside this room? You are some new breed of idiot, man.

He drums those stubby-nailed fingers on his sticky-out tum. 'Yes, I will come back later to hear you truly sing!'

'Wait!' I say. 'I cannot lie in this state unless you wish for me to soil the mattress. You will need to release my wrists and allow me some exercise and to use the pot until you return.'

'You think I would risk that?'

'Why not? There is no window to crawl away.'

He shakes his head again. 'I have risked enough in my life and no more. If you must be using that potty, you will do it right this moment while I am here, for I can only think a bird's shit is sweet-smelling like a rose!'

He unpicks these ropes and immediately I am up and trying

the door in the hopes of darting out, all of which appears to please him. His eyes gleam.

'A-ha! You rogue bird! You would try to escape the cage! And am I not treating you well? I have given you some fine red wine, and what more can a girl want? Ah, I will have all the fun of the fair with you, dear. This bird needs taming!'

I sit upon the pot and piss in a long stream of stinky urine, glowering at him all the while. My heart is doing a bad, bad dance inside of my chest and I wish to be anywhere but here.

'Do you know, sir, my friends from that troupe will be hunting high and low.'

I am imagining my Ambrose and Maria, and those acrobats and the juggler, all trampling the countryside, not resting till their old friend Tibb is found. Then I imagine no one looking for me at all. Not even Ambrose.

'And they will never find you, dear! Not here.'

He shoves me back on to the bed.

'That was the last of my money and I think I have spent it wisely,' he mutters while he ties these knots. 'I might have less in worldly goods than Lord Fielding and those rich friends of his, but who, might I ask, owns a songbird?'

He stands and rests his hands on his hips. 'Yes, it was no gamble, dear, buying you.'

'Birds must fly, Mr Manners.'

He is about to say something, and then he comes over all wild-eyed like a big idea has just popped into his sweaty head.

'Yes!' he says, and 'Yes, yes, yes!'

A pair of fine wings

Rooves are not all sweet, Ma, and I have certainly mapped every peeling-patch of this one. Mr Manners was telling the truth: there is no way out of this dingy cage. Nor the terrible mistake I made in trusting Signor Perero, that little serpent-creature. That man did despise me so much because of the no-fucking situation. O, cry with me, Tibb, since the world is getting blacker.

What will Mr No-Manners do to me? I think it is worse than what my own ma did suffer in her days of charging-for-it. Namely the ambition to disembowel me like a capon and eat my entrails. What else is the reason for this banging and clattering which is clamouring through the house and into this cage-room besides? I should think he is preparing his battering-tools.

Well these tears are hot down my face and I do not need these ties because the snake is so heavy coiled on top of me that I could not stagger up in any case. My thoughts are all soupy inside of my skull like there is too much going on in there, and all of them bruised and banging against one another. My colourful and long-limbed Ambrose. How will he ever find me here?

Then I am thinking of the kind and beautiful face of Ivo. I am remembering those days we did share in Norfolk and in Suffolk. The sand-hills and the oyster caves and the soft marshes with their hiding-eggs, and the sea-bathing and our stars-watching and our nightly fires. Why would you think of all that, Tibb?

If the big-man was real then I should ask him now: 'Please would you have those people called my friends find a girl named Tibb Ingleby? She is in the no-windows room in that no-servants house of a bird-enthusiast named Mr Manners who has some great problem with the foolish sport of gaming, sir.' But he isn't up there so why bother asking? And here is some other streak of terror slinking its way into my own roily thoughts. That voice of Farmer O hissing at me all quiet so my ma did not wake up: 'You will get that just reward, Tibb.' Quite right, Farmer O, since it is all working out just exactly as you said.

'Good evening, my little songbird! Now I must show you what I have fashioned this day for you!'

Mr Manners prances in all spruced up in his good breeches and a shirt, though when he comes closer I can see they are in fact filthy with stains and creased up like chicken skin. He was telling the truth when he said his maids were released. Are you washing your clothes in a puddle, sir?

'But where is the light in here?'

This fool-man says it like this darkness is my own silly fault.

'That candle did die some hours ago,' I say, and he is running around the house to find another. What is the thing he has fashioned? I am picturing some horrible brace to wear.

Finally he returns and he starts that grand entrance again, all sweaty with glee.

'Wings!' he says, carrying into this prison-room two pieces of thin metal and some hanging ropes. He holds them both up, leaning them against his tum. 'A pair of fine wings for a lovely little bird! I have been hammering them all day.'

No shit, sir. I heard the noise of it but this person is no skilled blacksmith. The wings are each the size of a fawn. They have been cut like triangles, the thin point at the bottom and the widest part at the top though one wing is bigger than the other.

It seems he has tried to make the appearance of feathers, the outer edge all wiggly, but that attempt is what my ma would call crude-as-a-bluetit's-shit, Tibb.

He locks us in and pockets the key, his tongue flicking in and out. 'Now I will release you and you will try them on for size!'

Release me again? There is some thought in my head to lunge and kick but I am thinking he had some keen-enough strength the last time.

He puts both hands around my neck and says into my ear, 'Don't you think of anything naughty, my pretty bird, since you would live to regret it.'

I think this person is reading my own mind. If only he were not such a great lump, I might stand a chance.

Well those wrist ties are unpicked and his fat tongue is lolling between his lips again while he concentrates. He is fiddling with the ropes, wheezing out his heavy breath. It seems he has cut two holes at the top of these wings, on the long, straight edge, and he has threaded his thin rope through.

He spins me around so he is looking at the back of me. 'Bend over!' he says and he is resting the first wing against my back and tossing one end of the rope over my shoulder so it is hanging down by my bulbs and the other end he is tucking underneath my arm. Then he reaches round, tying them together into one big knot in my arm-pit which stinks by now. Then he does the same on the other side, all with the air of a nursemaid putting a cape around a small child, his tongue lolling out sideways. His breeches are bursting like he has a little worm trapped in there.

'A songbird indeed! Did you not tell me that birds can fly?'

So this is *my* doing?

He pushes me forward because he is excited now and my forehead is touching this cold wall. He is fumbling with those breeches. 'Now let me hear you sing, dear!' he says, and this no-rushes floor is swimming beneath me because there is no way out and these wings are heavy like lead. And I am thinking of my own ma who did this thing for money more than once. And I am wiping those tears but nothing is happening and in fact that sobbing sound is not coming from my own mouth.

I turn.

Mr Bad-Manners is sitting down on the mattress with his breeches round his ankles and these tears in his eyes are something quite unexpected.

'I'm sorry!' he warbles, and his grey face is crumbling. Then his head is in his hands and his body is heaving up and down and there are some streams of mucus flying out of his nose. 'I'm sorry! You are all I have now! You know my wife left me because I am a good-for-nothing wretch who has fallen foul of the dice and the deck. I am a laughing stock! And everyone knows she has found a new man called Simon who I am told is a merchant of spices.'

More blubbering, and I am piecing together a better picture of this man. His tiny prick is sleeping between those white thighs and he is pushing that toe of his into the floor and making a little well in the clay, and his nose is all creased up in his puffy face. O, Ma. I should say nothing in this prison-house is making much sense and perhaps the world is hanging upside-down like a bat.

'Those friends all wonder why I do not entertain them here any more. But I cannot have them see this grand house all empty. And to think I once kept peasants on these grounds who called me Master, and now it is all left to ruin!'

He descends again into that wailing and here is the owner of some dark feelings, Ma. He is a little boy under all that bluster and I am sitting beside him and putting my arm around his shoulder because it seems he has his own snake there to boot.

In time he wipes his greasy nose and pulls up his breeches. 'You will fall into love with me in your own sweet time, dear, and then we might consummate the union.'

Well this man is a bigger dunderhead than I thought.

I swallow and my throat is dry and it has swelled up besides so perhaps I am swallowing an apple just now. 'Perhaps she will come back.'

'No, dear, she will not come within an inch of me. You see, when one has a problem such as that of the dice and the deck, then everyone they know is dirtied with their own bad name.'

Some little chunk of my heart does stop still at those words. Dirtied. I think of Ivo. Is it possible he left me in Peterborough so I was not dirtied by his own secret? Did he love me all along, just as Maria said?

'Anyhow I shall not pine for her now I have you. Much like you will not be pining for that coloured monster besides.'

That apple inside my throat is melting and now it's just tears. But perhaps everything is all as it should be, since I do not deserve those nice things like a husband-man or a daughter. Or a home. Because you are some devil, Tibb Ingleby.

He pushes his wiry fingers into my neck like he would stop the breath. 'Now I did not buy you to be a cry-baby. You know I don't wish for visitors unless they want to be here. Otherwise, I can make their life far worse . . .'

That note of threat in his voice is making me shrink. This man is up and down so quick, I wonder he did just bounce upon two strings.

'Well ask me, then.'

'Ask you what, sir?'

'Ask me if you might stay.'

My forehead is bunching. 'But I don't want to—'

'You need to ask me!'

I narrow my eyes. 'May I stay?'

He waves a hand and brings out a pack of cards. 'Dear, of course! I have a fine deck from France and I will show you all of it! But I might ask a little favour of you in return, that while you are in my own home, you will wear those wings I did hammer for you since they were a gift and you should be polite.'

Spoil a nice game

'I won at a fine house in Tamworth once – with this very deck in fact – and then I made the almighty mistake of playing again and that should be my downfall every time. It was soon after that my wife left this place for good.'

I have been here a few days now but I can't know how many because I was not given all the brains by the big-man-God to be counting up the hours in the day. I have been thinking a lot of Ivo and that small glimmer of hope that he does love me still, but how do you think those thoughts should help you now, Tibb?

We are in my prison-room with one flickering candle and these cards are all lined up waiting but that means nothing to me. At least I have persuaded Mr Manners to allow me to wear my parrot dress under these wings, though the ropes are still rubbing under my arms. We have for our refreshment some stale wafers and he has drunk a bottle of that bad stuff so his lips are tinged with red. This is my own plan, Ma: get him fucked on liquor and then I might smash him with my wings.

'I knew you would learn to like it in the end, my love. You are improving fourfold.'

Is he mad? He is speaking like we are two married people just here.

He chortles. 'It is so nice to have someone here and you are staying of your own free will so you must love me a lot, dear.'

'But I am not here of my own will—'

He holds up a hand. 'Why must you spoil a nice game, when we were getting on so very well?'

Fuck, this man has troubles inside of his head. There are fishes swimming around in there and birds flapping their great wings and insects crawling. Would you hold your nerve, Tibb?

I say, 'More of the hard stuff, sir?' but he holds a hand over that wood goblet and says, 'Now, I have learnt through error to keep my mind lucid.'

This dolt is more clever than I supposed.

'Sit upon my lap, would you?'

'Your lap?'

'Yes, dear.'

I perch there while he starts kissing at my lips like he is a sparrow with a beak. Perhaps I will spew.

'Call me a king,' he mumbles.

'Sir?'

'Call me a king, would you? If not, then a duke.'

'You are a king, sir . . . of many wealthy palaces.'

'Bigger than the Lord Fielding's?'

'Much bigger, sir.'

He puffs out his cheeks. 'Are you in love with me yet?'

I shake my head.

'You are hurting my feelings,' he says, and he shoves me off. 'You have asked to stay after all.'

I bow my head.

'Say sorry.'

'Sorry,' I tell him, and he is restored at once. He is dealing those cards again.

'Play!' Mr Manners shouts, and he tosses the dregs of his wine in my face.

Leominster, Herefordshire

The King is playing with him. Surely he should have arrived by now, sentenced them all to die and been on his way? It feels like he has been months in this place, though of course it is only a matter of days.

He wishes to be drowned instead. After all, he's been drowning his whole life.

Or hanging. He imagines the rope, squeezing around his neck. Squeezing every part of him, his guts forced up and out of his mouth, like the devil being evicted from his body. His father spoke of that before. Exorcism. Of the repulsive desires inside of him needing to be coaxed out.

Evil. Is that truly what he is? Unnatural? Is his love for Flavio something wicked?

He thinks of his parents' marriage in contrast, their loveless union. Two separate lives lived in the same home. Lives of toil, restraint, discipline. Abstinence. These are the words that float around the nave of every church in England. But what about joy? What about love? Passion? He thinks of his uncle too. The person who took him in and offered him a new life. The person Ivo always suspected was hiding the very same secret as his.

He wavers between feeling inherently sinful, and the next entirely free of guilt. As though Tibb's view of the world has nestled into his own head and started a revolution there. What would she say to that?

If only he might speak to her again before the end. He cannot bear to think of it; those slender, pale limbs of hers manhandled around the pole. Never mind his own end – it is hers that truly plagues him.

The warden brings more watered-down beer and Ivo shrinks in the light of the lantern, his hands in front of his eyes.

'You were fooled like the rest of us,' he is told in whispers. 'You know God is still on your side.'

He stares at the walls and the water trickling down them in skinny streams. Is it true? Is God on his side after what he did? When he is what he is?

Those thoughts he had of a revolution, of being entirely free from sin, are slipping away so quickly, it was like they were never there at all. He thinks of the crowd who jeered at Samuel and Ewan. All the faces contorting in just the same disgusted way. He thinks of the cold hard facts; that if everyone is so sure that God spurns sodomites, who is he to question it?

The warden shakes his head, tutting. 'Can't say the same about that false-angel. You know some of the crowds out there are calling her the Holy Maid as though she was sent from God! I heard those wings were made from metal, Father.'

The word pricks his skin and then softens, seeping into the hay beneath him. He hasn't heard that word since he arrived at this hellish place.

Father.

Always a river

It is now or never, Tibb. The man is not slurring as I hoped, but I am planning this move of mine nevertheless, with these great wings behind my back. And here is Ma saying, 'Well I have taught you something, Tibb Ingleby!'

'I have an idea, sir.'

'Well speak up! If there is a game you like to play better then you should make it clear. I have been in a dozen gambling rooms and there is not one game I haven't tried my hand at.'

It is some effort to keep my face from wrinkling up because the words which are about to spill out of my own mouth could make the beetles crawl backwards. 'Well it is no game as such, but I should rather like to start the fucking now.'

His baggy eyes do jump out on stalks and those white parts are all mottled like the shell of a gull egg. 'Already! But I have made you fall in love with me quicker than I ever imagined!' He pokes out his pigeon-chest and smooths that not-much-hair-left to the side. His yellow teeth are like little kernels of corn and I have the urge to pluck them out like a blackbird might.

'I only wish to take off my wings, sir, as I should want to lie down on my back and see you all the better.'

'Ha-ha!' he says. 'But of course you wish to look upon my face.'

Slowly, Tibb.

Yes, Ma.

Well he is unpicking those ropes and then I am wily like a fox, pulling these wings and spinning to bang the metal against his thick skull till he is on this no-rushes-floor but he is slapping me and grabbing my ankles like this is a grapple between two cats. The man has strength. More than his fat body would let on or the empty wine bottle might tell me, and he is smashing me back into the wall and all the air is winded from my chest. I wish to sprint out of this room but the key is in his waistcoat and I can't grab that thing.

'RUDE!' he pants. 'You asked to stay. And you should be polite!'

We are like two writhing snakes on this floor and I am bashing the metal wings against his skull some more but he is pulling them from me and now they are his.

The man is up and he is more nimble than I thought, those metal wings outstretched, and I am dodging these blows of his and thinking this is some shit place to see before I die. It is worse than a rich man's scullery, Ma, and I am catching my breath but there are drums inside of my head and my skin is puckering up with coldness.

'I should have kept you tied up!' he says, then he thwacks me on the skull and those bitten-down fingers are crawling around my neck and pushing in and I am thinking he will stop the air. Ambrose and Ivo are slipping away from my head-thoughts and I'm thinking this is it, Ma. The end, except I'm not in a hole like you are.

And then that sound saying 'Tibb!' is racing through this house like I am surely going mad. My poorly-mannered captor is all stiff about his dripping-like-wax body and his ears are pricked so that sound must in fact be real.

'Ambrose?' I shout, pushing him off, and Mr Manners lunges again.

'Tibb!'

'He is certainly dead?' I say.

'O yes, Tibb.'

Now we are crouching over this big dead man, since my own kind and beautiful Ambrose did come crashing through this door at a run, and he did finish Mr Manners off by way of the wings, slicing them into his flabby neck till he was spitting blood.

This is some lovely reunion to boot, despite the problem of the corpse beside us. My own husband-man did think to come here and save me and all the warm things are huddling in my chest like sunlight and hot bread and pies. He looks terrible though, bent double and with two black eyes and gashes all down his arms.

'What happened to you?' I say because I think Ambrose has had some wrangle with the fuckers.

He shakes his head. 'That's a story for later.'

'How long have I been here?'

'Five days. And I would have been sooner, Tibb, but this place was hard to find. I was in the village nearby just this morning, asking directions.'

I think he has climbed mountains to come and save me here because I was never more loved than by this kind person, except maybe by Ivo but he is long-gone.

'What now?' he says and I do have the answer to that one.

Always a river, Tibb, because water does cover up the mischief of a lifetime. Countless times I did help my ma to drag those fuckers to a river with their necks sliced through while she cried, 'They are all the same, Tibb!' and 'Don't you know that?'

Ambrose hauls that man called Mr No-Manners out by the ankles like a dead cow, through this no-furniture but cobwebs-everywhere house and out to the garden which is overgrown, and I wonder if these tall-as-me weeds have eyes. He is like a hooked fish with that mangled neck of his and the sun beats down like it would say: 'Tibb Ingleby, I see you!' There is no river here but a well. That sun is blinding.

I bend, shaking, for a stone, and that pretty splashing sound echoing up this great cavern says, 'Get on with the job!' And I will, but first I am stripping off his filthy clothes I might flog for monies because I learnt from the best and would you watch a penny roll into the mud, Tibb?

From her own nipple

This town is going by the name of Worcester and I am paying for this lodging room with Mr Manners's clothes. It is owned by a cheese-making woman and she does let out these rooms for extra money, so she said, and there were many promises to flog us some of her good cheeses at half the price but I could not give two shits about cheese when my Ambrose is hovering far too close to being cold in the ground.

Now he is groaning on the wood floor. This journey has finished him off. We did hitch a ride on a hay wagon and paid the driving-man far too handsomely, I think, with one pair of shoes belonging to a dead man.

'Tibb,' Ambrose whispered while we sat amongst the hay-bales, 'Signor suggested to Lord Fielding's friends that I was in the market for a beating, so they dragged me out to the forest and had their fun till I was black and blue.'

I can well believe it owing to those oozing gashes across his chest and arms which I spied when I swapped his murdering-shirt with one of Mr Manners's.

'And they took the money I had been saving up for our life too, and perhaps that is the worst thing, Tibb, since I wanted to give you a roof so much.'

I am squeezing his hands because his own flesh-and-blood means more by far than any roof he does speak about.

'But not one of those cruel men suspected I should rise up and wait till I caught Lord Fielding alone. And then I had him by the neck till he told me where you were. But why did Signor hate us so much when it was you and I who brought in all the crowds, Tibb?'

Well I know the reason to that, sir. That jealous arsehole thought to pay us back for doing the fucking game which I would not do with him. But I have never told my Ambrose all that because maybe I enticed Signor and his little worm like he said I did, and like I did the same with Farmer O.

Now it is dark because I have placed an oiled-cloth over the little round window of this lodging room. That bright world outside is no friend and my head is full up with thoughts of Ambrose who is mostly just purple and laid out like a corpse. O, I could cry with the clouds, Tibb! Me too, Ma.

I do not like the sweat-beads dripping off his lovely face or the way he is wincing in his sleep and puffing and holding his breath at times. And I am all blood-red in the eyes due to a lack of sleep and an excess of murder. My Ambrose did have the good sense to clean up the blood stains on the clay floor of that middle-of-nowhere prison, but perhaps Mr Manners might begin to stink in the well, and someone will send a bucket down and meet solid flesh. Or perhaps he was not truly dead at all, and in fact he will wake up and climb out and tell the world, 'Those fuckers tried to kill me!'

There is a very dark cloud hanging over me which I have not felt since I first arrived on that Norfolk beach and slept for five days straight. Because I am not putting this person in a hole too. And there is Farmer O to boot saying, 'Come-uppance, Tibb!' since he has not left me well alone these last ten years.

'Cheese!' says that lady who runs this house.

I open the door.

'No cheese for me, madam, but I require beer for my own husband.'

She comes in, bending over him like a nurse-lady herself. I already sent her to an apothecary with Mr Manners's waistcoat as payment and she came back with some dried leaves for a draught and a fat lot of good it did.

She rests her thick wrists on her hips. 'He's getting worse! You need a priest, my lamb!'

'A priest?'

'Of course, that's the only person who might save him now.'

Well the big-man did not ever help my ma when she needed it, and yet I would try anything to keep this lover-person alive.

Outside this grand stone church there is a long line of people.

'What are they waiting for?' I say and the cheese-lady crosses herself.

'Ah now, we've had a wonderful miracle of recent weeks. The priest here is a truly holy man!'

She pushes in and we stand in this great nave which is cool and quiet save for some sobbing and muttering at the front. My ma would be hunting out that wine already but the cheese-lady calls, 'Father!' and she is looking around for the man-in-the-dress.

That snake's tail of people is hugging the stone wall of the church, all the way to a little statue at the far end which is a stone sculpture of a woman. The God-hunters are kneeling there, far back from the statue and behind a rope, saying of their prayers and crying besides.

'What's going on, madam?' I ask.

She says, 'Ah, the Virgin Mary. For ten days now she's been leaking milk from her own nipple! The foodstuff of Jesus Christ! Didn't I tell you this is a most holy priest we have here at Worcester?'

Now this is making no sense to me and I do have a wish to

see that statue for myself. 'Wait your turn!' they shout at me while I push to the front, and I say, 'Fuck off!'

Behind the rope, that stone sculpture is certainly leaking milk from the nipple, in slow droplets which are all falling like raindrops into a cup. I narrow my eyes, looking at the head of that woman carved in stone because there is certainly a dent there and this magic is fucking obvious.

'Ha!' I say, because of course the priest-man has drilled a tunnel from the top of her head and right down to the nipple. He will be pouring in the milk from time-to-time and passing it off as magic! But why can't these God-seekers see it?

'You lot should put away your monies!' I warn them, and I step over that rope as the waiting-people gasp and I point to the hardly-there dimple upon the head of the statue and another right in the middle of her drippy nipple.

The priest comes out then from a little room at the back and he sees me there right up next to his statue and he calls out, 'Stop! You are too close, madam! This here is a miracle from the Lord, in my own church. Would you be respectful?'

The cheese-lady is giving me looks that say, 'What the fuck are you up to? And come right back here!' So I do.

She pinches me in the side as my punishment then she says, 'We are requiring your help, Father, since we have a sick man at my lodging rooms.'

He nods. 'Well I can pray for him, certainly.'

'Thank you, Father,' the cheese-lady says, and she pinches me again.

'Thank you, Father,' I say.

He produces a bowl and I am all dazed, like the man would offer me some nice bread pudding all steamy in there.

He coughs.

The cheese-lady says, 'Well? Give him the coins, child!'

'O,' I say, digging them out, though I am thinking this is

the biggest waste of money I ever did hear of. And I am thinking of the oftentime carolling of my own dead ma about the rich and the poor being two foul opposites.

'I would say, though, that to ensure he does not pass to the realm of the dead, you would be wise to purchase a small dose of milk from the Virgin also.'

He gestures over to that shit ruse in the corner and I am some sick fool too, for I am handing over the very last of the coins I got from selling Mr Manners's sweaty breeches. Have you lost your head, Tibb?

Some family

'It was cow's milk, Tibb,' Ambrose said, all rasping in his voice. Of course it was, sir. Now he's moaning even more and burning up and the cheese-lady is back to collect her rent which I do not have. I cannot hand over those blood-splattered wings for melting down, else she will know what we did and that she is housing two murderers on the run.

She looks all worried for me, speaking of rich men's kitchens and how I might beg for work at one, or else offer myself to the candle-maker's in town which may or may not have a job for me, but we don't have time for all that shit.

'You truly have no skills, dear?'

'No, madam, though I was an actress in a troupe-of-sorts.'

'A troupe! I did see one just a few days back, passing through this city.'

Now my heart has woken up from its slumber. 'You did?'

This cheese-lady is bright-eyed and dreaming. 'Yes, my lamb. A big woman up on stilts and some good acrobats too. Finest players I've seen!'

A big woman on stilts? Acrobats to boot? Here is some great dagger to the heart and a griping in my innards.

'You are sure?' I breathe.

'Quite sure,' she says, eyeing me closely again.

And so here is the bare truth of it: those so-called friends of mine are carrying on just the same though two of their own have disappeared. Though Maria did tell me oftentime, 'Tibb, I am mighty glad to have a girl-friend at last.'

The cheese-lady says, 'But you've come over all funny. Now

listen, is there no one who might take you in, as an act of charity?'

'No one,' I whisper, because the world is full of fuckers and there are no fine ideas creeping into my head.

'Where will you go, then? You must have *some* family . . .'

Family. I can't even bother to rattle off that old horse-shit about the no-family up in Leicester because in fact Ivo is the only family I have left. 'There was a person called Ivo once,' I say.

'He was family?'

'Sort of. But he did leave me. Though perhaps he did that because he loved me.'

She looks confused and I could knock on that grey head of hers and tell her, 'Yes, dear. And you're not the only one!'

Like a pointy turret

This moment is dark in the same way that mud is dark. Ambrose is shivering on the wood floor though I have draped him with a blanket from the cheese-lady. It is something too sore for my eyes to see this big and strong giant-man curled up like a dying dog because those fuckers did get him after all. I lie there too, and he draws his knees up so I am all cocooned by his great body and how does it make sense that he is stroking my own face with that cold finger of his? Like he would care for me even when he is the one who cannot stand?

'I can't believe they did this to you, Ambrose,' I whisper, and there are tears wanting to climb out of my eyes.

He puts his arm over me and squeezes my hand.

I say, 'It's like those fuckers won.'

He clears his throat, speaking in a slow croak: 'They never won, Tibb. Because they are all sick inside their minds and we are not. Is that not strange? I am the one covered in these birthmarks and yet they are the ones who are truly scarred, just inside of themselves?'

I am not thinking that at all. In fact I am wishing that this kind man was not covered in these purple marks because if he were not then the Lord Fielding's friends wouldn't have kicked the shit out of him and left him there for dead. Then again, if he didn't have those purple stains he would not be the same Ambrose who is in fact beautiful and we would never have met in Signor's troupe. These thoughts are hurting my head because I'm not sure what to think now.

'I am just glad I found you in time,' he rasps, pulling me in closer so we are really just one person. His heavy breathing is filling up this room and I am turning to glance at the green juice which is weeping from these sores across his arms and his chest and around his blackened eyes. There is some terrible tone to his words, like he would prepare for the end, and I did hear the same words in a barn from that dead person called Ma.

'Ambrose,' I say quietly and I am thinking of taverns and men and the fact I don't have flies for tits. 'You know there is something quick I could do for monies—'

'No, Tibb,' he says, and there is a finality in his voice that I haven't heard before. 'I would rather be six feet under the ground than see you do anything of the sort.'

We are in silence then and I am full up with the image of him lying with the worms six feet in the ground.

'Don't leave me, Ambrose,' I whisper and of course I am thinking of Henrietta who died beneath a hedge and Ma in the hole at Newmarket. His hand creeps into mine again and these tears are too hot when he is so cold and isn't life something cruel, Ma?

'Tibb, I would never leave you. I am always inside of your heart.'

He is pressing his head against my back and I think the birds would go dumb forever if Ambrose were to die too. Inside my heart is not enough, sir.

The cheese-lady wipes her hands on her apron. 'Well I must go over to Leominster to my husband's creamery since there is a great deal of fine cheeses waiting there. I should tell you to be gone by the time I return, unless you have come into some more money that is . . .'

Leominster. Now here is a word I have heard of before. I am wiping those tears from my face and my body is still.

'Well?' she says. 'Have you?'

'Leominster,' I repeat.

This word is sticking up like a pointy turret inside of my head, poking at my brains.

'Are you quite well, dear?'

Ivo. Ivo said that word. He did speak of a kindly uncle one time in the land of Leominster. Is it possible he went there, to the only family who still did like him?

I say, 'Madam, this Leominster . . . it is close?'

'Of course! A day by horse-cart. Why?'

A day? My mind is galloping. If Ivo is in Leominster, then perhaps he will help me keep Ambrose alive. Perhaps it was all planned, Ma. Perhaps I have marched west across this kingdom like I was coming to see him all along! I think the sun is shining out of my chest bulbs and lighting up the whole of this dingy lodging house. Everything seems different.

'Madam,' I say. 'We're coming with you!'

Her eyes are all wide like I have smacked her round the face with a fish. Who could love *you*, Tibb Ingleby? O, would you fuck off, Farmer O?

Rector of the fine church

Well here I am at the land of Leominster, which is some pretty-enough little town, though I should think a shit-hole would look like home so long as it was named Leominster. That cheese-lady was less than delighted about the prospect of Ambrose dying under her roof. 'Don't you know a dead man will haunt your lodging house and no one will pay a penny to stay here ever again?' I did tell her with my ghostly voice. 'And perhaps that spirit will turn bad and curse you to the Hell-place.' She did go cold at the thought and grasp at her apron since she was riddled with that thing called superstition if our trip to see that hoodwinking priest and his cow milk was anything to go by. Superstitions will be the ruin of fine brains, Tibb.

Ambrose can hardly stand. He is leaning against me and this is some heavy weight around my neck and so is the bag with the metal wings all splattered with Mr Manners's bad blood. Sweat is dripping down between my chest bulbs and I am stinking worse than Signor Perero ever did which is saying something grim.

The sun will be slipping off to its bed-time house soon and the sky is lit up in orange, but I am picturing my old friend Ivo popping up in front of me any moment. I have not seen him for three years and what should I say to him now? Hello, Ivo, remember me? Go away, Tibb Ingleby. Did you not take the hint?

The breeze is sweeping over my skin and making those white hairs sit up. I am smoothing down this sweaty sheet of hair and wondering if he isn't here at all and these jumbled houses are bulging in their frames like they have eaten too much for dinner.

I stop at an inn which is not teeming with fuckers yet. 'Good sir, you will know of a golden-haired man going by the name of Ivo, since I believe that he lives around these parts and he is hard to miss, being quite beautiful.'

That landlord – and he is frowning like there is a moon turned upside-down on his face – says, 'Ivo? Ivo what?'

Now here is a question I had not anticipated, and in truth I do not know any other name belonging to my oldest friend. Would you ask me another, sir? I could tell you the exact motion by which this person Ivo pulls up his crab-line when there is something wriggling on the end, and the very way his legs tuck beneath him in his sleep.

'I call him only Ivo, sir.'

He shakes his head. 'Well I cannot help you much then, dear.'

Ambrose is lolling against me like he is a rag-doll and I do stagger with the weight and the landlord is looking over like my husband-man is riddled with the pox.

'And I cannot offer a room to that man in case he has the consumption.'

A beer-drinker rises and he is quite drunk upon his bandy legs judging by all the swaying he is doing. 'Miss, the only Ivo around here is the rector of the great church we all attend.'

There is some murmur of agreement from the landlord, like the penny just dropped. But a rector? That would be a fine joke after what we saw in Peterborough.

'No, sirs! This is not the same Ivo who I am after.'

Outside these street children are flapping about my ankles and this bag is heavy with the metal. Perhaps I got it wrong. Perhaps Ivo is not in Leominster after all.

'Ivo, you say?' those men shout down to me. They are standing up there thatching a roof and scratching their heads. 'His other names?'

'I do not have one for him, sir.'

'Well the rector here is named Ivo. Young man. Blonde hair. Is this him?'

'No, no!' I say, though the description fits just right. 'No, it is not the one.'

I stand a moment in this lane, thinking and sweating. Ambrose's limp arm feels like a sack of marrows around my neck. What else did Ivo say of his uncle? I am trying to dredge up that conversation from all those years ago, and I believe my Ivo did tell me his uncle was a *man-of-the-cloth*. I wonder that I did just swallow some beetles and now they are frolicking round-and-round inside my belly.

I walk back down that lane and look up again, a hand over my eyes since the setting sun is blinding me. 'Good sirs!' I shout up. 'What is a *man-of-the-cloth*?'

Ivo. A churchly man? The world is turning somersaults, Ma, and now I can't tell up from down but that church is beckoning and the beetles are still dancing a jig inside my belly just to vex me. 'Stop,' I say, and 'It is only Ivo.' And to Ambrose: 'We are nearly there!'

This is some mighty fine church settled in a large green next to the town and the river, and with a big bell up in that flat-on-top tower. It is locked though – even the rabbit-door – so I stagger down the path to the vicarage-house beside it, dragging my Ambrose with me. It is a nice stone building with glass windows and a swelling orchard wrapped around it like a wreath. And these flower petals are all pink like cheeks since July will soon pop its head up on this land of England, and the apples are turning some good shades of red. So red I should wonder that a sneaky painter has not brought a ladder and stood to paint them. An apple for the bad times, so said my ma. I wonder she did not eat more apples.

I turn a full circle because I cannot think Ivo is truly living here at this almost-palace house. And he was the one who said rooves are not everything, Tibb. And it is people not rooves which make a real home.

Does he keep a cook these days? Maids? Who else is in there with him? I would not have thought Ivo would do this job for all the money in the world.

There is a rosemary bush beside this vicarage garden and I am laying Ambrose under it, since this bit I should do alone.

'I'll be back,' I say and I give that man a kiss. 'Soon you'll be shown that lovely bed.' But there are players gathering their drums inside me because did I not leave Henrietta under a bush besides?

Would you knock, Tibb?

This is some long wait. Longer than I ever did wait in my oyster shell to make that grand reveal. Longer than I waited for Ma to wake up after a night-on-the-bottle. Longer than that morning I spent with my ear on Henrietta's blue lips outside a dairy-farm in Norfolk.

Well this person who answers is Ivo all right, but this is not the Ivo I remember. He is beautiful still, that striking jawline of his, but where is that chopped-with-an-oyster-knife beard? And those clear blue eyes are empty somehow, and that lovely face is lined all over.

'Tibb!' he breathes.

This is an older-than-his-years person, hidden in some sullen church garb. Where is that warm smile just for me?

I say, 'Will I come in here, Ivo?'

One troubling lie

Well I have been given a big cup of water and this is not made from wood. I imagine that the Lady Margaret Beaufort herself takes her morning milk in a pewter cup like this. It feels cold and heavy in my hands and my ma would have stuffed it in her pocket already and run. Ivo sits across from me in his own high-backed chair.

'You keep a large house these days, Ivo. This is a far cry from that beach we made our first home at King's Lynn and ha-ha-ha.'

He doesn't laugh at all and I think it is much too quiet in this grand house.

'Yes, Tibb,' he says, but why doesn't he look at me?

'I imagine you have a horde of maids for your own convenience to boot!'

'No. I sent them away. I prefer to be alone.'

Since when, Ivo?

We sit a little more together and I am wringing my hands and scratching a map into my palm.

'Ivo, you gave me a fine idea you know, which has become my employment over the years. I became a human-pearl of sorts!'

Now here is an opening for some nice conversation, but he shrugs like he doesn't care – like he forgot about that pearl – and he stares very hard at the floor and the little crumbs between the flagstones.

'Why are you doing this, Ivo?' I say more quietly. 'This priestly business, I mean?'

'I received a calling from God.'

A *calling*? Well this is not making one single slice of sense to me. Did the big-man-God call down from the sky?

'I have missed you, Ivo,' I say, and I am sure enough of our old friendship to reach and touch his hand over this fine wood table but he pulls it away like I just poked him with a pin.

'I haven't much time, Tibb,' he mutters. 'What can I do for you?'

My palms will bleed with all the scratching. Men will let you down, Tibb. Even the good ones turn out to be fuckers. Well perhaps you were right there, Ma.

I clear my throat. 'Will you show me around?'

This house-tour is done in silence, around all these many rooms with no one in them. It is some well-built place with good stone floors, though it is smaller by far than the Lord Fielding's house. And it doesn't have anyone else inside of it except Ivo. There is a smell like dust and it feels too quiet and still for my old friend. All these empty rooms with big wood cupboards and chests, each one laid out differently than the last. The kitchen is the only room which is showing any signs of someone living here at all and that is because the wood table is piled up with bread and cakes and buns. There is such a lot of those baked things that my head is spinning because I cannot imagine Ivo would eat so much.

I follow him up the narrow stairs and he doesn't look back at me because I believe I am some great inconvenience to him just now. And I am watching my feet and telling my eyes to stay dry, won't you?

Upstairs there are four rooms with beds in, as though one person could sleep in four beds at once! And all the windows have thick curtains over them and the fireplaces are bare as bones and layered with more dust. Folded blankets and stitched-with-wool cushions have been piled up on the mattresses but

I do not have one single urge to jump on and see how it feels to lie down amongst all that soft stuff.

'So many rooms, Ivo,' I say with a not-real laugh. 'I can't imagine what you use them for!'

He says in a flat way, 'Whoever is the rector here is given this vicarage. Sometimes I receive visitors from the Church . . . not often though.'

'We could have done with a house like this back in Norfolk and ha-ha-ha!'

Well he doesn't answer that and the silence is making me clench my fists because this is all wrong. The blood is pumping in my ears. I look at that golden hair of his as he descends the wood staircase and I say, 'For a long while, Ivo, I did think you left me because you couldn't trust me with your secret.'

He stands at the bottom.

'What secret? There is no secret.'

He is looking up with this black expression like there is no one in there. And like the heart of him was wrenched out.

'But you said—'

'I said nothing. And we were children, Tibb. Children dream up all sorts of silly ideas.'

My eyes squint. I wish to say, 'That was nothing so silly, but the inside feelings of your heart!' Ivo is all different and distant though, and I can't say that thing to this straight-backed, frowning person.

'Then why did you faint that day at Peterborough?'

He looks away. 'I fainted due to the heat.'

'I see.'

I do not see a thing.

He is gazing up at his one-time friend and I can tell there is something bruised and dark inside that lovely head of his.

'Ivo, it occurred to me that you did not leave me under that bridge because you didn't love me, but because in fact you loved me very much. Too much, even.'

And now my breath is held because the thudding inside of my heart is hurting, and my eyes are stinging with that thing called hope.

He thinks a while.

'Tibb, I left because I didn't wish to be with you any more.' And I am touching this solid stone wall like it should hold me up.

'Ivo?'

He sways down there like a terrible shadow in that shaft of orange light. 'There were more important things than to spend my days doing nothing with you, Tibb. And I had a calling from God, so I came to learn from my uncle who was the rector here.'

'You had the calling under the bridge?' I ask. This is all one troubling lie.

He waves a hand. 'In any case, my uncle died last year and I am now the rector in his place. This is why I am so busy these days and the reason you should leave, I think.'

'But Ivo, I need your—'

'Tibb,' he says in a not-like-Ivo voice. 'Move on. This is my home now, and it isn't yours.'

Well I am all caught up in despair and those bad thoughts are rising up like a big flood. Because he doesn't care a bit for me. And Maria did not care the same.

I clear my throat but these words are crackly anyway. 'I have a husband-man out there who is quite sick and this is why we made the journey. And I think he will die unless he is resting and warm by a fire. We have nowhere else to go.'

His eyes bulge just a little. 'A husband?' he breathes, and he loses that coldness just for a moment. 'But that is so good to hear.'

I should ask him: 'Why, sir? When you do not care for me?'

He stands still and then he goes to that leather purse on the side and says quietly, 'I can give you money, Tibb.'

And maybe that is the worst thing he did say to me so far.

'I do not want your money, Ivo.'

A false-Ivo

A dark heaviness is creeping in and I should think to bury myself into the ground like a dormouse and block out all this stuff. My eyelids are baggy but there are no hollows here.

We are both of us under the rosemary bush, but Ambrose is sleeping and I am lying beside this man like we are two roots entwined, and my tears are making that shirt of his all wet too. His breath is shallow and soon he will die here, like my own sister died beneath a bush. This rosemary is confusing since the nice scent does not fit with my dark mood or the fact that the end is nigh, Tibb. Close your eyes, for this place called Leominster has nothing but badness inside of it.

This night does pass too slow and my thoughts are swirling like the wind picked up, such as my ma being dragged into a hole in Newmarket by a cordwainer who didn't keep his promise. And then I am thinking of the grave-place of my own baby sister which I never did see upon the beach at King's Lynn and what kind of a person does that make me? And where will I bury Ambrose? And how will I ever leave him there alone? And then I am thinking of Ivo who swatted me away like a fly with all those many lies of his. And Maria who left. That farmer was right, because only someone with a black-as-soot heart could have all this shit happen.

I am on my way to the half-life when those big bells are pealing from the church tower and making the ground shake and the birds fall off their branches. That watery sun did rise a while back and now I am watching as Ivo stands solemn at the church door with that great gold hat upon his head and a cross around his neck. Things are gone awry and this world is shaken like a tincture and quite fucked-up, Ma.

'It is all corrupt, Tibb,' he did say at Norfolk. 'Faith has been taken over by cruel men and made into something fearful.'

Are *you* a cruel man, Ivo?

There is a small queue of early-morning people gathering at the church door and I notice the way they are adjusting their clothing and smartening up ready to take his hand. Ivo is like a God himself in this town and many more thoughts do mull around inside my head because of it, including thoughts like: you cannot trust anyone, Tibb.

When those people are all squashed inside, and when Ivo too is gone from the door, I sneak in. At the back I stuff myself into a pew, right behind a stone pillar, because I need just one last look at my no-longer friend called Ivo.

He is standing in front of the congregation with his arms outstretched, directly under that high-up balcony which has a lovely wood screen hanging a little over it, painted with some hovering angel-babies. Not the angels which Ivo did tell me were sitting in the sky as stars and without their own bodies, but chubby pink ones with golden wings, and I think of Henrietta who did not have rolls of flesh like theirs. I wonder who that balcony is for and who did think to paint it so carefully. And I wonder even more who climbed up to that high ceiling above me to place those criss-cross beams. Such a fine echo to be had if I did shout up something rude, though I am not in the mood for all that mad foolery. My ma would say this building would be a sweet-enough bed-room for vagrants since it is not too big and it is nice to look at besides, but this is not the right home for a man named Ivo.

He says, 'My parishioners, would you join me in prayer?'

I have never attended a church service though I have heard snippets of what-goes-on from when Ma and I would wake up in a hiding-place, such as under a pew or in the vestry-place, and have to scurry away quick. Even Ivo cannot make these lengthy Latin prayers amusing. I fear he has lost all his sparkle. Is there nothing remaining behind those lovely blue eyes? Is there nothing left of that curious crab-catching person who would take such delight in shells and sunsets and birds?

We are all told to stand up by way of Ivo's hand signal. Then to sit again. Then to stand. Then to sit. All the time with these cloying smells wafting up my nose. I should think I will pass out, the air is so stuffy in here.

And then comes the sermon. Now this part is in our own language but the words my Ivo speaks are all wrong.

'The purpose of your lives, good people of my parish, lies in the avoidance of temptation. God teaches us to repel the desires of the flesh. That abstinence is the most holy state. Was not a virgin required to carry the most purest person, Jesus Christ? And if you cannot make yourself celibate as a priest must be, nor to confine yourself to a nunnery or a friary to do God's work in the purest way, then you must fight the pull of lust, for this is the ruin of humanity and it will be punished in Hell-fire. Make that act of begetting children both holy and quick, and do not feed that earthly and base desire, for it will turn you like a poisoned apple. Think of higher things, which are namely faith and prayer.'

I am come over all sweaty at these words and those white hairs on my arms are quaking too. There is a great deal of guilt scudding around in the air of this vaulted building. How many of these people are secretly gambolling around like rabbits each night as Ambrose and I have done so frequently? And what is wrong with that besides?

'Ivo!' I want to scream to these rafters. 'Ivo, you do not believe a word of this pulp!' He cannot want everyone to live all cold and austere. Not my Ivo! He is a loving person. A maker-of-seaweed-belts person. A person who told me once: 'I will always love you, Tibb.'

At the end of the service there is a great clinking of coins and a collection is done for God. I wish to enquire: 'How should God like to spend the money, please?' Then everyone starts leaving and shaking hands again with Ivo at the door, and I am sneaking into a big wood box to wait it all out, but when they are gone he pulls aside the curtain of my new hiding-home and looks right at me.

'You knew I was here?' I say.

'You hardly blend into the congregation, Tibb, with that hair of yours. I could see you from my pulpit, hiding behind a pillar.'

'What is this thing for?' I ask, climbing out.

'It's a confessional.'

'And what purpose does it serve?'

'To confess one's sins, Tibb.'

'And have you confessed yours, Ivo?'

Now he goes red like those fine apples outside. Else like the crabs we used to catch when we were the best-of-friends.

He walks away and starts to organize small things on the altar-table. Things like beads and books and candles, all of which appear to have a certain order that must be observed upon this lace tablecloth. I stand in the aisle between the empty pews and watch with these sunken eyes of mine.

'I don't believe you, Ivo. That you left because you didn't like my company.'

He pauses.

'No?'

'No,' I say, and my voice does echo up to those wood beams. 'You loved my company.'

I fish out that little pearl, holding it in my palm for him to see.

'You kept it?' he says through watery eyes.

'Of course,' I tell him. 'And neither do I believe that you had a calling from God. Not once did you pray for anything when I lived beside you.'

'A calling is a calling, Tibb. It can happen to anyone.'

I raise my eyebrows.

'And you are happy? In this calling, I mean?'

'Yes.'

Now this is another lie! But this one is making me sadder than ever.

I say, 'I watched how these town-people worship you. You are invincible in this role. You are here because you will never be suspected of that word *sodomy* while you wear these robes. And you are to be a celibate man to boot. It is a way to refuse yourself your own pleasures. Tell me I'm wrong!'

He looks around him like there will be peeping eyes lurking in those high stained-like-ink windows and listening ears in the walls which are formed of stones.

'Whatever you think about me is wrong, Tibb. I told you.'

'Then why did you tremble like a jelly at Peterborough?'

'It was barbaric . . . and I was sympathetic.'

'Then you are caught up in the wrong kind of work, sir! I hear the church is not a forgiving place.'

His face hardens. I think he is tensing all his chest muscles under that robe.

'How can you bear it? To work for this churchly-place which punishes people like you? People who wish to seek out that thing called love? Here you are in the lion's mouth! Admit it, Ivo, that you are miserable here – that you have left everything of yourself back at Norfolk, and now you are a false-Ivo and these robes you wear are a shield to your own happiness!'

He is looking at me square in the face and his eyes are blazing and his fists are clenched beside him. Words are clamouring to get out of him – that terrible and wonderful truth he is keeping all to himself. I can almost see those words hammering against his lips for release but all he can say is: 'Tibb, you have invented a story and none of it has a shred of truth.'

He might as well have taken a poker and pierced it through my skin.

'It's time we left you alone, Ivo. As you said we should.'

I stand up, a bad kind of lightness inside of me, like I have been emptied of all my blood and bones and guts and now I'm just skin.

'Wait!' he says. 'I can help you – I can help your Ambrose too—'

'Why, sir?'

I am walking out of this place with its dusty pews and its table of free-for-the-taking refreshments and I can hear Ivo behind, following me down this stone aisle to the church door.

'Where will you go, Tibb?' he says.

'Why should it concern you, sir? When you did up-and-leave me long ago and I have been all round the country since then? And when you do not trust me enough to tell me the real truth?'

He reaches out and puts a hand on my shoulder and I close my eyes a moment before I shake him off and turn around, because his hand is something I have not felt for so long. 'But your man – Ambrose? Let me help him, at least—'

'I can look after him.'

Ivo's forehead bunches. 'How, Tibb? You said you have nowhere to go . . . no money. He could die—'

I shrug. 'I just remembered I have something to sell after all, Ivo.'

Business with whores

Why didn't I sell the pearl already? I have been trudging this land with a small treasure and I was so stupid to think it had some sweet meaning inside of it. In fact it doesn't mean one thing apart from money, Tibb. Did you listen to your ma at all? This man Ivo did spit you out like the rest of them.

That image will be scratched into my mind forever, I think. Ivo – or a shadow of Ivo – standing at the door to his own church, his arms hanging by his sides while he watched me disappear. What was running through that once-lovely mind of his? Fears and worries and the thought that he cannot trust his old friend Tibb one piece. The fact that our own life in the land of Norfolk meant nothing at all.

Goldsmiths' workshops are few and far between in this place – these town-people are only interested in one big auction for chickens out there – but I have found a good-enough shop and the goldsmith man is standing in front of me, spying at this pearl with one eye shut, holding it right up close to his face. His nose is pink and he is reminding me of a mole I did see once in the land of Yorkshire.

'Did you steal this, child?'

'No, sir!'

He is smirking at me like I just told a fat lie and I want to ram my fist into his mole's nose.

'I was given it.'

He looks me up and down, like still he doesn't believe a word of it.

'Given it?' he says slowly, and he lowers his voice. 'You know I do not conduct business with whores?'

'Sir! I was given it upon a beach by a friend who found it inside an oyster.'

Friend. That word sounds flimsy because in fact Ivo is no friend to me.

The goldsmith splutters. 'Well that is a most unlikely happening, child! To find a pearl inside of an oyster is something of a miracle!'

'Well perhaps it was just that, then,' I say.

He narrows his eyes, hmm-ing and haa-ing to himself and turning over that pearl which my fingers know back-to-front like he would find some new clue inside of it.

It is strange to see it there in this man's dirty fingers. There is a feeling like dread inside me – like I want to lean forward and snatch it back – because this has been my companion since our beach days and once it is gone then it is gone forever. But I think of Ambrose under the rosemary bush and the fact he needs saving besides. A good tincture and some fine ale to make him better and a warm fire to sleep next to because I am not burying one more person in a hole.

'Very well,' the goldsmith says. 'I will take it for half a crown and I won't give you a penny more.'

I am about to tell him, 'Then we have an agreement, sir,' and I am about to pocket that money when the door is flung open and Ivo is there at the threshold, his chest heaving.

'Father Ivo!' the goldsmith gasps, and he does away with all that looking-down-his-mole-nose bluster and he almost bows to this shadow-of-Ivo like the maybe-murderer King Henry himself did just enter.

Ivo ignores him, coming to stand in front of me.

'Don't do it,' he says quietly, and his blue eyes look like they mean it too.

'Why not?' I say.

He shakes his head as though to tell me, 'We can't talk here, Tibb,' and then he takes the pearl from the goldsmith man and says, 'She will not be selling it today, Robin,' and he steers me out of this shop.

Outside he pulls me by the hand into a small alley behind this line of workshops so we are all alone. I am remembering the way he pulled me along the beach to run away from the man who said we would fornicate.

'Stay with me?' he says.

'Why?'

'I've taken Ambrose into my house. I can help him. You should come and see to him.'

My eyes narrow. 'But it won't be the same if you are lying to me, Ivo.'

He looks exasperated, like he is holding back rude words. 'There are no lies, Tibb.'

Of sweet frumenty

Ivo wasn't lying. He has brought Ambrose into his house, all the way up the stairs, and laid him in one of the big beds with wood posts at each corner and heavy cushions and sables all piled up. He has lit a nice fire in that fireplace and he has drawn those thick curtains too.

'See, Tibb,' he says. 'I will have your Ambrose better in no time.'

Ivo did make a bowl of sweet frumenty and he is sitting beside Ambrose on the bed, offering spoonfuls of that steaming stuff to my own husband-man. How strange it is to see two people who I have loved so close together like this. I wonder two fingers did not reach down and flick me on the arse for all my startled blinking.

In the bed Ambrose is taking small amounts and swallowing it with some difficulty, all the while with his eyes closed and that green oozing liquor looks bad in this low firelight. His breathing sounds like a bull but at least he isn't doing that shivering or that terrible moaning any more.

'You don't have to,' I say to Ivo and my voice is knotted like that rosemary bush outside. 'If you had let me sell the pearl then we wouldn't need to be here at all.'

He doesn't answer that.

Ambrose wheezes, 'Thank you, Ivo,' with his eyes still shut.

Ivo doesn't look at me but continues raising the spoon to Ambrose's lips like he is all decided that making my husband-man better is his own duty now. Such a change in him. Did the tides stop still too?

'Sir,' he says to Ambrose. 'I would do anything for someone who has cared for Tibb.'

Why are you saying those kind things, Ivo? When you tried to get rid of me with your money and when you will not tell me a single sliver of truth?

Ivo asks, 'But why is he so bruised and battered?'

I shrug. 'Ah, this was a bad beating, but I think it was words which did cut the deepest.'

I can imagine those friends of Lord Fielding did say much the same as those troupe-watchers who would cry, 'Look at the devil on his lute!' rather than shutting those holes-in-their-faces and listening a moment to the sweet melody.

'Words?'

'O, my Ambrose is often cursed at like that, all because of this wonderful colour dripping down his body like he is half-covered in berry juice.'

'People can be cruel, Tibb,' Ivo whispers as he pokes another spoonful into Ambrose's mouth. 'And you know that as well as I do.'

Those words are making me angry. He is pretending to be a friend, but friends tell each other everything and Ivo is lying through his teeth.

I snatch that bowl from his hands because I have had enough of this child-play. 'I shall do it from here, Ivo,' I tell him and there is not one note of softness in my voice. He nods his head, that sadness in his eyes again, and I want to shake him by the collar and holler like a stuck pig: 'Just speak the truth, Ivo!'

When he is gone then Ambrose and I are together in this room and it feels too quiet apart from the crackle-logs in the fire.

'That's a good man just there, Tibb . . .' he does whisper into the warm air.

I am ignoring those words. 'We will get you better, Ambrose, and then we'll be on our way.'

'Tibb?' he says with one eye open. 'But you spoke so kindly of Ivo—'

'I was wrong. He is not the friend I thought he was.'

Good saltwater

We have been a week here in Ivo's vicarage-house but he still feels like a stranger to me. It should be like one big dream to be living underneath a good thatch roof and eating off plates at a table and with my dearest friend Ivo here to boot. But this place feels colder than an open barn in that bad month called January.

Ivo has me trussed up like an old matron with my hair in the scarf whenever I leave this house.

'If you are asked, then tell them you are my new housekeeper, Tibb, and that you are hired to look after an old friend of mine who is wounded and receiving alms at my vicarage.'

He had that fear in his eyes again because this whole life of his is all wrapped up in lies.

'And why is that, Ivo?' I asked.

He shrugged. 'It is strange to have a young woman inside my home . . . People could think the worst . . .'

Well I could have said a dozen things to that. Like: 'And you are happy, Ivo, to work for this church-place and be scared of people thinking bad thoughts that could be the end of you because the big-man hates love and fucking?' But those words would not have made a sound since Ivo is lost to me now.

Most of the day he spends in the church next door and otherwise he is coming into the room to tend to Ambrose's wounds. He has been mixing up bowls of good saltwater and he has gone to the herb-wife besides and bought all the things to be feeding Ambrose a fine draught each day. He says things like, 'These cuts are healing well, Tibb,' and 'Soon enough he'll be jumping around like a hare and ha-ha-ha,' which sound too distant from Ivo's mouth, and we might as well be strangers in the street.

Right now he is using a little square of linen to wipe the saltwater all over Ambrose's chest. Those gashes are healing up and they are not oozing any more with that green stuff, and the skin around his eyes is not so black.

The two of them do talk a lot while Ivo tends to the cuts – words about music because Ivo has a great interest in that now he has an organ-player coming to his own church. They talk about the land of Kent besides – what they remember of it – because my Ambrose used to live there with the family who did not love him enough and Ivo did leave his home in Kent too.

'And how did you come to be here?' Ambrose asks, and he has colour in his cheeks again.

'My uncle – he was the rector but he died last year.'

'I am sorry for you,' Ambrose says and Ivo just shrugs.

'He was a good man – I think we understood each other.'

And what is *that* supposed to mean, Ivo? You think *I* do not understand you?

The two men look each other in the eyes and there is some tender moment between them but I am waiting here like a fool on the outside. I cough loudly.

'Thank you, Ivo,' Ambrose says.

'No trouble, my friend. I owe you everything for looking after Tibb.'

I want to pummel my fists into his chest at these too-confusing words.

When he is gone back to his church then I lie down next to Ambrose and he puts his big purple arm around me.

'You know, Tibb, whatever you feel towards Ivo just now, he's a good man. I can see why you wanted to put the sign up outside our home.'

I shake my head. 'Don't say that. He is all changed.'

Ambrose looks disappointed, like I just told him that the bees did quit and there will never be a pot of honey again in this world.

I sit up on my heels. 'Ambrose, he does not trust me any more, though I am his oldest friend. He thinks to lie to me about his real feelings, and to deny himself all the goodness he could have in this life.'

Ambrose sucks in his cheeks like he is thinking hard. 'About loving other men?'

I nod.

'It must be hard. This world can be so unkind . . .'

No shit, sir. I did see two men bloodied in a farrier's tent because of it. But surely there are ways around it? Surely the answer is not to give up altogether?

'Ambrose,' I say, 'my own ma did tell me, "When it rains won't you dance like a mad dog in it?" And she did tell me you should make the life you want.'

I don't add that she did not ever quite manage that herself.

Ambrose is looking very intently at my face.

'Anyway, didn't you tell me yourself that a person must hold their head up? Well my friend Ivo is burying his inside a very big hole.'

He squeezes me some more. 'Give him some time, Tibb,' he says, and 'Who knows the battles people are fighting inside their heads.'

I think of that image like he sewed it with threads. Like those tapestries pinned to the wall of Lord Fielding's feasting hall. I am picturing tiny armies gathering inside people's skulls and slashing each other with spears and swords till their limbs fall off. I think everyone could see the big battle in my ma's head since there was no hiding that stuff.

My eyes trail over all these no-use-for-them things coated in dust like leather-bound books and wood stools and more thick carpets. And what is going on inside *your* head, Ivo?

When Ambrose is doing his sleep-breathing then I slip out and over to the church in my housekeeper's garb.

This church service is just like the other one and these people are dangling on Ivo's every word. Perhaps it is the most devout congregation in the whole of this shit land called England, although there are not many priests who look so beautiful as Ivo and maybe they are come just to stare at him.

'Back again, Tibb?' he says when they are all gone home, and I can hear that worn-out note in his voice, like he is starting to fray. 'Perhaps you are discovering God yourself . . .'

Again he rearranges things on his altar-table and I walk down the stone aisle towards him and I am noticing that there are words etched into these big-and-little flagstones on the floor because there are possibly dead people under here.

'No, Ivo.'

He pauses. 'Then how might I help you?'

His shoulders are up around his ears and I think his hands do shake while he moves that golden candlestick.

'I just wanted to see again this lie you are living—'

'Enough!' he says and that startles me. He turns and throws that candlestick down so it clatters on the floor then he sits on the altar-step with his beautiful face in his hands, and there is a quiver in his manly voice. 'Enough, Tibb, you're right! I'm here for that reason. To protect myself. To stop myself too. Are you happy now?'

I sit down beside him because my dear Ivo is crying and he has blotted my tears many times before so it is my turn now I think. 'I am not happy, Ivo, because *you* are not happy.'

He says quietly, 'Do you think me unnatural?'

My brow furrows because this is a strange question. 'You could be anything, Ivo, and that is exactly who you should be.'

He waits and then he says, 'I had those feelings since I was a boy and my papa found out too. I couldn't marry that girl they brought for me. You know I left in the night.'

I say, 'I think you did the right thing to leave that family who would make you marry a girl.'

He bows his lovely head. 'Why are you come here to cast your judgement on me, Tibb? You do not know what it's like.'

'To be different, you mean? You think I do not know what that's like, when I have been a vagrant all my life and when I look this way?'

I hold his hand, and I am surprised that he squeezes mine, just as he used to. I put my skinny arm around his broad shoulders.

'But how will it serve me to admit these unnatural feelings and be flogged or even killed for it, Tibb? Should you like that better?'

I hold his face in my hands like he used to do to me, and I feel that warm skin of his. I feel his heart beneath that robe and it is thudding away. There is nothing unnatural about you, my friend, and, 'Ivo,' I say, 'I am going to save you, like you saved me.'

He takes my hand. 'I didn't save you though. I left you. Will you ever forgive me?'

'I have already forgiven you.'

He is looking into my eye-balls. 'You know I have thought of you every day, Tibb. Every moment of every day. The beaches . . . those were the very best of times.'

I rest my head on his shoulder. 'Yes, my friend. And perhaps we will have those times again.'

Like an angel up there

This vicarage table is too grand for one-time vagabonds called Tibb Ingleby, but Ivo has made a great dinner of a partridge and turnips to put on top of it. There is something of the old Ivo creeping back in, and I should say there is a big weight lifted from his shoulders to have finally said those things out loud.

'I cannot reach a thing from here, Ivo!' I laugh, because this table is so wide, and he says, 'Then I shall serve you, Tibb, and I shall sit beside you too since that is something I have wished for.'

This bird is tasting delicious because Ivo is here with me. And there is a shit-load of bread on this table. Two fine loaves and then a long plaited one which I think the angels made.

'This is as light as air, this here bread!' I say. 'I will be taking a good portion up to my Ambrose besides.'

Ivo's lovely cheeks are all rosy in this candle-light. I crane my head and I can see that his kitchen is once again chock-full of other baked goods like there are four families living here with him. Rolls and nice buns and tiny cakes all studded with fruits. Great piles of them, Ma!

'I think you have some hankering for bread since you became a vicar, Ivo?'

He laughs and then raises his cup. 'Here's to you. And I am mighty glad you found a husband, Tibb.'

O, me too, sir.

After that partridge we eat some very fine cream and some berries of course, and then he says, 'Would you tell me about your time spent in that troupe? I would like to imagine you there and doing the pearl act you mentioned.'

Ah, but where to start?

'Ivo, I was travelling with a great many people and doing some grand performances in towns and such. I had a costume which was in fact flour and water and a great many white linens wrapped around me. And I thought I made some friends – one in particular – but in fact they did fuck off without me.'

My voice tails off and Ivo looks sad about this to boot.

'Anyway that troupe boss called Signor Perero – though he was hardly Spanish, Ivo – did sell me off to a man named Mr Manners who bought me at a feast though I was not for sale. And he was no kind man which is why I have these bruises still—'

'I cannot hear of it, Tibb,' he says, and his knuckles are all white around that fine silver spoon. 'Tell me this person's whereabouts and I think I will go myself and kill the man.'

'Well you would be too late, Ivo, for Ambrose did it for me.'

He smiles like the real Ivo again and not much like a priest who should say that killing is one naughty sin, dear. 'Truly, Tibb? Then I owe this man even more than I thought.'

This warm silence is like it used to be, and he holds my hand in the yellow candle-light.

'He is in fact the roof I needed, Ivo, and which my ma did not ever have. And you were right. It is a different love than our love since our love is a friendy-love.'

He smiles so softly as he always used to and he says firm, 'Yes, Tibb, that is exactly right.'

'Would you take me to that church again, Ivo?' I say after dinner. 'I am mighty curious to see all those grand parts of it and those things that are important to the godly-people of the parish of Leominster.'

Well we are running down this short path like we are two vagabonds once more, and we are both a bit drunk by now on that tasty apple cider from Ivo's own orchards.

Once I have sat on every pew and stood at the pulpit like the priest himself, then I say, 'Tell me you do not punish the adulteresses in this place. Because you know that dance needs two people and they probably did it out of love because they were pushed into some shit marriages besides.'

He shakes his head. 'Never, Tibb. And nor am I charging monies for seats in Heaven and such.'

'Then you are an honest rector,' I say. 'Do you remember that toe-nail we did see at Norfolk?'

He nods and nods. 'Tibb, I have seen hairs and stones and all sorts sold off. It is the power we have and these words being all in Latin. Truly we can pretend anything.'

I tell him of that milk which was just cow milk and he is shaking his head again in a serious way.

'But, Tibb, there is a lot of goodness in this faith, and this has been a great surprise to me.'

'Really?'

'It's true. From how I see it, I think there is a God somewhere, and that he wants a peaceful world and a more compassionate one than this.'

'You think he would be compassionate towards men like *you*, Ivo?'

He thinks long and hard, like this is some very difficult question which I suppose it is. 'I do, Tibb.'

I smile. 'That is good, Ivo, that you have found a sort-of-faith again.'

Then I am exploring some more and asking all manner of interesting questions, and I am pointing up to that small balcony with its angel-babies above it and which hangs down at the front of the pews like a nice eyebrow of a rich woman.

'What is that part called?'

'That's the rood-loft, Tibb. It separates the congregation from the altar, as you see. There should be a choir there, but the monks boarded up that room to the side so no one can reach it any more.'

'Ah, but I do climb like a goat,' I say, and I am pulling myself up the pillar beneath that small balcony, then hauling myself over the wood railing and, 'I like it up here!'

Down there in the aisle, Ivo looks up at me, smiling. Like a beautiful young man again without that thick garb and all of the world's weight upon his manly-shoulders. And he says, 'You look like an angel up there, Tibb!'

Even higher

Not once did I think my roof would be a vicarage but the three of us are living this small life together and I should say it is something quite special. To think I was so wretched when Ivo suggested I might be his maid back in the shit land of Peterborough. I think being his housekeeper is the best apprenticehood I could ever have, Ma!

Some weeks have passed and this summer weather is settling in and my Ambrose has chased off the worst of his leaking wounds. Each night we are all three of us eating together at the big table and I have never been so well fed in my life. The vicarage-house has become a little piece of paradise, all full up with laughing and talking, and Ivo's shoulders are not pinned around his ears any more but at the usual place on top of his chest.

Sometimes I do watch him at the church-place too. It is something strange to sit at the back of the pews with all the God-lovers, my head wrapped up in a scarf and with a walking-cane for good measure, and I can't tell what the fuck he is speaking about most of the time but I just like to look at Ivo.

Now it is night-time and Ambrose, Ivo and I have come into this church and up the spiral steps from Ivo's own vestry so we are some hundred feet off the ground on the flat roof of the bell-tower. I did have a good look on the way up at the little landing where the bell-ringer should stand and the big holes in the stonework for that sound to sneak out and wake up all the birds.

There is just a low wall of stones around this roof and then a sheer drop to the ground but we are lying on our backs and looking up at the night sky which is mild and silent. It is peppered with those bright stars and they are dangling so close that I am reaching out with my hand to catch them.

'I think this is the tallest place I have ever been,' I say, and it feels nice to have Ivo at one side of me and my own Ambrose on the other.

'Yes, Tibb, and far from everyone else. We could be on a sand-hill again here.'

I reach for his hand. 'True. But this is even higher.'

Ambrose says, 'I think you were both the luckiest people to have found each other when you did upon that beach.'

I am thinking about this. We *were* lucky. Then my mind is thinking of Henrietta who is still there and all alone and there is a part of me which wants to dig her up and bring her here to this place too.

'You know, I think you were right about the stars, Ivo,' I say. 'The fact they are dead people up there, but without their bodies. Just their thoughts.'

He smiles, like this is funny.

'I have been chatting to my ma more than ever.'

'Do you see her tonight, Tibb?'

I squint. 'Not tonight, no.'

Ambrose squeezes my other hand. I should say the two of us have been making up for all the lost time by way of the fucking game. It is something fun to do that naughty thing in our very own bed and not in a barn or in a tent. We have been bouncing around like two tumbling rabbits.

Ivo says, 'It is mighty fine to have you both here. And to have love brightening up my vicarage. I admit this has made me think a great deal on this strange life I lead.'

I roll to face him, and those eyes of his are all glassy in this blackness. I do not like that sad look inside them, and, Ma, I am thinking no one deserves love more than Ivo, and not just the friendly kind.

I say to him: 'I wish you would find yourself a person to call husband, Ivo. It is some nice-enough word for the tongue, let me tell you.'

He is blushing and the moonlight is lighting up that pink smear across his cheeks so he can't hide it a bit. He glances over at Ambrose and I do think my friend Ivo is scared that this man is going to declare him a sodomite, but he does not know my husband-man well enough.

'There is no one for me, Tibb,' he says quickly, and he puts his arm around me. 'You think about things more simply than I do. Perhaps you are the bravest person I know.'

Now that is not something I have ever thought of. Are you speaking in tongues, sir?

And milk tarts

The next morning when I wake up, Ivo has already taken an early service at his church and he has since come back and prepared for me a nice bowl of porridge all speckled with raisins.

'I am off to the bakery, Tibb!' he calls in a while.

He has told me the same every morning and he comes back all laden with yet more pastry buns and milk tarts and little ginger cakes and honey loaves. So much food, Ma. You would be stuffing it down your throat saying, 'Tibb, would you eat it before the fuckers do?'

'Ivo!' I say, and I am running down the corridor to see him at the door. 'We are crammed full of baked things! Have you not seen the kitchen?'

He laughs a little bit. 'Ah, I have a big stomach as you know! And anyway, I can take the rest to church this evening for the people to be having their Mass.'

I grimace. 'Not the cakes, Ivo! I have stolen from many a church and I did not ever find cakes on the altar-place.'

He laughs again but he is not giving me any straight answers.

'The ducks, then. Perhaps they would enjoy the stale parts.'

Ducks, sir? When you have lived like a vagabond? This stuff is not making a single morsel of sense to me.

'I am coming,' I tell him.

His eyes widen. 'You are?'

I nod.

'There's no need—' he begins but already I am coiling up my white hair and stuffing it into my scarf-hood because if there's a rat, Ma, you can be sure as fuck your own Tibb will stink it out.

People hardly notice this red-and-yellow-costumed person in their town because they are just looking at Ivo. They are all stopping in the lane and parting for him and lifting their caps to say, 'Morning, Father!' and crossing themselves like the bigman just swooped down from the clouds. They might as well drop to their knees and kiss the ground where he walks like our own King Henry VII who does not suffer vagrancy.

This town is like a spider's web of crooked lanes and the bakery-shop is hazy with steam in the middle of it and that is something sweet to my eye. I tuck those last wisps of hair into my turban and my Ivo is all twitchy as that bell says: come on in!

Ha! The smell of a baker's shop, Ma. You did always like that too, though you did linger round the back and plump up your tits for the baker-boys while your own Tibb slipped in and out again like a white-as-snow ghost with pockets rammed full of pastries.

This one is the finest and I stand still on this sawdusted floor a moment, trying not to think of those times I did find a bakery with my one-time friend called Maria who was interested mostly in meat florentines and flans. I am watching that grunting-like-a-boar man with no hair on his head, fetching of hot rolls from his ovens. His apron barely covers half of him. Ivo's need for buns is growing more confusing by the moment, then a voice says, 'Father? Can I help?' And I turn to peer behind a great pie-stack.

Well here is someone quite beautiful, Ma, and I think he is not from England! He is all dark-skinned and good-to-look-at and kindly in the face. Muscly but not so tall, just like Ivo. Here are two peas from the same pod, except this one has dark features unlike my friend Ivo. And those black eyelashes are so long, I think I could sweep the floor with them. These men are staring at one another like they never saw another person walk upon two legs.

Ivo is finding his voice and that is proving tricky. 'A bun and a loaf, please, Flavio,' he says.

Flavio. A Spanish person!

That man nods and smiles, and then he says quietly, 'As always, Father,' and I can't miss that little lisp, like he cannot form those silky *s* sounds quite right. This is someone truly Spanish, unlike the man Signor Perero who was one big hoodwinker.

'Anything else, Father?'

Well Ivo is standing here and I can tell he doesn't want to move so he is adding to the list three of those cheese tarts and then a sponge cake of berries.

I think Flavio is moving extra slow to stop the time inside this warm bakery. That grunting baker-boss is shuffling in and out of the oven room.

'And a slice of the pie there, Flavio. And a small helping of your thin wafers, please.'

He has filled an entire bag, and now the world is making a lot more sense to me besides.

Outside, Ivo says, 'You see it was just a quick trip to the bakery, you really needn't have come!' but there is a spring in his step – like he could take off from the mud with every stride and flap his wings like those marsh-birds we lived beside in the land of Norfolk. 'Ah the air is fine today! Rain perhaps later!' He rips some of that roll with his teeth and he says, 'Would you have some bread, Tibb?'

Painted into my skull

'I have sniffed out your secret, my friend.'

I am saying this to Ivo later, when he has done his evening service at the church and when we are sitting like two ducks on top of this fine tower. The summer breeze is something cool but I can see that my Ivo's chiselled face is glowing in the moonlight.

'Secret, Tibb?'

'Yes, sir. This love you have for a certain baker's man. Flavio, I heard you call him.'

He shakes his head, and he does look away from his old friend Tibb. Up into those twinkly stars which are in fact just corpses.

'No wonder you are buying that delicious bread each morning and all those treats. I think you are going to the bakery every day just to see him and I cannot blame you!'

He glances round like there are people watching but we are on top of the tower and there is no one to hear us except the dead people and the moon. 'It is all silly,' he whispers. 'It is all in my head, Tibb.'

'Not so, my friend! I could have scooped up all that love with a spoon and made a fine broth with it!'

He looks flushed – like this is all too much – and then, 'Tibb, I came here to be a vicar . . . to have no temptation in my way.'

'And yet here it is, Ivo! A great temptation right in front of your face.' I think I could whoop and holler for my old friend.

He puts those hands on my shoulders like he would have me truly listen and he does say, 'Tibb, I would be strung up and killed. Don't you remember what happened? And don't you know those two men in Peterborough had it easy? This world is painted in black and white and love is only for a man and a wife and even then it is not really encouraged. Men cannot be in love with other men and especially not if one of them is a priest.'

Well I do remember what happened and I remember the blood which ran from the farrier's tent like that stuff is painted into my skull. But there are other things I remember, like how much those two men did love each other.

'And the worst thing is that I am meant to preach against any kind of transgressions and inflict those punishments myself!'

'You know you do not have to be caught, Ivo. And my ma did say you just have to play the fuckers at their own game. There must be a way—'

'Tibb!' he says, and his eyes are full up of that terrible thing called fear. 'Sometimes there isn't. And I am happy enough with this nice exchange we have each morning.'

He is looking at me like I should be content with this too, but this truth is clawing one big hole in my sail. O, I am not content with it, Ivo, and this is one small life so you must try and make your heart sing. Wise words indeed from that woman my ma whose heart was not singing very often.

Later on I am lying in our fit-for-a-king bed with my Ambrose beside me who has been making up for those feeling-ill times by stuffing his perfect face with all the pies and pastries from the kitchen.

'My friend Ivo is in love,' I say to him. 'He cannot waste that!'

'Don't you think that is for him to decide, Tibb?'

'No.'

He raises his eyebrows.

'Ambrose, did you not tell me that people must hold their own heads high, not hide away? It is some doleful thing and I think I could cry with this wasted love.' I throw my legs over his body and my arms around him like I am a limpet upon a rock. 'I intend to do something about it if Ivo will not.'

'This is not your battle though,' he says while he does stroke and stroke my back.

O, all this talk of battles! Don't you know that sometimes you must stand up and holler and shout?

This night is hot and I can't lie here when there are horses galloping inside of my skull. I climb out of bed with that candle and I am sitting in the great arm-chair which has leather stretched across its wood frame and which swallows me up whole. I dangle my legs over the arm.

In the bed Ambrose sits up. 'Would you come and sleep, Tibb?'

No, sir. I am thinking of all the clever plotting that my ma did do oftentime and all of that sneakery she taught her own daughter besides. Lessons to live by, Tibb!

He says to me, 'What are you planning?'

The man suspects me of foul play and wicked deeds which will ruin the life of my oldest friend Ivo. I glance at this long bookshelf beside me with all these heavy books and their creased spines and their dust. Godly books. I take one.

'I am reading a book,' I tell him.

'Tibb,' he whispers. 'You cannot read.'

True.

Choose between two

In the morning Ivo is off to take his early service and I am jumping out of bed the moment I hear the door shut down there. I am rushing out into the town with my hair coiled up into my matron's scarf and my old-lady's cane click-clicking on the cobbles. Those watching-men did shift this bakery in the night and I can't get there fast enough.

'I am requesting to speak with a Master Flavio,' I say when I am inside the door.

'Well?' says the porky baker-boss. 'What business would you have with my baker-boy, madam? He is busy all day at the ovens making pies and loaves and I cannot afford to spare him even for a moment.'

I smile. 'There is a need for a cook of general-means and the bread baked by your man here is some of the best.'

'As I told you, I need him here.'

That man wants me out of this shop but Flavio is looking at me like I just bumped down from Heaven with this news.

'Ah, sir. But don't you know this message is come from Father Ivo?'

The baker-boss's eyes are round like two coins which I do not have in the pocket of this red-and-yellow dress. 'Father Ivo?'

'That's right, sir. I am the housekeeper-woman at the vicarage, and Father Ivo is in need of a cook since his days are busier than ever.'

He looks like he did see a ghost creep through the door because of course he is thinking of the big-man and when the priest does dish out orders then you have to follow them.

I nod to Flavio. 'And so your man?'

We have eaten some stew of mutton, and those two are holding hands under this table like they think our heads are all stuffed with wool and like we didn't notice that thing with our own eyes. I can feel a great rushing inside of my chest, as though there is a tree growing there and forcing all its wiggling roots into the soil. Ma, I could not wish anything more than for my friend Ivo to have a grand and riotous time this night, and not to have a single wink of sleep.

While Flavio and Ambrose are laughing and talking over that sweet wine then I am standing with Ivo in the kitchen as he pretends to tidy up the plates, and his face has changed and he is pale in the flames from the hearth, like a thought did poke down and pinch his smile. There is a cold-enough doubt slithering around inside me like perhaps you fucked it up, Tibb.

'What's wrong, Ivo?' I whisper. 'You aren't happy about this?'

The other two are laughing ho-ho-ho in the dining room and that noise is whistling round the house and making it warm.

He smiles a little. 'O, I am, Tibb.'

'Then what is it?'

He sighs and maybe that sound could turn the skies black. 'I think I must choose between two now. This lovely man Flavio who makes me feel like life just started, or God himself.'

I whisper, 'Now I have not been much of a follower of the big-man as you know, Ivo, but I can't see how any God is worth praying to who thinks that love is something evil.'

He thinks about it a long time. 'Perhaps,' he says and I can tell he really wants to believe it. And I am trying not to think of those two nice men called Samuel and Ewan who were squirming on the ground at Peterborough because perhaps you have been dreaming, Tibb Ingleby.

To eliminate all sodomites

I have been some new shade of happy now Ivo has his lovely boy-friend living with us. I am seeing my beach-Ivo back again and that is some sweet mead. How many times he has told me: 'Thank you for bringing Flavio here, Tibb' and 'You are a true friend.'

Friends. First, a good-to-look-at Spaniard. Second, a beautiful priestly man. Third, a much-recovered Ambrose who is far bigger and more colourful than all of us, and last, that pale and odd-looking girl who is called Tibb Ingleby.

Friends such as these are like pert tits in a nunnery. You don't find them often – not ever in my ma's case – and didn't Maria and the others leave us for dead already? We must stick together. In fact, Ivo has made Ambrose his very own church-warden, which he says means a guarding-person for the church and a helper of all the godly things. 'There are eyes watching everywhere, Tibb, and we all need accounting for. Now I have a housekeeper, a cook and a new church-warden.'

Flavio is a great skills-man with a pan and a fire, and he has been making all sorts of good stuff like rabbit coated in pastry and I did think of that carcass which was waiting for me under my tree-hollow. And Ambrose is content in his new churchly job because he is a fixer and a do-er of good things and he has all the wisdom of a hundred men besides. 'But I shouldn't want to cause a stir,' he did say. 'I have travelled around playing the lute after all and my colouring has proved to be something of a distraction over the years.'

'Perhaps it is a good thing,' Ivo said, 'for these people to see that not everyone is cast from the same clay.'

A few people have asked already, 'Who is that man?' and Ivo had some taking-no-shit tone in his replying voice, like: 'Mistress Little, it has been my own pleasure to nurse this man who is an old friend and who came to me for alms not long ago. Now he is better I have seen it fit to employ him as my church-warden because this person is more devout than any.'

Well she eyed his skin like it was crawling with ants. 'But he doesn't look better at all!' she said.

O, would you find something new to comment upon, dear? People have the imagination of flies.

Now here we are, the four of us, lying on the flat roof of this bell-tower and gazing up at the black-like-ink sky. But this place does not feel the same tonight and there is a tightness inside my chest. I can see some flitting bats but not one star. Are you up there, Ma, or are you just asleep?

I wonder we have all held our breath these last few weeks. Like such a perfect life inside a vicarage cannot last forever, and there are memories scratched into my head to convince me of it besides. Then this morning, Ivo had a scroll of parchment brought to him by a messenger boy. And that parchment was from a certain Father Brian.

Priests in this southern part of England! it said. *Beware the abominable vices of men who will go against nature for their pleasures. Eliminate all sodomites from the land. Vigilance always!*

'Is it from him, Ivo?' I asked after he read out those terrible words. 'The very same Father Brian?'

He nodded and the world seemed to bulge with its own tears besides. 'He's a powerful man around here, Tibb.'

We have not talked about that parchment since but I breathe in this cool night air and I say that thing which all of us are thinking: 'We can't stay here forever like this.'

'No,' Ivo whispers back, and his eyes are brimming with worries. 'I can't be in this costume much longer. We need to search out a new home because living in a vicarage is dangerous.'

'Where will we go?' I say, and there is a sliver of panic running through me that perhaps this lovely man will up-and-leave you again, Tibb.

Here is a bad silence because no one has the answer. We need an acrobat to turn a somersault and lighten this dark mood but what good will that serve, Tibb?

'Flavio,' I say, 'would you tell us about your home in the sunnier lands?'

Flavio leans back on his tanned arms and says, 'Ah, my father and I travelled from Spain to Portugal since he was a fisherman and he was always looking for work. We would sail off the coast there and into the ocean. Just the two of us.' He smiles like this is some sweet memory. 'He was an adventurer, and we would take his good sturdy boat and set sail for a number of weeks. Once we lived a whole summer upon a tiny island which was all white sands and glistening waters and we lay in the sun and ate fish for every meal.'

'Truly?' I say and I look to Ambrose because he did speak of those hidden beauties hiding in faraway countries and which we would not ever see. His eyes are wide like mine are.

Flavio nods. 'We had everything we needed and my father taught me how to make that water quite drinkable, and remove all the salt. And we ate figs and oranges and all those good things.'

'*Oranges*, sir?' I say, because this is a stranger-word as much as *sodomy* was.

He bends towards me and it seems there are oceans and mountains and forests lurking in those big brown eyes. 'Sweeter than apples, Tibb. All dripping with juice and puckered with tiny dots.'

Well I am imagining just that and I cannot move on account of the momentous idea which is sneaking into my thick skull. It is sprouting wings of its own and feathers and a great long tail. This thing has scales and claws and teeth, Ma! I sit up.

'Tibb?' Ivo says, because he knows me too well.

Ambrose puts his hand on my shoulder. 'Tibb, what are you thinking?'

'Could you find it again?' I ask Flavio. 'This island?'

This Spanish person does blink and blink those dark eyes like there is a little knocking on his head. He says slowly, 'Well there are lots of islands, Tibb. And they are not drawn upon the maps but I have a good knowledge of those parts from my fishing days. Why?'

O, Ma.

Ambrose is gathering up his thoughts and he has that heavy look about him which says, 'I do so hate to disappoint you, Tibb,' because he did wear this same look on his face at the Lord Fielding's house when he told me, 'I wish I had all the monies now, Tibb, and you would not have to do this stupid play of virtues for these spoilt people.'

'Flavio,' I say, 'did you ever see anyone else there?'

He shakes his head. 'Not a soul. Those places were our secret.'

They are all looking at me like *I* am the mad one which is quite fucked-up.

'Don't you see?' I breathe. 'Why are we *here*, when we could be *there*?'

Still they are all vacant and staring with their eyes glazed over like buttery buns. I lean forward as my ma would do when we were sheltering in woods and she had something wonderful or terrible to tell me, like: 'Tibb, I have met a man this day.'

'Listen. My one-time friend Maria did tell me once: "Make

your own paradise, Tibb, since this world is no sweet place for people like us," and those were some sage-enough words for me. So we must end this shit half-life, running from the fuckers and living under rooves which don't want us. My friends, we could be eating fruits and lying on the white sand and never working one day of our lives. And free! And by that I mean you would be holding hands with Flavio whenever you wish, Ivo, and Ambrose and I will not be stared at all day like we should be ashamed to show our faces!'

I stop to allow them to cheer like lunatics but they do not make a single sound. Nothing. Why are these people not hollering as I am? Flavio has that hint of something-like-hope but the other two are shaking their heads.

Ivo reaches out for my hand. 'Tibb, now that could never ever happen.'

Do they mean to burst the excitement like a bubble?

'Why?' I say, jumping up. 'Would you give a reason, sir?'

Ivo says gently, 'You cannot just sail across the seas to an unknown island, Tibb. It's absurd! We'd have no money for any of it. A boat! Do you know how much it would cost? And the journey could kill us all . . .'

I am looking at Ambrose now. 'Tell me you agree with me?'

My big man looks like he is stuck somewhere between those places called wonder and doubt, a hand rifling through his reddish curls.

I peer around at my friends, all three of them gazing up at me. Pitiful, as though I have gone mad, and I can't bear their looks.

'*You* are absurd,' I say. 'Because you cannot see a good thing when it whacks you on the arse.'

Leominster, Herefordshire

Flavio has stuffed rolls and buns into every pocket and Ivo takes one, biting into the soft dough which is spiced and spiked with currants. At least he might die on a full stomach, and yet he is not hungry for much.

'What are the crowds like?' he asks, his voice hoarse with dryness. Does he want to know the answer?

'Huge,' Flavio says quietly. 'And growing.'

Ivo thinks of it. This small town on the border of Wales teeming with people. Overrun, because of him. His own church surrounded, crowds swarming. Wrapping up the truth in sticky strings. He thinks of that bowl of coins his mother kept at the door. Hasn't he always loathed how the priests corrupt truth? Trading their false promises for pitiful savings? And now he has done just that, seduced by the possibility of what it could buy.

'And the vicarage?'

'They're still in there, Ivo.'

He nods drily, imagining those enemies living in his own house.

'And you've been sleeping in the kitchen still?'

'Of course. Like any good kitchen hand.'

'I'm sorry.'

Flavio trails a finger across Ivo's cheek. 'Sorry? I should be in here with you.'

'You should run. The priests will be after anyone associated with me. They'll know you played your part in it all.'

Flavio doesn't say anything. Why won't he run? There is nothing noble about staying put and being condemned to death.

They sit together, hands entwined, and Flavio doesn't retch even though this place stinks and Ivo stinks too.

'Is she suffering?' Ivo asks into the darkness.

Flavio looks worried. 'You know how she is. Just . . . Tibb.'

They stare into each other's eyes and Ivo thinks of her at the church. Tibb, who truly believes that there is a place for people like him in the world, though she has never belonged herself.

They don't speak until the warden's footsteps return. 'Would you give her my love?' Ivo whispers quickly. 'Would you ask her: does she still have her pearl?'

Shit in a nest

This pew is rock-hard and I have had better cushions for my bony backside on the floor of a stable. It is night-time and I am watching Ivo do his priestly duty and talk at this crowd in his very own place-called-church. He looks like some handsome prince up there in front of that great book, but I am thinking of the island. Why had my friends thought it so ridiculous? If Flavio found it once, he could surely do it again. And it was Ambrose himself who spoke of all the beautiful sights around the big world that the rich people did tell him about and which we might not ever see.

Ivo has spied me at the back here and he did flash me that look which says, 'Tibb, would you be careful?' because my good friend does worry too much. Can't he see I have perfected this hair-turban and I am clutching this walking-stick for my own amusement, and I have told those nosy parishioners who wish to know me: 'O, I am the new housekeeper at the vicarage'? My own ma would have said more than that besides, like: 'What the fuck does it matter to you, sir?'

'Good friends,' says Ivo, and, 'would you kneel to receive a blessing?'

I kneel like the rest of them, but there is nothing holy about my thoughts. In fact, I am looking at Ambrose who is lighting candles at the back of this church like a very pious churchlyman and I am picturing myself rolling around on top of him in the white sands of the island we are not going to sail to.

Ivo is flicking some water and saying of prayers in the language of Latin, and then he says, 'Now for the sermon! Good people of Leominster, I should speak to you today about the receiving of God's word, and of the importance of opening yourselves up to messages from Heaven. The Lord our God did many miracles through his son Jesus Christ and we are told of them in the holy book.'

Something has happened to my Ivo right now in that he is misty-eyed, and I can see he is speaking from a truthful place.

'Had Mary not opened her heart to the angel Gabriel, then how should she have known she was carrying a very son of God and that she was the mother of Jesus himself? And so we must open our hearts to all of God's signs. A fine harvest. A sunset!'

Once those people are gone to their own warm beds, then Flavio does come over from the vicarage and us four are climbing up on to the bell-tower roof.

'That was some nice sermon, Ivo,' I say, when we are all lying on our backs and staring at the sky. 'I think you meant every word of it.'

'I did, Tibb.'

Wink-wink says Ma from her high-up house, but this is no time for smiles. I wonder she is even closer tonight. Perhaps she will come hurtling into this very bell-tower and I will throw my arms around her lovely neck. But I sit up. I should say I am frozen solid like a piece of ice, and with these stare-eyes of mine.

'Tibb?' Ambrose says, but I can't answer because these thoughts are racing around inside my skull and some mad idea is forming which is causing me to sweat and I need to concentrate. My palms are wet like two puddles.

Ivo shakes me by the shoulder. 'Tibb!'

I hold up a hand. An *angel*, he did say.

'Ivo, tell me again what you said. About that angel called Gabriel.'

'Well,' he says, all furrowed across his forehead, 'he was sent to Earth since he was a messenger that reported to God.'

'And there are more of him, in that great book?'

He cocks his head like he is very confused still. 'There are more, Tibb. Some of them cherubs. An archangel named Michael too.'

Such a swooping inside my chest. Ma! Do you see what I see? I laugh and laugh and she is getting brighter and wider because she has been in on this all along when she told me, 'Tibb, don't you know I was knocked up by the big-man himself?'

'Tibb?' Ivo says. 'Would you explain yourself?'

'Come down with me quick!' I tell them, because they all need to hear this plan which is ready to climb out of my mouth. And, 'Thank you, Ma!' I shout as I run down these spiral stairs like the snap-dogs are back.

Inside the nave again, I haul myself into that rood-loft balcony by way of scaling the pillar with some help from Ambrose who shoves me up by the backside. I look down on these three men who are scratching their heads.

'Tell me again what you said when you saw me up here, Ivo.'

'I believe I said you were looking like an angel yourself, Tibb. Though I think I am not the first person to come up with that.'

'Exactly! Now I am no clerk of big numbers, my friends, but I should say I certainly do not have enough fingers and toes on my body to count the times I have been mistaken for an angel, and this is due to my pale skin and this sheet of white hair.' I cock my head. 'Would you believe me if I tell you that I have a pair of wings fashioned by a not-so-polite-man and those things are in your vicarage as we speak? Here is some fine stroke of luck, wouldn't you say?'

Ivo is all confused and he looks at Flavio as though to tell him: 'She is destined for the madhouse!' But I can tell Ambrose is piecing all these parts together because he did see the metal wings for himself.

'Tibb,' Ivo says, 'you do not really think you are an angel?'

'Of course not, Ivo! But I can pretend!'

Again that lovely forehead of his is crinkling up. 'But why should you need to pretend to be an angel?'

Why is my Ivo so slow today?

I smile as I lean my elbows on this wood railing because my own ma would be proud of her sneak of a daughter.

'Ivo, do you not remember the toe-nail and the money that priest was making from it?'

He narrows his eyes.

'And just recently, I saw a stony icon of the ma called Mary which was dripping milk and it was all a great falsehood but you should have seen what those people were paying! Can't you see? I can be your miracle, and we can raise the funds for our island life! Didn't you ask me how we might pay for a boat?'

Ambrose is wearing a little smile, like he is quite proud of a girl named Tibb, and Flavio is just staring like this big church is full up with bats and cats and monkeys. It is Ivo who looks like there are wolves prowling outside.

He runs a hand through that thick yellow hair, glancing around like we are peeped-upon. 'Would you truly risk everything with such a deception? A blasphemy like that would be punished by death if we were caught. I think we would be dragged before the King himself and have all our insides ripped out!'

I shrug. 'All the priests are doing it, Ivo. The King cannot be checking up on every one. And Father Brian is more worried about other stuff like love and fucking. We just have to keep it quiet and do it quickly—'

'Enough of this talk!'

There is some panic in my friend Ivo's eyes and that note of finality which sits like a shit in a nest.

Not so many eyes

My friend Ivo and I are gone into the land of Wales for the purpose of seeking out our new roof. Flavio and Ambrose were not allowed to come because that might look suspicious, or so said Ivo. A priest with friends? Ha! Is the sky turned green to boot?

He is trying to be cheerful about this shit idea of his. 'A life of quiet in the countryside . . . away from town. We will be more private there, Tibb.'

'Like we were private in Norfolk?' I say, remembering that man who caught us and chased us from the beach with the promise of branding a V upon our foreheads.

He sighs.

His not-so-grand plan involves leaving the Church and setting himself up in some small home, perhaps as a carpenter, and with Flavio, Ambrose and I living close by so that he might visit on occasions and not be suspected.

'We can live freely, Tibb. It will be a nice roof besides, and you did always want that.'

I am not smiling back at him because I don't fancy separate rooves, or any roof in this fucked-up country at all, because that is not freedom in my own mind. But I am not saying much any more because he doesn't wish to hear about that island and its white sand which would in fact solve all our problems.

We stop at the place called Pilleth for ale and then at some other villages which are much smaller than Leominster. Sometimes Ivo points around to yellow wheat-fields and sheep like I haven't seen those things before with my two eyes. I am thinking back to the pink sunsets I watched with Ambrose in our troupe-days and the lambs and the rivers we walked along just the two of us. Back then I did think those sights were something quite beautiful but in fact it was Ambrose who was beautiful and my ma was right all along. Those nice things like sunsets and meadows are all owned in this kingdom by the rich, and people like us will not ever be welcome to call them ours because this land is made up of two bad opposites and if you are not one then you are the other. Worse still if you are something different altogether.

'You see, Tibb, there are not so many eyes watching here.'

I do not like to add that I did wander in the countryside with my ma before she died in a hole and she found plenty of eyes along the way to show her tits to.

Churches creep past and little monasteries with stone arches and gardens because this land is stuffed full of them and my ma did say: 'Monks are not to be trusted, Tibb, and neither are nuns since they are some sly folk. And don't you remember we do not ever beg?'

Well there are country people swilling around this one like the ants found the butter. Something is happening and Ivo pushes forward. A feeling like panic is crawling around my neck because I am thinking of that grim day at Peterborough. 'Ivo!' I say, and I am reaching for his hand.

There are some stocks in front of this small stone monastery and a man has been locked in them, his head poking out the wood hole like a rabbit from a burrow, except his head is covered with a woman's cap, all laced and white. He is writhing but he is stuck fast.

Now I have seen people pilloried more times than I did steal fresh milk – for those rascal deeds such as vagrancy and not-wearing-a-cap-in-the-big-man's-house – but this crowd seems angrier. Theirs is a different kind of hatred and it is reminding me of that day at Peterborough. And these people are carrying all manner of vegetables and turned-rotten foods and they are raising them ready.

'Perhaps he stole a chicken, Tibb,' Ivo whispers hopefully but we both know it is something worse and that laced cap is in the middle of it all.

'The Church is to smite all people like you!' The monk there is stuttering and fat and bent over in his brown dress like he could use my matron's stick just now. His saggy eyes are wide like two great walnuts have been stuck upon his face, like he is frightened too, though he is the one to declare the punishment. I am remembering Father Brian who did smirk a lot at Peterborough, and whose silky movements told me his heart did not speed up at all. This monk looks nervous like a shrew.

The rabbit-man says, 'It was just a mistake, abbot! I misplaced that wool cap of mine!'

'Enough, sir,' the abbot says, but his eyes are roving across the muddy ground like he would rather be anywhere else. 'You have been caught twice in these clothings by your own God-fearing wife who judged it against nature . . . as I do!'

The woman called his wife nods a lot to the crowd and tuts, 'And finally you listen, abbot!'

'Ivo,' I whisper. 'Do something!'

The old abbot-man clears his throat and he is gaining some volume. 'We must be more vigilant to vice of all kinds,' he says and he glances back at the other sleepy monks who are gathered at the stone door and who are watching this thing like a clap of thunder did just crash over their own heads. I am thinking this old man did receive the same message as Ivo and he is shit-scared of Father Brian just the same. Perhaps he wishes to ward off the man with a scene such as this one. Who knows what other bad stuff like drinking and fucking those monks are up to in their fine stone house?

'You have not heeded the words of the Book of Deuteronomy, in which it states that the woman shall not wear that which pertaineth unto a man, neither shall a man put on a woman's garment: for all that do so are an abomination unto the Lord thy God!'

Now there is a striped hood shoved upon the poor man's head instead of that laced cap and this covers his face too, and Ivo is breathing quick and then holding his breath like he did back in Peterborough when we were witnessing such a cruel thing as the mutilation of those lovely men. And the crowd is jeering and throwing their wares, making that poor man call out.

'Please, Ivo!' I say. 'You are just as powerful!'

But I can see that tear roll down his cheek because of course he cannot speak up.

'Come, Tibb,' he whispers. 'We should go.'

And so we do.

We run. Like we did run from that beach except this is so much worse than the thought of a V upon our foreheads. I would take a V upon every part of me if that man could be spared the stocks. All because he thought to dress up like a woman and why should he not if that does make his heart sing?

Ivo stops in this copse and his muscly chest is heaving like there is a big dog jumping on it and we are shaking our heads since this is a sombre day. And that big sky above is crying too with a spit-spit-spit at first and then a downpour so we are sheltering under these trees.

There is a tumbling inside of me like the world just sneezed and now the snake is doing its squeezing game once more and there is a space between my ears which is getting larger and filling up with air and perhaps I will float away too.

Slowly Ivo puts those hands on my shoulders and he looks at me with those blue eyes all round.

'Tibb,' he says. 'Let's do it.'

'Do what, Ivo?'

'The boat. The island. All of it.'

Place a carpet

'It is a wonder of the world that you fit in there, Tibb!' or so says Flavio who does not know me well enough. Tomorrow is the day, and we are practising this trick yet again. For the fourth time I am stuffed here between the two wood screens that hang a little way over this rood-loft. Ambrose did shove me up here into this position, and the wings which have been washed of Mr Manners's blood are thin enough to fit in behind me.

'Just try it one more time, Tibb!' Ambrose shouts up once he is back on that stone floor.

'There is a certain tree-hollow in my memory which was smaller still!' I call down to him.

'And oyster shells, Tibb. I think you are well practised by now!'

Yes, sir!

I have my back against one screen and my flat feet against the other and I am folded up in between so there is some creeping feeling in my legs.

'Now!' he calls and I drop down into the rood-loft like the real human-person I am and I can't deny that big thud which is bouncing off the long windows and making the cats howl. The distance is only around five feet, or so said Ivo, but I have bruises under this costume already.

Ivo looks pale as he paces down the aisle. How quickly worry replaced all his sureness, and perhaps he is having those things called doubts about our money-making plan but he isn't saying, 'Enough, friends!' and 'What was I thinking?' because really he wants this as much as the rest of us.

'You are making too much noise,' he says, biting on his fingernails. 'And there is nothing angelic about it! Why can't you simply be here when they all come in? You could stand behind the altar there, and when I pull back the curtains, you will be facing us all?'

Would you ask this same question one more time, sir?

I lean over the railing. 'People are not stupid, Ivo. The congregation will just assume you have installed me there overnight. I must fall to Earth in front of their eyes and you must be taken by surprise just as much as they are. That way, there will not be one finger pointing at you if it all goes wrong.'

He does not seem to like the image of it all going wrong.

Ambrose says, 'I know! We simply need to place a carpet!' and he is slipping out of the oak doors into the night and returning from the vicarage with a small square of woven wool.

'See!' he says as he lays it out in the rood-loft. 'It's so thin it fits into this balcony like it was here all along.' And even Ivo can't deny that my landing is much quieter now.

Ivo has us all in the vestry afterwards to go through every tiny moment of the service tomorrow, though we know this plan like it was scratched on to the back of our hands, and mostly I am smoothing down this angel-costume so that thing is not entirely creased by the morning.

Flavio, that clever baker-man, has fashioned me a new dress. 'We cannot go into the tailor since he attends this church and he would recognize his own handiwork at once,' he said. So instead he has made me this gown all sewn together from his own white shirts and with a high neck since this is very churchly-looking, then of course those wings are poking out the back and the ropes hidden underneath. And tomorrow I will brush out my hair so it is white and silky like a curtain, and pull a white hood over my face so there is hardly an inch of me on display. A true angel of the highest godly order, Ma!

'You're sure this will work?' Ivo whispers once he has run through all the details yet again just in case the rotting people underneath this church did not quite catch them.

I bang him on the back. 'Ivo, all the priests across England are up to these naughty japes. Only ours will be better! It is just a little trickerie, you know.'

He widens his eyes like maybe this isn't much comfort to him.

'Anyway,' I add, 'it was you who did say that people will believe anything the priests tell them to.'

'That's true,' he says but he says it with a sad face and a sad voice and Flavio is studying him carefully.

'Can you think of a better way to make the monies for our run-away plan than a good miracle?'

'A false miracle, Tibb.'

Now I don't like this umm-ing and aah-ing too much when everything is all perfectly in place. 'The thing will be done so quick you will forget about it in a few days,' I say with a little laugh. 'I cannot think it will trouble you when you are sailing off to paradise, my friend!'

No answer, and I ask quietly, 'Ivo, are you in or are you out?'

He thinks a while. Too long in fact, and I am observing his carved-by-a-sculptor face and then the floorboards in this vestry which are all uneven.

'I'm in,' he says, but his voice is trampled-on like those clay paths my ma and I did take in search of the big-man's houses.

'Food!' Flavio says before anyone might change their mind, and off we go to the vicarage, though I cannot think even one of us eat will eat a piece of the roasted bird or the pottage this good man has stirred up because the morning is shuffling closer, Tibb.

Coming of the Lord

The seas have filled up and emptied again, and the birds have all flown south: this is how long I have been here, stuffed into position between these rood-screens. I am all trussed up in my costume and smelling of the rosewater which Ivo flicks around this church-place so often because angels are no common folk, Tibb. I rubbed that stuff into my skin so the sultans might sniff me out from Constantinople.

Finally the last of these slow-as-slugs parishioners come in and that chatter is stopping and they are all grunting to settle into their pews. Now I am just waiting for Ivo's little handbell and that smoke which means: almost ready, Tibb!

We have agreed that I should fall down some way into the sermon. Mostly, Ivo says, because people are deathly-bored by then and so a shock will be most welcome and all the more surprising since it will wake them from a half-slumber.

I can only see the church-goers when they are right below me but I can hear their chatter and my Ambrose saying, 'Yes, I am the new church-warden,' since these people have more snouts to poke in each other's business than a whole cattle-wagon of pigs.

Finally it begins, and Ivo is speaking of the suitable foods which a good and faithful person might think to eat. How complicated it all sounds, with this so-called abstaining ritual and the no-flesh-eating on those holier days, and I am thinking that you are some bad sinner, Tibb Ingleby. And then I am thinking that my legs are shaking and it is high time this angel did arrive. Fuck, Ma. And do you see me here?

Now, Tibb.

O, I am coming, my friends!

A bump. That is the noise I am making; just a bump to Earth from Heaven and that gasp below sounds like a wave. Like the water did crash upon the sand and all the gulls just stopped their shrieking. My heart is banging away and perhaps it will burst through my ribs.

Slowly, I stand, and I am adjusting myself and blinking heavily, peering down upon that congregation who are starting to stand up on their leather-booted feet. Some are pointing now, and some are cowering and others are whimpering at this sight and clutching at one another like I am a flesh-eating ogre. If I had not acquired such a thick skin in this oftentime-cruel life of mine, I should be quite offended by these horrified faces. I can see the fat baker-boss who I paid off and that landlord who directed me to Ivo and this is making me feel a little bit sick but 'An angel!' they start to say. 'An angel there!'

Now this is all going perfectly to our own plans, and such a hubbub below me. Tibb, you are a fine, fine actress.

Someone says, 'Quick, ascend to her, Father!'

'That chamber is boarded up, as you see!' says Ivo, pointing. 'And if she is a holy maid then we must keep our distance so as not to frighten her!'

'Father, Father?' the people say, and 'Who is this being? What is the meaning of it?'

Ivo puts a hand on his heart, his hat askew. 'I cannot know!' he says. 'Will I ask her?'

In fact, Ivo is turning out to be a decent-enough actor himself. I guess that is down to years of pretending to be someone-he-is-not. I peep at him from under this hood, and he is gazing up at me with that look of love in his eyes. The same way he did look at me when he said, 'Tibb, I buried her.'

'From where have you come, holy maid?' he shouts to me.

Well I do not answer because we practised this. Angels do not engage straight away. We are some wily folk besides.

'Are you an angel of some holy order?'

I incline my head. 'I am, Father,' I say, and there is a great hollering and a hoot-hooting from the audience.

This angel-voice is what Ivo calls *sincere*. 'Deeper, Tibb!' he said last night. 'And slow it down, would you? Angels are not in any rush, after all.'

Down there the people are all gasping still and speaking of Hail Mary and the prophets and the coming of the Lord upon the good Earth. This is easier than I expected – there is no convincing to be done!

'Draw the curtains, quick!' Ivo orders, and some of the church-going men are jumping up and pulling long curtains over the wine-coloured windows so they are all wearing their dresses too. Keep it nice and dark and there is less room for errors. So said Ambrose, who thinks of all the clever things. These clumsy metal wings do not need any hawk-eyes on them.

'Kneel everyone, at once!' Ivo says, and he rattles off a great deal of Latin prayers and a great many outpourings of gratitude for this present from the Almighty. And then he orders everyone to shut up with their chattering and listen and then slowly – very slowly – I am saying this: 'I am sent to you here by the God who reigns over you.'

'Sent to us?' Ivo repeats, a hand on his heart. 'We are humbled truly that we are the chosen people!'

I nod again. 'God is pleased with the piousness of the people here, and as such has sent me as a gift to fulfil your prayers.'

Another gasp from my audience and Ivo shakes his head like he cannot believe his own eyes and he turns to these starry-eyed watchers sitting in the pews. 'The Lord has thought it prudent that we are the congregation most deserving.'

Another hoot-hoot breaks out and Ivo raises a hand. 'Please, keep this news of our angel-guest close to your chests, my friends. Here is a secret for the people of this town alone. We cannot risk the angel becoming frightened and leaving us, and speaking to God of our poor charity and our bad hospitality. Might I trust you?'

Now there is a rumbling: 'You may!' I hear the churchly-people are well practised at saying things in perfect unison.

He tells them to make a good line outside. 'And when she is ready, then everyone might come and have a private audience, until she sees it fit to return to her place in Heaven.'

When that door is shut then I am swinging down like a monkey and my Ambrose does have me up on those broad shoulders of his. Such a fine and silent jig we are doing around this darkened church. We are lunatics in here with our shaky legs and our fists punching and our hoo-and-haa, and my cheeks are hurting from all this mad smiling. Ma, are you seeing this? A by-the-sea and under-the-stars roof is coming our way!

When we are all breathless enough from that panting dance and all the kicking then Ivo says, 'Now up you go again, Tibb. And remember – only take from the rich ones.'

'Stay with me, Ambrose,' I whisper down. 'You will have to be the angel-protector now.'

He says, 'Tibb, I have always been your angel-protector, even when you didn't know it,' and my heart is singing because of those kind words.

'Make a line!' Ivo is saying outside, and, 'Ladies and gentlemen, make a line!'

Very terrible thing

Those village fairs did always have a fortune-teller and my ma would make us stand in the line with the village-folk and wait our turn. I can remember just the way she would lean across and snatch her money back if she did not like the strange words being spoken, and swipe those picture-cards to the floor in a big rage. 'You are guileful, madam!' she would hiss, and 'Do you think I am stitched in wool?'

Well now I am that fortune-teller, except I don't have the clever skill-of-card-reading to entertain. I only have this placid nod and this empty promise of God's own redemption but it appears to be working just fine. I cannot much blame these people for falling for my bad trick; finally they might see something real for all their believing.

Most of them wish to kneel down and shout up names to me like Old Aunt Maud and Long Gone Papa. Dead people who I might watch over in the place-called-Heaven that they are all so very definitely sure about. Others wish me to speak with God about their nearly-dead relatives who perhaps don't need to die so soon, and that money I am collecting by way of payment is glinting in the candle-flames and I think that boat will come quicker than we did imagine.

'We could hardly have hoped for a better outcome, Ivo,' I whisper down when he does pop in here and eye-ball that great bowl of coins himself.

He nods slowly, like he did not ever see money before, and there is a greyness to his face. 'I can't say I feel too happy though, lying this way, and to good people besides.'

I think this man is one-foot-in and one-foot-out of this bad trick.

'Ivo,' I say firm. 'You know I am only taking the money from the rich ones because I am a vagrant at heart and I do know too well how the world is cut up into two halves.'

He sighs. 'Amen to that, Tibb.'

'Calm, please,' Ambrose says outside to the long line of angel-waiters, and 'Do not trouble the angel with your pushing and shoving out here, else she will surely depart!'

Now here is another couple asking for divine help and the good word of the angel-person. 'O, holy one!' they say, all dazed in their eyes, 'we have heard much of people who have come into wondrous things such as letters from saints, or who have woken up amongst a pile of Heaven's bread, but never an angel! We are blessed indeed!'

I do fancy a piece of that bread just now in fact.

They are speaking then of a small child going by the name of Elizabeth, which is my own real name too, and who is very poorly in their home.

'We are undone with our despair that she might be taken up too early and we are praying for your intervention, angel.'

'The Lord hears you,' I say, and I have said this very same thing to every visitor who is come here to stand between the pews and gaze up at me this morning, since I am of the opinion that the less-said-the-better because who knows how angels truly speak?

Now they are crying because these are some powerful-enough words to them. But my own ma is sitting on my shoulder and saying, 'A mug of beer solves all the problems of the body, Tibb, else a good tincture of herbs!'

'Have you given that child a nice tincture?' I ask.

'We cannot afford a thing.'

'Then would you poke your noses into that collecting-bowl and take out a good handful on your way out?'

Don't you know I am the Robin Hood of Leominster, Ma, and ho-ho-ho? O, I am having some warm feeling trampling up my spine as those people leave because life is some hard-enough plod in this shit kingdom, Tibb, and perhaps a false-angel is not such a very terrible thing.

Use the baker's box

There is some rumbling in my belly which is saying, 'Would you feed me, Tibb?'

'Go carefully,' Ivo says to my last visitor, 'and be sure to keep this secret to yourselves.'

He locks the church doors and finally I might quit this ridiculous expression. Angels are some mighty patient people to be so serene all the time.

Ivo and Flavio, those two sweet love-birds, are gripping each other around their necks and kissing on their lips and kicking their legs like the world is all a song.

'Ha!' I mouth, and 'My friends, we did it! Look at the money, we have filled up three vessels already!'

I climb over the railing and then hang off this balcony, sliding down the pillar beneath into Ambrose's arms, which is no angelic sight.

'Tibb, it is all working!' Ivo says, and he throws his arms around me. 'This thing will not take as long as we thought!'

That relief sprawled across his lovely face is something truly sweet and maybe he is settling into this fuck-the-world ruse at last.

I pull up my angel-sleeves. 'But will I come to the vicarage now and eat? I am hungry like a hunter. I did not think I would be so long up there—'

'No!' they say, and these faces are all lined with frowns while we stand together in this nave and the sound of people out there is trickling into my own ears.

'Why are they still out there, Ivo? You told them to leave and to keep quiet.'

Ivo puts those heavy hands of his on my shoulders and he smiles a little smile. 'Tibb, as someone who has not often done as you are told, you can surely imagine that those parishioners will not heed my words exactly. There will be people lurking till it is late, I think. You are a miraculous visitor after all.'

Hmm. Well this is a fine point and here is some worrying problem to boot, since you should consider your stomach first, Tibb. I did have my eyes upon those nice apples in the orchard and some of Flavio's fine cooking.

'But, what will I eat?'

Ambrose says, 'I will fill my pocket and I will bring for you a good meal later.'

'A good meal from your pocket?' I say, all slanty-browed like this is sounding not-so-good at all. 'Well do not scrimp on that nice bread of Flavio's. And I like it all slaked with butter and salt as you should know.'

Time is some slow beast and I am bored-stiff in this cavernous building, all lit up by candles since the world is quite shut out. The gnawing in my stomach is getting louder and so are those excited voices out there which are not filling me with happiness.

I have run my fingers over the keys of this organ-instrument, and opened my mouth as though to sing one of my ma's ditties such as the roof-song she did sing in her better moods, or the end-of-the-world song which she howled at the worst-of-times and which did mention those fuckers in every line. I should like to see her tonight, up in her sky-house, but Ivo said, 'Do not go out on that roof, Tibb, since you are visible to everyone up there.'

True, my friend.

Well I do have a little play at whipping my fingers through the candle-flames and would you come back now, Ambrose, with that dinner you promised?

I have rummaged amongst those wine bottles again which are hidden in the vestry and I have stood at the pulpit like Ivo does and waved my angel-hands about but this hungry feeling is shouting and screaming like a stuck pig which is no kind thing.

'What took you so long?' I say when Ambrose and Ivo finally return. 'I am famished! I think you have forgotten my stomach is a true mortal-stomach and it is now empty like a begging-bowl.'

In fact they look all nervous like two creeping vagabonds themselves and I cannot see any food bulging out of their pockets.

'We have been inundated with questions out there, Tibb,' Ambrose says, and he does put his big arms around me. 'You wouldn't believe the stir.'

'At this hour? Lift me on your shoulders, my man, and I should like to peep out myself.'

He lifts me up and I am nudging just a tiny inch of curtain to see all those angel-hunters surrounding this church. They are standing there in their numbers with their flame-torches and their lanterns and all of them wide-awake and watching this church like perhaps the big-man himself might just burst out the roof.

'Fuck!' I say. 'But they do not look like they are going home any time soon. Are they to starve me out?'

He rummages in his breeches and hands me over a piece of bread which is all mangled and squashed and with no butter on top of it.

'Just this? I will faint and there is nothing angelic about that. Besides, I have drunk every drop of water in that font-place and all the wine upon the altar a long time back.'

'Tibb,' Ivo says. 'We cannot bring you great joints of meat in our pockets, or a big bottle of beer. Those people might notice.'

Ambrose looks like there is a flame lit in his eyes. 'I know!' he says. 'We can use the baker's box!'

Off he goes into the vestry, returning with a large wooden box which has a good lid and which I have already checked for crumbs and morsels. 'I have noticed you, Ivo, carrying the bread over here for the Mass-taking each day.'

There is a sideways glance from Ivo's beautiful blue eyes, like he cannot tell where this is all heading.

'Flavio shall simply fill it at the vicarage with fine bread whenever you are hungry, Tibb, and Ivo will bring it over like a wolf in plain clothing, since this is an ordinary task of a vicar!'

Ivo looks like he is contemplating this plan, but what is there to contemplate, sir?

'Ah, Ambrose,' I say. 'Yet again you have proved yourself the very finest brain in all of England.' And I am chewing on my squashed dinner and swallowing it in two mouthfuls.

'But how will I use the pot when that urge is coming upon me? Surely those people will clear off soon enough so I might stick my white backside out the door of the vestry?'

Neither one answers this question.

Ivo grits his teeth. 'Tibb, I think these people won't be going away for some hours.'

This thought is something worrying but Ambrose says, 'I will pack a small pot each time, Tibb, and this is for your secret-doings. All you must do is replace it in the box once you have eaten the food and I will collect it later.'

‘Well then, we have an answer at every turn!’ I say, but my dear friend Ivo is coloured in grey like a pillar of marble and I don’t think he will look like Ivo again until this naughty trick is finished for good.

‘I wonder if we bit off more than we can chew,’ he whispers, and Ambrose and I are pretending we did not hear that part.

Doubled in size

Those shut-eyed curtains are not helping me decide when morning is arriving, but I am judging it by that shaft of light which is inching under the great wood doors and those birds outside which are singing, and then the people chattering too. By the sounds of it, there is a too-big crowd and I am thinking these people did not shut their mouths about me as Ivo did predict.

I rest my head on Ambrose's chest while those criss-cross beams above make themselves clearer. He slept in this church beside me because he did promise, 'Tibb, almost losing you to Mr Manners was too much to bear and I will never sleep a night without you again.' I think maybe he will regret that promise soon enough though because I am starting to smell like a barn.

That kind man Flavio does bring me some breakfast by way of the baker's box. This naughty trick is in slick operation already so at least I am not starving. Late last night I did peer in to see a feast fit for a king. Flavio's fine bread and also a fat hunk of cheese and a jug of beer. And I did give them a nice little treat in return because you are an animal, Tibb Ingleby.

'I have counted the monies from yesterday, Tibb,' Flavio says while I am eating this morning-food. 'And it amounts to a big fortune. A few more days and we will have enough.'

A feeling like hope is building and building in my innards. But how do these people have such a great number of coins? O, the world is some market for the rich, Tibb. Now here is something not-so-unfair any more, Ma.

'Enter quietly, my friends,' I hear Ivo say once I am all ready with my wings on, 'and let us hope she remains!'

That key is turning and the doors are thrown open and the sunlight is making me wince.

Well the people of Leominster do not shake Ivo's hand like last time they did come into this church since they are too busy pushing and shoving and gazing up to the rood-loft like they are stuck inside a trance.

'She remains!' they are saying, and 'The angel remains, Father!'

Well not one of them is watching their feet so they are bumping into each other in that aisle. And I am stiff like a pillar though my eyes are roving under this low hood and my heart is banging around like it would say: 'Tibb, would you let me out?'

There are so many people flooding in that they cannot even fit upon these pews, such are the big numbers of angel-hunters. So much for keeping secrets; I should say that everyone has told their sister, who has told their aunt, who has told their friend, and now we are full up to the brim in here. There are people spilling into the aisle and out of the door! That sunlight streams in and I am thinking of my knocked-up-by-a-rude-man wings and the fact they are not so convincing in the daylight.

'I see my congregation has doubled in size,' Ivo says at the pulpit. 'On account of the angel that has graced us, no doubt.'

I can hear that bad note of worry in his voice and I should say I am sharing the same. I did not imagine this thing would grow so very large, and I have not been an angel two days yet.

'And so we see that this precious angel of the Lord is with us still.'

An old man stands from the pew and holds his cap to his chest. 'It is your own faith, Father Ivo. Your faith and your kindness is such that a Heavenly sign is gracing the likes of our own parish.'

I think I can almost see my dear friend shrinking at that, and the blood inside my not-very-angelic body is faltering and swimming backwards.

'And so let us begin our prayers,' Ivo does say, and I am thinking that you have made a criminal of a good man, Tibb Ingleby.

One of the parishioners stops Ivo as he leaves. 'Your new warden,' he says, pointing over to Ambrose. 'I think I did see a lute-player with just this colouring, not far from here . . . in Redditch perhaps . . .'

'Not this one,' Ivo says with a laugh, but here is some dark feeling slinking into my bones which my own ma would call menacing.

Rather lovely cushions

'Now for the evening Mass, Tibb. Would you put those wings back on?'

'Fuck, Ivo, there's *more*? I'm exhausted!'

Today we did make six more bowls of monies and Flavio has been counting it all inside the vestry. I must have held over a hundred interviews from up here. More mothers all lined in their faces with worries about sickly babies and the Heaven-place and the expensive seats there. I did want to tell them: 'You think a real God-person would have you pay for peace?' This stuff they believe is all thin like dripping-sand, and yet they are still lining up outside because of it. I did not take monies from those mothers of course. Nor did I take it from those people who I had a little suspicion were wanderers like me, owing to their not-belonging faces as they trod with their bare feet on the stone floor.

From the rich fuckers I did demand coins, though, because I don't have shit for brains. The searchers of more and more. Searchers like the cordwainer who want more money and more land and more women to chew up and spit out. I can sniff out those people like they do carry a smoking taper behind them.

Then there was one woman who looked up and asked me, 'Would you have my tits swell up to twice the size, angel? Since I have struggled to find a husband with no tits to boast about?' And I did stop myself from winking and leaning over this railing to tell her, 'Now my ma did beg for bigger ones just the same. And you should see the fine bulbs on my one-time friend named Maria!'

This evening congregation is bursting out the doors, and these Latin prayers are sending me off to the land-of-dreams but angels do not yawn, Tibb. Nor do they have hog-breath either. I have a hankering for some of that fine wine they are all gulping from Ivo's goblet. No wonder these people all like the big-man so much.

When it's over at last there are two stragglers who are sitting on the back row and I can see they are not moving one tiny inch. And they are looking to me and then to Ambrose who is doing his warden duties until he sees them and then he stops quite still.

'Goodnight, my friends,' Ivo is saying, which is a nice way of asking: 'Would you fuck off?' But I am holding up my angel-hand because I can see exactly who those people are with my own two eyes.

'Father Ivo,' I say in my best angel-voice. 'God would have you lock that door.'

Well I should say these angry thoughts are scampering around inside of me, and I am swinging down from my loft-home with a face like a thunder-clap once that door is locked, and Ivo is staring at me as though I am gone mad. What are you doing, Tibb? he is thinking. And would you get back up there already? But he does not know these people like I know them.

'Ambrose!' they are saying and they are reaching up to wrap their arms around his neck and he is smiling back because he is the owner of that kind thing called forgiveness.

'So,' I say, with my arms crossed in front of my chest. 'Now you turn up for your old friends?'

'Tibb?' she whispers. 'Is it you?'

'Of course it is me, Maria.'

Well she laughs some belly-laugh and throws her heavy arms around me but I am not moving a muscle and John the juggler is looking like he has seen a real ghost-person.

'Tibb?' she says again.

Fuck off, Maria. That sentiment is sprawled across my face so I don't even need to say it.

'Listen, Tibb. We woke in the morning at that great house in Wilmcote and you and Ambrose were both gone, and Signor said that you had decided to leave together at once because a friend of Lord Fielding offered the both of you to be installed at his house as entertainers. To be paid a mighty wage each week for the pleasure!'

Well this is some horse-shit just here.

'And you believed him? You do not think I would have said goodbye to you – my dearest girl-friend?'

She is all red in her cheeks like when she lifts haybales and groans with the great weight. 'I know it now, Tibb—' she starts to say but I am too riled up to listen.

'I was sold, Maria! Sold to a very un-mannered man to do very un-mannerly things. A gentleman-friend of Lord Fielding. And Ambrose was left for dead!'

Ambrose is watching me and he lays his hand on my shoulder because he can see I am all shaken up with my rage.

Maria looks so anguished, I wonder if the ants did crawl beneath her skin and pull her face in all directions.

'Really we should have known it, Tibb,' says John. 'But we were just pleased for you and Ambrose to have been offered such a hand of fortune. Then we were performing at Kidderminster just yesterday and we heard some talk of an angel-woman with such strange colouring at Leominster and this sounded too familiar.'

'So what did you do?' I ask.

'Well all of us confronted Signor Perero who tried to weasel out as usual, and we added two and two together,' Maria says. 'The acrobats tied those scaly hands behind Signor's back and covered his eyes from this bad world and his mouth from shouting, and it was me who had the great pleasure of tossing him in the back of a potter's cart bound for Scotland.'

Well this is sounding more like it. Signor tossed into a wagon and sent up the country to the land of prickly heather and snow and warrior-people which my ma did tell me of. Surely it is some fitting end for that not-so-Spanish man?

'Then the acrobats took the tents and they are travelling down south as we speak to hop upon a boat to Calais,' John continues. 'With all their best regards for you, since they are fed up with this place just as we are.'

Maria says quietly, 'Am I really, Tibb? Your dearest girl-friend?'

My chin is still jutting upwards. 'Well I thought so once,' I do mutter through gritted teeth, and now I have those great bosoms in my face and here are two rather lovely cushions and don't you know frowning does give you wrinkles, Tibb?

'O, my friend,' she says once we are finished with this tight-enough embrace, 'I will not be leaving you ever again and you can trust me on that.'

Well this is some beautiful thing to say, and I am feeling that lump in my throat like this world just got a little bit brighter.

'But what about those nice dreams you had, Maria?'

She waves her hand and shakes her head in a not-very-Maria way.

'That place of my dreams does not exist. At least not in England, and so at least I might surround myself with friends and that will have to be enough for me.'

Now I am thinking there is something very wrong about hearing those giving-up words from the mouth of my big friend Maria. They are so like those words Ivo said just recently about the separate-rooves plan. But mostly I am thinking that these two people must love me very much to have come back for a girl named Tibb.

Tents, Ma?

Here we are, Ma. One patchwork man and that is Ambrose, one dark and good-to-look-at baker which is Flavio, one handsome vicar, one haystack-wielding Flemish woman, a tall and thin juggler named John and a false-angel. And we are sitting in the vestry and Maria and John are both open-mouthed at our grand plan.

'And not one of us will work a jot, except you of course who would take some delight in that, Maria. Instead we will be fishing those warm seas and eating fruits and we will be living as Ivo and I did live in Norfolk which was the happiest time in our lives.'

Quietly, Maria leaves and slips back in with the almost-empty wine vessel from the altar, and she holds it up regardless. 'To us, my friends. I have seen enough of everyone else for a lifetime.'

Now here's something to drink to, Ma! Those crowds outside sound like they would pour a cup and take a sip to boot.

'Tibb,' she says, 'you know I have brought you that crown. I would have melted it down if I hadn't found you. And would it not be the finishing touch? A fine halo?'

Here it is too – the crown which Signor Perero did have knocked up at a blacksmith's tent. Well I am ramming it on my head and observing my face in that metal goblet and if I looked angelic before, then now I must be the mother-called-Mary herself.

'How many more days of money-collecting, Flavio?' I ask, since he is the counting-person.

He says, 'I should say just one, Tibb.'

'But that is perfect! The thing will be done so quick!'

Ivo swallows hard, shaking his head. 'I am losing my nerve. I didn't imagine there would be so many people. You know some have even brought tents, Tibb. They mean to sleep out there to be first in tomorrow. How do we ever get you out of here, when we are surrounded at all times?'

Tents, Ma? Now this is no pleasant thought.

'Ivo,' I say slowly because I do not have shit for brains, 'I have been thinking of this exact problem. And here is the answer: when we have made enough monies, then I shall just be disappearing off to Heaven, and by that I mean I will run up to the bell-tower and hide out there. And when those people of your parish come in for their service, they will say: "Such a shame she is gone but at least we might be the only town in England to have been visited by an angel!" '

Ivo looks grim, like he is not feeling so good about this escaping-plan, but we do not have another, sir.

He says, 'I wonder it is best to get you out while we can. People will begin to ask questions. The very fact that Maria and John have found you here . . . Shouldn't you hide up in the bell-tower tomorrow morning?'

Tomorrow morning, sir? This wine has stopped half-way to my own lips. Is he serious? Would he stop short of collecting the funds for our life-of-bliss when we have come this far? I catch Flavio's dark eyes which are heavy at the thought of wasting all these efforts, and I place my hands on Ivo's shoulders. They seem to droop down with the weight. 'Ivo, it is just one more day and then we are quite finished.'

He nods slowly, but there are thoughts squirming around inside that lovely head that he is not sharing, and I have seen this same expression on my Ivo's face before when I did drag him to a rabbit-door in the land of Norfolk.

★

When my friends are all gone to the vicarage, Ambrose takes off my wings and we lie on our backs in this rood-loft home of mine. He has brought me some cloves and a tooth cloth to rub on my teeth because of the stinking-like-a-hog problem and he has told me, 'That is far better, Tibb,' which is quite probably a lie. And even that rosewater does not cover the stench of my own arm-pits and in fact I need a long soak in a cold river, or just to dance in the rain which my ma did swear by for more reasons than just ecstasy.

I study the criss-cross beams high up in that ceiling and my Ambrose is falling straight to sleep with his arm around my shoulder. Those crowd sounds are trickling in here under the door but I am thinking of that secret hankering for a little person of our own named Henrietta who I would look after much better this time, Ma. How I did like that hot heaviness in my arms.

'Perhaps, Ma,' I whisper up towards those beams and I can see her lovely face in my mind too. Those kind and frightened eyes which wanted a home for us so badly, and all that guilt inside of them when she did spend the monies on beer instead.

I can hear that low chatter rumbling out there but this is something like a lullaby. My hair is all spread out around me and I have undone these robes to scratch at all the sweaty parts of me. There is a calm sort of happiness gathering up inside my guts and I am thinking of rooves. The best kind: the by-the-ocean and under-the-stars kind, and with the people who are really the roof themselves.

Perhaps she was right. Perhaps it wasn't my fault, what happened with Farmer O. Because if I was so very bad as he did put it to me, then I wouldn't have this good fortune by way of an island, but only bad rewards. That is how it works – so said Farmer O – the big-man does punish all the baddies so perhaps I'm not one after all. Now here is something sweet to dream of, Tibb.

Leominster, Herefordshire

His dreams are startlingly clear in here. As he drifts in and out of wakefulness, his brain tired from the lack of food, he finds they are burgeoning and swelling and he can't decipher which are real and which are false. He dreams of a Spanish baker. The dark softness of his skin; his thick eyelashes. Is he real, or just imagined?

Familiar images lumber past and then an island – he sees it clearly. An island bathed in sun, secluded in the ocean, wreathed with strange and wonderful trees and glistening shallows. A place like this is surely too beautiful to exist, and yet he is sure that Tibb said they would run away to it. Run away. But is it running away when you are so delighted to leave?

He imagines the warm air, the salt on his skin. The feeling of the ocean around his ankles. He imagines the puckered skins of bright fruits. The fresh fish he would eat. Is he there now? Is this the reason for these pungent smells?

He stirs, wrinkling his nose, rubbing his face and the beard which Tibb used to cut with an oyster knife.

'I'm sorry for you,' the warden said earlier. 'You're a good man, Father, as I said all along.'

Is he?

Perhaps he feels so wretched down here in this cellar because he allowed himself to imagine a place for people like him in this world. A real home. An island, where he might be free. Why did he let himself believe it? People like him must live only inside their heads. Folding in on themselves till they become so small that nobody can see them. Tibb has stars in those blue eyes. She deals in perfect visions of impossibilities. She doesn't notice the rabbit-holes hiding in the meadow, only the lush grasses and the flowers, though she has found herself in many rabbit-holes in this life. He should have put a stop to it. A greeting in a bakery each morning is surely better than nothing.

The question is crystallizing in his mind: is it better to live in a small way, or not to live at all? He cradles his head in his hands like this would stop the thoughts, because how many times can a man ponder the same bloody question?

Little eye-glasses

Such a yawn, Tibb, the flies will fly in. I should say I am awake before the sun, and with Ambrose in this cosy loft beside me. The good people of Leominster are jabbering out there like geese already since they did camp outside. How's that for a birdsong, Mr Manners?

Eventually Ivo and Maria unlock that door and they do pant in like they have muscled through a herd of cows. O, I do not like this grim look on my dear Ivo's face, or this churning in my stomach like this is all your own fault, you devil-child.

Ivo says, 'Bad news. We are to be visited any moment by two rectors from parishes nearby at Eyton and another from Kimbolton, who have heard about you. They're coming to stay with me, and I cannot turn them away since we are suspicious enough already!'

Fuck.

'Well how long will they stay?'

He shrugs.

'We can hope they won't trouble us long,' I say, and 'They must be busy men, besides!' but my voice is flat like a pancake.

It is some woeful thing to see Ivo's broad shoulders so tense and high around his ears again. And suddenly I am not much liking the sound of those crowds outside. It seems I am surrounded in this place and I am feeling something like panic creeping up my throat because of it. Live the life you dream, Tibb! Well I am trying, Ma, and yet it is one thing after another to stop us.

He says, 'Just keep doing what you were doing, Tibb. More than anyone, we can't have priests casting doubts over this.'

Constancy, Tibb. Constancy is what you must have before you whip out the blade. Give no cause for alarm. But there is cause for it and my head is full up of worries for my dear friend Ivo.

He shakes his head. 'I should wonder they are jealous, since they are not garnering any money from their relic tricks while everyone is come here instead. It takes a fraud to know one.'

So many thoughts are swarming me at once. I would bat them away if they had wings and I am resting my fingers on my temples like this would make them stop but it doesn't because I think we might be teetering on the edge of being royally fucked.

'So this is the angel,' they say.

'Speak softly, Fathers, I beg you,' Ivo tells them, opening his arms like a big bat. 'Behold the miracle we are sent.'

Their churchly-garb is the colour of wine and they are both far older than Ivo, staring up to me not so much with that misty-eyed look of awe which I have grown accustomed to, but more like studying-of-the-stars people with their foreheads bunched. They are taking out their little eye-glasses and shooting up stares, squinting in the candle-light like they would thread needles.

'Father Ivo, you received her here like this, up there in the rood-loft?'

'Yes, Father Cuthbert, when she came down to Earth in the middle of a service.'

'There were other witnesses to it?'

Ivo nods. 'My whole parish in fact.'

This Cuthbert priest has a very long and pointed nose which he is stroking with his index finger and this is something strange to me. Would your nose like a cup of milk besides? It is unsettling how close he is; standing there almost underneath me. Perhaps they might see the scratches on this not-so-fine crown and smell my clove-breath.

'She entered through the roof?' he asks, peering up into that narrow space where I did wait. 'But there is no hole up there in the stonework and that gap between the screens is too small to fit a *dog*. How on earth did she pass through?'

Ivo chuckles like he expected that and he says, 'Well that's just it, Father! She is no earthly being and she moves in supernatural ways.'

Would you breathe quieter, Tibb? You are a dead person after all. I think the fishermen will hear my breath in the seas of Constantinople.

'And she hasn't left the place since?'

This is the other one, and I should say he looks like a scribing pen. All skinny with his little ankles poking out the bottom of that dress.

Ivo shakes his lovely blonde head. 'No, Father Reynolds. A few days now she has graced us here.'

I am wondering where my clever Ambrose thought to hide that bowl of monies I made just this morning. I did demand a great sum from one so-called physician who wore two golden ear-rings and who my own ma would have called a leech. And more still from those shady London merchants who flog their wares for twice the price, Tibb.

'And she prefers the dark?'

Those priests cast their eyes to the drawn curtains and the flickering candles which Ambrose is replenishing daily.

'As you see,' Ivo says. 'The quiet and the dark.'

'How long will she stay?'

'I cannot know. She is staying in God's grace.'

There is some trail of terror slinking through me. Sweat is

gathering on my forehead where that hood and my new crown are sitting because I know my Ivo is quaking on the inside.

'Well then, she is an angel of vast generosity,' Father Reynolds says, and there is something disbelieving about his tone. 'I am surprised though, Father, that the Lord would single out this church, because it has come to our attention that you are not scrupulous in the correcting of your parishioners.'

Ivo stiffens.

'In *our* parishes, Father, it is a weekly ritual that adulteress women are brought forward and shamed with the shedding of their clothing and the holding of lighted tapers. But I have not ever heard of such rigorous scrutiny here . . .'

My Ivo is not responding.

'And you will have heard there is an even greater mould sprouting amongst our people which must be scraped off – worse by far than the transgressions of women and their natural inclination to whoring and adultery. Worse than any other sin of the flesh.'

O, Ivo, I can hear your breath from here.

'Sodomites,' Father Reynolds says.

Well I wish to remove this heavy crown and rest my head on this wooden rail. Ivo is like a marble gargoyle down there. He clears his throat and says, 'But I am always alert to such crimes against God, though I've seen nothing in my parish yet.'

They turn their attention to Ambrose who is loitering at the door and they grimace which is nothing new. 'And who is *that*, Father?'

'Well this here is my church-warden,' Ivo says quick, though even that seems to raise their suspicions. I do not like the way they ogle Ambrose; like he is a fly for swatting.

They pace between the pews and rub at their faces as though they might find some answers in those crevices and Father Cuthbert is stroking and stroking his nose.

'And you are certain, Father Ivo? You are certain she is truly from God?'

Ivo gasps. 'What are you suggesting, Father? You will blaspheme in this way, in the Lord's own house? You would think to deny this servant of God?'

They say, 'No!' and 'No, Father!' since ours is a scary world where naysayers are strung up for bad words pertaining to the King and the country or else the big-man-God. But those heavy-lidded looks and those furtive glances are still passing between them. My face is aflame beneath this hood which is not helping the appearance of death.

'She speaks?' they ask Ivo.

'She speaks sparingly.'

'And which language?'

Ivo says, 'Our own tongue, English.'

'Hmm,' they say, 'I should have assumed it would be Latin that she spoke since this is God's own language.'

I can see that twitch of Ivo's shoulders and that give-away clearing of his throat. Would you pull it together, my friend?

'Yes, it is strange and perplexing but God works in mysterious ways, I have found time-and-again.'

They nod to this. 'Of course, of course.'

Ivo says quietly, 'My brothers, this goodly angel has chosen my church and to speak with my own parishioners, and I shouldn't wish to stand in the way of God's plans. While she is here we must respect her privacy. Please, use my vicarage as you will. There is plenty of food on my kitchen table and I keep a fine cook.'

Those men are rubbing their tums as Ivo shows them out, but there is a wet slick of sweat between my bulbs and across my head because Father Cuthbert and Father Reynolds will be in the same house as Ivo and Flavio who are in fact in love.

Trace of you

Would you let a cat take the kippers, Tibb? No, Ma, and only a fool would toss pennies in the mud. Even on the worst-of-days, because who knows when next you might come across one?

I have those rich people tipping their coins into the big collecting-bowl, and when that is full, into an urn from the vestry. All that fine metal is catching the candle-light and glittering up on the ceiling like the fireflies did swarm the place.

'Would you pray on that business of mine, angel?' that rich man shouts up and I do not appreciate the tone of it or the fact that his wool cap is still perched upon his fat head. Manners are free, sir. Did you know that?

'Your business?' I ask.

He nods and nods. 'My own flour mills which are plentiful in this land of Herefordshire. I should want to make triple the fortune this year!'

'Sir,' I say, 'an offering of money might help me remember your prayers,' and he is nodding again like he expected that. Mostly I am thinking of the crowds which are getting louder and the priests who are still here and who are not showing one sign of leaving. Maria and John are circling this town for the purposes of listening-for-opinions-of-the-angel and quelling-any-doubts.

'What are those wings formed of, Father Ivo?'

Father Reynolds and Father Cuthbert have been popping in here all day between my audiences and now those eye-glasses are out again, glinting in the candle-light.

'How can I know?' Ivo says quick. 'It is all Heavenly stuff of course.'

They say 'hmmm' and 'hmm' like they aren't too sure and they do peer at those collecting-bowls like two greedy magpies.

Ivo clears his throat. 'Now, my friends, I wish to have some privacy so I might sit in prayer with the angel,' and those two priests have to leave because this is Ivo's own church and not theirs.

'Come to the vestry, Tibb!' he whispers up to me.

Down I climb and, 'Tibb,' he hisses, 'what's going on? We agreed no more collecting!'

'Well I am only taking from the rich ones, Ivo—'

'No!' he says, and he is forgetting to whisper now. 'Those two priests are turning green over this—'

'I'm just thinking of the boat!'

He has his head in his hands. 'I'm scared of these men, Tibb. They are all-powerful.'

'You are powerful too, Ivo. This is *your* church.'

He takes me by the shoulders and he speaks slow, like I am not understanding quite well. 'Don't you see? It's not the boat we must worry about now, but our lives.'

I think my Ivo is panicking.

'We've got to end this thing. The longer you stay, the more chance the priests have to find fault with it, and I do not like all their whispering and their questions. And soon enough we will attract even more of them to poke holes in this ruse.'

I nod because my Ivo is right of course. 'Then I'll hide in the bell-tower, Ivo. I'll do it tomorrow.'

'It won't do, Tibb,' he says, and his voice sounds like the sun did pack up and fuck off for good. 'Those two priests will be checking everywhere once they see you are gone. They will be searching every nook of this place with their eye-glasses – we mustn't leave a trace of you. Already they are walking the perimeter of this church like guarding-dogs.'

My eyes widen. Now here is a feeling inside me called terror, Ma, and this is making the hairs on my arms jump up and shriek.

'But, Ivo, if I can't get out, however will we end this piece of trickerie?'

Do these men mean to smoke me out like a rabbit?

He rubs around his eyes and then his neck. 'This is exactly the problem, Tibb,' he whispers, and it is some dreadful thing to see this scared expression on such a handsome face as Ivo's. He looks like a too-old Ivo again with those eye-bags and his brow bunched. The whole world is on those lovely shoulders and that is all my own fault because I did draw him into this great deception, though my Ivo is no bad fucker like Tibb Ingleby.

'I will solve it, Ivo,' I offer thinly, and 'Think of the island-home!' but this is some feeble dream just now. I believe he is thinking mostly of the noose.

Their hawk-eyes

Ambrose and I are like two weeds in this vestry, all tangled round each other.

'Tibb,' he says, 'don't lose hope. I know we'll think of something.'

What makes this person so sure, when in fact the end is glaring at us in the face? Ivo was right – if we can't finish this thing soon, it's not the island we will be waving goodbye to, but life itself. The truth is, we are surrounded on all sides and I am trapped in this church-place without an escaping-plan and those priests are not going anywhere fast.

I run my finger around the edges of the baker's box and lift those stale crumbs to my lips which are dry and flaking owing to the not-much-to-drink problem. Ambrose's flecked-with-gold eyes widen like he just saw a ghostly-person.

'Ambrose?'

I watch as he pulls the box towards him, though I have eaten every part of the contents already, and he says, 'Tibb, don't you remember when you first showed Signor the talent you have at making yourself very small?'

I can't think why he would mention it now. Signor has been carted up to the bare lands of Scotland to be eaten by all those terrible beasts which do lurk in the heather.

'Yes, sir,' I say. 'Though I didn't see *you* watching.'

'I was, Tibb. And I remember it now – it was around the same size as this box.'

This grand idea is hopping from his own head to mine and

now I catch your meaning, sir! We are staring at one another like the words have floated through the air between us.

'Try it,' he says, and I think neither of us are breathing much.

Well I am climbing in and lying on my side with my knees up round my ears and I tip my head down into my chest so I am the shape of an egg and Ambrose slides across the lid.

'Ha!' he says, though that sweet sound is muffled from in here. 'I knew it! This is perfect, Tibb! This is how we can get you out. I will simply carry you like I did when you were in the oyster shell. I've been carrying this box to-and-fro for Ivo's Mass services each day, or rather for your sustenance!'

He removes the lid again and stares down at me. The thought of escape is whistling through my head-thoughts and making this building turn all shades of yellow.

'You truly think so, Ambrose?'

He lifts me out. 'Of course! It's perfect—' he begins to say, and then we see them. My metal wings which I cast off and which have caused my skin to peel red raw under my arms and against my shoulder blades. Here is a silence for the night-beasts, Ma.

'There's no way they can fit in the box too,' I whisper and there is a feeling like all my blood is trickling down to my feet.

Ambrose is nodding quietly and thinking, his fingers pressed against his head, but what's the point, sir, when there is no possible tincture for this new problem? We can't carry the wings out underneath a robe either. Not with the prowling priests and their hawk-eyes. They're too bulky. That fucker called Mr Manners did not have one skill at metal-work, much like he did not have a skill at the dice or the deck.

Ambrose's lovely eyes wander this building, as though he might find a place to hide two enormous wings, but of course there is nowhere.

He says slowly, 'Perhaps we could hide them up on the roof . . .'

I shake my head. 'Leave no trace, Ambrose. Didn't Ivo mention that?'

'At least *you* would be safe, Tibb—' he begins to say, and I am imagining the priests sifting through this place once I am gone and finding the wings and condemning my own friends to death because of me.

'No,' I say firm. 'I won't hear of it.'

Most generous patron

Two more days did pass because I cannot escape this rabbit-burrow and I stink like a goat and those two priests show no signs of leaving. In fact, more priestly-men are cropping up like this place caught the pox. Half a dozen today, or so says Ambrose who has the skill-of-counting. They are all the same in their wine-coloured robes and their bejewelled fingers and their saying of 'It's a miracle!' when in fact they mean, 'We do not believe a word you say, Father Ivo, and we will have your not-so-little trick all revealed.' Here are some jealous-as-fuck priests who are taking notes for their own false miracles and their money-stealing. O, Ma. I should not have kept collecting – I think I did make this bad trumpery altogether worse than it already was.

'This trick should have been over by now,' Ivo whispered this morning with his lovely head in his hands. Yes, my friend, but here is another day with an angel and I can't see a single way out unless the rain does fall and have those tent-people and these nosy priests fuck off inside. This summer drought did come at just the worst time, and now that sorry word and this panic feeling are one bad potion inside of my body.

Father Reynolds tells these new priests, 'Do go over to the vicarage, there is a very fine cook who makes all manner of sweet buns and cakes. We are enjoying our stay immensely with such a grand spread of refreshments!'

He says it like this is his own house and like Flavio is his own slave to order around. You are taking some fucked-up liberties there, sir. And don't you know the show is over?

While our old friends Father Reynolds and Father Cuthbert return to their task of being guarding-dogs outside, those other priests follow Ivo to the vicarage to stuff their faces, all of them dribbling at the thought of pastries and pies. Except one. Now here is a grey-haired straggler we didn't bargain for.

Ambrose says to this left-behind priest, 'Father, we will let the angel rest now,' but that wrinkly man is fingering his chin and the wiry hairs which spring from it like he should pull out those thoughts one-by-one.

'I must tell you,' he says, and I don't much know who he is speaking to, 'that I have been puzzling over a strange event. You see, I am from the church at the village of Inkberrow.'

I do not know how this should interest me, sir. Would you fuck off besides?

'There is a gentleman in my parish who has been a regular to my confession-box these last few years owing to his great need for the gambling table. A Mr Manners, he is called.'

That name smacks against the pews and makes them all shake. Fuck, Ma. Ambrose and I are looking at one another but without moving our heads. Only our eyes.

'But then he stopped coming so I checked upon him and do you know there was nothing left in his house? And he had a friend who came also to enquire, since Mr Manners had missed two gambling parties. A most generous patron of the church at Wilmcote, not fifty miles from here – a Lord Fielding.'

Well I am gripping this wooden rail like the world might melt and turn to oceans beneath my feet. And my poor Ambrose is looking for words – I think he is burying a hole to Constantinople in his search – but those things are all stuck inside his throat.

The priest rocks on his heels. 'I told the Lord Fielding, "Sir, even the most faithful to God will take their own lives – and Mr Manners was a troubled soul," but perhaps I was too quick in my judgement. You see, the Lord Fielding was full up of tales of a gambling party where Mr Manners bought a girl fair and square and he seemed to think this person marked the demise of his good friend. A pale girl with white hair. Tiny stature, so he said. An actress.'

His eyes drift up to this rood-loft house and I wish to tug my hood lower and hide every part of me, and didn't I teach you about the fuckers, Tibb? The crows will dine on our own heads like kings, Ma.

'The Lord Fielding was told by her previous owner that this girl was an impertinent thing. A little viper . . .'

Ambrose is all shiny and staring at the eyes. He clears his throat and he says, 'This is an angel of God. She is not an actress, Father, nor a viper. She does not know anything of Wilmcote or Inkberrow since she dropped here from the skies and there are witnesses to attest to it.'

The priest nods and nods. 'Well quite, and I admit it did not once cross my mind when I set out to meet an angel yesterday morning. I confess I did not spare a thought for Mr Manners all the way here, with the reins in my hand and the wind in my hair. But you see there is another small detail which has my mind in knots. The thing is, I heard from some of my parishioners that not long back there was a certain stranger, coloured in by Satan they said, who was poking around the village for directions to Mr Manners's house. I hear he was bloodied and quite desperate in his search – he terrified my good parishioners—'

Fuck and fuck, Ma. I think I am formed of feathers up here and my head is full of air and the panic flooding my mouth tastes like a butcher's shop. That priest is glaring at Ambrose like the cat did find the mouse, then he pokes him in the chest with a bulbous finger. 'And so you see I have two reasons now for my doubts. What do you say in answer to *that*, sir?'

Ambrose is choking on his words. 'I have not been to any such village since I am a church-warden just here with Father Ivo.'

'Ah, sir. But I hear whispers out there – a certain lute-player that people are reminded of.' He narrows his eyes. 'Who *are* you, sir? And who is *she*?'

Speak, Ambrose. Anything!

The priest laughs. 'Well if you will not provide an answer then there is nothing else for it. I shall fetch the Lord Fielding himself, and there we have our proof. How does that sound?'

Hot meat pies

There is an image hanging in this vestry like the devil-person did sew a tapestry. My friends at the block and the axe-man waiting behind. Can they see it too?

Ambrose says, 'We can't have that man reach Lord Fielding and bring him here – that would be the end of everything.'

Maria and John are open-mouthed since they did watch the exchange from the vestry, and we are like four crayfish stuffed in pastry, all limp and pale. I am thinking of Lord Fielding turning up here, saying, 'That's her! I would recognize her anywhere! And there is the coloured-in man who gave me two black eyes! And the big woman who danced on the table in my gambling room!'

We are quiet and then Maria stands slowly and I don't much like that look upon her face. 'Here is a task for a Flemish woman, my friends.'

'Maria?' I say.

She flexes her muscles. 'I mean to track down that carriage, Tibb. And I shall make it my business that the priest inside of it is not reaching the Lord Fielding any time soon.'

'But that man will be far away from here already.'

'Ah, now don't you know I'm a big country girl? I did run the sheep into pens in the land of Antwerp.'

There is something sorrowful about Maria's face when she says, 'See you soon, Tibb. And don't you let them get you,' because she knows about the fuckers as well as I do.

When she and John are gone then I put my head in Ambrose's lap. You are some sour-hearted bitch, Tibb Ingleby.

Don't you know you are putting your friends in the way of danger? Don't you know a man called Mr Manners is dead because of you? And a baby named Henrietta besides? I did always know that farmer had it right.

My halo is digging in above my ears. Standing so long with all this metal-work and these heavy robes is some troublesome thing and I am thinking of that priest who has sewed up the clues and who has gone to fetch the Lord Fielding himself. My Ivo said, 'Tibb, continue as the angel for the time being. Keep them believing while we consider our plan for your escape.'

What plan, my friend? I cannot think of a single way out of here.

'I will recommend you to God,' I tell that person down there. How many times will I promise the same empty stuff? And with no coins to make it bearable either.

News is some quick-spreading thing. Like the pox, or so said my own ma. It is making my guts writhe to hear of the long journeys each angel-pilgrim has taken. 'We are come from Shrewsbury, angel, for this end.' Else: 'We have travelled from Tettenhall to be here.' One man I am told is coming from the area of Devizes. So long as you are not coming here from Wilmcote, sir.

'These people are not going anywhere,' Ambrose hisses up in between my interviews. 'In fact, that crowd is getting bigger and bigger. There are hundreds of tents outside now, Tibb, and the priests are checking everyone in the line like we are all in cahoots. There are water sellers out there, and a woman selling hot meat pies. She's racking up a small fortune.'

This yawn would have the cats howling because I did not get a wink of sleep last night. One bad image was keeping me awake, namely Lord Fielding clambering up the pillar and prising my eyes apart. Then I was picturing Mr Manners who is dead and who we killed. I was picturing him waking up at the bottom of that well and coming here to tell those priests exactly what they wish to hear. 'This girl is a murderer, not an angel!'

Ambrose opens the door for the next pilgrim and here is one slick-as-ice feeling inside my bones, like the sun did just drop out the sky, because this skinny-as-a-rake man is something quite unpleasant to my eye though I am not sure why.

He is removing his cap and warbling on about the weather and the water-logged grasses and then he says, 'O, and angel, would you kindly have God see to it that I might acquire a great many more cows since mine were lost.'

Lost? Well now I am realizing exactly who this fucker is and the reason for the no-sun feeling. My fingers are seizing up around this balcony rail and perhaps those candles will fizzle out besides. Here is the man who was the death of my own dear sister Henrietta. That bloody dairy-farmer who had me spill her milky-dinner and cut her life short because of his snapping dog-wolves. And come all the way from Norfolk just to see me?

I should call it a small eruption, this feeling inside of me. Revenge, Tibb: this is the spice of life. Yes, Ma, and how I would dearly like to lean my head over this rail and to spit down upon this bean-man from my great height and tell him, 'God is frowning, you fucker!' Or else vault over and twist that chicken neck. But that thing called revenge is ruinous too and we have bigger things to consider just now, like how to get out of this fucked-up mess.

'I will ask God the very thing, sir,' I say with my angel-teeth gritted. And I should say my fingers are interlaced so tight that the blood has stopped flowing.

Before he retreats from this church he turns though, and he

squints up to this rood-loft like his memory is doing somersaults, and then he shakes his head and replaces that cap.

Ma, this fat trick has grown legs and is running towards that cliff-edge like it has a wish for death and Ivo has spies in his own vicarage because of me and who knows where Maria has got to?

Scrupulous and probing gentleman

Father Cuthbert bursts into this nave. 'Father Ivo,' he says. 'I have taken the liberty of inviting another friend of the cloth.'

My Ivo's shoulders seem to sink five inches. 'All are welcome here, my friends,' he says wearily and I am weary too because I am thinking of Maria and whether she and John did catch that priest and I am thinking of how we can end this thing before we are all dead in the ground.

Father Cuthbert strokes that long nose of his. 'The man keeps the highest standards for the King and country, upholding the letter of the law for all of us. And such a *scrupulous* and *probing* gentleman, he will want to see the angel more than anyone.'

Now I do not need to have the great skill-of-reading to read between *these* lines. Father Cuthbert wishes to have his friend come here because it sounds like the man will uncover our naughty game if anyone can.

'But, Father,' says Ivo, 'are you suggesting the angel is some kind of fraud?'

'Certainly not!' he says with a sneer and a hand upon his not-in-there heart. 'It is only that Father Brian will take particular delight in seeing the angel too.'

Father Brian?

My innards are slipping down to my feet. It is some small mercy that this place is lit only by candles, since I am turning every shade of grey. Father Brian is coming to Leominster? The same Father Brian who ordered Samuel and Ewan, those two good men, to be mutilated like cattle in a farrier's tent? O, would you throw open that door, Ambrose, since this place is burning?

'You know of him, Father Ivo?'

Down there, Ivo is pale like a ghost. This is the same expression he had when he dragged us from our beach-home and told me, 'Run, Tibb! And do not look back!' And that scene from Peterborough has been carved into his skull, and now the man named Father Brian is coming here because of me. Why did you think this deception was such a fine idea, Tibb? This shame will turn me to ash.

Ivo says, 'I think I received his messenger boy here just recently.'

Father Cuthbert nods and paces up and down like he owns this building. 'Father Brian presides over the great city of Peterborough. He is a true agent of God and he is quite relentless in his search for sinners. In fact it is the pious Father Brian who has raised awareness about those ungodly men who would fornicate together like husband and wife. He has spread the word across the south, and does it not show his dedication to the priesthood?'

Ivo nods so slow, I wonder his lovely neck is turned to iron. 'It does, Father,' he whispers.

Once Father Cuthbert is gone and the door is locked, Ivo sits down in the front pew, gripping at the wood, his eyes staring. I clamber down and slip in beside him and rest my head on his shoulder.

'I'm so sorry, Ivo, that you will have to set your eyes on that cruel man Father Brian again. I would never have wished it upon you, and yet I have brought it all about myself.'

That thing called guilt is swelling inside of me and there is a feeling like I am unravelling, and the world is unravelling with me.

'I should not like to have this man anywhere near us. He

should be locked up for the thing he did at Peterborough, or, better still, on a pyre. This is why I am surprised you have found your faith, Ivo, if these things are what faith amounts to.'

Ivo says, 'O this is not faith, Tibb. These are not faithful people. Religion is a very peaceful thing as far as my uncle taught me, but these people have corrupted it.'

'Perhaps life is not so very simple as I once did see it, Ivo.'

He turns and grips me by the shoulders and he says firm, 'Don't talk like that, Tibb.' Then he is easing up the corners of my mouth ever so gently with his warm fingers.

Leominster, Herefordshire

Ivo blinks, straightening up from yet another half-sleep to see Father Brian's face looming down on him, cut like glass in the lantern's glow. Every hair combed into its glossy curtains. How out of place he seems in this cellar, his polished boots tapping on the sodden hay.

'I wished to see how they were keeping you,' the man drawls, his nose wrinkling with the stench.

Ivo clears his throat, swallowing the terror which this man inspires. 'In no great estate, as you see.'

Father Brian smirks, the corner of his thin lip curling upwards. 'Well it is certainly no home for the righteous. But God is fair.'

Is that so?

'How are you enjoying my vicarage?' Ivo asks. 'And is the angel still at my church?'

'How dare you carry on this way?' the other man hisses. 'You have been caught in the act! Your heinous trick is all revealed and we are simply waiting on the King's word.'

Now he hasn't a retort to that.

Father Brian gathers himself, smoothing down his hair though there is no smoothing to be done. 'I imagine you are regretting your choices?'

Ivo shakes his head. 'One does not choose to be visited by an angel.'

'Ah, but I am not speaking of that.'

Ivo stiffens, looking right up at him, into those cold eyes. What does he mean?

'I am speaking of your choice of cook, sir.'

Cook.

His blood feels like it is freezing inside him. There are shovels inside his head, clearing out all other thoughts except for this word and this image. Flavio: his cook.

Father Brian tuts quietly, enjoying the terror which is spreading across Ivo's face. 'I would not have thought to look twice at him, though his bread has kept us all nicely fed this past week. But then he started slipping out at all times and I had no choice but to follow. How strange to have a cook so enamoured of his master that he would bribe his way into a locked cellar. More than once too.'

'He is a loyal servant,' Ivo breathes.

Father Brian spits on the floor and crouches low. 'Ah, but we both know he is more to you than that, sir. And did I not say I would rid this country of evil?'

Ivo feels tears gathering in his eyes, panic searing through him. The silence settling in this cellar could stifle cities. 'Please,' he whispers. 'Don't hurt him.'

The other man smiles, his face just an inch from Ivo's. 'I have him in my keeping, sir, and I will hurt him as I please.'

Those words pierce his skin, making his head feel hollow. He has done this; if it wasn't for him, Flavio would be working at a bakery and not subjected to the mercy of Father Brian.

When the priest has gone, Ivo's head rolls back. He pants, twisting himself into a ball, hitting out at the wall.

'Flavio!' he cries into the rank air. 'I told you to run!'

That hater-of-love

That hater-of-love slinks so quietly through those doors into Ivo's own church, I hardly notice him. He is no large man, but a black cloud drifts in behind him and this is filling up the nave like the world would turn to cinders. The ducks would drown if he passed a lake and the fish would float to the surface. There is some chill inside my bones at his darting eyes and those crisp robes and that no-hair-out-of-place. I think the man has never lost sleep over anything.

'It is like a siege out there with all these tents,' he says, and each word is spoken so clear and slow, I wonder he will shatter the windows. He wipes his shoulders like the people outside have dirtied them. 'The whole of England is come. There must be thousands of people surrounding this place, Father . . . what was your name again?'

'Ivo.'

'Father Ivo,' he repeats, and he narrows his bead-eyes. 'I think you are new to the cloth, since I have never heard of you once.'

'True, Father. I inherited the parish from my uncle just last year.'

Father Brian squints his eyes like I am a tiny currant up here, but his face doesn't wrinkle because he is made of wax. 'You are an angel?' he says, and this false-enough smile is making the tree-trunks bend and the butterflies plummet to the ground.

He comes to stand in front of the rood-loft, looking up, and I am looking down on his no-hat head and wondering if that straight parting might part the sea. He drums his fingers on the pew-end and I am seeing such evil about this person, like it is dripping off him.

'Father Ivo,' he says with that milky voice. 'This kingdom of ours has been corrupted at some alarming rate with poison. Sinners of all kinds, and I make it my business to seek that poison and do away with it.'

'You would say an agent of the Lord is poison?'

The man's eyes flash. 'Stranger things have happened and been proven false.'

There is some clarity settling in here, like every breath of mine is too loud and my angel-fingers are too dirty under the nails. I can feel those ropes pulling there, making welts under my costume, and the head-crown digs in. Father Brian looks at me too long. Then he looks around this church slowly, examining the curtains which have been drawn over the long windows since I tumbled into the rood-loft. He looks at the empty font and at the wooden pews and the dripping candles which we are replenishing every day. He is studying this place like he would scratch everything into his forever-memory.

Ivo says, 'You would not deny a sign from God, since that would be heresy, Father?'

Father Brian just raises his eyebrows.

I know what you did, Father Brian! I wish to scream. And if there really is a Hell-place then you will be the first fucker shoved through its door.

Angels' food

The hour is late and I am thinking of Father Brian's part-the-sea hair and his oozing voice and the fact he will be staying in Ivo's vicarage all because of me. My stomach is whining like it should cry too. How will this thing ever end?

My Ambrose has a new job in this church and that is called the wiper-of-my-tears. 'I do not know what I should do if you were not here beside me,' I tell him, and then I think about the fact I have rolled him up into this deception just the same, and does that sound like love to you, Ma?

'What's happening over there?' I say when Ivo finally brings that baker's box. My teeth are not ripping at the bread like they did before because I am too nervous to eat and in fact I am stuffing half of it into my angel-pocket for later.

'Flavio is plying him with wine and all sorts at the vicarage. Such a lot of questions that man has for me. He is a spy in church-garb, Tibb.'

He rummages in that thick sandy hair of his. The hum of the crowd creeps under the door of this vestry and that hasn't stopped for days.

'This has become quite something of a ruse, Tibb. It has gone on longer than we thought and it has grown bigger than we planned.'

True, my friend.

'Perhaps it is time I did hold my hands up and you might all feign surprise—'

'Tibb!' they say together, and Ivo says, 'That is not the person I know!'

The gentle heaviness of his arms around me is something sweet.

'Who is that person, Ivo? Once I was a vagrant and a sister and a daughter and now I am none of those things. And I have been a pearl and a goddess and a songbird and an angel since then . . .'

He shakes his golden head. 'We must keep up the pretence, till Father Brian and the others are content with it. That's all we can do. Else we can pray they might get bored and leave.'

It sounds unlikely, sir.

Afterwards, he takes the empty baker's box and there is no naughty gift for me to hide inside of it because I am eating less-and-less and maybe soon that thing called an appetite will dry up completely.

I go back up to my rood-loft house. But as he unlocks the door and steps outside, there is a darting hand, cat-like, and a silky 'Ha!' and the lid of that box clatters on to the floor along with all my crumbs.

'I knew it!' says Father Brian, stepping into the nave, and he doesn't raise his voice one bit. 'I saw you fill that box just this evening, Father, and now it is empty. The congregation did not partake of a Mass, and so it is that you are supplying this non-mortal being with mortal-food.'

There is some light feeling in my head. Blackbirds are circling and stormclouds do block out the sun. Would you close your eyes with me, Tibb, since this world is turned some ugly shade?

Ivo is stuttering and bending to put the lid back on to his box and those two other priest-men Father Reynolds and Father Cuthbert are coming in too and pacing around, poking out their chests under those robes like *they* were the ones to work it out.

'Such falsehoods, Father Ivo! You are a fraud! Father Brian

has barely been a day here and already he has uncovered your secrets!'

Father Brian could have ten eyes the way they are roving but the rest of him is deadly still. He holds up a hand like he would tell them: 'Leave it to me.' His syrupy voice says, 'When the King is hearing of this he will have you strung up on the gallows, and you know that angel will have her guts pulled out?'

I am clutching this wood rail till my knuckles are white. My guts? If he mutilated two men in a farrier's tent, I cannot think Father Brian is lying one piece.

'Falsehood?' Ambrose says, stepping into the nave. 'But this is no falsehood.'

Why does he sound so calm? There is no clawing back from this, Ambrose! My Ivo is watching him as though to say: 'My friend, what plan have you got here?'

Father Brian smiles a little, and I am staring down upon that parted hair again.

'And who are *you*, sir?'

'The warden here,' Ambrose says. 'I have been tasked with guarding the angel at all times.'

Father Brian eyes him carefully, all over his purple parts. 'Well then, you can hardly deny that this box was full of bread for the angel?'

I am glancing down to see that Ambrose hasn't cowered at all. He is standing with that great stature of his as though our tricks are not currently being laid out in all their glory for the magpies to peck at. 'I am saying no such thing, Father. But are *you* suggesting that the host once it is blessed is merely bread? This is the flesh of Christ and thus immortal.'

Ha! What a fine stroke of quick-thinking and I wouldn't expect anything less from this always-one-step-ahead man. I could swing down from here like a monkey and throw my arms around him.

'You are not truly telling me that Father Ivo blessed the bread?' Father Brian asks, those smooth words spilling out his mouth like they are formed from butter. The other two priests do hoot-hoot with disbelief plastered across their faces.

'I did,' Ivo says like he just caught up. 'And do you deny, Father Brian, that the bread is truly the body of Christ?'

It is some small piece of bliss to see that smirk wiped clean off Father Brian's face, and those two priests stumbling and muttering behind him like they are very ashamed of themselves.

Ivo is gaining confidence now. 'This angel must have sustenance the same as anyone, but hers is a spiritual sustenance, not an earthly one. It is angels' food from God, of which she received the same in Heaven.'

I am rather thinking thank fuck they did not open it this morning when there was a piss-pot in there and a fine shit waiting to be tossed in the mud.

'Well if that is so,' says Father Brian, 'how is it she is getting the angels' food, as you call it? Is she flying? As far as we know, angels are flying-creatures much like birds. I can see those wings behind her back.'

'She is not flying, Fathers.'

'No?' he says. 'Then how? As you tell us, she has not left that rood-loft, and so how is she getting it?'

Ivo is losing that calm – I can see he is all out of answers – but Ambrose steps forward. 'There is another way she receives that magical food, and it is not by flying. And if you would join us tomorrow for the service, Father Ivo will encourage her to take the host with everyone else and you might witness it yourself.'

'Fuck, Ambrose!' I want to shout. This is an impossible thing you are promising! But Father Brian and those two priestly men are looking like they have three mighty bird eggs dripping down their faces.

If not a crab-wire

'What shall we do?' So says every one of us in this vestry. This place is fast becoming our secret plan-making house but right now there is not one plan on anyone's lips.

This church is stuffy since it is high summer out there and I can hear that afternoon crowd gibbering away like they aren't going anywhere. It is giving me some bad stomach feeling to think we are surrounded. And there is some tightness in my chest like the snake is back because these lovely faces of my own dear friends are strained with that thing called fear. And those pigeons outside are doing all the talking like hoot-hoot-hoot and how will you wriggle out of this one?

Ambrose is rubbing his temples under that curly hair. 'We need to clear Ivo's name. We need to pull off this Mass-trick.'

I say, 'It sounds so simple when you put it like that.'

Silence again, and I am holding my head in my hands because you have put a man as good as Ivo in danger this way.

'I am so sorry, Ivo,' I whisper. 'This is all my fault.'

I can feel his fingers crawling into my palm though I don't deserve his kindness.

'I wager you wish you had never met me on that beach.'

'No, Tibb,' he says, and he wipes that tear, just as he did when I was kneeling on that sand-hill and shouting at the sky. When will this person turn around and tell me: Would you fuck off, Tibb? I think you ruined my life!

'And I bet you wish I had never walked along that wet sand towards you.'

'No, Tibb,' he says again. 'No' and 'no', like he really means it, but my head is perching on one side.

There is Ivo in my mind's eye. That nearly-a-man boy with his thick fair hair and his rolled-up breeches. He is there and smiling and sitting on the rocks with those tanned forearms while I was just a shell on the sand and carrying a dead baby for company.

'Tibb?' that kind man named Flavio says, but I am looking at Ivo and blinking. Thoughts are gathering up their belongings inside of my skull and bells are ringing in my own two ears.

'You were fishing, Ivo,' I whisper. 'Don't you remember?'

He says, 'Of course,' like this is making no sense, and 'We fished for crabs more than once, Tibb.' But the ringing in my ears is getting louder because here is some fine party of clever thoughts forming a line inside of my head.

Suddenly he has his warm hands around my face and we are staring into each other's eyes too and he is saying, 'Tibb, you clever thing!' and Flavio and Ambrose are none-the-wiser and saying, 'What?' and 'What?' because they did not share that lovely Norfolk life with us where we did fish for crabs and pluck oysters from wild beds sometimes.

'I still have it, Tibb!' Ivo whispers. 'You know I do have it still.'

Now it is evening, or so I am told because how am I to know? Those long curtains are drawn all the time and I should place a coin on each because those are some heavy eye-lids to boot.

Flavio and Ivo are plying the enemies with wine at the vicarage. Those priests will be tucking into some fine pork about now too, else taking turns to walk around this church, navigating their way through all those camping-out people. But here I am with my own Ambrose who must love me a lot, and we are practising this trick like our lives depend on it, which in fact they do.

'Shall we try again, Tibb?' he says.

It is something quite special to see him down there, gazing up with all that love and those colourful limbs and saying, 'Slower, slower!' and 'I can see your hands moving.'

Here is the thing: this fishing wire is wound around my finger with my angel-sleeves pulled right down, then it is sneaking over the balcony rail, all the way down to the place below me where Ivo puts that bread in what he calls the pyx box, to hand out to his parishioners. The end of it is fastened round a piece of bread.

'How about that?' I whisper. 'Is that good?'

My hands are clasped and I am wrapping that wire round my finger with the subtlest of movements, so that piece of bread is rising smoothly through the air. This is no thrashing crab, Ma, and when it has floated up to my own home then I reach out and take it.

'Tibb, this fishing business . . . I am fearing for the morning.'

'Fearing? Why so, my man? It is all working out well enough from where I am standing!'

Ambrose is passing that almost-invisible wire between his some-of-them-purple fingers and saying, 'I am thinking that this wire could be too visible in the morning since that door there is always hanging open for the people outside to see in, and if only we had something even thinner and barely-there.'

These wriggling doubts are not welcome to me. 'But if not a crab-wire, then what?'

I swing down from here with that dragging feeling and he stares a long time at me, like he should find the answer in my own face. Then he leans forward and he is plucking one of these long white hairs from my own head and he is pulling it taut between those fingers of his.

Mass for all and sundry

Ma and I did some nice sneakery on Twelfth Night. 'The world is feasting, Tibb, so would you take your moment?' And she did toss me over a chicken pen to steal a bird of our own. 'Such a lark!' she said with those chicken-bones stacked up. 'Distract the fuckers and you shall have the cherry!'

Wise-enough words from that woman called Ma, and it is not the Twelfth Night now but distraction is some good-enough friend. Flavio has been flapping about lighting incense all morning and whipping up a great plume of smoke, and now there is a misty haze lying low in this church. A lovely screen to cover up all naughty deeds, and specifically those almost-invisible head-hairs which are knotted together and stretching down already, fixed to a piece of bread.

'Please give room for the Mass to take place!' Ivo shouts as he opens the doors. 'And we shall see if the angel who has deigned to visit us will partake also. Here is a Mass for all and sundry!'

Such a great fuss of pushing and shoving down there to reach the front pews, and children are being sent forward under arms and between legs to save spaces. And Father Reynolds with that always-sharp expression of his, and his pointy hat on top. Does he wear that hat to shit? They are tumbling in like those sea-waves which my own ma did like to dance in, and they are calling at one another across the nave and in the aisles and squabbling over seats and squashing their big-and-small arses into the pews for the service. The place is like a theatre. Perhaps we are in the land of Rome and those flaming chariots which Ambrose has versed me on will soon come crashing through the windows, and those fat bulls behind them. We are treading right close to the edge here, Tibb. My heart is thudding yet again. Joy and despair have been taking their turns with nothing in between and I am feeling like my poor ma must have suffered a lot in her life.

'Settle down!' Ivo is saying, and 'Do not startle the angel!'

He looks like he has not slept one tiny wink.

That church door is wedged open and Ambrose was right not to risk the crab-fishing line. This smoke has put a cockerel in my throat though, and it is wanting to warble its merry tune but angels do not cough and splutter, Tibb Ingleby. Would you fuck up the whole thing?

There is something unnerving about the way Father Brian stands so still, unlike Father Reynolds and Father Cuthbert who are practically hopping. I am ogling that hater-of-love beneath this hood but my attention is all caught up in the feel of this save-our-skins-hair around my finger. I wonder there isn't a band of gold just there.

'Friends!' Ivo is saying, lifting off the lid of the pyx carefully so as not to break the thin hair-wire. 'God's angel remains here for we are chosen disciples in this good parish at Leominster, and it has been asked of me, "How does she eat?" And she eats, as you will see, through the immortal flesh of God, and by that I mean the Mass!'

My hands are clasped already, but they are shaking now and perhaps this will break the hair. I am preparing my fingers for the first soft tug.

'And so, I will invite my angel to take the first bite of Heaven's bread!' he is saying while those hundreds of people do hold their breath, and the ones outside in those closing-in crowds who are all hush-hushed besides. These trysts, Tibb – these are the making of a life!

Are they, Ma?

In fact there cannot be an inch of movement. Not even an inch between my hands else the people will see that motion. And I cannot pull the bread up too slow and risk them spying the hair, but neither can I pull too vigorously or the hair could snap. And there cannot be a moment's pause between that bread appearing at the railing and my taking it. One thousand things might go wrong, and only *one* must go right.

'You will see now, good people of my parish, that the Mass food flies up to the angel when she summons it,' Ivo says. 'And this thing I have seen each day with my own eyes.'

Careful, Tibb. I am wrapping this hair around my finger so softly and I am standing so still, I wonder the whole world has paused besides. The sultans of Constantinople are frozen on their chairs and the King himself has gone dumb. I can feel this bread-weight on the line like here is a fish to end all suffering, Ma. And so here we go.

Slowly, Tibb. Just like you did practise it.

I think every part of my insides like my heart and my stomach are dropping to my arsehole just now. The bread-morsel is rising up through the air and there was never a crab of such grave importance as this.

Down there, the audience is in raptures and leaning forwards, and there is such a hush descending because of the extraordinary and inexplicable scene of the floating-through-the-air bread. So many open mouths – the flies will come from Calais! Up it rises and I am keeping this motion slow and slow until that crusty morsel is inside my palm and then inside my mouth and there is some deafening silence before every person has their arms up in the air like they just saw the big-man crash down from the sky. And those priests could wipe the floor with their hanging-open jaws but Father Brian is looking like a bird did shit on his perfectly parted and smothered-in-fat hair.

Ivo says, 'The angel must have a moment of recollection and silence after the Mass.'

O, I can hear that sweet relief in your voice, my friend! He is eyeing Father Brian though, and then he is looking up here at me.

'I fear she is becoming weary with God's work,' he says heavily. 'If we wish to have her stay, then we cannot overwhelm her, and the sharing of the bread and wine amongst us will take far too long with so many new guests in my congregation.'

There is some grumbling disappointment down there since all these people are clamouring for a nice gulp of wine as much as I am. Then there is the usual pushing dance as too many people are leaving from this place and the atmosphere is jubilant like there has been a real miracle done today.

'We did it!' I mouth when that door is locked, and Ivo is on his knees.

'Did you see those priests?' Flavio whispers once we are gathered in this vestry. 'They were stunned to silence! They will be wringing their hands since they cannot piece it together at all!'

'My friends,' I say. 'I think we have pulled off the greatest falsehood the country has ever seen.'

Ivo smiles but that is not the eyes-closing smile I know. 'Tibb, I would rather like to say it is the very *last* falsehood the country will ever see. We need these priests to leave before any more demands are made.'

He shakes his blonde head like there are too many thoughts going on in there. 'It is a special thing, you know,' he says quietly. 'The bread and the wine. I so wished to be a more honest priest, but in fact I am just the same as all the rest.'

The little un-Spanish crook

The crowds outside are swelling and swelling, or so says Ambrose and he is the man-on-the-door. 'You cannot see beyond them,' he says, and I can hear as much. Those flying-over-England birds must be seeing some strange-enough sights too: one small building with its flat-roofed bell-tower, all packed in by a thousand-strong crowd.

Ivo did say, 'Would you carry on with your blessings, Tibb? Soon enough those priests will be gone.' But we all know that is some wishful thinking and these must be the blandest blessings in my short career as an angel since my belly is turned to shreds and I need this lie stuffed in a coffin and buried underground while my Ivo is in the clear and before that shady priest returns with Lord Fielding shouting, 'Lies!' and 'They did dance at my own house!' O, Maria, what is taking you so long? Is it possible that she and John did stumble upon some wickedness in their grand plan to save us all? I have been painting some sick-enough pictures inside my head involving vagrants and sticks and Maria and John lying dead in a ditch.

'One more pilgrim, and I will tell them you're tired,' says Ambrose, before he ushers in the next.

Who is it now? This shuffling old man will want to speak of his own seat in Heaven if I'm not wrong. Would you get on with it, sir? And such a wide-brimmed hat; you should remove that for an angel to boot!

Well he does that thing with slug-fingers; like he is drawing it out on purpose. And then he looks up at me and my insides are trying again to escape out my arsehole and the church is spinning, Ma.

Signor Perero himself. Right there.

'Got you!' he says, and he smirks under that greasy grown-out moustache then he laughs like the wolves returned.

O, there is no hiding this what-the-fuck expression of mine, or the fact I am gripping this wood railing like I should tumble to the floor. Why is the little un-Spanish crook not roaming around the moors of Scotland with the beasts and the prickly heather? Revenge, Tibb – that thing can be as clever as you wish to make it. Too true, Ma, and yet perhaps this revenge was not clever enough.

The man is half-starved and dishevelled like he has walked here across the seas from that place named Antwerp which Maria did speak of oftentime and he has grown one tufty beard. I should say he is gazing up here like I am some pretty sunset.

'Nice crown,' he says. 'But that does not belong to you, dear.'

I am bowing my head. I have an urge to pull the hood right over my face and throw off this stupid head-piece. A tightness is creeping round my neck and I have the sense that grubs are skulking around on my own skin. Would the ground sprout teeth and swallow you up, Tibb?

'Ambrose,' he says, extending his weed-arms. 'Do you have nothing to say to your old friend Signor?'

Ambrose is not answering that either. He is ashen-white there in the aisle – even that lovely purple part of him is a little bit paler.

'Well, it is good to see you both nonetheless,' Signor continues. 'Might I stop a while?'

He slithers into a pew and puts his little feet up on the bench in front. Such a grin across his newt-face and tap-tap-tap say his fingernails on the wood. I think they will hear that tapping in the land of Constantinople. There is sweat gathering in my arm-pits and on my back and the stench is rancid.

He tuts, picking food from his teeth. 'This tall tale of an angel. That description did match up too well, I had to see for myself. But how did you escape your owner, dear? And I thought they left you for dead besides, Ambrose.'

Signor tuts again, then: 'Reveal yourself, Tibb Ingleby!' he bellows up to the vaulted ceiling like he should wish to raise the dead.

Shut up, man! I am bowing my head to this floor like my neck does bend upon a hinge.

He stands. 'Take down your hood, woman!'

Shut up! He is so loud that those priests outside called Father Reynolds and Father Cuthbert and the awful Father Brian come panting in.

'What?' they say, and 'What is it?'

Ivo and Flavio are rushing in behind.

Signor Perero stands and bows like this is his own moment to perform. Have you waited long for it, sir?

'This is not an angel, for this woman I know well. She is a contortionist of sorts, though even that is a stretch, since she has little talent beyond dressing up and passing herself off as something she is not. And it is all because of *her* that my own group of strolling-players ran off and stole my props!'

He throws his scaly head back and there is nothing real about that hooting laugh. Then he rubs his hands on his too-tight breeches which are coated in mud. 'Fathers of the Church, this is some unruly little bitch.'

Father Brian looks like the sky has burst and all his dreams are coming true and by that I mean the right corner of his mouth is curling ever-so-slightly upwards.

'Mind your words, man, in my church,' Ivo tells Signor, 'for here is an angel. Just today we have seen a most holy and inexplicable taking of Mass. A miracle in fact, which cannot be denied.'

'Horse-shit,' says Signor, 'for this woman is known to me as a certain Tibb Ingleby. And she is more than well acquainted with that patchwork man, I should say.'

There is a cold worm burrowing around inside of me and making everything feel hollow.

'Blasphemy!' Ivo shouts. 'The words you speak in my church are shameful and poisonous and you will answer for them, denying the angel with some strange tale of props and strolling-players? We have a madman in our midst. Restrain the nay-sayer, since this is heresy!'

Ambrose is so big and tall that it is an easy thing for him to have Signor's skinny arms locked behind his hunched back.

'I want my shells back!' he shouts, kicking his twig-legs. 'They were crafted specially! And I want my tents returned besides!'

The *shells*? Why should he want the shells back? Who else does he think will do the oyster show like Tibb Ingleby?

My poor Ivo's face is strained with worry but he is trying to retain the air of being the-man-in-charge. 'To the stocks with this sinner who has denied an agent of God!'

Ambrose drags him out while Signor Perero is still bleating on: 'The girl is a common thief!'

It is some comfort to hear the stragglers outside boo and holler at this angry little man but inside those busy-body priests are mulling it over and muttering together like a coven of witches.

'The angel is attracting all of God's creations,' Ivo says, 'even the mad ones.' His face is even paler now. I should say there is no blood left inside of him.

'You judged the man to be mad quite fast there, Father Ivo.'

'But of course, Father Brian! You saw the Mass – there are no doubts over the angel's magical properties and so it is unlawful to be denying her. You saw the bread of the host levitate into her mouth, did you not?'

The other two priests are pondering this but Father Brian says, 'Unless, of course, there were some evil and unholy trick at play.'

Ivo looks like he is broken already, like little parts of him are cracking and falling off. 'But that is to blaspheme, Father.'

'I simply want to check that *you* do not blaspheme yourself, Father Ivo. The man had such a strange and wonderful tale of shells and tents and a name for the angel too, I struggle to think he made it up, and we would not want you, nor the good people of Leominster, to be taken as fools.'

There is something chilling in Father Brian's calm demeanour. I am remembering the way he flicked a hand to have his henchman beat poor Samuel like a dog at Peterborough. This man spreads evil so quietly, he hardly needs to open those thin lips.

Ivo says, 'But of course he made it up, since he was a madman!'

'Then if you are certain, you will not mind that we check? And to check is merely to see that now the angel has taken of her Mass, she will not require the services of the pot.'

'Father?'

The faintest smile works its way up Father Brian's face again while the other two are walking around like plucked hens with their heads bobbing. 'Well as an immortal being, she cannot be relieving herself upon a pot like an earthly person. That is our sure way to check if the man was speaking the truth, or if he is in fact mad.'

Ivo throws his hands up. 'Of course she is not relieving herself! Which angel have you heard of that will bend and piss upon a pot? You are unbelievers. I have a mind to have that crowd outside march you to the stocks as well.' But I can hear that sliver of panic in Ivo's deep voice because he is saying all the right things and yet he is clearly thinking in his head that this poses a very big problem indeed.

'Now, Father,' says Father Brian's sickly voice, and he folds his hands gently. 'We want only to guard our kingdom from the flickerings of evil.'

'This is an angel of God,' Ivo whispers and Father Brian nods as though he expected those words. His smirk is lopsided, like a sparrow did fly down and pull up one corner.

'Well if you're so sure, Father Ivo, then there cannot be any problem with us waiting outside. The purpose being to ensure no excrement is leaving this church, because angels do not shit, Father.'

O, Ivo. Even if I were the owner of that great skill-of-counting, I would not be able to count up the sorry-words which are piling up inside of my head.

Open the floodgates

By the evening, there is some mighty ruckus gathering outside. Discontent has been trickling under the wood door of this church since Signor Perero's bad words. I should say they did open the floodgates, and now those secret doubts are being spoken of out there, and these doubts are wriggling through those crowds and gathering up armies.

'That false-angel in there thieved the milk from my dairy-farm!' a man's voice is shouting. 'And she lost me half my herd! I knew it as soon as I saw her!'

The dairy-farmer. I did think he stopped to stare too long.

'I want my money back!' I am hearing now, and 'I think I have seen that woman before in a troupe of players!'

'Yes! That angel was a pearl! In the same troupe as the colourful man! It is all one big falsehood!'

But there are voices besides which are ragged and desperate and they are saying something of the opposite. Like: 'Would you explain that miracle, then?' and 'We have been given hope by that true angel!'

Here is some prickly heat on my face and the snake has returned to its old home around my neck and it is squeezing there like it never stopped. Ivo and Flavio fight their way in, leaning on that door like they have slain some dragons outside.

'Will we go to the vestry, Tibb?' Ivo says.

O, what is the point, sir?

We are sitting here on the floorboards like four lambs to the slaughter around this candle, and I have some gnawing emptiness inside of me. Would you shut your eyes, Tibb? I can hardly bear to see my dear Ivo's perfect face looking so full of fear about that dreaded noose. I am beginning to think this noose has been scratched into his head-thoughts for all of his life. He is holding Flavio's hand like that person would be torn from him too.

'Not everyone out there disbelieves us,' Flavio says hopefully with his Spanish lisp. 'Many are still on our side because of that great miracle with the bread. You know they are calling you the Holy Maid of Leominster?'

I say, 'Perhaps, but there are a great many more who have had their secret doubts confirmed and now they are digging tunnels in this trick, as if we had room for that.'

Tears are trickling down my face and these are hot like wax. Perhaps they will burn me and I will shrivel up to a cinder. Blood and sand, Tibb, as my ma would say oftentime when things went awry, though I never really knew what it meant. Blood and sand in any case, though rather too much blood than sand just now. That island did long since sink into the sea and now we are sinking with it, waiting for the bad water to fill up our lungs.

'It seems I am in need of the pot more than ever, Ivo,' I whisper.

In fact I have been needing it all morning since I was not able to do my urgent business last night in the clay pot and place it into the baker's box as before. Now my nerves are all shredded.

He holds my hand because he is a dear friend.

'Tibb,' he says. 'You do your business. Do not make yourself uncomfortable.'

Back-note of an unpleasant smell

'Child, you could not find a cow in a haystack, such are the soggy brains in your thick skull, but that evil inside you is something much worse.'

Farmer O, you were right, and this bleak thought is swirling around in my belly and making my head hurt too, and I deserve this sour tincture. Stupid and evil is no fine blend for victory, Tibb.

'I have made a decision, Ambrose,' I say while he lies with me in our high-up house in the evening. It is smelling badly of my own shit which is hidden in the vestry under one secret floorboard. There was no choice about this thing, since I was called upon by Mother Nature, that wait-for-no-man beast.

'And what is that?'

'Well,' I say slowly, and that word sounds shaky, 'I think you should fetch Ivo and Flavio, and you should all run off and save yourselves, and find Maria and John, wherever they may be, and take them too. And you should go ahead to that fine island in the sun, since this crime was my own bad idea.'

Ambrose wraps those long arms around me and says, 'Tibb! How could I ever leave you? Besides, there is always hope. After all, I was sent out alone as the son of a witch and my life has gone in many far-flung directions since then.'

This is not making me feel any better because in fact there is no hope left at all. The truth is, this church will be surrounded by more and more nay-sayers till we admit our bad deeds. There is no way out. Ambrose's mottled-like-egg-shell eyes search mine and I like the colour of those reddish curls so much.

'Sleep, Tibb,' he says and he guides my head on to his chest, but how can I fall asleep when tomorrow we are in the same no-way-out problem? There is a panic feeling inside of my head. A kind of spiked emptiness like I did feel when that farmer-man shuffled under those sheets and held those wiry fingers round my jaw and when he pulled up my own dress and whispered, 'Shut your mouth, child, because you asked for this.'

Soon Ambrose is dozing off so I am really alone with these roily thoughts. Such a fine dream you did have for me, Ma. About beating the fuckers and getting my own roof and all that perfect stuff. What would you say if I told you they won and that rooves don't matter when you're dead anyway?

Really I am like an eye-glass, such as those that the sneak-priests wear, except this one is not looking outwards but inwards. Right into my thinking-brain in fact. This glass is looking at my own ma or at least the always-picture of her which is propped up inside of my head. Slumped by that thick tree and saying, 'No roof for us' and 'Would you call it the end, Tibb?' All this because she did not get that thing called revenge. She was ruined by that fucked-up tale I did tell her, but in fact this thing was my fault to start with, since Farmer O was right and I did encourage those dark deeds I did with him. Ma – it was me you were looking for all along.

Now the eye-glass is peep-peeping at Henrietta under that hedge when she was grey and stiff. And it was me who did not keep her alive, which is another piece of proof that I am in fact the spawn of the devil-person and no angel at all.

Life is something fleeting, Tibb, and that was true enough, Ma, and I was all mad for this ruse and the island-dream because of it. But in fact I have put all my friends in a sinking boat and they will die because of me. O, Ivo was right about the world being not-so-simple as I see it. And perhaps speaking once a day in the bakery was as good as it could get. And finding two separate rooves in some shit village in the land of Wales was enough besides.

'We will think of something, Tibb,' Ambrose mumbles.

'When?' I whisper. 'There is no time to think of a thing.'

I can hear the crowds outside. Those priest-men will be trudging round the church on their night-patrol besides, as though they need any more evidence that I am, in fact, entirely human. If I strain my ears perhaps I might hear their footsteps like one million claps of thunder in my ears while we are trapped in this building like prisoners with a shit under the floorboards.

'Tibb,' he says gently. 'Would you close your eyes?'

No, sir. Because you do not deserve love or friends, Tibb. You don't deserve any of it. And you have brought all this bad luck on yourself. There is no arguing with you, Farmer O. You win.

The next morning Father Brian and his two lapdog-men are in here and they are all three prowling around the pews saying, 'Do you smell that, my brother?' and 'Surely you can smell it?'

Such glee in these words being exchanged. They might just as well fetch a net and scoop us up because we are caught already. Flavio has been swinging the incense all morning, but no amount of that musky stuff and rosewater will mask the smell of human shit which is lingering under that floorboard in the vestry.

Ivo ignores it as he prepares for his service and flaps about at the altar, pretending to be busy. This is some weary-faced person my old friend has become and that is the worst thing of all.

'Yes, the back-note of an unpleasant smell is gracing us here, and we will locate it, unless you have any objections, Father Ivo?'

'No, Fathers,' he says quietly, since he can hardly say otherwise. 'No objections.'

Off they go, the three of them, sniffing like dogs. They are even going up to the bell-tower, like I should have done my doings there.

'It is simply a rat that will be dead in that wall cavity somewhere,' Ivo suggests when they have been looking a while.

'A rat that smells like shit?' Father Reynolds asks.

'Or perhaps,' Ivo says, 'it is the case that this angel is disturbing the dead who are buried in this very church.'

'Enough!' Father Brian barks, and a little hair comes loose from that smothered-in-fat helmet and hangs over his forehead.

Sheddings of a fraud

In the evening, Ivo is back. He did gabble like a goose through the service today since he was racing against the spreading stench of shit which does not much like to be contained. 'Such a shame,' Father Brian did say. 'There were so few prayers. And I have never heard such a short sermon.' Now Ivo's eyes are so red, I wonder the whole world is on fire out there. And I am here in the pew with my head in my hands because all is lost. The stupid halo is tossed to the floor and my head is pulsing where it sat for so long.

'I'm so sorry, Ivo.'

He sits beside me and he holds me by the shoulders like he always used to and he says, 'Tibb. Would you stop that? We will find a way.'

'How can you still speak to me when I have dragged you into this mess?'

He takes these heavy wings off by way of untying the ropes, and he rubs my shoulders where they have cut in and made some sores. This thin skin was given to you by the angels, Tibb. Well that is something quite fucked-up given the situation, Ma.

He says, 'Tibb, without you in Norfolk, perhaps I would have returned to my family and married the girl after all. But you gave me a new life on those beaches, and you made me feel like I could be myself for the first time. And now you are come again to me, and you have brought me Flavio and you have brought smiles and possibility, and I need some of your courage. Perhaps this angel trick is the test.'

My eyes are filling up because it is nice to hear these things.

'Come on,' he says, and he is leading me by the hand to the bell-tower.

'Why are we going up here?' I ask.

We slip past that bell-landing quick since the stonework around it has cut-out holes for the noise to carry. I can see the shady outlines of the crowds from here and they stretch so far that I can't make out anything beyond. Some have made little fires in their camping-sites and that is reminding me of the troupe. Bile is clambering up my throat like it has somewhere to be. Then we are at the top.

'Ivo,' I say. 'You do not mean to climb up there and lie down like we used to? Surely they would see us?'

He shakes his head. 'No, but you have been too long without that wise mama of yours.'

He slides across the little hole-in-the-roof, and that is some pretty sight. I have not seen the sky above me since we began our hoodwinking and I should say I did forget how big it is.

The moon streams in and this is making the white hairs on my arms sit up. I always did like the covered-in-stars roof best, and one big lump is forming in my throat because my dead ma is so close tonight. She is bulging out of the sky and winking at me like she came especially. And would you have some courage, Tibb? Would you let the fuckers win?

'Is it her?' he asks me.

'That's her, Ivo.'

He smiles and it reaches his eyes.

'Thank you,' I whisper and he puts his arms around me. And we are standing here at the top of these spiral steps and beneath this hole-in-the-roof, staring up at that great star who is in fact my own dead ma. There is some odd sense of calm just now. Until there isn't.

'What was that?' I say.

One mighty ruckus if I am hearing it right. Some hollering which is crashing off the stone walls down there. Priestly voices all sharpened like knives and ones I recognize too.

'Ivo?' I hiss, and I am grabbing his collar. 'Do you hear that? It does not sound like it is coming from outside.'

But he is deathly white because those voices are getting clearer.

'She's gone!' they are saying. 'She isn't up there!'

Here is some dark truth: these voices are hooting their bad tunes from inside this very church.

'Fuck,' I whisper. 'Why has Flavio let them in?'

My dear Ivo is not answering. I should say he is frozen here on these steps like those saints in the windows.

'Ivo, if they come up here, you might say you found me, wandering the building. Who's to say what angels get up to when they are left alone?'

Still no reply. He is just shaking his head, and nodding to me like I should understand. Then: 'Your wings, Tibb,' he croaks. 'Your halo.'

I feel for those things like these hands are someone else's. These hands are feeling for those ropes under my arms and that heavy halo on my head, and my stomach is tumbling to my knees because I left those things in the pews. The wings hammered by Mr Manners are sprawled out in the nave like that place is some cabinet-of-terrible-things, and the halo is there too, tossed to the floor.

'Do you see this, my brothers?' Father Reynolds is hollering in his shatter-the-glass voice. 'Wings! A halo! Is that not proof enough? These are the sheddings of a fraud!'

'Well, sir?' they are asking Flavio. 'You have been in these meetings with the so-called angel. Would you own up already?'

It sounds like Flavio is not giving one answer. Now those

grating voices are sailing up these spiral steps and bouncing off the stonework. They must be in the vestry now.

'Where is she?' Father Cuthbert demands of that kind baker. They mean to interrogate him.

'Why don't you speak, sir?'

Father Brian's silky voice sounds more clipped than usual. 'She will be here somewhere, since this place is surrounded. She cannot have got out. There is foul play at work from that little criminal and now her time is up.'

Here are boots on these stairs and I think my head has gone all heavy on my neck, like it is made up of brass. And these stone steps feel so rough beneath my bare feet. Why didn't I notice that before? We could be on the shingle at Suffolk just now.

They are calling up to us amongst their panting: 'It will be worse for you if you continue the trick. Just own up! Show yourself!'

I can feel a light breeze in this tower. It is lapping around my neck and brushing those parts of me where the ropes have puckered my skin, and, 'Ivo,' I whisper. 'You know we could be on the shingle just now?'

He holds my hand because this is the last walk.

Those oily words

My breath is too noisy.

'This is the Lord's own house, Father. Why should the angel need wings to reach Him?'

That is Ivo speaking and I can hear the terror in his voice, but only because I do know him so well. My legs are shaking and I am gritting my teeth because here is some cramping feeling besides.

Those priests are spluttering like they swallowed their meat all wrong but Father Brian's quiet voice is like a knife through butter. 'This is some filth from your own mouth. How could she possibly remove her wings at leisure, and by the way of ropes no less? Might you remove your *legs*, Father?'

Ivo says, 'Who are *we* to know the workings of the angel's anatomy? I think you have not met many others, my friends?'

Father Cuthbert says, 'Those wings down there are metal, as I always suspected! Is there a blacksmith in Heaven? Admit it! You are defeated! And why are you up here anyway? Is this not something suspicious?'

'Not a bit, since I was polishing up my bell,' Ivo says, 'which I do each week. The last I saw, the angel was down there in the rood-loft. Perhaps *you* have scared her away.'

'Without her wings?' Father Brian asks again.

O, would he fuck off about the wings?

Now, I can fit myself into small spaces such as oyster caves and wood shells, beneath hedges and in hollows of oak trees. Even that tight squeeze between the rood-screens, but here? This bell is all the wrong shape. 'Tibb!' Ivo did say with his eyes all shiny like two polished leather boots, and 'Get in quick!'

Well I am stretched inside it with my feet on one side and my hands on the other, or one hand in any case since I am holding on to that pendulum so it doesn't swing. Would you get on with it, Ivo, because my legs are shaking and my hand is slipping, and soon I will poke out the bottom then topple to the floor and the noise of this bell will have the hens cold dead in their barns.

Father Cuthbert cries, 'Look, there's a door up there! He's let her out. To take another shit, I reckon!'

No, sir. Not today.

'Be my guests,' says Ivo, and, 'Perhaps you are wise to check.'

Now I can hear them climbing, and my Ivo last of all because he is speaking extra loud so I might hear. 'Up we go, my friends,' he is saying, and by that he means: Tibb, time to move.

I can hear him slide that wood door back across and I am falling from this hiding-house so quick, that pendulum is almost thwacking on the side of this great bell.

'Do you believe me now?' Ivo is saying from out on the roof, and I know he will keep them up there as long as he possibly can.

Run, Tibb.

O, I am running. All down these steps – tripping down some and riding on my heels, and this breath coming out of my mouth is like dog breath. Then I am shoving on the wings and the halo and clambering up the pillar to my too-long home like that dairy-farmer's wolf-dogs are back which is true in a way. I am still panting when they return from the roof-tower.

'She's there, as I thought!' Ivo says as they come again into the nave and that laugh of his is no sincere thing, Ma. 'I cannot think what you were talking of, Fathers! Are you all quite well? Would you go to my vicarage, and calm yourselves with a bun and some milk?'

A sliver of fury crosses Father Brian's stone face, just as it did when he condemned those poor men to the farrier's tent in Peterborough, but he waits before he speaks so his voice is not jagged. 'O, I do not have any wish for a bun, Father,' he says quietly, and he slicks down his hair.

There is one silence then, save for my panting which I am trying to stifle, and Father Brian paces up and down the aisle like he would calm himself this way.

'Though I have been intrigued by the calibre of cook you keep and I thought to make my own enquiries.'

Ivo freezes. 'My cook?'

Father Brian nods. 'The baker in town informed me that he was quite inconvenienced to have given up his apprentice. He said your housekeeper was the one to make the appointment, Father. And yet I am staying at this vicarage a while now and I don't see a housekeeper . . .'

His eyes are drifting up to me, and the corners of his lip are curling up too. I think you can hear the beetles crawling along the leaves outside and the apples falling from the trees in the orchard.

Ivo begins to tell him: 'My housekeeper had to leave quite suddenly—' but Father Brian raises a hand.

'It is all one lie too many,' he says. 'Whether she is a strolling-player or a housekeeper, you, Father Ivo, are a hater of God himself and I believe it is your turn for punishment now.'

These words sliding from his mouth are turning to mud in my ears and this world is all wobbly. I wonder that I am being submerged in water up here.

Now they are throwing open the doors and summoning

the biggest men from the crowd. 'Restrain him, please,' says Father Brian and those oily words are flooding into my skull. 'The man is a danger to his own people.'

I think the birds have formed an army and they are pelting down towards us and their beaks are piercing my skin and pecking out my heart. Where will they take him?

'You cannot do this!' Ivo is saying. 'This is my own parish!'

Father Brian does not care about those rules.

I cannot see much from this balcony, but I can hear those crowds have gone as quiet as church mice as the rector is marched out like a common thief though Flavio is hollering like he would raise the dead, all in Spanish, and that is some terrible dirge. I think those dark eyelashes of his will close forever and block out the world.

'God is angry,' I say, and this voice is all rough.

'O, would you shut up!' Father Brian says. 'It is time our good King Henry hears what is happening at this unholy place. Send someone to court with the message since this thing has gone far enough.'

Leominster, Herefordshire

The image tortures him. His beautiful Flavio, locked up, but where? What has that evil man done with him? Is he starving him? Mutilating him like he did Samuel and Ewan? Where does the man's cruelty stop?

He thinks of Robert, the boy from school who first taught him love. Perhaps he is content with his wife in Harrogate. Perhaps he has found a kind of peace there. And perhaps Flavio would have found his own peace as well, had he not been called to work at the vicarage. He could be married to a kindly girl who would eat his pies and cakes and tell him what a fine baker he was. Flavio could have buried those feelings and lived the life of a husband and a father. At least then he would be alive, and not condemned to the flames. He thinks of their greeting in the bakery each morning. It was enough. Wasn't it?

He is still thinking these things when footsteps approach the cellar. Who now? Father Brian again, come to gloat? The guard? The Justice? The King himself? He finds he doesn't give a fuck about his own fate any more. He only cares about Flavio. About Tibb. The people who accepted him. As the door yawns open, he sees a well-dressed man, holding a lantern. Someone he recognizes from the congregation at church.

'Well,' the man says, his voice wiry. 'You know you are lodging in my home?'

He has a sharp, pointed face; his eyes narrowed as he studies Ivo. So this is the man who lets out his cellar for criminals to be penned in. Ivo nods. Does this person expect to be thanked?

He lowers his voice, glancing back up the stairs. 'Listen, I don't know what happened in your church, but my mother is still convinced that woman's an angel.'

Ivo is shocked. He hadn't expected this at all.

The man crouches down, his waistcoat crumpling so the fine gold thread of the lining is just visible. 'She's desperate to hear it from you, Father, since that angel promised to watch over my old papa and she hasn't slept this soundly since he was dead.'

Ivo grimaces. Part of him wants to say the truth, because everything is lost now anyway. Of course she isn't really an angel! How many angels flutter down to Earth and make their home in a rood-loft? He wants to throw his hands up and call this man stupid. A fool.

'Of course,' he says quietly. 'Tell your mother that of course she is really an angel.'

Sunshine streams out of the man's face, lighting up this dank cellar, but Ivo's mind is whirring, taking in the fine clothing. Considering this person's high status.

'Listen,' he says. 'If you believe the angel is real, then why would you keep me here as a prisoner?'

That face goes dark just as quickly as it lit up. The man shakes his head, incredulous. 'Don't you know how much I'm making on you, Father?'

Of course.

Money.

Just blood

Well the time is night but it is never quiet anyway since those crowds outside are all testy again. And some are saying, 'Believe it!' and some are saying, 'Don't!' but in fact I am deaf to all of that shit.

Softly softly, Tibb. Up these stone steps which are grainy and cold under my bare-again feet and this is not feeling like shingle now. Up this thin spiral staircase and I am thinking of Ivo. That lovely man has been taken as a prisoner because of a false-angel and a fool named Tibb Ingleby. Flavio did sob, 'Sorry!' and 'Sorry I let them in!' and he did tell me of the way those priests forced back the door in an ambush. But this is my fault and not his.

How cold I feel in this dress which is in fact the thin slip from underneath my angel-costume. I am all rock-hard at the tits but this is no bother since I will be painted upon the ground soon and those crowds will see more than my fine bulbs. They will see all those mortal things inside me like bile and blood which angels do not have, Tibb. And they will see the marks around my shoulders where those ropes did pull from my wings, and the scabs above my ears from that digging-in crown which is no halo but some shit prop knocked up by a blacksmith in the town of Stratford-upon-Avon.

Flavio's anguished words are floating around inside my skull like one cruel ditty and I wonder I should sing along. 'They have him in a cellar, Tibb. Like my Ivo is a murderer.' I should have asked him: 'Why are you crying on my shoulder, sir, when I am the one who did this thing?'

Step and step, Ma. It would be something strange to think these were my own last steps, but I do not think that because there is no more thinking to be done. Only the doing. I should say Farmer O is waiting up the top with his arms outstretched and saying, 'Of course, Tibb Ingleby. Did I not say you were formed of evil stuff?'

I don't glance down to those huge crowds as I slip past the bell with its cut-out windows. I will see them all soon enough when I am splattered amongst them.

Well I am climbing the ladder and sliding across that trap-door to the roof, and such a coolness is rushing in. The full moon is poking through the little square hole like it would say: 'Tibb, will you come on in?'

Somewhere down there, those not-sleeping people are chattering like the fun is just beginning, but that is all muffled from here. Would you haul yourself up, Tibb? Once you're on that roof, then there's no going back, since that flat surface is open to the world.

It will be one long fall of course, but that thing is some road to redemption for those kind creatures called friends. And one of them who I like to call a husband-man too. Well I can imagine them now and this is some comfort. Their voices saying: 'No! She was a false-angel? But we were fooled just the same!' Then Ivo will be released and this is the least you can do, Tibb Ingleby, since you have done enough bad deeds in this life. Perhaps they will still make it to that island in the sun.

My head is poking up through that hole and I am quaking like a leaf.

Blood and sand, Tibb, but mostly just blood. Or perhaps sand like poor Henrietta who never stood a chance with me.

My arms are flat on this roof too, and soon I will be lit up by the moonlight and they will all be craning their heads to see me fly.

Now, Tibb.

Yes, Farmer O.

But here is a purple hand upon my ankles and this is pinning me to the wood rung. And the angel-person here is pulling me downwards and he is scooping me up in those long-and-colourful arms and carrying me down these spiral stairs like a baby-child, but I can't see much because my eyes are leaking.

More than loyalty

Would you look up, Ma? Right here in this pretty loft which is poking out over the nave of this fine church. Your own Tibb Ingleby, or the Holy Maid as they are calling me out there in this land of Leominster and further besides, but this thing has travelled far from a joke. My lips are peeling and my arm-pits stink and the whole place is smelling like shit.

Ivo has been gone for three days now and I have only a few morsels of consecrated bread left in this vestry and that's all angels eat, sir. 'I can't go blessing the Eucharist in another man's church!' said Father Brian and that grin could have touched the clouds. No other food is coming in since those watching priests have swivelling heads like some bad-enough owls and I think I am something close to starving. The wine kept in the vestry is down to the dregs.

'She looks hungry!' So said Father Brian just yesterday with that look like pity and that false scratching of his forehead. 'I cannot think why she doesn't return to Heaven.'

Ambrose and Flavio have not been bothering to fling open the doors and invite the people in one-by-one because they would surely be hurling eggs or cabbage leaves my way. Else those people would climb to this rood-loft and poke me with a stick to see that I am warm flesh and blood. Their chants are spilling under this door and Ambrose says, 'Tibb, you know there are two factions out there still, and they are fighting something terrible.' And these words sound strange to me because as far as I can tell, those chants seem to start and end with: 'Down with the angel!'

Flavio might well have risen from one of the grave-places beneath us because he is all dead inside. His eyes do stare ahead at nothing and he is muttering in Spanish all the time, slumped in the pew.

At late morning time, Ambrose is pacing the floor with that lovely two-colours face all crumpled with his worries, and I am hanging my head over this railing like I am placing it down for the axe. Father Brian knocks and my Ambrose lets him in, and those two eye-glass-wearing priests do trot in behind, holding their noses because of the high stench in here.

'Yes?' Ambrose says. 'Can I help you?'

'I see that again you are not holding interviews, though you have pilgrims who wish to come in.'

'No, Father Brian. This angel is disappointed in humanity.'

'Then why doesn't she fly back?' He taps his chin. 'O, wait, it is because her wings were hammered by a blacksmith.'

The other two priests guffaw. Perhaps they would jump off the peak of a mountain if Father Brian were to do it first.

'You know Signor Perero remains stuffed in the stocks in town?' Father Reynolds says, ogling me up here. 'His story hasn't changed a bit either – I think he has half the crowd listening now. All about your travels and your costume and your nights spent committing devilry with this ghastly-coloured man.'

My stomach is growling and this thumping in my head has some terrifying beat since there is no tankard of water in sight to stop it.

'Out!' says Ambrose. 'I am still the angel-protector, and this is not your church, Father Brian.'

That hater-of-love looks up at me. 'Nor will it be yours soon enough.' He doesn't raise his voice but these placid words shatter the windows. 'Only an evil witch would do something so much against God. You know, I have seen witches dragged by horse-carts on their bellies, and then thrown into rivers to go the hard way with a great weight attached to their hair. Else thrown upon a pile of kindling and lit up like a beacon. I think that crowd outside would enjoy to see the colours too.'

Lit up?

Ambrose says, 'O, you are the God-denier, sir,' but there is not a single grain of hope left in his voice.

Now Father Reynolds shakes his head and I wonder if it will fall off that stalk-neck. He pokes his spindly finger out towards Ambrose like it is a jabbing-stick for pigs. 'The King is coming, you know.'

Father Brian holds up a hand to that man like he would say: 'I shall deal with this, dear.' He stares at Ambrose, and he does only need to raise one eyebrow to show that slick of disgust across his wax face. 'You will be burning beside that witch up there. Don't you know there are people who say you are a lute-player and not a warden at all?' He shakes his head. 'You are undoubtedly the spawn of a sorcerer yourself with this tainted skin, and it is clear as day that you are colluding together in the meetings you host so often in this locked place. Do you think us all idiots?'

The spawn of a sorcerer? My poor Ambrose has spent his life shedding those evil words. I wish to scream out: 'You are one prize fucker, Father Brian! And have you blood running in those veins or only ice?'

Now he stops, because Flavio is sobbing there like he would cry out a river and have us all swim upstream. And Father Brian is swaying over him and narrowing those cruel eyes, like he did when he stood over those sweet men named Samuel and Ewan. That sliver of disgust is creeping out of him on legs and crawling up the walls of this dark building, leaving behind its trails of slime.

'I have been thinking,' he says, his face contorting with a

smile, 'that it is something quite unusual to have a mere cook so very upset about his master's incarceration.'

Flavio stiffens in that pew and his lovely Spanish skin is turning to sand. 'I am a loyal servant,' he says.

Father Brian laughs and I think that soft sound could topple mountains. 'But I wager it is more than loyalty, sir, for a cook to be visiting his master who is a prisoner now.'

Perhaps I am dead because my own heart has ground to a stop. How does that man know where Flavio went so secretly? Was he following him? Even at night? My halo is slipping to the side, and the ropes of my wings are digging in.

Now the man is pacing. Leisurely, like he would take a ramble as Ivo did call it on the beach at Norfolk. All down the aisle and back. 'It had me thinking about the kind of life you must lead in that house together. The two of you alone so often. It is a strange composition for a vicarage, don't you agree?'

Well here is a silence falling on this dark church and I should wonder the cloud people did smother it. He squats down slowly in front of Flavio. 'I have known men like you—'

'No, Father—'

He smacks Flavio round the face, that cat's paw swiping so quick I hardly see it move. 'If there is depravity then I will find it. On behalf of the King – because, you see, *I* am the loyal servant here. Now get up. I have somewhere I mean to put you, since I cannot risk you running before the King arrives to hear of your sick lust.'

The Lady Margaret Beaufort herself

The noise out there is deafening. So much prattling and hawking, and it seems to have got louder and more insistent, like those people are scaling the walls and bellowing through the weak spots in the stonework saying, 'Tibb Ingleby, you are some bad fucker!' And that rain is not enough to send them away, and instead it is hammering against the windows like it would ask us: 'Will you open the curtains and let me through?'

'They've locked him up in a room at the vicarage, Tibb.' That's what Ambrose said about Flavio and this image is making my head feel hot and then cold and this guilt is fourfold heavier than my stupid wings. Two good people imprisoned because of me. And a baby named Henrietta in a hole too and those things do add up and say: 'Do you hurt everyone you love, child?' I do, Farmer O.

There is an inch of wine in this very-last-bottle and this stuff tastes like vinegar. And there were some stale morsels of bread in my angel-pocket but these are long-gone since yesterday. Perhaps I will starve before they coax me out and kill me but who cares anyway since I deserve all that. My body feels like a lump of lead and I am sitting very still on the stone steps of the altar-place with the snake for company and my knees up against my bulbs which have shrunk.

'I wish to bring you food, Tibb, but they are checking my pockets every time.'

My head is thumping with the nothing-to-drink situation.

'Let's own up,' I mumble. 'At least Ivo and Flavio could feign innocence.'

I can imagine flinging off all this false stuff and telling those fuckers: 'You win,' and, 'It was all my fault and not theirs!'

Ambrose shakes his head. 'We'll find a way.'

Why does he say that shit when it is clear everything is lost?

'You should have let me jump,' I whisper, but he shakes his head and sits down beside me and he holds me close. 'Tibb, we're in it together.'

'Ambrose, the King is coming. You know we will all die for this thing?'

He isn't answering that. Instead he stands up all quietly like he is thinking some big and important things, and he disappears into the vestry, returning with a small brass pot. 'Tibb,' he breathes, his lovely face opening up, 'why didn't we think of it before? The rain!' And he is running up the spiral steps to catch me some rain from that hole-in-the-roof so that I might not die of thirstiness. And what did I do to deserve this kind person, Ma?

Later on, Father Brian and his lapdogs come banging on the door and Ambrose opens it. I did have one nice drink of water before the sky dried up thanks to his clever plan, though I can hardly stand up straight in this stupid high-up home since all my strength is sapped into the mud with the worms. They pant into the nave, brushing down their still-damp clothing like they just fended off the wolves, and Ambrose forces the door shut on those angel-pilgrims who are losing all their manners.

'Such a scene out there. Such a ruckus you have caused over nothing. Are you pleased with yourselves?'

Ambrose asks, 'What is it we can do for you?'

I am thinking they would say: 'The King is here. Would you ready yourselves for the end?'

'The King is otherwise engaged on a hunting excursion.'

There is some glimmer of hope in that, but why is Father Brian not frowning about this piece of news? What are those streaks of jubilance painted across his face?

'He is sending someone else instead.'

Someone else?

Those three priests exchange their smiles like the sky just rained with currant buns. 'In fact, it is even worse for you, since the King's mother, the Lady Margaret Beaufort herself, will attend this church.'

'The Lady Margaret Beaufort?' Ambrose repeats slowly and Father Reynolds is hopping on those skinny ankles.

'The very one. She has recently set up a council for cases such as this. False miracles, though none so audacious as yours. You could say she is something of an expert, and she will quickly decipher this one. The Lady Margaret is not a woman to be trifled with.'

Well this news is the final cry. Did you hear it, Ma? All the bats did screech their last song and all the roses withered. I think the name Margaret Beaufort is bouncing off these stone walls and burrowing into those velvet curtains and will I remove the wings right now?

'Her preferred method is burning of course. I thought it prudent to have the pyres erected in advance, since that angel looks like she might die of starvation any moment, and I do so wish to see her little feet writhe.'

Leominster, Herefordshire

He can smell smoke. It is permeating down into this cellar, burrowing into every small crevice as smoke does. He is reminded of the beach fires he used to make, to cook crabs and marsh-birds and tiny fish for Tibb. But this is different.

One of his hands is tied to the metal ring in the wall, making him agitated like a caged bird. His face streams with tears as the smell of burning wraps around his body. He punches at the wet wall with his free hand like he might have the stones crumble and form a tunnel. An escape. He pictures himself sprinting out; pulling Flavio from the fire and shouting to the world, 'So you call this a sin?'

When the warden finally appears, bending to present the day's crusts, Ivo reaches out and grabs him by the collar, sending him reeling. 'Tell me who's burning!' he shouts. 'Tell me now!'

'I don't know, Father!'

The two men grapple and even with one hand bound up Ivo has more muscle and less dormant flesh by far. He is weakened though from the days spent in here. Faint light floods in as the owner of the house appears, sumptuously dressed again, squinting down the steps and into the cellar.

'Marcus!' he shouts. 'Marcus, what's happening? Does he need restraining further?'

Ivo's free arm drops; the cellar is spinning.

'It's fine!' the warden calls back up. 'Lost my footing, that's all!'

When the master of the house has gone and this place is plunged into near-blackness once more, Ivo says, 'I'm sorry.'

The other man nods, righting his shirt, handing over the food he has smuggled down though Ivo hasn't eaten these offerings in days. 'It won't be long now, Father. They're saying the Lady Margaret Beaufort is nearly here. A matter of hours.'

'The King's mother?'

'That's what they're saying.'

It makes sense. They say the Lady Margaret is such a pious woman she may as well be a nun.

He leans back to rest his head on the wall. Whoever his executioner is, it is a strange relief to have something definite. A time. A name. He finds his mind is emptying itself ready.

Stand up like wheat-sheafs

'Ambrose?' I whisper, half-toppling down the pillar. 'What is this mad smile about? Didn't you hear what they said – the pyres are being built already?'

That curly ginger hair is falling over his eyes and he is gawping like he is walking down the path to madness – and I did see that same thing cross my own ma's sweet face oftentime. Mostly just before she would say: 'Tibb, will we take off our clothes and frolic in that rain-storm since we don't need a roof to be happy?'

He holds me, those strong arms wrapped around me like he would never let me go and in fact I would like that very much just now and any day besides, and then he stops and looks me right in the eye.

'Tibb, I am smiling because this is the finest news we could have hoped for!'

O, this riddle is having me cock my head and grit my teeth because soon after my own ma had frolicked in the rain, then she would curl into a ball and cry about the no-roof problem, else the urge to do throat-slitting, and everything seemed much worse.

'I have a little tale that will make your hairs stand up like wheat-sheafs.'

A tale? He would tell me a tale when the King's own mother is coming here? When the end is eye-balling us in the face?

He lowers his voice to a deadly whisper. 'Do you remember I told you that I found some employment a few years back, which was to play my lute at the house of the Lady Astor?

She was a wealthy woman and a regular person to attend the court of the King, and a particular friend of the very same Lady Margaret Beaufort who is coming here today.'

'Yes. And how is the Lady Astor in any way useful to us?'

Ambrose's eyes are all round and shiny like two nice coins.

'Well, while I was playing for her that summer, in her fine house in the county of Berkshire if I remember right, her good friend the Lady Margaret Beaufort paid a visit with a great retinue of ladies. I would play on my lute and sleep in the kitchens with all the scullery-folk but I found it much too hot. One night I decided to walk around the gardens of that grand place for my lack of sleeping, and who did I come across in the dead of night but the Lady Margaret Beaufort herself in a small chapel by a lake.'

I cannot think where my man is going with this strange tale.

'And she was kneeling upon the stone floor in front of the great cross, Tibb, and whispering all things to God. Words which I confess I stopped to eavesdrop upon.'

'Yes?' I say and I am getting impatient to hear the end. 'Would you go on?'

'Tibb,' he says, and he rests his big hands on my shoulders. 'I heard something so damning that night, that I have kept it to myself all these years, since this thing would be treasonous if passed to the wrong hands.'

I think my eyes are bursting out from my head. 'But what was it that she said, Ambrose?'

More wild falsities

The door is thrown open.

'Well? Where is this so-called angel?'

The Lady Margaret Beaufort's raspy voice is no sweet melody and it is screeching into the church like an axe was thrown. 'Show yourself!'

That tiny shrew-woman stands in the doorway, all lit up thanks to our own bright moon tonight and those small lanterns that her following-behind ladies are carrying. In fact, she has arrived in perfect time like a very well-mannered banquet guest, just when those on-the-clouds people have blown the sun out to help us. And the angel-enthusiasts who have been chattering out there all night have gone quiet. The crowd seems to stretch on forever, all their torches and their candles held aloft and their mouths hanging open like a whole host of hungry birds.

'I haven't time for your ridiculous child-play!' she does howl into this nave and it is clear this woman is vexed to have been called to observe another plot-against-God. And at such a late hour besides. She waves her hand in front of her face. 'But I can hardly see!'

And I can hardly see *you*, madam, under all that white powder and that map of wrinkles across your face. She is dressed like a nun to boot in a black gown and hood, covered right up to her chin. But of course she is a very poor nun indeed if her deeds are to speak for themselves. Really she has done something secret and terrible and Tibb Ingleby knows all about it.

Behind, her retinue of ladies-in-waiting are squinting up at the empty rood-loft, all expectant, and Father Brian's not-so-soft-any-more voice seems to rise above the throng. 'Where is she?'

I can just see him stepping forward. That strand of hair has escaped again from its oiled curtain and is dangling in front of his eye and he does not bother to push it back.

'She's been in that rood-loft, madam,' he says, 'I swear!'

And the Lady Margaret tuts and says, 'Well she is not there now, sir. What nonsense have you called me to?'

Those tendons in Father Brian's duck-neck are so tight, I wonder they have been stretched like a catapult – the kind my ma did think to make in happier times – and soon enough a polished-up conker will ping out and have us all cold dead. O, it is some sweet tincture to see him sweating like that. And Father Cuthbert and Father Reynolds, those thorns-in-our-backsides, loitering behind him too, but they are all soupy in the darkness of the doorway.

'I am coming in!' the Lady Margaret announces to this black haze, and that foot of hers says tap-tap-tap on those cold stones and her ladies tell her, 'Careful, madam. Do you think it is quite safe to enter?'

She swats at them. 'Safe? Of course it is safe! Don't you think I have seen more wild falsities than this? Stay right there, since I do not need your assistance in these matters.'

If I was not so shit-scared then I could laugh aloud at the way she teeters on her little trotter-feet, edging her way down this aisle like the floor might crumble away.

'It is far too dark and smoky! What ill-will is going on?' she says, waving a heavily jewelled hand in front of her face.

Learn from your own ma, Tibb: darkness hides all shady deeds. Well we have not lit one candle in fact since there are some shady-as-fuck deeds to see here, sir.

'And why does it smell so *strong*? It is like a whore's bedchamber, this church.'

Now that one is easily explained, madam, since we have been burning all the incense in the vestry to cover the smell of shit which is rising up from the floorboards.

Father Brian calls from the doorway: 'I swear, she is *always* in the rood-loft, My Lady, and now she is gone! Perhaps I might come in and assist you—'

'No, sir!' she orders, and 'Stay right there! I am not requiring your help, since you have solved precisely nothing so far!'

I can see her a little better now and she is thin like a reed, this old mother-of-the-King. If I were that rich I would cram my face so full with ham pies that Ambrose would need to roll me into the bedchamber like a barrel every evening.

'Show yourself! Do I make myself heard?'

O, you do, madam. I am hearing these shrill words loud and clear since they do sound like a bitch in season. The crowds out there have grown silent with this royal arrival. Their fire-torches sway, all of them grainy under the smoky haze.

'Perhaps she is in the vestry?' calls Father Reynolds from the threshold.

No, I am not in the vestry, my simple friends, because I am right above you. I am wrapped around these wood beams in the darkness of the ceiling like a big moth with my wings fixed tight, and Ambrose is here too, all dressed in black and blending into his own beam like he is carved of wood besides. I have dangled us into this puddle-of-water hoax so now I plan to get us out, because my own Ivo did teach me to swim.

Spooked like a deer

'Show yourself!' the woman says, with her beady eyes roving around the pews. 'Else I will search the place from top-to-bottom. You cannot fool me!'

Ah, but this is exactly what I plan to do. Just a little further down this aisle, Your Greatness-of-Terrible-Deeds, and I shall be floating down to meet you as angels do. What I have to say must be whispered into an ear-hole and not called out from the rafters.

My heart is banging against my rib-cage like it does have its own escaping-plan and I am tugging on this crab-fishing wire since that is our secret-sign and my clever man and I have practised this enough. The crab-fishing wire is stronger by far than a hair-wire but we have weaved it into what Ambrose calls a *plait* to be extra sure. He has fastened it around my chest and under both of my arms where the ropes from the wings are hiding too. And he is holding the other end because he is called the puppet-master here.

'You are like a feather, Tibb,' he did say when he practised the precarious art of lowering me down from his perch in the rafters. No shit, sir – I have half-starved in here. It is not invisible like the hair was though, and that is why we did befriend the darkness today.

Ambrose glances at me as though to say: 'Tibb, the time is nigh.'

The whites of his eyes are glowing and even in this hold-your-breath moment he has that quiet calm about him. And so lower me down, my big man, for this is the only hope we have of ending this stretched-out and fucked-up piece of trickerie.

Now, Tibb.

Letting go of the wood beam is no easy task. Would you put your trust in a glass horse, Tibb? No, Ma, and yet now we would trust a plaited wire with our own lives. I take my hands off the beam and I can feel the wire go taut which is some sweet relief.

Well my breath does stop as I float down, upright, with my hands clasped in prayer, and I think every breath in this kingdom is held just the same. Up there, Ambrose will have tied that plait around his wrist and he does let it out inch-by-inch so I am not falling splat on to the stone floor like a bird-shit. This wire is tightening around my chest and under my arms and perhaps all the blood will stop flowing. My hands tingle.

The Lady Margaret's mouth opens like a baby bird but no sound is coming out except a whimper like 'O!' and 'O, my Lord!' and I do think we are in business, sir. Now she is holding on to her no-bulbs chest as I come to float down beside her currant-face like a spider, hanging there six inches off the ground, this glaze-eyed stare on my un-angelic face.

'Not too close, Tibb,' Ambrose did warn me. And he did not need to add the words, 'because you stink like a barn, dear,' since that much was obvious and my husband-man is the fine owner of those nice things called manners.

'My Lady,' I whisper. 'I have waited to receive you.'

Well her face has gone all shades of holy-fuck and I am wondering whether those cloves which Ambrose brought me to chew upon have not quite done the trick. Is she recoiling because of my own breath-stench? Or is it possible I am streaked with sweat and dirt from all the climbing we have done this day? Ambrose did wipe my face up with the last of the rainwater because it isn't every day you do meet the mother-of-a-king but perhaps I look like I just bathed in a pig trough.

'God has seen your deeds and that thing which is locked inside your conscience.'

This plait-wire will surely stop my blood from flowing. And perhaps we did practise one time too many and we did weaken the thing. This halo is slipping to the side and I am cocking my head so it doesn't clatter to the floor.

'Deeds?' she breathes and she does choke some noises like the words are wedged inside of her throat. She has splayed her hands over her eyes and I am studying those rings which are stacked up on her wide-knuckled twig-fingers. 'I do not know what you speak of.'

I think she might keel over in fright for she is spooked like a deer.

'Just let me see that angel, madam!' Father Brian calls from outside and this skinny woman bellows, 'Shut up!' from somewhere deep down inside of her guts which is no ladylike sound.

Those ladies and priests are hanging back some yards in the doorway and open-mouthed too, and that crowd beyond is all hushed to silence. I did not imagine those fire-torches and lanterns from the crowd-people would be so bright though. If only a gust of wind might come and blow them all out. O, would you keep your nerve, Tibb?

'I believe you know exactly what I speak of, madam,' I tell her in my whispers. 'Something which you did to two innocent children. I am an agent of God, and even those things you have not told a soul are known well to me.'

Her face freezes. In the doorway her ladies are edging forwards and she turns round and barks again, 'Back! Stay out, you rogues!' because this woman is an expert in the art-of-deceit and in the keeping-of-secrets and she does not want anyone to hear of her naughty past. Well those women are wide-eyed and affronted because these rich-as-kings people do not often get told no. I can see that Father Brian has slunk back too, fury sprawled across his face as he does stand upon his toes and call again and again, 'But Lady Beaufort, would you hear me a moment?'

Ah, but no one is spared from that thing named authority, Father. Won't you know your place too? It is no time for laughter, Tibb, though I think I could howl with it. Above me, Ambrose will be lying across the beams, his face all strained with his efforts.

She tells me, 'I don't know who you speak of, angel,' and still she holds on to her no-bulbs like they might fly away too.

'Madam,' I whisper, so only she can hear. 'I am privy to the secret of your heart, and the foul deed pertaining to those two princely boys within the Tower. The fact that their disappearance was your own doing. You killed them, madam. Do not offend him further.'

Now she is swooning on that stone floor, scrambling with her stick-legs. 'No,' she is croaking at me, 'I will not offend him, Your Holiness.'

Those fat ladies are calling, 'Madam? Would you allow us to help you?' and Father Brian is saying over and over, 'If I could just come in, Your Highness, I am certain there is something unholy at play!' but this woman on the floor is swatting at the air and shouting to those pissed-off watchers, 'Stay back, I said! Or I will have my son ship you all to Calais in exile!' And she is pulling up that too-high collar like she would cover her face if she could.

'Do not offend him,' I repeat and I am touching my halo which is the signal to Ambrose to pull me up quick, sir! 'Do not be long down there, Tibb,' he said to me. 'We can't be sure how well the plait will hold.'

This is one slow ascent, but I am peering up at those beams

and then back down to the Lady Margaret who is plastered on the floor like a black puddle. 'Go!' I want to shout at that woman. That door needs closing and soon because I am thinking that there is nowhere to hide once I am up in the rafters, and which angels do you know that sit like birds on a branch? We did not think too hard about that part, Ma. I glance up at Ambrose and he looks like those same thoughts are rattling through his own mind too.

'Leave me to God, madam,' I say, 'while you consider everything I have said this night.'

The Lady Margaret Beaufort is nodding and nodding and crawling out of this church on her hands and knees. Such a hush among that crowd outside, I should say there is a blanket thrown over them.

'It is an angel!' she announces, staggering to her feet with the help of her wizened old lady-friends. 'This is a true angel in here!'

Such a gasp – I wonder every ocean did draw back from the sand. I reach for the beam and swing myself up but muscles like Maria's would be something helpful just now. I am slipping and sliding all over the place with my sweaty hands and Ambrose is pulling that wire because in a moment I'll topple to that floor after all and those still-peeping-in priests will have won. He inches forward, reaching to push me up by the backside with his big purple palm till I am lying flat on top of the beam again, wrapped around like a snake. The two of us are catching our breath and listening hard.

'What did she say?' the priests are asking, though I can't see them any more, and Father Brian's crisp voice is louder than any. 'What did the false-angel frighten you with, madam? That thing is all a ruse!' Suddenly he darts forward a few feet into the aisle, searching this place with his empty eyes. 'Is that another person I see upon the ceiling? A man?'

Fuck, Ma. I am pressing my body against this beam but I am white as a ghost and my heart is like thudding away and perhaps Father Brian will hear that too.

'How dare you?' the Lady Margaret says. 'Out! I said everyone out! Do not presume to cross me, sir!'

They are not so dense to argue with this woman who all but rules the country for her weakling son and she slams the great wood door shut at last so this church turns black again, none of that torchlight whispering in.

From his next-to-me beam, Ambrose reaches out and takes my hand and I can see the relief in that shut-eyes face and in the hand-squeezing he is doing.

'In there is an angel!' the Lady Margaret is announcing to the crowd and my ear is pricked like a dog ear. 'A real holy angel, and that is of no doubt! I have proof!'

'What proof?' some are hollering back like they did forget their manners in this kingdom called England which cares very much about respecting the rich. 'What is the proof?'

The Lady Margaret's voice carries over the hushed-up crowd: 'That is my business. The angel requires the peace of the empty church. No one is to speak to her again, and I demand this church to be left fallow for three months at least, and if the angel has not retreated to Heaven by the time it is opened again, then I will demand you wait until she has.'

Of course you will, dear. To who else might I tell your little-big secret?

Ambrose squeezes my hand some more and his smile is reaching those shaped-like-an-almond eyes.

Now I can hear that syrupy voice of Father Brian. 'Madam, madam. Please, let's speak properly on the topic of the angel,' but she cuts him off with a big un-ladylike screech and a stamp of her trotter-foot.

'Here is my law on the subject: not a soul might enter – not even you, sir – and these crowds are to leave this instant. Anyone lingering around this church will be brought to the stocks in the town square of which I am told about.'

'What about the priest, Father Ivo?' the crowd shout back. 'He is caught up in a cellar in the town!'

'And that is another crime! Fetch the man back, and take these priests instead since they are the true offenders of God. Father Ivo might decide their fate. Now take me home!'

'Madam?'

'Take me to my chapel, since I have a good deal of praying to be doing there.'

Now *that* you do, dear.

Leominster, Herefordshire

There are people coming. They are descending the staircase to this cellar with purposeful strides. An army of men, come to drag him out and throw him on to the fire because of course this is the end. The Lady Margaret Beaufort has arrived and has judged the angel to be, in fact, entirely human. She has seen the sick deception that was conjured up and now she will condemn the depraved priest who fakes miracles and fucks men, and she will have him thrown on to the flames too.

He feels a thin stream of urine trickling down his leg; his head feels heavy, lolling on to his shoulder. Maybe it was always coming. Perhaps he was wrong to consider a loving God who is tolerant and kind, and this is the punishment for his subversive nature. Just like they said.

'Perhaps there is no God,' he said to the warden earlier.

'Father! How can you say that?'

Where his mind was busy – populated by images – now it is simply bare. He is a fruitless tree. Have Tibb and the others already faced the flames? Will he smell their flesh in the air?

The iron door creaks open and a faint light trickles in, spreading its half-circle on to the grime of the floor, and he buckles for the end.

Run across the rooftops

Flavio and Ivo walk into this church like they would come to the altar and marry. It is something rapturous to see their sweet faces again. Ivo looks tired and pale and he says, 'Tibb?' like he isn't too sure because I am all trussed up as his housekeeper once more in this old headscarf and a long coat. Ambrose has fashioned for me two dark eyebrows and some whiskery hairs to boot with his clever lute-playing hands.

Well the guilt is swelling up inside of me and I think it will come steaming out of my ears and my nose and I am glaring down at my booted-up feet like these are something truly interesting.

'Ivo,' I whisper. 'I'm sorry.'

It is quiet then, only the sound of the breeze against the big windows, and I wonder if my oldest friend will ever forgive a girl named Tibb who almost had him on a pyre. But he steps forwards, and those warm fingers – which once did prise the dead baby called Henrietta from me, and which did make a straggly seaweed belt for me, and which did point out my own ma in the big sky to me – they are now wiping away these hot tears.

'Tibb,' he whispers with a very-Ivo chuckle and he holds my face in his hands. 'You did it!' And we are laughing like we did on those sand-hills and my Ivo is saying hoo-and-haa to boot and we are hanging on to each other's necks like monkeys. 'I sent those prying priests to stand in the stocks at their own parishes, Tibb. You should have seen their faces!'

Well I like the thought of that, and especially of Father

Brian pelted with eggs, though he deserves much worse. For Samuel and Ewan and for those black marks around Flavio's lovely eyes which were caused by that fucker's own fists, I think.

'And Signor was chased off just as soon as he was released, because no one wishes to suffer that man's strange tales now the King's mother has confirmed there is an angel in the church here,' Flavio says. 'The people of Leominster will be talking about their resident angel for years to come, and how they never doubted her even for a moment.'

How sweet it is to dance around this church in a line, holding on to each other's shoulders and throwing our legs in all directions and hooting up to the rafters.

'It is mighty fine to see you without those wings and robes,' Ivo pants when we are done with this mad jig. 'But why the costume?' He peers out the window. 'There is no one hanging around outside this place since the Lady Margaret has spoken. I think we might run across the rooftops and no one would notice!'

I tut-tut and I say, 'Now I am not too fond of risks, Ivo, and have you ever heard of a thing named prudence?'

I think my friend could turn over milk urns with that face.

Not one evil thing

This fine leek pie is half-way to my greedy mouth when Maria returns two days later. She clatters into the vicarage with John at her side and she stands there in my skinny-armed embrace saying, 'I heard what happened, my friends. You fooled everyone! You did it!'

She wishes to know it all and we are having some fine meeting of memories around Ivo's grand table.

'Whatever happened to that run-away priest, Maria? And why did you take so long? I have been painting all sorts of terrible stories inside of my head involving dark lanes and vagrants and scarlet bodies dead in ditches.'

Maria chuckles. 'Ah, now that one is a story to warm the flanks.'

John leans forward, watching me all the while. 'We followed him to a travelling lodge, Tibb, and it was there that we witnessed his antics for ourselves, and that is no celibate man, I can tell you. So many whores were stuffed into the inn, and he was trying out every single one up in his lodging room. He had them brought up, one after the other. The man has the stamina of an ox!'

Maria says, 'Ha! But then I did knock upon his door and he was surprised to see a big Flemish girl at the threshold and not his next maid with her corset half undone already. "You?" he said, and his face went white. "Yes, sir, it is I!" I told him. "And you are caught up here!"'

'And?' I say. 'What happened then?'

Maria shakes her shiny brown hair so it falls down her back.

'Such a fear of Father Brian that man had, Tibb, and he begged to know what might be done to have us keep his secret. So we named our price there and then – no further talk of Mr Manners.'

'Maria!' I say, because this person has the cunning for all of England.

'And we demanded his horse-cart too, just for good measure.'

Well this story is something amusing and wonderful and I am laughing till my sides ache. 'You are two good friends,' I tell them. 'Though we will not be needing a horse-cart where we are going. You know we are quite ready to sail away!'

In fact, that boat is calling from its little mooring on the River Severn and saying, 'Tibb, would you hurry if you wish to see the sun before you're old and shrivelled up like the Lady Margaret Beaufort herself?'

'Yes, Tibb,' Maria says, but she is not really looking at me now and I am getting the sense that there are certain things not being said in this loaded-with-questions silence. It looks like there is something sharp and pointy shoved up her backside. She glances to John with those big brown eyes. 'In fact, to own a horse-cart is a fine thing. We have made good use of it these past few days . . .' Then: 'Tibb,' she says quietly, 'could I trouble you to put those wings on just once more?'

'My *wings*? I should rather not, Maria. I was hoping never to wear those things ever again!' And here is some chortling from my own mouth but Maria isn't laughing with me.

'Maria?' I say because something strange is most certainly going on.

She says, 'Tibb, while you all had your work cut out here, I have been doing my own type of work, since idling is no friend to me as you know, but *you* are a friend to me, and that is why I did it.'

This is a riddle which is not fitting inside of my skull and that leek pie is going cold on the plate. 'I cannot think what you mean, Maria.'

She tucks her chestnut hair behind her ears and she runs her fingers over her face like this is some tricky thing for her to say. 'The truth is, after we had dealt with the run-away priest, we took a journey in the horse-cart, and that's where we have been these past few days. Looking for someone.'

'*Looking*? Looking for who?'

'Well,' she says, and she puts those big country hands on my shoulders and shoves me on to the wood chair.

'Tibb,' she says, kneeling down in front of me. 'John and I took the horse-cart down to the town of Weymouth, the home of the farmer who you spoke of and I have never forgotten it.'

Farmer O? Some great banging is happening between my ears and my blood feels like it is in fact ice-blood. 'Maria,' I breathe, 'that was no business of yours, and don't you think Ma and I went back there? He moved on!'

She nods, glancing again to John. 'But we found one person who knew of his movements, and I must tell you that we tracked him down.'

'Maria,' I whisper. 'Why would you do it? It was you who said: "Do not loiter in the past . . ." '

She takes my hands into hers and they are all cushiony and rough with calluses from her lifting hobby.

'That is all well and good, but there is unfinished business, Tibb, and revenge to be had, and that is a medicine which I think your ma never got to try.'

Well that is something true right there but my own head-thoughts are drowning and then coming up for air.

'What did you tell him?'

'Only that had he heard of the angel, which of course he had, and that the angel wished for an audience with him.'

Well I am gulping down this great lump in my throat, and here is my belly going round-and-round like there is a barrel of mead inside of it.

'He is here, Tibb. At Leominster. And I think you should see him, because there is not one evil thing about you, my friend.'

Like death warmed up

'O, Heavenly one!' he says.

This man has aged like a piece of leather but I would know him anywhere. That tufty moustache and the full beard and those cruel eyes. Those hands which did poke and prod where they were not wanted. I am grasping this wooden railing like I cannot trust my own legs and there is some muffled noise inside my ears because those frightened feelings are flooding back thick and fast. You are six-or-thereabouts, Tibb, and he is come to do that thing again.

'Angel?' he gasps. 'Is it really you?'

I nod once, and I am pulling this hood lower down over my face with a shaky hand and I am thinking that I should never have agreed to this. Now there are two colours which are loud inside my mind and one is white because that is fear and the other is red for all the shame which is cropping up while I remember what happened back then. I do remember the pulsing of his prick inside my child-hand and the taste of his beer-breath in my ear. And then there is Maria's voice while she did put my wings back on, over the sores from the ropes and the crab-wire, rubbing oil on my skin as she did it, like this was a sort-of-apology.

'Just once more, Tibb,' she said. 'You have to see how small he is. You have to see it or he will be large in your mind forever when in fact he should not be taking up an inch.'

I didn't answer her while she placed the halo on my head, rubbing more of the oil behind my ears.

'I can't look at him,' I whispered and she held me tight by the collar like she might knock me out herself. 'You have to,

Tibb,' she said, her teeth gritted. 'Promise me, you will look him straight in his eyes?'

O, Maria. I hope you are right in this last-of-all scheming of yours.

'Farmer Oswyn,' I say, and I am wincing at this name as it does echo around this stone building because I have not said it out loud or thought it even once. 'I wanted to see you, since I have tidings from that holy place.'

'You do?' he says.

I am forcing myself to look at him. At the greying hair sprouting from his nose. The way his arms hang down by his breeches like two limp onions. In fact, the longer and harder I look at him, the smaller he seems down there. One small and sad man. A pin-prick in this vast world.

I nod. 'The thing is, sir,' I say, and I can hear some note of sureness in my voice, 'they all had it wrong. I am not from that holy land called Heaven, but the other one.'

'The other one?' he says, and that is the same creased-up face he did pull when he told me: 'Tibb, you know you have lured me to these sheets again?' But that was all one big lie, wasn't it?

'That's right, sir. I am come from Hell.'

Now I am lifting down this hood. My own face is painted so I am like death warmed up. Flavio has smeared white flour in some places and ash in others, such as around my eyes, for this very effect. There is some strawberry juice too so that I am dripping with blood. That little man gasps like there is truly some evil spirit in this church.

'You are no angel, then?' he stammers, grabbing the pew.

'O, I am an angel, sir, just a bad one. An evil one in fact. I am the source of all evil sent from the devil himself, and that is why I am come to you, because you are evil too.'

'No!' he says. 'Not me!'

I lean forward, and I think there is a hot current rippling through my veins and a feeling like rage which could bubble over and scald the world.

'You are, sir. And I am here to recruit you to that place called Hell since you will be there soon enough anyway.'

'No!' he warbles, a hand on his heart. 'I am never going there!'

'O, you are, Farmer Oswyn. And I will bring you there myself.'

'Then I will run!' he shouts, twisting his body like he is caught up in a trap. 'I will run!'

I watch as he stumbles down the aisle, his knees giving way, his hands reaching for the wood doors.

'But I will find you!' I call after him. And, 'Do not forget, I will be always one pace behind!' as he drops his hat and curses and runs like the bulls are pounding behind him.

Ma – did you see it?

Now those friends of mine are stepping out of the vestry and Maria does throw her hands up. 'You did not let me kill the man, Tibb?' she cries, like she is truly disappointed.

There is something like power trickling into my body and I breathe very deeply and the air smells different, like all the dust did fly away. 'No, Maria.'

These shoulders of mine have never felt lighter.

'But I was ready!' She flexes her muscles. 'You know I am a big country girl.'

I smile at this but I am shaking my head because the little hobby of throat-slitting did not ever shift the clouds for my ma.

Ambrose comes and leans down to look me in the eyes and he is all riled up like my friend Maria, those gentle fists clenched. 'Tibb,' he says quietly. 'Let me run out there and give him a grisly end. I think I won't rest till I've done that.'

I smile. 'O, I already did it, Ambrose,' I say. Because I know what that ugly thing called shame can do to a person.

Parting gifts from an angel

'Come on, Tibb!' my old friend Ivo is saying the next day. 'We are to be collecting our sturdy sailing-boat at the River Severn and we will want to start our sea journey while this fine weather stays.'

Well I am coming down these stairs all ready in my red-and-yellow parrot dress once again and my good leather boots, but that once-mane of white hair is cut off to my neck for I will want to feel the wind around my face in those high seas. And Flavio has used walnut shells and tree bark to dye it this shade of brown because you can never be too careful when there is a perfect island waiting on the horizon.

'We could be sisters, Tibb!' Maria says.

We are off to somewhere even the most Spanish of people cannot find, Ma, let alone Signor Perero who in fact is not Spanish in the least. He would be searching till the seas freeze over and the sun turns cold.

What a fine thing to see Ivo smiling again, and looking like he did in those days at Norfolk. All unshaven and dressed simply in a linen shirt and breeches. He has that Bible tucked into his belt too because faith is something different than they tell you, Tibb.

'I should want to buy a little hat on the way,' I say. 'Since I am grown out of the shirt-turban of our Norfolk-days, and the sun will be hot where we are off to. And a new lute for my Ambrose besides when we come across the good city of Hereford.'

'As you like it, Tibb.'

Ivo leaves that door swinging open for the next rector who might move in here.

'Wait,' I say, once we are out of this vicarage with its lovely orchard and on the path-to-a-new-life. 'I need to do one last thing in that church which is of great importance to me.'

And those five friends of mine are waiting in this pinched horse-cart of ours while I am rushing in.

Here is some shuffling around in the vestry and some moving of floorboards. Some scrambling up to the rood-loft which was a home to me for far too long. And this is a nice gathering of gifts once I am finished, all lined up in that balcony-place: a pair of not-so-fine wings hammered by a very bad man; a metal crown of no great expense; a long string of white hair, knotted in places; a rolled-up and plaited crab-fishing line; and a receptacle containing one of those naughty things which I did store under the floorboards. These, my parting gifts from an angel.

I am about to leave this place by way of swinging over the rail as is my little way, but I stop. I run my hands over the railing, feeling the coarse wood beneath my palms. Not gripping it like I did when Signor turned up, or when Father Brian arrived with his part-the-sea hair, or when Farmer O thought to take me back to Weymouth. I run my hands across it like the piece of dead-wood it is. And I look down upon those empty-for-once pews and imagine all the people who have crammed themselves into this church-place to sit and gaze at me up here. Thousands of them, I think. And perhaps just some of them do have a good memory of it, like this strange thing called life is a little bit sweeter after they did meet a real angel.

Down in the nave I stand in the aisle and I look at those wood doors where Ambrose did usher in all the angel-pilgrims with their sad requests for my own kind help, or else their greedy demands for more and more, please, angel. And I look at the altar-place, the same table-wearing-a-skirt that you do find in every church in England, and which my ma liked a lot. On the wall behind it the cross is hanging up and I am wondering if maybe the God-man is real after all, because it is something like a miracle that we are not all dead in the ground. And it is something like a miracle besides that now the man we called Signor is hushed to silence about the real truth and in fact he is turned vagabond though he did threaten me with that word long ago. I can imagine him roaming this shit country like I once did, without his tent or his whore-money. And have you heard of just deserts, sir?

'Thank you?' I whisper at the cross, like that is a question. Then I blush like a fool because who the fuck knows if anyone is listening at all?

My eyes linger over the criss-cross beams high above. I can imagine Ambrose up there, his face straining as he inched me up and down for the Lady Margaret Beaufort to swoon at. You're a lucky person, Tibb, if you find a man who does love you enough not to chuck you out on your arse. Well I found one, Ma, while I was hiding in that tree-hollow. Or perhaps he found me.

My friends are waiting out there but I can't help climbing the stairs up to the bell-tower. These stone steps seem closer together than they were. I stop at the bell which I hid in once and I am thinking of the bells which interrupted our beach days in Norfolk and Suffolk and which Ivo never liked to hear. I run my hand over that smooth metal and I am wondering when this thing will be singing next, since the Lady Margaret did declare this place a fallow field.

At the top of the stairs I reach up to slide across the wood door to the flat roof, and I do gaze at the blue sky which was one small comfort to me when I was trapped in this burrow like a rabbit. It was there on that roof that I did have the big thought of the island-home, and when I did think of angels and the plan for our great ruse. And where Ivo took me to see my own ma when we were neck-deep in that bad jape.

Ma. I am thinking of you now. I am thinking of how you did tell me: 'Live the life you dream, Tibb!' and 'Would you let this short life slither past?' Well maybe we will reach that island-place or maybe we won't get there at all but nothing can be worse than this kingdom called England and would you let a ripe apple roll on by, Tibb?

No, Ma. I would not.

Outside they say, 'Are you ready now, Tibb?'

'O, I am ready, my friends, and I am bound for island-life with you fine people. Those waves are calling and all those juicy fruits and those swimming fish, and I think we shall never look back!'

And here we are in this horse-cart which Maria did acquire by hooks-and-crooks since we are the best-of-friends, and we are riding out of this nothing-in-between kingdom like we mustn't miss the fair. Hoo-and-haa, Ma. And do you see me here?

This little hand

Somewhere in the middle-of-nowhere but off the coast of Portugal

The sea is calm like a mill-pond in the shallows around our something-like-paradise island, and the sun is shining down as though it wishes to fry us all like fritters. Thank goodness I thought to buy this fine straw hat with our Robin Hood money, since I would be all burnt at the edges otherwise.

So, here I am: bad-girl, hoodwinker and one-time-angel Tibb Ingleby, walking along like the Queen of Castile herself. All around this floury beach which wreathes our secret island.

Ivo says two years have passed since we arrived at this Heaven-on-Earth place but who is counting years when years are so very perfect? In fact, I should like to count backwards, and give ourselves *more* time to live.

In the water there, Flavio, who is a most clever man, has created a net from reed plants and he is wading in those shallows and catching us another delicious dinner of fish. And afterwards, my dear Ambrose will be playing on that lute of his, as has become our tradition every night.

'Tibb!' Flavio calls when we go past. 'We shall be enjoying a good catch this evening. Do you know there is a crab in this net?'

'A crab?' I say. 'Now Ivo will be pleased about that!'

On we go across this beach with that sparkly water glittering beside us. This little hand in mine is gripping on because walking is something new and difficult and this feeling inside of me has wide-open wings like an eagle.

Maria is standing and laughing by these tall-as-a-tower trees where she has built a great tree-house, because her skill of lifting and her great ambition of house-building have been put to the test. And there is her son inside of it and he is a beefy thing already and smiling with his two coming-in teeth.

She waves and waves. 'Look, Tibb!' she shouts. 'I have built a little roof just this morning.'

A roof. A roof especially for our own tiny children.

'Fine work, Maria!' I do call out with that small frog sitting inside of my throat.

On we go, and this place is all stuffed with orange trees as you can well see, Ma. I have found that oranges are the king-of-all-fruits, though if I am sick of them, then I might nibble upon figs or pears or an olive or other such vegetables that Flavio does make it his business to grow. He sees to it that we are all full up with delicious things every day and I should say I am growing round and fat like a bun which is pleasing me a great deal. And these tits of mine have bulged out to boot. You are a woman of the world, Tibb Ingleby.

Yes, Ma.

I walk a bit further round this bay where I find my Ambrose doing some good patching of the boat with John. We use that thing sometimes for the purpose of fishing excursions, or else to seek out a sunny place to eat upon an even-smaller-island. Or an off-to-the-mainland journey which takes longer of course. We are truly in the middle of the ocean here.

'Tibb!' Ambrose says. 'We have hatched a great plan to take you all to see the flying-fish!'

O, Ambrose, you God-of-the-sex-kind, I could jump upon those lovely long limbs of yours any day of the week, and who knows what day it is since this does not matter one piece?

Ivo, who was napping under a palm tree, wakes up with the big-man's book on his muscly chest and he says with a smile,

'Tibb, I think I see that small daughter of yours walking in perfect straight lines,' and this compliment has me turning from pink to red.

'Well she is, Ivo. She is getting the hang of it quick. Would you look at that trail of little footprints?'

Now Ivo is bending down in front of this person who I did not name Henrietta, because Henrietta was a person too and that would be to replace her. This one I have named Angela because it is some perfect name for an angel.

Ivo is taking those two pudgy hands and he is leading that daughter of mine into the shallows and he is swinging her up and down in a sea-dance so her little feet skim the surface and she likes that a lot. And would you dance with me, Tibb? For these are the days and I should say they were always coming.

Acknowledgements

A big thank you to all at Penguin Fig Tree for taking a chance on my debut novel; I feel extremely lucky that Tibb and I ended up with you. My editor, Helen Garnons-Williams, you are such a pleasure to work with. From the beginning my experience at Fig Tree has been amazingly positive and you were so considerate of the fact I had a new baby competing for my time. I really appreciate you being completely in tune with the story and for pushing me to make it stronger. I couldn't have wished for a kinder editor. Thank you also to Ella Harold for your insightful comments, ideas and support. Another huge thank you to the wonderful marketing and publicity team: Kayla Fuller, Olivia Mead and Alexia Thomaidis. Thank you to my copy-editor, Sarah-Jane Forder: your eagle-eyes are truly remarkable and I am very grateful for your hard work and your generous comments. I have loved being part of an all-woman team.

Thank you to my agent, Katie Greenstreet – surely the best agent in London! Your support has been invaluable. Again, I feel very lucky that you took a chance on me. You have given me so much time – jumping on Zoom to explain submissions and pre-empts and contracts – and your unfailing enthusiasm and professionalism have made the whole process of selling the book a joy. And thank you to Felicity Blunt at Curtis Brown for suggesting that Katie might like to read it in the first place!

I am enormously grateful to my course mates at Curtis Brown Creative. I think we got very lucky with our group. It means so much to be in a gang of writers who are rooting for each other all the way. Thank you to our tutor Charlotte Mendelson for whipping us all into shape and to Norah Perkins for reading the first extract and for saying you had an inkling I would get there. I really needed that.

A huge thank you to Professor Mills at UCL for answering my (many) questions about representations of sexualities in the Tudor period, emailing me back with such thorough and thoughtful replies.

Thank you to Danna, Chally and Tay who were still my friends even when I stopped coming downstairs and mostly sat in my room writing. I'm glad you stuck with me! Thank you to my sisters, Hattie and Vee – I realize how fortunate I am to have sisters as best friends – you have been behind me all the way through the ups and downs of writing a novel and have celebrated every success like it was your own. I am so grateful to have you both. Another big thank you to my parents, David and Cathy, who, when I decided to have a stab at writing a novel, went out and bought me a desk and then came round to un-flatpack it . . . I'm a very lucky daughter.

Finally, thank you to my husband, Oli, who has been my greatest cheerleader all the way. You have always believed in me – much more than I have ever believed in myself – and I am so fortunate to have you by my side. And last – but not least – thank you to our beautiful son, Rex. I can't wait to read you stories.